Praise for *Abducted*

"TOP PICK! Ragan executes this spine-chilling thriller with such razor-sharp precision readers are left breathless."

–Romantic Times

"The satisfyingly frightful episode of a calculating cutthroat."

–Kirkus Reviews

ABDUCTED

T. R. RAGAN

Text copyright © 2011 Theresa Ragan
All rights reserved.
Printed in the United States of America.

Published by Thomas & Mercer
P.O. Box 400818
Las Vegas, NV 89140

ISBN-13: 9781612185095
ISBN-10: 1612185096

For Ruth Cole Cunningham
my beautiful, one-of-a-kind mom

CHAPTER 1

Sacramento, California
Saturday, August 17, 1996 6:47 p.m.

Tall, dense oleander provided cover within the shadows of the night as he watched the front door to the Andersons' house. Behind him lay a field of tall dry grass, which would be useful in keeping him hidden when it came time to get to his car parked on the other side. The dry grass was a fire hazard. If this were his neighborhood, it would have been taken care of already. One thing he'd learned from watching the area for the past two months was that the people who lived here were complacent. No "Neighborhood Watch" signs. No regular meetings. No communication.

Idiots.

Didn't they know that the best protection against crime was an informed public? Be vigilant about what's going on in your community, people. Be observant. Be alert for strangers or unfamiliar vehicles. He shook his head.

The media "experts" insisted the recent killings were about control and playing God. It wasn't about that at all. It was about patience. Not only did he have the patience of a saint, he was a saint. He wasn't a maniac or a lunatic or any of the things the reporters liked to call him. If he were a "crazy lunatic," he'd go

1

after each and every one of those so-called "experts" and call it a day.

Retired FBI agent and now author Gregory O'Guinn referred to him as a loser, asserting that he was an outcast…a failure who thrived on torturing the innocent. Gregory O'Guinn gave Harvard a bad name.

But what did he care what O'Guinn thought? He knew the truth. He knew what he was doing and why. He knew the difference between right and wrong. If the author spent more time investigating the lives of the dead girls, he'd see that they were far from innocent—they were bad girls. They were disrespectful teenagers who had forced him to take action when no one else would. If O'Guinn knew the whole story, he'd be calling him a vigilante, a hero, a man obligated to ignore the due process of law and execute justice on his own terms.

He kept his gaze fixated on the Andersons' front door. Glancing at his Rolex, an Oyster Perpetual Sea-Dweller, he swallowed the irritation nipping at his insides. Despite having an aversion to all forms of water—sea, ocean, pool—he'd always wanted a Sea-Dweller. His dad used to wear one just like it. With thirty-one-jewel chronometer automatic movement, the watch was water-resistant at 1,220 meters. It was solid. Not as heavy as those beefy Omegas. The watch had been milled from a solid block of ridiculously expensive 904L stainless steel. The dial was easy to read, even in the dark. A gift to himself for a job well done—three girls in three months—all menaces to society.

He narrowed his eyes. *Where was Jennifer?*

For the past eight weeks, like clockwork, Jennifer Anderson's parents went to dinner and a movie every Saturday night, leaving their sixteen-year-old daughter home alone. What they didn't know was that within five minutes of leaving the house their daughter crept out the front door and walked to the neighbor-hood park to meet her boyfriend. Shame on her.

Convinced she would sneak out eventually, he decided to wait as he thought about the other girls he'd recently disciplined. The experts had speculated that he got his kicks out of torturing the girls, which was ridiculous. He got more out of the morbid curiosity of the public than he did out of taking the girls home and doing whatever he had to do in order to teach them a lesson.

Was he the only one who refused to let insolent, spoiled teen-age girls rule the world?

Saturday, August 17, 1996 7:00 p.m.

Lizzy Gardner crept down the stairs, hoping to escape unnoticed, but when she reached the landing, her sister's lipstick dropped from her hip pocket and slid across the tiled foyer.

"Where do you think you're going, Elizabeth?" Dad asked from the kitchen.

She sighed and looked his way.

Mom stood behind Dad and waved a dismissive hand through the air, letting Lizzy know it was OK. Dad was just blowing off steam the way he always did before she went out with her friends.

"It's my last night with my friends," Lizzy lied. "Emily and Brooke are leaving for San Diego tomorrow."

"It's a good thing," he said. "You need to start hanging out with people your own age. Who's driving?" He opened the front door and looked outside.

Emily waved from her convertible VW bug. "Hi, Mr. Gardner!"

Dad grunted and shut the door. "You don't need to go out tonight. There's still a killer on the loose."

Not this again. The notorious teenage killer hadn't struck in months, but after killing one fifteen-year-old and two sixteen-year-old girls in a three-month period, the maniac had managed to turn perfectly normal parents into fearful worrywarts.

"Dad. Please?"

"I want you home by ten."

"Tom," her mother interrupted. "I told Lizzy she could stay out until eleven thirty. This is her last night with these girls. After the bowling alley, they're all going back to Brooke's house. You've met Brooke's parents before. She'll be fine."

"I don't like it," Dad said, shaking his head.

"Go ahead," Mom said with a wave of her hand. "We'll see you later tonight."

Lizzy didn't need to be told twice. Forgetting all about the lipstick she'd dropped, she ran out the door and didn't look back.

Saturday, August 17, 1996 11:25 p.m.

Lizzy didn't want the night to end. As Jared drove toward her house, she looked out the front window. It was a dark and wonderful night…a perfect night.

Jared took a right on Emerald Street.

"Do you mind pulling over up there?" she asked, pointing to the curbside at the end of the block. "I'll walk the rest of the way. If Dad sees you dropping me off, he'll kill me."

Jared drove his dad's Ford Explorer to the side of the road and shut off the engine. Lizzy unlocked her seat belt. She leaned into him and pressed her lips to his. When she pulled away, her eyes watered.

"What's wrong?"

"I don't know," she said. "I just hate this feeling…like I'm never going to see you again."

Jared pulled her close and kissed the tip of her nose, her cheek and chin, and finally her lips. Every kiss felt like the first. And now he was leaving for college. Life was so unfair. "I wish tonight would never end," she said.

"Me too," he said before kissing her again, deeper this time.

She loved everything about Jared Michael Shayne: the way he looked, the way he made her feel, the way he smelled, and the sound of his voice.

"Jared?"

"Hmm?"

"You're not going to forget about me, are you?"

"Not a chance."

There was a long pause before he laughed and said, "Look at us, acting as if we're never going to see each other again. I'm going to Los Angeles, not Mars. A five- or six-hour drive tops. All you have to do is call me and I'll be there."

"Promise?"

"Promise." He kissed her again.

The clock on the console read 11:25 before he parked the car. Dad was probably already in a frenzy. "I better go." She turned away to open the car door.

His hand stopped her. "I love you, Lizzy. This isn't the end. It's the beginning."

She managed a smile. "You're right. I love you too. Call me in the morning before you leave, OK?"

"I will." He looked at the street ahead of them. "Let me take you closer to your house. It's too late for you to be walking alone."

She liked that he worried about her, but he had a tendency to treat her like a little girl sometimes. She had spent enough Sunday night dinners with Jared and his family to know that his father could be bossy and controlling. She didn't want Jared or anyone else telling her what to do. Besides, Dad would ground her for a month if he saw Jared dropping her off when she was supposed to be with Emily and Brooke. Lizzy planted a quick one on his mouth, then turned and climbed out of the car. "I'll be fine," she said before shutting the door and blowing him a kiss.

He threw an invisible kiss back at her.

Feeling better, she headed for home. Before making a right on Canyon Road, she looked over her shoulder, but Jared was already driving the other way. She waved anyhow.

Her house was at the end of the block.

She could see the silhouette of the willow tree her dad had planted in the front yard.

The clicks of her shoes against pavement sounded loud enough to wake the dead. She stopped and slipped off her shoes. Now the only sounds were the croaks of a zillion frogs looking for mates in some distant creek.

Zap.

A streetlight went out. She looked up at the light as she passed by. She hadn't thought it could get any darker, but she was wrong. Even the stars had abandoned her tonight. God, she'd forgotten how much she hated the dark. The only thing she hated more than the dark was being *alone* in the dark.

Jared was right. She should have let him drive her closer to her house, or maybe she should have just let him take her home and walk her to the door the way he usually did. She could have told her dad that Jared had picked her up from Brooke's. Dad would have believed her. He always believed her. Her stubbornness was the reason she was out here now...alone...beneath an inky black sky.

A rustling noise sounded near the side gate of one of the neighbors' houses. Chills crawled up her arms. She stopped and listened, hoping to see Fudge, the chocolate-brown lab that loved to lick everyone to death. A couple of steps later she heard it again. The *thump thump thump* of footfalls.

"Jared? Is that you? It isn't funny, you know."

She swiveled about on her feet. The street was empty behind her. The neighbors' lights were off; no one was peering out their windows as far as she could tell. No dogs barking.

That was a good sign, wasn't it?

You're getting yourself all worked up over nothing.

She started off again, one foot in front of the other. And yet the sensation flowing through her was the oddest thing. She could feel it…sense it…somebody was watching her.

Her father always said, "Trust your instincts, Elizabeth. If something doesn't feel right, then it probably isn't."

But then again she'd also been told she had an overactive imagination.

A cool breeze grazed her arms. But there was no breeze tonight, was there?

She should run. She should have started running the moment she'd felt as if she was being watched.

Thump, thump, thump. She whipped around so fast she nearly lost her balance. A man charged straight for her. Her brain shouted RUN. Too bad her legs wouldn't listen. It was as if her feet were glued to the cement.

Whack! Whack!

Something solid hit her leg and then the left side of her head. A hot, searing pain shot through her skull. Her knees buckled and all she saw was black: black jacket, black mask, black sky.

CHAPTER 2

Sacramento, California
Monday, August 19, 1996 9:12 a.m.

Lizzy opened her eyes. An intense pain ripped through her skull, making her wince. She was on her stomach with her hands tied behind her back. The rope was thick and coarse. Her wrists felt raw. She could hardly move. The bastard had taken the time to wrap the upper half of her body in rope, around and around, pulled so tight she could hardly move, let alone breathe. Her ankles were also tied.

Where was she?

It was difficult to see clearly. Her head, all the way to her eyebrows, was wrapped in gauze. The man had bashed her in the legs and head and then covered her head with gauze? He'd talked to her too, through some sort of weird microphone that made his voice sound like the Robinsons' robot on reruns of *Lost in Space*. The voice had sounded eerie, especially coming from a man wearing a mask straight out of an old Batman movie.

How long had she been here? A few hours, a day, two days?

As her eyes adjusted to the semidark room, the pain became more of a pounding on the top of her head and less of a sledgehammer crushing against her skull. Shapes began to take form.

The room was about the size of her bedroom. Dark blinds covered a rectangular window, but light squeezed its way through tiny slits. Cobwebs, with an array of silky designs, stretched from the corners of the window to the ceiling.

Chills crept up her spine.

Fear threatened to swallow her whole, but she knew she didn't stand a chance in hell of getting out of here unless she stayed calm.

A pile of cardboard boxes was stacked high to her right. She tried to wriggle her arms. It was no use. She didn't want to die. How many girls had been reported missing? Two? Three? More importantly, how many had been found alive?

A big fat zero.

A creepy crawly worked its way up her leg. She could feel it moving. She stopped breathing. Whatever was on her leg stopped moving.

Why did it stop? To take a bite of her?

A shiver shot up her spine. She wanted to cry out, but that might get the maniac's attention, and then what?

The creepy crawler was on the move again. A spider with the body of a cockroach, she decided, since she could feel its heavy belly against her skin as it moved along, slow and steady.

She fought with the ropes; tried hard to wriggle her arms, her legs, her hips. It was no use. Her stomach heaved and gurgled.

You are not going to be sick, Lizzy. Stay calm. Breathe. Just because the other girls couldn't find a way out doesn't mean you can't. Think.

Focus. She had watched *Oprah* recently, a show about what to do under extreme situations, like if your car went under water. The number one thing to do was stay calm.

She shut her eyes, inhaled, then slowly exhaled. The stab of nausea left her. When she opened her eyes again, she saw a spider skitter across the wood floor within an inch of her face. And then another…and another.

What the hell was going on? Where were they coming from?

She turned her head as far as she could. Shit. Only a few feet away was a giant aquarium filled with insects. Not just spiders either— scorpions and centipedes too. The insects all climbed on top of one another trying to find a way out. Just like her, they were trapped.

Whatever was on her leg had inched its way past her knee. *It's just a bug…a stupid bug. Get a grip, Lizzy. At least it's not dark.* More than anything, she didn't want the maniac to come back. She didn't want to die.

Images of the other girls came to mind. She squirmed like a fly caught in a web, ignoring the white-hot pain as she tried to get a feel for where the ropes intersected behind her.

Suddenly an eerie calmness settled over her. Her will to live was bigger and stronger than the monster who had tied her up. The maniac, now and forever dubbed Spiderman, obviously didn't know she was double-jointed. She could bend her limbs and joints in ways the sick bastard probably never imagined. The smell of her own stale blood made her stomach churn. She couldn't pass out now. She needed to get untied and get out of here before he came back.

Forget about Spiderman.

Concentrate.

A little more pressure on the left shoulder should do the trick. She had popped her shoulder many times to impress her friends at parties. The doctor called it positional nontraumatic dislocation. If she could do this…if she could maneuver her arm just so…and a little farther to the left… *Focus, Lizzy. Crack.*

A tear dripped down the side of her face, across her cheekbone. *Thank you, God.*

The throbbing ache from dislocating her shoulders was nothing compared to the agonizing pain in her head and the burning sensation in her leg where he'd hit her with something hard and solid. She slid around on the floor to loosen the bindings, then bent her chin into her chest and used her teeth to pull on the rope. It was working. The ropes loosened. She pulled her right hand free. Yes! The rest was easy.

She flipped over, sat up, then used her right hand to untie the ropes around her ankles. With no time to waste, she used her right arm to draw her left arm close to her chest and coaxed her shoulder back into the joint. Relief followed.

She scrambled to her feet. Adrenaline kept her moving, kept her from passing out. A spider fell off her head and landed on the floor in front of her. The eight-legged beast was big and hairy and brown. Barefoot, she used her toe to brush it aside, then frantically brushed bugs from her tangled hair. She'd been bitten twice, maybe more.

Spiders were everywhere. They crept over the floor and around the pile of boxes. She held still and waited for the dizziness to pass.

Go, Lizzy. Get out of here.

Her leg nearly buckled on the first step, but she managed to cling to the wall to steady herself. She couldn't worry about injuries and pain. She needed to get away.

She peered through a slit in the blinds. Iron bars framed the outside of the window. She hobbled to the door, surprised to find it unlocked.

She listened. Somebody was talking. Voices. A television was on. Quietly she stepped into a hallway lined with thick carpet. The house looked new: fresh paint, new carpet, nothing on the walls.

One step at a time. Quiet. Slow. Her gaze connected with the front door, an ordinary entry door with a peephole and a chain. Her heart beat triple time.

Oh my God. Oh my God. She wanted to run for the door, but she refused to make any quick movements and attract unwanted attention. The chain on the door looked thick. Someone had bolted the chain with a heavy metal lock. Swallowing, she looked around the front room. A commercial for dog food was on the television. Her tongue felt thick and swollen. And then she saw him.

Holy shit.

The maniac. The monster. Spiderman. Right there.

He was on the couch…asleep on the couch.

She would wake him if she tried to undo the lock and go through the front door. There had to be another door in the house. It didn't take her long to find one. A sliding glass door situated between the kitchen and a small informal dining area. She would escape and she would live to see another day.

She hobbled toward the door. And then she heard a child's cry…a long, drawn out, pitiful moan.

Boy? Girl? She had no idea. But someone else was in this house. She gnawed on her bottom lip. Outside the sun was rising, lighting up the sky. From where she stood, she could see a future. The dawn of a new day in reach…but there it was again.

"Aaaahhhhhhggg."

Shit!

Limping back to where she'd just come from, her gaze fell to the man on the couch. He hadn't moved. His eyes were closed. His neatly trimmed beard failed to hide a boyish face. His hair was dark brown and cut short around a big dopey-looking ear; he had no gray. He was on his side. She could see only half of his face, enough to see a high cheekbone and a deep tan. There it was again. The cry of a child. Not as loud this time. Why couldn't she pull her gaze away from the monster? He didn't look like a maniac. He looked like a businessman, someone she might pass on the street and say hello to. He looked "normal."

She forced herself to go. She hobbled down the carpeted hallway, once again ignoring the excruciating pain in her leg and the pounding in her head. Mostly she ignored the fact that she was a fool. And damn. She was going to throw up.

Three doors. One was the spider room. The other two doors were shut. She took hold of the knob to her right and twisted it slowly, careful not to make any noise as she peeked inside. It was a guest room. A perfectly normal guest room with a bed half covered with a patchwork quilt. There was a bedside table with a light and a handmade, frilly looking lampshade, the kind her grandmother used to crochet. Nothing in this house made sense. The house of horrors with fresh paint and handmade quilts. She headed for the next door, and the moment she opened it she smelled something musty and moldy.

She put a hand to her mouth at the horror laid out before her. The odor was sickening: rotted eggs and dead rodents. A bed took up most of the small room. Propped on the top of two of the four bedposts were skulls…not the kind of skulls she'd seen in the doctor's office. These skulls had stuff hanging off them. *Skin? Hair? Oh God.* She gagged.

A movement caught her attention—the source of the noise. There was a child on the floor. Thirteen? Fourteen? The kid's arms and legs were nothing but bones, bound and tied to a bedpost. It was hard to tell whether the kid was a boy or a girl, but going solely by the silver necklace around the neck, she guessed female. Her light brown hair had been cut short at weird, uneven angles with a blunt knife. She was so thin. Her face was pale, her brown eyes large and round, bulging. The girl's clothes were torn and bloodied.

Lizzy was pulling off ropes with her hands and loosening knots with her teeth before she even realized she'd moved toward her. Tears streamed down Lizzy's face as she worked. The girl couldn't stand on her own, so Lizzy picked her up and ran out of the room and down the hall, grinding her teeth to stop from screaming out in agony.

She didn't stop to look to see if the man was still on the couch. She needed to get the hell out of there. She ran toward the sliding glass door where she had no choice but to set the girl down so she could use both hands to unlock and open the door. When she finally picked up the girl again and stepped outside, she was blinded by the bright light of the sun. The branches of a big oak reached out to her. Other than the tree branches, she couldn't see a thing.

At least not at first. It took a moment for Lizzy to see him.

He stood by the fence.

Waiting.

And the girl in her arms must have seen him too, because the strangest sounds were coming out of her mouth.

CHAPTER 3

Sacramento, California
Friday, February 12, 2010 6:06 p.m.

Lizzy stood front and center in the multipurpose room at Ridgeview Elementary and pointed a finger at the young girl in the front row. "Heather, what's the first thing you should do if you think somebody is about to abduct you?"

"Draw attention to myself."

"Good. And what might be a good way to do that, Vicki?"

"Scream and kick."

"That's right." Eight kids had signed up for Lizzy's class tonight, all girls under the age of eighteen, but only six had actually shown up. Not bad for a Friday night. She'd been teaching kids how to protect themselves for the past ten years. She'd definitely had worse attendance, including a roomful of no-shows. It was easy to see who had been paying attention for the past hour and who had not. "How about you, Nicole? Come up to the front, please, and show us what you would do if somebody tried to take you against your will."

Everybody waited quietly until Nicole was standing in the front of the room.

Lizzy used her chin to gesture at Bob Stuckey, the local sheriff, whose daughter was in attendance tonight. Bob had a stocky build and stood at about five foot eight inches, only four inches taller than Lizzy. He had entered the classroom ten minutes ago. He, along with a few other parents, waited patiently for the class to end so they could take their daughters home.

"Mr. Stuckey, would you mind helping me out?"

He hesitated, then shrugged and headed toward the middle of the room where Nicole stood with both arms straight and stiff at her sides.

Lizzy gestured for Bob Stuckey to go ahead and wrap his big, beefy arm around Nicole. Although Sheriff Stuckey was clearly uncomfortable putting his arm around the girl's neck, and rightly so, he did as she asked.

"OK, Nicole. What would you do if someone grabbed you, like Sheriff Stuckey is doing now, and told you to get into his car?"

Nicole swallowed. "I don't know." She made a feeble attempt to wriggle out of Sheriff Stuckey's grasp, but she couldn't get loose. "This is freaking me out," Nicole said. "I don't even want to think about it. I don't know what to do." Tears gathered in her eyes. "Please, let me go."

Lizzy raised a brow at Bob, letting him know now would be a good time to let go of Nicole.

He quickly dropped his arm.

The girl obviously needed a few more sessions before Lizzy used her as a guinea pig. Lizzy pointed to the back of the room where one girl sat as far away from the others as she could possibly get. The girl couldn't be much older than sixteen, maybe seventeen, but the five piercings on each ear, one on her nose, and one on each brow made her look older, tougher. Her black hair was short and spiky, and despite the February chill in the air, the girl wore a dark blue spaghetti-strap top, a miniskirt, and worn sneakers without shoelaces. A tattoo of an angel on her collarbone stood out on her fair skin. *Ouch.*

"What about you?" Lizzy asked the girl. "What would you do if someone grabbed you?"

The girl chewed her gum, blew a bubble, a great big bubble that she managed to suck back into her mouth without leaving a trace of goo on her face. *Impressive.*

The cold and calculating look in the girl's brown eyes was supposed to cover up what Lizzy guessed to be a severe case of loneliness.

"What's your name?" Lizzy asked.

"Hayley Hansen." She pulled the wad of gum out of her mouth, stuck it to the bottom side of the desk, then stood and headed for Sheriff Stuckey, who looked more than a little worried by the girl coming toward him.

"Go ahead," Lizzy told Sheriff Stuckey when Hayley stopped in front of him and turned toward the class.

Sheriff Stuckey put his arm around the girl's neck, locking her in by grasping his other hand around his forearm.

"OK," Lizzy said to Hayley. "You're in the park and this guy has just walked up behind you and put a stranglehold on you."

Hayley looked bored out of her mind.

"What would you do?"

"I'd bite a chunk out of the motherfucker's arm." And then she went on to demonstrate.

"Ow! Shit!" Bob Stuckey yanked his arm away and jumped back. "Jesus." His long-sleeved shirt was torn, and blood began to seep through the cottony fabric.

Lizzy ran to the other side of the room and grabbed the first aid kit. She handed the plastic box to Sheriff Stuckey and ushered him toward the bathroom.

Parents murmured worriedly to one another.

Once Lizzy found her place at the front of the class again, a few random giggles erupted on one side of the room. Jane Stuckey, Sheriff Stuckey's fifteen-year-old daughter, turned toward the other girls. "It's not funny."

"No," Lizzy agreed, "there's never anything funny about someone getting hurt." Lizzy looked at Hayley, who had returned to her seat at the back of the room. "Hayley, I'm going to give you the benefit of the doubt and assume you didn't mean to hurt Sheriff Stuckey, but I am also going to remind each and every one of you," Lizzy said, making eye contact with every girl in the room, "that this is serious business. And for that reason I'm going to use what Hayley just did to Sheriff Stuckey as an example of what you should do in this type of situation. How many of you think Hayley would have gotten away if she was attacked?"

They all raised their hands.

Lizzy nodded in agreement.

One of the teenagers' mothers, who had been sitting at the far side of the room through the entire class, bolted to her feet and said, "I don't see how biting an officer of the law could ever be used as an example of the right thing to do."

Lizzy sighed. "That's because you, Mrs. Goodmanson, have never been held against your will, have you?"

Mrs. Goodmanson opened her mouth to respond, but Lizzy didn't give her a chance to say anything. "Were you ever told to do something you didn't want to do, something you knew was wrong? Were you ever touched improperly? Have you ever had a knife put to your throat, Mrs. Goodmanson, or a gun held to your head?"

The woman shook her head and sank back into her seat.

Lizzy turned back to the kids, whose eyes were now big and round and curious. For the first time since they entered the class-room, Lizzy had their full attention. "Swear, curse, bite, kick," she said loudly, sternly as she paced the front of the room. "Do anything you have to do to get away. Yell at the top of your lungs, 'HELP, I DO NOT KNOW THIS PERSON!' If you're on a bike, do not get off or let go of the bike. If you do not have a bike, run in the opposite direction of traffic and scream as loud as you can."

Lizzy anchored loose strands of hair behind her ear as she continued to pace the length of the room, using bold gestures to make her point. "If you can't get away and you do somehow end up in the abductor's car, roll down the window and scream. Scream every bad word you can think of...anything that might get somebody's attention. If you come to a stop sign or stop light, jump out of the vehicle and run! If the car is moving and you're in the passenger seat, grab the keys from the ignition and toss them out the window or toward the backseat. While he goes to retrieve them, get out of the car and run."

She let her gaze roam slowly about the room before she asked, "Do you understand me?"

The giggling had stopped a while ago. A severe hush floated across the room.

Every kid in the room nodded, except Hayley Hansen, who looked as if she already knew everything there was to know about bad people in the world. Bad people who did horrible things to innocent people for no reason other than to hunt and victimize, reliving their grotesque fantasies in their minds until the next time.

Sacramento, California

Monday, February 15, 2010 9:12 a.m.

Lizzy squeezed Old Yeller, her faded 1977 Toyota Corolla, between two cars parked on J Street, climbed out, and headed down the sidewalk toward her office. Although it was past nine a.m., a layer of thick fog still floated below the bare branches of the tree-lined street.

The cold nipped at every part of her. Lizzy rubbed her arms, and then shoved her hands deep into her coat pockets. She was cold. She was *always* cold. Her sister, Cathy, said it was because she was too thin and didn't have enough meat on her bones. Maybe so, but one of these days she was going to move to Arizona or Mexico, maybe Palm Springs, somewhere hot, where she wouldn't have to wear gloves and two pairs of socks. Her hands were just getting warm when she pulled them out of the warmth of her pockets so she could open the door to her office.

She admired the newly etched sign on the door: "Elizabeth Ann Gardner—Private Investigator." A much-appreciated gift from her sister.

Lifting her elbow, she tried to wipe a smudge from the glass, but the door came unexpectedly open. She wasn't expecting any clients. She wasn't married. No ex-husband. No boyfriend. No kids. One vacationing intern. One fourteen-year-old niece and one sister, neither of whom had a key, which meant she had been burglarized.

Poking her head inside the front room, she heard the faint rustling of papers in the back room. Change the phrase "had been" burglarized to "was being" burglarized.

She slid her hand beneath her jacket and felt her Glock .40 snug within her holster. She unsnapped it and brought the gun to her side. Although Lizzy had never had to use the gun before, she'd been wearing one for ten years now. It was her friend. It made her feel safe.

The doorjamb showed no sign of forced entry. She opened the door wide enough to squeeze her way inside without making any noise. Despite her niece's attempt to fatten her up by shoving Rice Krispies treats down her throat when she visited, Lizzy had lost another three pounds. She wasn't trying to lose weight. She just wasn't hungry. Food didn't turn her on. Sometimes she wondered if anything turned her on, although she did have a weakness for peanut M&M's.

She glanced at her desk. Computer was off. Papers scattered in an unorganized mess. Half-chewed pencils sticking out of a weird-looking jar her niece had made for her; everything was just the way she'd left it. Not even a burglar would attempt to find anything of interest in this mess.

But little did the burglar know that her sister had forced her to start writing a daily journal all in the name of catharsis, figuring if she barfed up all her emotional baggage onto paper, then she'd be restored to a better, newer, purer self. Her sister considered writing in a journal to be an emotional cleansing. All that electrifying enlightenment was right there on her computer saved under "stuff." And to think the burglar thought the goods were back in the safe.

She took quiet steps toward the back office, which was really a large closet in disguise. The rustling noises grew louder. Somebody was definitely a busy little bee.

Lizzy's adrenaline pumped in earnest now. A little adventure, a little excitement—just what the doctor said she didn't need. Yep, her sister, Cathy, wasn't too far off when they'd argued the other day and Cathy had called her "one sick puppy." But Cathy wasn't the local girl known as the "one-who-got-away" either. Cathy hadn't spent two months of her life with a sick-minded, spider-loving maniac.

Lizzy's gaze shifted to the floor. No signs of wet or muddied footprints, only ugly beige carpet that needed a good cleaning. She had her priorities though. And cleaning the carpet was pretty much the last thing on her list—right under scrub the shower tiles, shop for groceries, and take the car in for a long overdue tune-up. If anyone was going to get a tune-up it was going to be her, not an old car with a broken tailpipe and a mind of its own.

The file drawer clamped shut with a bang, giving her a start. The door to the back office/closet was ajar. She could see a pair of boots. Somebody was leaning over the bottom drawer of the file cabinet.

"Put your hands up or I'll shoot!"

Two hands shot up. Papers flew. "It's me, Jessica. Don't shoot." Lizzy pushed the door wide.

Jessica looked relieved to see that it was only her, but even so, she kept her gaze glued to the gun's barrel while she held her arms straight up in the air.

Lizzy frowned and lowered her weapon. "What the hell are you doing here? I thought you were on a plane headed for Jersey?"

Jessica Pleiss, psychology student at Sacramento State and brand-new intern that Lizzy didn't need or want, but who she'd "hired" because Jessica had a knack for talking people into things they didn't need or want, dropped her hands to her sides and said, "Jersey didn't work out, so I thought I'd spend my week off from school organizing these files. Did I leave the door open again?"

Lizzy nodded, too tired and too cold to bother lecturing the girl.

Jessica bent down to gather the papers she'd scattered across the floor. The girl had been working with Lizzy for only six weeks—and only when Jessica's busy schedule permitted, which wasn't often. Mostly Jessica ran to Starbucks and got them lattes and mochas.

Now that Lizzy thought about it, the girl was costing her more money than she was worth…or could afford.

Jessica pushed herself to her feet. "That gun's not real, is it?" Lizzy had already put the gun away. She nodded. "It's real."

"Cool. It's probably a good thing you carry one, considering all the weirdos you work for."

Lizzy didn't know which of her clients Jessica referred to, but neither did she care. She also knew she should probably ask Jessica why her trip to Jersey hadn't worked out—boyfriend problems, lack of funds, perhaps—but she really didn't want this "relationship" to turn into some kind of girly-girl, talky-talk social thing. Although Jessica had school and homework and family, underneath it all, she was clearly a needy, lonely young woman.

It took one to know one.

Lizzy didn't want anyone looking up to her, counting on her, confiding in her, because sooner or later that person might really need her, and then what the hell would she do? She'd feel guilty, that's what. And feeling guilty was right up there with always being cold. And afraid. It sucked.

Lizzy headed back to the front room. "So did we get any phone calls?"

"Two. Mrs. Kirkpatrick from Granite Bay High School wanted to know if you could give a talk to three hundred students. And a guy named Victor called—wouldn't give his last name. He asked a lot of questions about hiring somebody to follow his wife. I told him we didn't do that sort of thing, but he's one of those guys who can't seem to take no for an answer."

We? The girl hadn't yet clocked twenty hours and she was already using sentences with *we.* "Did he leave a number?"

"Nope. He said he'd call back later."

Five hours later, Jessica was gone and Lizzy was typing in her journal for the day. She didn't like writing down her feelings, but her sister had asked, make that *begged,* her to give it a try. Write anything you want, Cathy had said. Anything at all. Let it all hang out. *OK,* Lizzy thought, *here goes.*

Day Five: I hate writing in this journal. It's cold and foggy today. Not misty fog but the thick kind you can't see through. I prefer the other sort.

This wasn't a journal—it was a damn weather report.

I really like the sign my sister had professionally etched on my door. It's real nice.

Lizzy chewed on her pencil as she thought about what to type next and then dropped her fingers to the keyboard.

There's this girl taking my defense class. Her name is Hayley Hansen. She's tough. I like her. She reminds me of me. What's not to like?

She stared at the screen and tapped her fingers on her desk. She was getting really good at making a galloping noise with her fingertips. She sighed and forced her fingers to the keyboard.

Writing in a journal sucks big wampums. How is typing "this sucks" over and over every single day going to help me become whole again? Was I ever whole? Who knows. Until next time, Liz.

Lizzy hit the "save" button, shut off the computer, and breathed a sigh of relief. Writing in a journal ranked just under sitting alone in the dark when it came to the list of things she didn't like to do.

The screen turned black.

Cathy was right. Lizzy felt better already. Not because of anything she'd written, but because she was finished writing in her journal for the day.

Lizzy snorted and tossed a pencil into the jar. The phone rang. She picked up the receiver and listened to a man ask for her by name. "Yes, this is her. What can I do for you?"

Hmmm. It was Victor, the caller Jessica had mentioned earlier. Lizzy propped her feet on her desk. "Yes," she answered, "Jessica told me you called. I'm afraid I'm not going to be able—three hundred dollars a day?" She raised her legs and plopped her feet to the floor, listening to Victor rattle on about his wife and his daughter. Lizzy didn't do domestic cases. Mostly because they made her feel anxious, bad, and depressed. She did car accident investigations and product liability cases. Slip and falls were her favorite—helping companies deal with people who went around the country pouring oil on the floor, then slipping and falling and pretending to be hurt so they could sue large companies for even larger sums of money.

But a girl had to eat. And she'd have to be pretty stupid to turn down three hundred dollars a day to sit in her car all day and watch a woman betray her husband. Lizzy grabbed a half-chewed pencil from the jar and took notes while he talked. When he was finished she said, "Why don't you give me a cell phone number where I can reach you. I'll sleep on it and call you in the morning."

"I'll call back in a few days," Victor said. A *click* and a dial tone followed.

"OK, never mind, Victor. Don't give me your number. And maybe I won't sleep on it." She hung up the phone.

She read over her notes. Victor said he was an attorney. He talked like an attorney—fast and full of himself.

Lizzy shrugged. Something told her he wouldn't be calling back. She crumpled the note and tossed it in the wastebasket under her desk, then leaned back in her chair. Her gaze connected with her desk drawer. The same drawer where she kept all her private files…all of her secrets.

The phone rang again. She let it ring for a moment and then picked it up on the fifth ring. "Listen, Victor, I don't appreciate your hanging up on me."

"I've missed you, Lizzy."

It definitely wasn't Victor. "Who's this?"

"You promised you'd never leave me."

A cold chill swept over her. "Who is this?" she asked again.

"Because of you, nobody's safe, Lizzy."

She kept the phone to her ear but didn't say a word. Instinctively she reached for her Glock and looked out the window. Her gaze swept over the gray building across the street and then over the cars parked at the curb—all empty. About a block away, a woman exited a hair salon, pulled keys from her purse, climbed into her BMW, and drove away. Whoever was on the other end of the wire was still there. She could hear his faint breathing.

She held the mouthpiece away and took a deep breath, regained control of herself. "Is this you, Spiderman?"

A short, caustic laugh sounded on the other end of the line before he said, "You shouldn't have gotten away, Lizzy, and you never should have taken something that didn't belong to you. Too bad your mother didn't teach you any manners before she moved so far away. If I'd known you were a liar and a thief, I would have taken care of you long ago."

The line went dead.

"Shit."

She yanked open her bottom drawer and retrieved a file. She opened it and skimmed page after page of notes. Why couldn't she remember details of her time with that crazy man? What did he look like? All she had to do was close her eyes to remember waking up in the room with an aquarium full of spiders and then finding that poor little girl...and almost escaping. Almost. Close, but no cigar. Why hadn't she looked at the couch before she ran out the sliding glass door with that girl? If she had noticed he was no longer sleeping, she could have thrown a chair through the front window or maybe found a telephone to call for help.

She clamped her eyes shut. She could have locked him out of his own damn house. But she hadn't done any of those things. And now all of those days spent with him...all that time...the two months following her attempt at escape were as thick and hazy in Lizzy's mind as the fog outside her window. Two months of hell, and yet the only time she saw glimpses of the horror she'd experienced was at night, after she couldn't keep her eyes open any longer.

CHAPTER 4

Monday, February 15, 2010 4:00 p.m.

Back at her apartment, Lizzy opened the door and looked inside. She readied her gun as she listened and waited.

The only sounds were the padded footfalls of her cat, Maggie. "Meow."

Her sister, Cathy, did not like Lizzy living alone, so she'd given Lizzy a cat as a birthday present two years ago. Lizzy hadn't wanted a cat, and she had done everything in her power to keep her distance from Maggie, refusing to let the animal anywhere near her bedroom for the first six months. But Maggie was a determined feline, and she had persevered, making a permanent home for herself on a wide, cushiony chair in the corner of Lizzy's bedroom. It was Maggie's chair now. Maggie was her alarm clock too, waking Lizzy up every morning at six o'clock, give or take a few minutes.

It irked her to know Cathy had been right. Again. Because the truth was, Lizzy didn't know what she would do without Maggie. Maggie had become her friend, her family, her life…yet one more reason why she still needed therapy.

Maggie circled her ankles, wrapping her tail around Lizzy's leg as she meowed. She was hungry.

"Any visitors today, Maggie?"

"Meow."

Lizzy stepped inside and flicked on the light. "OK, if you say so." She locked the door, latched the chain, and slid one of the deadbolts into place.

The phone rang.

She jerked about and aimed her gun at the phone on the kitchen counter. Swallowing the knot lodged in her throat, Lizzy moved slowly toward the phone. For a moment, she just watched it ring. Finally, she decided to ignore the incessant ringing of the phone and feed Maggie instead.

She laid the gun on the counter and opened the refrigerator door, determined not to worry about who might be calling. Let it go, she told herself, afraid of what would happen if she allowed herself to believe Spiderman was back.

Retrieving an open can of cat food from the second shelf, she used a fork to scoop out the rest of the can onto a glass dish. She even hummed a little tune while she worked. The ringing finally stopped.

Thank God.

"There you go, sweetie." She stroked Maggie's soft fur.

The phone rang again.

Damn.

"OK, Spiderman," she said aloud. "Let's have it out once and for all." She picked up the receiver. "What do you want!"

"Lizzy, is that you? It's Jared."

She couldn't think. She was a jumble of nerves. "Jared Shayne?"

"That's the one. Lizzy, how are you?"

A wave of emotion swept over her. She hadn't seen Jared in a very long time. Maybe a dozen times since Spiderman bashed her over the head and took her to his lair fourteen years ago. She'd gotten away from him too. After spending two months in hell, she'd gotten away by using her brain. Mostly she'd used words, lots of words. All bullshit. She'd made the killer think she honestly cared about him, the oldest trick in the book, and then she'd gotten away.

And now, only weeks after her therapist said she was seeing progress, Spiderman called. And now, Jared was calling her too. *Coincidence? Or just bad timing?* Maybe if she could get more than two hours sleep at night she might be able to function like a regular human being.

She rubbed her temples. Night after night, she heard nothing but endless moaning, crying, sawing, and drilling. There was nothing she could do about it then, and there was nothing she could do about it now.

"Lizzy, are you there?"

Every single day she asked herself the same bullshit question: what would it take for her to be able to lead a so-called normal life? And every day she came up with the same answer: she wasn't going to get any sleep until she knew for sure that Spiderman was dead.

"Lizzy?"

"I'm sorry, Jared. Is it really you?"

"It's me, Lizzy. I'm sorry I haven't called before now. How are you?"

After returning from the bowels of hell, she'd told Jared to leave her alone. For the first six months, he'd ignored her request and stayed at her side, day and night. But in the end, he'd given up and did as she asked. "I'm great," she lied.

There was a pause before he said, "I'm glad. It's good to hear your voice. Unfortunately, I'm calling because we've got a situation here in Auburn. A missing girl. Is there any chance you can head out this way?"

She inwardly laughed. She couldn't help it. She'd heard from her sister that Jared Shayne had graduated from USC with a degree in psychology. Instead of becoming the best damn psychologist in the country, though, he'd surprised everybody by applying and being accepted into the FBI academy. Nothing could have shocked her more. Although Jared believed in truth and justice and everything his father believed in, he'd made it clear back when she was dating him that hell would have to freeze over before he'd follow in his father's footsteps. His father had been a police officer, an FBI agent, and a judge. Who would have guessed Jared would swim up the same stream?

"Are you there?" he asked.

"I'm still here. I hate to be the bearer of bad news, but I quit my position as a board member of the Missing and Exploited Children's Organization two years ago. I knew if I had to hear the details of one more kidnapping, had to watch one more family fall apart, I'd lose it for good."

She heard his exhale through the telephone line. Jared was having a hard time spitting it out. That wasn't like him. At least it didn't used to be like him. Why now after all this time? It didn't make sense. "I'm sorry," she said again because she didn't know what else to say. "Why don't you tell me what's going on?" *And then I'll apologize again and turn your offer down.*

"We've got a missing fifteen-year-old girl. Her name's Sophie Madison. The perpetrator came in through Sophie's bedroom window, took the girl, and left a note."

"Well, that's promising. They don't usually leave notes. Maybe that's a good sign and he'll be calling for a ransom."

"I wish it were that easy, but the note is addressed to you, Lizzy."

Monday, February 15, 2010 4:15 p.m.

Cathy Warner stepped out of the car and instantly got a feel for what the local weatherman had been talking about. The air was chilly, the kind of cold that seeped into her bones. On the news, she had seen a warning for wind chills in the Sacramento area, a combination of cold air and strong winds that would have the potential of causing hypothermia for those who stayed outside too long.

Cathy followed the other parents into the aquatic center, past the front desk and through double doors leading to the indoor pool area. Steam hovered over the water. The scent of chlorine was overwhelming. Most of the girls on the swim team stood on the pool's edge, wrapped in towels. A few girls lingered in the water.

Her daughter, Brittany, stood at the back of the group. Brittany's towel was wrapped tightly over hunched shoulders, her gaze directed at the ground while she sucked on the corner of her towel. Cathy wondered if her daughter was nervous about something.

Coach Sullivan stood a good foot and a half over the girls. He was powerfully built, in good shape for a man in his midfifties.

Although Brittany had been swimming competitively since she was five, the coach was relatively new. After finishing his spiel, Coach Sullivan shared a few words with the girls individually before they left for home. By the time Cathy reached Brittany's side, it was her daughter's turn to talk with the coach.

Cathy listened as Coach Sullivan talked to her daughter about what she needed to work on in the coming months. The first time Cathy met Coach Sullivan was two months ago. He had been personable and friendly, and especially great with the kids. Brittany tended to be shy, an introvert who had a difficult time making friends in school. Lately she'd been spending too much time on the computer. Her daughter needed the kind of camaraderie that a team sport provided.

"Brittany is way ahead of the pack," Coach Sullivan said directly to Cathy, yanking her from her thoughts. "Today she broke the record in the fifty-meter freestyle and in the fifty-meter backstroke."

"Wow," Cathy said, embarrassed by Brittany's apparent disinterest.

He smiled. "Now for the bad news. Unfortunately, as I told the other parents, I need to collect another hundred dollars from each swimmer due to increased rent at the aquatic center."

Cathy turned toward Brittany. "Dad's not going to be happy about that."

Brittany shrugged. "Dad's never happy."

Despite the chill in the air, heat spread over Cathy's face. "Not a problem," she assured the coach. "We'll bring a check to the next practice."

Once they were out of earshot, Cathy gave her daughter a stern look. "What's wrong with you?"

"I'm tired and these braces are killing me."

Cathy sighed. She'd forgotten about the braces. Of course Brittany would be in pain. As she waited outside the locker room for Brittany to change out of her bathing suit, she thought about what her daughter had said about Dad not being happy. Part of the problem stemmed from Richard's long hours. It didn't help that the economy was spiraling downward. She and Richard had been arguing a lot—usually about her sister, Lizzy. Richard didn't like Lizzy spending time with Brittany. He thought her sister was crazy, which wasn't fair. Poor Lizzy. She'd been to hell and back.

Brittany was right. Dad wasn't happy. Lizzy wasn't happy. She wasn't even sure if she was happy any longer. And the worst part was that Cathy didn't know what the hell to do about it.

Monday, February 15, 2010 9:00 p.m.

Brittany Warner signed onto her computer and saw that i2Hotti was logged on. Her insides did flip-flops. She instant messaged the boy known as i2Hotti, boldly asking him where he'd been for the past two days.

> i2Hotti: why? did you miss me?
> Brit35: no
> i2Hotti: admit it…you missed me
> Brit35: ok I missed u
> i2Hotti: have u bought a webcam yet?
> Brit35: mom said she'd think about it
> i2Hotti: don't u have $$ of your own?
> Brit35: i have a b-day soon
> i2Hotti: i know
> Brit35: how dyk?
> i2Hotti: dyk?
> Brit35: LOL acronym for "do you know"
> i2Hotti: i know a lot of things about u
> Brit35: Facebook?
> i2Hotti: ya

Brit35: ROTFL
i2Hotti: swim practice today?
Brit35: yeah lame
i2Hotti: why?
Brit35: new coach is a creeper
i2Hotti: what does he do?
Brit35: he stares
i2Hotti: because u r so pretty
Silence
i2Hotti: r u there?
Brit35: yes
i2Hotti: u should get a webcam
Brit35: why?
I2Hotti: cuz I want to see u when we chat
I2Hotti: then i can dream about u
Silence
i2Hotti: still there?
Brit35: i'm here
i2Hotti: anything wrong?
Brit35: i have braces now
Brit35: i look like a freak
Brit35: i don't want u to see me
i2Hotti: i like girls with braces
Brit35: liar
Brit35: hold on
Brit35: i have to shut my door
Brit35: brb
i2Hotti: brb?
Brit35: LOL
Brit35: "be right back"
Brit35: see, already back

i2Hotti: that was quick. parents r fighting again?

Brit35: yes

i2Hotti: about?

Brit35: lizzy

i2Hotti: lizzy?

Brit35: my aunt

i2Hotti: why?

Brit35: dad thinks she's a loony bird

i2Hotti: what does mom think?

Brit35: mom wants to help her

i2Hotti: what do you think?

Brit35: i like her

Brit35: she's hecka fun to be with

i2Hotti: i want to be with u

Brit35: my parents wouldn't like it

i2Hotti: they don't have to know

Silence

I2Hotti: think about it?

Brit35: i better go now

i2Hotti: tomorrow night, same time?

Brit35: i'll be here

i2Hotti: sweet dreams

Brittany logged off and walked to her window. She hadn't wanted to end her conversation with i2Hotti but she could hear Mom walking around upstairs. Mom liked to randomly pop in to see what she was doing. She didn't allow Brittany to lock her door. If Mom knew she was talking to an older boy, she'd go ballistic.

Brittany met i2Hotti on the Internet about a month ago. She'd never met him in person, but he sent her a picture after asking her to friend him on Facebook. If she ever did get in trouble for talking to him, it would be worth it. He was hot with a capital H. She didn't know why he liked her. She wasn't beautiful. Certainly not the sort of girl who stood out in a crowded room, although Mom told her she was a natural beauty and could easily be a model—something all moms said.

Outside, the wind was blowing so hard Brittany thought the oak tree in the front yard might fall and crash right through the house at any moment. She peered into the dark, scanning the street below to see if the SUV was there tonight. For the past three nights, she'd seen a man sitting in a blue SUV parked across the street. She rubbed her arms, glad to see he wasn't there. She couldn't help but wonder if it was Coach Sullivan. Next time she saw the car she planned to figure out exactly what kind of car it was so she could compare it to Coach Sullivan's car. Creeper.

Monday, February 15, 2010 9:32 p.m.

He looked at his watch. Time to get back to Sophie. Just one last look before he left. The light was on. He knew she was in there. *Come on, show yourself.* Too bad she was on the second floor. It would be quite challenging when it came time to take her home. He could use a challenge. Taking Sophie had been anticlimactic, but she would be waking soon and he wanted to be there when she opened her eyes.

Excitement rippled through him as he recalled the first time he realized he could make a difference. It was twenty-one years ago when everything had become so clear, and he'd discovered his life's purpose. He was a senior in high school—a young man trying hard to put his past behind him—when fate stepped in and made him watch Shannon die. That was the day he'd seen the light.

Shannon Winters, a sophomore in high school and the girl of his dreams, had consumed his every thought back then. Wanting to impress her, he had taken his time finding out things about her: her favorite food, preferred music, what she liked to do in her free time, et cetera. Once he knew her well enough, he waited for her after school. She always took the shortcut behind the school building, cutting through the baseball field, and then taking an alley to get home. He waited for her in the alley, surprising her with flowers and her favorite candy. Her brows had furrowed upon seeing him and that had confused him. Once she stopped frowning, she brusquely told him to keep the flowers since she didn't want to carry them home. Then she took the jawbreaker from him, her absolute favorite candy, and popped it into her mouth.

He told her he had something important he wanted to ask her, but she wouldn't stay still. She was already headed home, and she wouldn't slow her pace. He followed close on her heels. He was nervous, his palms sweaty. But he had prepared for too long to give up, so he spit it all out and told her how he felt about her. Then he asked her if she would go to a movie with him.

That did the trick. She finally stopped, spun on her heels, and gave him a you-must-be-joking look. It didn't take long for her annoying giggles to turn to full-out laughter.

She was laughing at him. She laughed so hard, she began to choke on the jawbreaker. He couldn't believe it. He'd bought her the big round jawbreaker because he loved her and now she was choking on it. At first, he figured the jawbreaker would pop out of her mouth, the mouth he'd fantasized for too long about kissing and sticking his tongue down. Assuming the candy would pop out eventually, he watched her face turn red. He knew she might yell at him for not doing anything to help her. *Whatever.*

Instead of feeling angry or scared, the whole crazy situation fascinated him. He especially enjoyed the way her big brown eyes bulged from their sockets as panic set in. He couldn't believe it when she pointed at her throat. The bitch wanted him to do something about her problem. She actually wanted him to help her after she'd laughed at him, humiliated him. That's when the whole wild scene began to make his insides tingle, especially his balls. He'd gotten hard quick. The redder her face got, the harder he became until he could hardly stand it. Then she turned blue and three shades of purple. She made some crazy garbled noises that made him want to pop the candy out and put something else in her mouth instead. He was hot. Nothing had ever affected him like that before. Not porn on the Internet, not Dad's *Playboy* magazines, nothing. By the time her fingers grasped onto his shirt, and her eyes nearly popped out of their sockets, he was as hard as granite. She died right there in front of him.

He'd never forgotten Shannon.

CHAPTER 5

Lizzy leaned into the steering wheel and tried to keep her eye on the divider. The road was curvy and slick from a light rain. Fog and a starless black sky weren't helping matters. She pulled to the curb, turned on the overhead light, and looked at the map again.

Even with the windows shut, Lizzy could hear around-the-clock traffic zooming across four lanes of freeway in the distance. She looked out the window, squinting to read the street sign in front of her. Vermont Street.

A cold chill crept through the crevices of her car. *See you soon, Elizabeth.* His voice kept creeping back into her subconscious. Damn him. She didn't want to think about the call she received earlier. She didn't want to think about *him*. Spiderman hadn't come back. He couldn't come back. He was either dead or in prison.

"Louie, Louie" belted out from the backpack she used as a purse. She shook her head at the new ringtone. Brittany, her niece, liked to play little stunts on her, like setting the alarm on her cell phone to go off at random times or reprogramming her ringtone to play goofy songs. She dug around in her bag until she located her cell at the bottom. It was her sister. "Hi, Cathy. What's up?"

"Where are you?"

Damn. Cathy was on to her. She knew Cathy would worry, but she couldn't lie. "Lost in Auburn."

"I saw the AMBER Alert. That's why you're there, isn't it?"

"It was on the news?" Lizzy asked. "Damn. I was hoping to beat the crowd."

"I forbid you to visit the crime scene, Lizzy."

Lizzy snorted. "You sound like Dad."

"Why are you doing this?"

"Because Jared Shayne is handling the case, and he called to let me know the kidnapper left me a personalized note. Either Spiderman is back in business, or I'm just really popular with the whole serial killer crowd."

Silence.

"I'm a big girl, Sis. I've been writing in my journal every day," she added with sarcasm. "I can handle this."

"Don't patronize me."

Déjà vu. It was as if Dad had taken over her sister's body. "OK, you're right," Lizzy said. "I'm sorry. But if Spiderman is back and he's leaving me personal notes, I can't very well turn my back on these people, can I?"

"I'm sorry for the little girl; I really am. It's tragic, but you can't do this to yourself, or to us. You've made tremendous progress over the past ten years, Lizzy. Just because you're the one who got away doesn't mean you're forever indebted to society and its victims. You've done your part, Lizzy. You've done all you can. It's over."

But I didn't save the girl without a voice. Hell, Lizzy thought, she couldn't hear an unfamiliar sound without seeing the girl's face in her mind's eye: big brown eyes and that horrible garbled scream. She squeezed her eyes shut, willing the images away.

"Cathy, listen to me. I can handle this. I'll be fine." And yet the truth was, not even Lizzy was convinced of that.

More silence, long and drawn out, until Cathy said, "What about Friday?"

"What about it?"

"Brittany is looking forward to seeing you."

"I wouldn't miss picking her up from school and spending the evening with my favorite niece for anything."

"She's your *only* niece."

"And my favorite." Lizzy glanced at the directions on her lap and realized she was closer than she thought. She pulled away from the curb and made the next left on Piccadilly. She could see the house at the end of a cul-de-sac. With all the emergency lights flashing it was hard to miss. A row of police cars served as a barricade and three unmarked sedans took up most of the sidewalk. She pulled up to the curb and turned off the ignition. "I've gotta go, Cathy. I'll talk to you soon."

She clicked her phone shut and dropped it into her bag. Outside, a thick fog clung to the sidewalk. Neighbors peeked through their curtains as she passed by. She walked toward the Madison house and found herself imagining the kidnapper walking this same path.

A breeze rattled the branches of the trees. The hairs on the back of her neck stood on end.

There were a few scattered bushes, but no fence around the perimeter or tall hedges to keep him hidden. Why would he pick this neighborhood? At the top of a hill? With only one escape route? Did he have a car? An accomplice? She'd seen enough of these cases from start to finish to know the kidnapper was probably in his early twenties or thirties, unless it was Spiderman, in which case he would be closer to forty by now.

If it was a serial killer who had taken the girl, statistics stated he would not be married. Most serial killers were alienated, lonely, and withdrawn. And yet there were always exceptions to the rule. One thing was certain: if the perpetrator picked a house on the top of a hill with hardly any tree cover, then he'd been studying the house and the neighborhood for some time now. The perp probably spent so much time here that by the time he broke into the girl's room he felt extremely confident and in control of the environment.

The houses lining the cul-de-sac all looked alike; each was dotted with a square patch of grass and lined with the same narrow walkway leading to the house. Lizzy made it as far as the front porch without being questioned, but that's where the fun stopped. A young officer, about five foot seven, muscular and compact, square jaw, stood before the front entrance, unwilling to give her the slightest peek inside the house.

She flashed him her PI license. He wasn't impressed, not until Jared made an appearance on the other side of the doorway.

The sight of him nearly took her breath away. Jared looked good in his dark suit, crisp white shirt, and dark tie. Standard fed attire. He should have mixed right in with the rest of the agents scouring the grounds, but he didn't. He stood out like Gerard Butler in a gay bar, or any bar for that matter.

"I've requested Ms. Gardner's presence," Jared told the officer. "Let her through."

She held her head high and walked inside, but not before giving the officer a smug look as she passed.

The outside of the house looked like it could use a new coat of paint, but the inside had an ultra-clean, recently remodeled appearance with wood floors stained a rich black walnut and cushiony furniture straight out of a Crate and Barrel catalog. To her left was the living room. A woman, most likely the mother of the abducted girl, sat on an oversized couch lined in tailored navy-and-white-striped slipcovers. She looked somewhat familiar, but Lizzy couldn't place the face.

An agent, or maybe a police detective, she wasn't sure, had made himself comfortable on a matching ottoman facing the woman. He had pen and paper in hand, and he was taking notes. To Lizzy's far right was the kitchen where a couple of crime scene technicians dusted for prints.

Jared gestured for Lizzy to head farther inside. Then he shut the door and stopped long enough to give her a quick once-over before he said, "Thanks for coming."

What could she say to that? "Thanks for inviting me" didn't seem appropriate under the circumstances, so she nodded and said, "Not a problem." Her gaze fell to his ID clipped to his front pocket. "Special Agent. I had no idea."

"Understandable, considering we haven't talked in a while."

She thought she detected a hint of hurt in his voice, and that surprised her, although it shouldn't have. Twice she'd let him down. After her disappearance, he'd put off going to college right away because he wanted to help find her. According to her parents, he spent every day for the two months she was missing in the volunteer center answering phones, distributing flyers, and calling the media to make sure they didn't forget about her. And then, against all odds, she returned and cut him out of her life as if he were a cancerous cyst. The flashbacks, the horrible cries of anguish, the torture, the mutilation, the blood: at the time, the images wouldn't stop coming—they suffocated her. Fearing she was losing her mind, she told Jared to go to college, get a life, leave her alone.

And after a few months of her continuous abuse, he did exactly that.

For the next ten years, Lizzy teetered on the edge of insanity. Hell, who was she kidding, she was still teetering; only now everything that had happened to her was a blur…unless she was sleeping. That's when shadows and faces came alive, just long enough to keep her from getting a good night's sleep and moving on with her life. Seeing Jared tonight made her wish things could have turned out differently between them. But such was life. Shit happened.

Jared was on the move, heading toward the back of the house. She followed him. He still had a nice ass. And she still remembered how the tightness of his buttocks had felt beneath her fingertips when they made love for the last time all those years ago. She could easily count the number of times she'd had sex since— and she only needed one hand. It didn't take long for the few guys she had dated to sense she had "issues" that needed to be dealt with before she could have any sort of meaningful relationship. Seeing Jared reminded her that nobody would ever compare to him. Apparently, he only got better with age. Pathetic. "Can I see the note?"

"This way," he said. He didn't turn around, didn't glance her way; he just kept walking, staying the course. One thing was clear: he hadn't invited her here for idle chitchat. This wasn't a reunion. He was a professional. He probably had a wife, two kids, and a house with a white picket fence. It was no business of hers, but that didn't stop her stomach from churning at the thought.

Shoulders straight and tall, she followed him down the hallway and into the bedroom at the end of the hallway. Another FBI agent was in the room talking on his cell phone. He was a few inches taller than Jared and at least two decades older. He used his chin to gesture a hello. He must have known she was coming because he handed Jared a note, which had been sealed within a plastic bag, and then he continued with his conversation.

Jared handed Lizzy the plastic bag. "That's Jimmy Martin. He has a few questions for you, if you don't mind."

Lizzy looked at the bag and tried to stop her hands from shaking. She hadn't allowed herself to think about the note until this very moment. If she'd learned anything from being abducted and subjected to some of the worst acts of extreme cruelty, it was how to swallow all the bad shit whole, tamp it down, and pray it didn't surface.

She busied herself with looking around the bedroom since she wasn't ready to read the note. The walls were painted a periwinkle blue with a funky chartreuse color accenting the wall space around the window. The window trim was painted a crisp white, with all the colors combining to give the room a fun, high-energy feeling. Brittany would love this room. There was a white built-in vanity with lots of space for makeup and other paraphernalia. In the far corner was a built-in desk with a large work surface and three deep storage drawers. The ceiling was covered with two rows of track lighting fixtures with halogen bulbs that shed a pure, white light around the room, which contrasted heavily with what had happened here in the past twenty-four hours. The cover on the bed was bunched up on one side and made of a white waffle-textured fabric. Throw pillows in shades of blue, chartreuse, and white were on the floor. A bedside table was littered with teen magazines and an open bag of potato chips. A magnetic board showcased the girl's myriad ribbons and awards for various school activities. The window treatments were modern Roman blinds topped by arched valances made from a checked fabric that included all the colors of the room.

The screen had been sliced open with a straight-edged razor. Lizzy looked at the note. She couldn't put it off forever. That's why she'd come, wasn't it?

I have missed you, Lizzy. You promised you would never leave me.

Liar liar, pants on fire. Nobody's safe and it's your fault.

I knew you would come. I know you better than you know yourself.

A man's face flashed through her mind, fast and startling, like lightning slicing through a dark sky. He peered through a mask that ended at the bridge of his long, straight nose. Beneath a wide forehead, his eyes were lit with excitement. He had thin lips. His skin was smooth and unblemished. No facial hair, no wrinkles.

Jimmy Martin said a curt good-bye. He snapped his phone shut and tucked his cell into the holder hooked to his waistband.

Despite her best efforts to stay calm, Lizzy's palms were damp and her hands wouldn't stop shaking. The note proved the one thing she'd been dreading all along.

He was alive.

She sensed the killer's presence as if he were in the room with her at this very moment. Spiderman had come back after all these years.

Or had he been hanging around all along, watching her every move?

Before a man named Frank Lyle was put behind bars, detectives had speculated that Spiderman had more than likely been incarcerated for another crime or that he had died. Serial killers didn't just stop committing crimes and disappear. They either went to jail for another crime, died, or caused more pain and death.

Jared made quick introductions.

According to his badge, Jimmy Martin was Special Agent in Charge. Although Jimmy looked less than pleased to meet her, he shook her hand and said, "Thanks for coming."

"No problem." She handed him the plastic bag with the note. "I don't know how I can be of any help."

"If this is the same man who kidnapped you," Jimmy said, "you were with him for quite some time. Did you ever see his handwriting?"

"I thought Spiderman was already behind bars," she said, testing him, since she had stated publically more than once that Frank Lyle was definitely *not* Spiderman.

"We'd like to think so. Until someone can prove otherwise, it's all speculation."

She shook her head. "I never saw his handwriting. He kept me blindfolded and bound. He also wore a mask."

"It says in your case file that you *did* see him."

"Once. He was asleep on the couch." *When she'd almost escaped the first time. When she'd almost saved the little girl without a tongue.* "I saw the side of his face. But if you read the file, then you know the rest." She thought about telling Special Agent Martin about the face she just saw flash through her mind, but Agent Martin didn't look like he trusted her, so she kept quiet.

"In his note he says 'it's all your fault.' Why?"

"Because like the note says, he knows me." She rubbed her arms, couldn't get the chill to go away. "He knows me well enough to know I'll feel responsible for anything he does."

"Why?" Jimmy's dark eyes bored into hers. "Why would you feel responsible?"

"Because I got away."

"Because he let you go?"

Why was this man trying to make her feel as if she'd purposely helped the maniac in some way?

Jared stepped forward, but she stopped him with a raised hand. "He didn't let me go. I got away. I escaped."

"Why didn't he kill you?" Agent Martin asked.

"I don't know. There have been days I wished he had." A young girl named Sophie was out there somewhere and there was nothing Lizzy could do to help her. Her chest tightened. *Breathe. Just breathe.*

Jimmy clasped the top of the bedpost behind her. She could feel the heat of his body as he tried to use intimidation to find out whatever it was he was after. "If it's your man who took Sophie, he's killed at least four young females, but he left your pretty little head intact...and you're telling me that after living with the man for nearly two months you have no idea why?"

"That's enough," Jared said as he took hold of her arm and pulled her out from under Agent Martin's intense questioning. "Like she said, it's all in the file. I didn't ask her here so you could rip her to shreds."

Jimmy ignored him. "Are you aware that Frank Lyle, the man found guilty for Jennifer Campbell's murder six months ago, has also confessed to killing all four of Spiderman's victims?"

Lizzy shrugged. "If the note you showed me tonight was from Spiderman, then Frank Lyle is lying. More than likely Frank Lyle has some pathological need for notoriety. I think Lyle is delusional. He's read and heard enough about the case to commit the facts to memory."

"He passed the polygraph test."

"If he believes he committed the crimes then you know as well as I do that he could easily pass the polygraph test. I told authorities months ago they had the wrong man."

"How can you be so sure?"

"I was there when they interrogated Lyle, watching from behind a two-way mirror. Nothing about Lyle struck me as familiar. Spiderman had a strong jaw and a wide forehead. Lyle possessed neither of those features. Besides the physical aspects, Lyle acted aggressive and hostile. I also saw the reports. Therapists describe Lyle as having little or no self-control. Spiderman is the exact opposite. He has patience. He's methodical and disciplined. Lyle is merely a wannabe. A guy who snapped after he lost his job and his wife left him."

"So, you're convinced that Spiderman is back?"

"I guess you could say that." She lifted her chin. "He called me today."

Jared looked perplexed, obviously wondering why she hadn't mentioned that when he'd called earlier.

Jimmy's scowl deepened. "What did he say?"

"He said I was a liar and a thief. He also said that because of me others would pay." Her gaze fell to Sophie Madison's desk where lots of pictures were taped to the mirror hanging on the wall. A bright yellow sign read, *You are a Star!* Below the star was a picture…a picture of Sophie Madison. "I know that girl."

Jimmy followed her gaze. His brows slanted inward. "You know Sophie Madison?"

"I've seen her in class."

"But you didn't recall her name before now?"

"I have dozens of students sign up every month. The class is free. I do recognize faces, though."

"When did she take your class?" Jared asked.

"A few weeks ago." No wonder she'd recognized the woman in the front room. "Oh my God." Her heart plummeted. "He is back. And he's pissed." *Liar liar, pants on fire.*

"Why?" Jimmy wanted to know. "What do you mean?"

"He knows I lied to him. He feels betrayed." Lizzy felt trapped. The room was stuffy, making it hard to breathe. She looked at Jared. "I have to go."

He ushered her from the room. "Come on, let's get some coffee."

CHAPTER 6

Monday, February 15, 2010 10:03 p.m.

Jared pulled his Denali to the side of the road and parked in front of a quaint Victorian house. Lizzy parked behind him and stepped out onto the curb. "This doesn't look like a coffee shop," she told him when he joined her on the curbside.

"Best coffee shop in the area." They headed for the house. "I grind my own beans."

"Impressive," she said, but her heart wasn't in it. Too much had happened too fast, making her feel as if the ground would open up at any moment and swallow her whole. She was having a difficult time wrapping her mind around the possibility that Spiderman had taken Sophie because of her.

Jared opened the front door and gestured for her to head inside. It was dark. Too dark. She stayed where she was.

Without questioning her behavior, he stepped around her and made his way into the living room, turning on lights as he went. He laid his jacket over the arm of a well-cushioned chair. Then he disappeared into the back of the house. When he returned he said, "It's all clear."

She stepped inside.

Jared took her coat and hung it in the entry closet. "You look good, Lizzy."

Impulsively she touched the flyaway hair framing her face. Realizing it would take an army of beauticians to make her presentable, she dropped her hands to her sides. "Thanks. You don't look too bad yourself."

His smile, Lizzy thought, didn't hide the worry etched in his eyes. He wanted to do his job, and yet he didn't want to upset her. "So," she said, feeling out of her element. "Why did you call me here tonight? You could have read me the note over the phone. It was short and sweet."

"We hoped you might recognize the handwriting. And I needed to see you—make sure you were safe."

Jared still had the same thick, dark hair. At thirty-three, he was lean and well muscled. Other than a couple of fine lines around his eyes when he smiled, he'd hardly changed. She followed him to the kitchen and looked around as he gathered filters, beans, and coffee cups.

"Do you think Spiderman is back?" she asked him.

"It looks that way."

"I don't think Jimmy Martin believed a word I said."

"I wouldn't worry about Jimmy. He's been dealing with criminals for too long. He's way past being bitter. He's downright acidic."

She smiled.

"I'm sure Jimmy hoped to retire next year knowing Spiderman was behind bars," he added.

Lizzy decided to let it go. She hadn't followed Jared to his house to complain about Jimmy Martin. In fact, she wasn't sure why she followed him here at all. "For the record, you don't have to worry about me," she said. "I have more than one deadbolt on the front door of my apartment. I've spent a lot of money securing all my windows and doors. And I carry a gun."

He scooped beans into a grinder and hit the ON button. Once he was finished, he said, "How's your sister?"

The aroma of crushed gourmet coffee beans drifted her way. "Cathy is doing well." She gave Jared a long look. No signs of a beer belly or thinning hair. Some guys had all the luck. "She has a daughter, Brittany, whom I adore."

"How about your parents?"

"Mom lives in Hawaii. I haven't seen her in a while, but I talk to her every few weeks. Dad and I don't talk much."

"I'm sorry to hear that."

After the finely ground beans were poured into a filter, he filled the pot with water and pushed another button. A pewter frame on the counter caught her attention. The picture was of Jared and a small girl she guessed to be about six years of age. She picked up the frame. "Is this your daughter?"

He shook his head. "Never married. No children. That's Ciara Gelhaus. My first abduction case. Found within twenty-four hours."

"Where was she?"

"Her neighbor's apartment, a woman unable to have children of her own. Five minutes before she planned to skip town with Ciara, we moved in on a hunch and it paid off."

"She's a doll."

"I keep the picture to remind me that there is such a thing as a happy ending."

Lizzy cocked her head. "Never married?"

"Surprised?"

"You always talked about having lots of kids someday."

"I was engaged once. It didn't work out."

"I'm sorry."

He reached a hand to her chin and tilted her head upward so she had no choice but to look into his eyes. "I'm the one who's sorry, Lizzy. I never should have let you walk home that night."

She took a step back.

His hand dropped to his side.

"Let's not go there," she said. "We could go back and forth with the 'I'm sorrys' until we're blue in the face, but it wouldn't change things. It is what it is."

"You have nothing to be sorry about," he said.

"That's not true. I lied to my parents. When I returned from the house of horrors, I told you to leave me alone. I fell apart. I couldn't see you. Not even after I began to see things a little more clearly. I thought about you all the time, but I never picked up the phone and called you. I'm sorry for all of that." And she was. More than anything back then she'd wanted to call him…mostly when she was in her deepest, darkest hour, because in the end, images of Jared were what helped pull her through the worst of her nightmare.

* * *

Jared watched Lizzy walk back to the living room. He hadn't expected to feel such a tumble of raw emotions. But the truth was, the moment he'd first seen her tonight, he'd felt guilty—guilty for not being there for her all these years. He was also surprised to see how much weight she'd lost since he'd seen her last. She looked thin, almost gaunt. Her green eyes still mesmerized, and yet there was no sparkle there. After she'd pushed him away all those years ago, his anger had turned to hurt before slowly fading into oblivion. He hadn't been sure what he'd feel once he saw her again, but now he knew. He wanted to wrap his arms around her and never let her go. He couldn't count the number of times he had wanted to call her. But in the end, he always rationalized it was best if he kept his distance, worried that hanging around her would only stir up bad memories for Lizzy. Now that she was here, though, he knew he'd been wrong.

Already he felt a strong desire to protect her. And yet he needed her to do the one thing she might not be ready to do. He needed her to remember, needed her to return to the very thing she'd been running from for way too long. He needed to ask her to dive into the deepest, darkest recesses of her mind and dig up all the seemingly insignificant details she might have missed.

He filled a mug with hot coffee. "Sugar and cream?"

She headed back his way. "Black is fine."

With coffee in hand, they made their way to the green vintage couch in the living room. She took a seat while he adjusted the thermostat. "It'll be warm in no time."

He took a seat beside her, and she looked at him over the rim of her cup. "Sophie Madison needs me."

Jared looked into Lizzy's eyes and realized he needed her too. It had taken him years to move on. And then he met Peggy Chambers, a lawyer. He had asked Peggy to marry him for all the wrong reasons. Every time she pushed him to set a wedding date, doubt clouded his mind. Peggy was a smart woman, though. She knew he'd never stopped thinking about Lizzy. So did his parents and his sister…everybody knew he had unfinished business with Lizzy Gardner even before he figured it out for himself.

"Yeah," he finally said. "Sophie needs you. I need you too. I need you to tell me everything you know about the man who abducted you. What was he like? Did he have any hobbies? Did he ever leave the house?"

"I've told the FBI everything I know."

"But you've never told *me*."

She sipped her coffee, her gaze shifting away from his. A quiet moment settled between them before she said, "Spiderman had an enormous amount of patience."

Jared watched her sip her coffee, waiting for her to continue. After a few moments, he wasn't disappointed.

"As you know," Lizzy said, "he was fond of spiders. The tarantula was his favorite breed, but he liked to talk about what he considered to be the most dangerous spiders in the world. He liked to place spiders on his victims' bodies. He would watch closely as the insects moved over smooth, unblemished skin. Hours would pass before he would provoke the spiders, pinch them, anything to make them bite into flesh."

"Sophie had an older sister who was sleeping upstairs at the time of her abduction," Jared told her. "Do you think Spiderman knew exactly which sister he was going after? Do you believe he followed his victim and scouted her out before he made his move?"

"Yes, of course. If this is Spiderman's work, he always knew who he was going after. By the time he kidnapped his victims, he knew them better than they knew themselves." There was a long pause before she added, "Except for me. I was a mistake."

"What do you mean?"

She gave him a wry smile. "You know—wrong place, wrong time, wrong bat channel."

"Yeah, I guess I do. He wasn't after you that night, was he?"

She met his gaze straight on, unblinking. Her eyes looked sharper now. "No. He wasn't after me. You know that. He wanted the Anderson girl. He told me that, and I told the feds." She sighed and then asked, "Any chance Sophie Madison was a family-member abduction and they wrote the note to throw you off?"

"There's always a chance, but from what we've gathered so far, that's not the case. Mrs. Madison can hardly stay focused and her husband was rushed to the hospital an hour before you arrived... heart problems. There are no uncles or aunts, and all grandparents are accounted for."

"Mondays really do suck," she said without much emotion.

He didn't respond.

"Are you and your FBI friends conducting a neighborhood door-to-door search?" she asked.

Lizzy didn't have a great deal of respect for the agency and Jared couldn't blame her. For over a decade, she'd been treated more like a criminal than a victim. "Should we be conducting a neighborhood search?"

She narrowed her eyes. "Isn't that standard procedure?"

With anyone else, he might play the game, but not with Lizzy. "You know it is," he said. "I'm only surprised you would ask."

She shrugged. "If I were the mother, it would certainly make me feel better knowing my neighbors didn't have my kid stuffed away in the back of their bedroom closet." Frustrated, she swept flyaway bangs out of her face. "If you've read the files, you know Spiderman is keen on disguises."

She looked over her shoulder as if she'd heard a noise.

He followed her gaze from the entry door to the front window. He was about to ask her what she was doing when she turned back to him. "If anyone says they saw a suspicious character around the area, I wouldn't bank on their description, that's all."

"I didn't see anything about disguises in your case file, other than the mention of a beard."

"That doesn't surprise me. Why take notes? From the start, the authorities have taken much of what I said with a grain of salt."

"That's because every time they interviewed you, Lizzy, your story changed."

Her eyes narrowed. "How so?"

Jared stood and disappeared down the hall. Moments later, he returned with a thick manila file and handed it to her.

She flipped through the pages, most of which were dog-eared. She skimmed page after page of notes, starting with the day she was found and ending with a few recent articles, including an interview with her father. She stiffened. "I didn't realize Dad agreed to talk on national television."

"When was the last time you saw him?"

"I haven't seen him in years. He wants nothing to do with me. He blames me for everything bad that has ever happened in his life."

Jared remained silent until she finished reading the article. "After you escaped and were picked up on the side of the road, you said a couple of things that turned out to be false statements. You told Betsy Raeburn, the woman who found you and drove you to the police station, that you had been sexually abused." Jared paused. "The fluids on your undergarments matched my DNA only."

Her cheeks flushed with color as she continued to skim the contents of the file.

"When you were interviewed by the FBI you stated that the killer forced you to swallow poison, that he burned you daily with cigarettes and hot pokers, and that you were forced to—"

She tossed the file on the couch to her side and stood so fast her knee knocked into the coffee table. Coffee sloshed over the rim of his cup and onto the table. "Fuck you and all of your FBI friends. It all happened." She pointed a finger at him. "I don't care if you or anyone else believes me, which begs the question: If you people don't believe a word I'm saying then why the hell did you call me here? Why are you asking me questions I've already answered a hundred times? Mostly, Jared, why are *you* doing this to me?"

Jared stood too. He put a hand on her arm, but she knocked it away.

"I believe you, Lizzy. If you say it happened, I believe you."

"Bullshit."

"OK, let me rephrase that. I believe that *you* believe these things happened to you, but they couldn't have happened, Lizzy. Rattlesnake bites leaves scars. Your blood was checked for poisons, and yet the results showed you were clear of toxins. And there are pictures, Lizzy. Pictures of your arms, hands, legs, stomach. They're all in the file…taken days, if not hours, after you returned. No burn marks. No insect bites. Why is that, do you think?"

"I don't know."

It was quiet for a moment, the tension thick.

She raised her hands, and then clasped them behind her neck. Clearly frustrated, she dropped her arms to her sides and began to pace the room. "Listen, I want to help you find Sophie, but I refuse to be treated like a criminal…or a liar."

Jared sat back down. He hated to get her riled. He knew she believed these things happened to her, but they hadn't. But that didn't mean she wasn't verbally and mentally tortured for two months. For two months she was gone. Missing. That much was certain. And when she returned, she was malnourished and dehydrated. That was also a fact.

Before joining the FBI, Jared majored in psychology with an emphasis on criminology and victimology. He had a theory about what had happened to her, and he realized he was going about this all wrong. "Lizzy," he said, his voice calm, "you could have experienced a form of countertransference—what some people call bystander's guilt or survivor's guilt."

She stood silent in the middle of the room, her arms crossed.

His chest tightened. "You said you wanted to help Sophie. I've read the files, but I need to hear it all from you. I need to know we're not missing something crucial." He exhaled. "You mentioned Spiderman wore a mask."

"That's right. He did." Lizzy moved toward the front window. The blinds were closed tight. She opened them slightly, allowing moonlight to squeeze in through the crevices. She turned his way and said, "Besides the mask, he never looked the same: a beard one day, a mustache the next. Same with his hair: long, short, blond, dark brown, or black. Never the same."

Lizzy came back to where Jared was sitting and put a hand on the back of the couch. "For the record, I think he left the house sometimes because days would pass where I didn't see or hear him walking around. In the beginning, I was always scared. As the days and weeks passed, I was more hungry than I was scared. Toward the end, I was hungry, cold, and pissed off."

A twitch set in her jaw. She clutched the back of the couch and looked him in the eyes. "Did you know that my father blamed my mother for letting me go out that night?"

He nodded.

"Then I'm sure you know they divorced within a year of my abduction."

He reached out and covered her hand with his.

She flinched but didn't pull away. Her skin felt soft. She was trembling. He didn't like the ache gnawing in his gut. Although she put on a tough act, she was fragile.

"If I had done as my father asked," she said, "none of this would have happened."

"Spiderman would have found someone else."

"Perhaps." She looked at him long and hard. "So what's the plan?" she asked, her eyes sharp, her voice less heated. "The feds think he's going to come after me, don't they?"

"If that was Spiderman who called you today, I'd say it's more than a possibility."

She lifted her chin. "For the record, I'm not afraid."

"I'm afraid for you."

"Don't be." Her eyes lit up with determination. "I made a decision on the way over here tonight."

"A decision?"

"I'm going to find Spiderman," she said. "I can't keep hiding and jumping at every little sound. I'm going to find the sick bastard before he can make his next move."

"And how do you propose to do that?"

"I'll contact the media and send him a message of my own."

CHAPTER 7

Monday, February 15, 2010 11:59 p.m.

He thought about popping another Klonopin. His hands were shaking. His hands never used to shake. Turning away from the Sophie girl, he headed for the door, then pivoted on his feet and said, "Boo!"

Her eyes widened. Beneath the duct tape, he heard a gasp.

He sighed. Is that all she had? "You never should have cussed at your mother," he said with a pointed finger for emphasis. "Especially in public." He shook his head. "Only bad girls dress like sluts and curse like sailors. Do you know why I chose you, Sophie?"

She shook her head. Tears dribbled down her cheeks.

"Because you don't have any respect for your elders. If I ever dared to talk back to my parents, do you know what they would have done to me?"

She shook her head. Her entire body was shaking as if she were a damn Chihuahua. Not only did the teenager have zero respect for her parents, she had no spine.

"My father would have taken a razor to my flesh," he said with fervor.

Her eyes nearly bulged right out of their sockets.

Better.

He went to the dresser and opened the top drawer to view his collection of surgical knives and straightedge razors. For Sophie's benefit, he held up an exquisitely sharp curved blade, manufactured in England and made for precise incision.

"Should we start with this one, Sophie?"

She closed her eyes. Her lips quivered. He guessed she was praying to some invisible God who couldn't hear her.

He stopped to stare and wait.

Why didn't he feel anything?

He counted to ten. Nothing. His breathing was calm and even. Not one tingle rippled through his loins. The girl was a bore. At that moment, she opened her eyes and looked right at him with big brown puppy-dog eyes. Eyes that reminded him of why she was here, why he was forced to do the things he did. His pulse roared in his ears, hitting his senses like a thirty-foot wave crashing against jagged rocks.

He moved toward her, his fingers rolled into fists, his insides swirling in a state of frenzied activity: temples throbbing, pulse erratic, blood flickering through his veins like an electrical current. He had every intention of carving her eyeballs out of their sockets.

Whimpering, she squeezed her eyes shut.

Damn. Open your eyes. "Are you scared, Sophie?"

It was hard to tell if she nodded or not with all the violent shaking going on. The girl needed to develop a backbone. Man, oh, man. She had a lot to learn before he killed her. What happened to the ballsy girl with the big mouth? His shoulders dropped. He watched her for another moment before finally turning back to the dresser. He put the knife away and slammed the drawer shut.

Her eyes were still clamped shut as he headed for the exit. "I want you to think about what your punishment should be. I'm going to go rest for a bit while you think about it."

Shutting the door behind him, he made his way to the front room. Sophie should have been asleep. He'd given her enough sleeping pills to keep her out for another two or three hours at least. She was an odd duck, all shivery and quiet.

And those eyes…disturbing.

Every muscle in his body ached. He had yet to hit forty, but today he felt like a seventy-year-old man. He plunked down on the couch and let his head fall back against the cushions.

If he'd learned anything last night, it was that all those experts were right about one thing…he could never stop.

Tuesday, February 16, 2010 10:12 a.m.

Cathy had shown up at Lizzy's place thirty minutes ago, and they were already arguing.

"You need a bodyguard," Cathy told Lizzy.

"Don't be ridiculous," Lizzy said. "For the past fourteen years I've done everything you've asked of me. I see a therapist every other week, a therapist I can't afford, I might add. I also write in a damn journal every day. I hate that."

Cathy rolled her eyes. "Putting your thoughts to paper is therapeutic. It's a healing process, a pathway toward understanding yourself."

"Writing in a journal is bullshit. I have deadbolts and locks on every door and bars on every window," Lizzy said, spurred on by Cathy's blasé attitude, since her sister had no idea what it was like to be scared shitless twenty-four hours a day, seven days a week, for year after year. "I carry a gun. I never step outside without checking behind every bush and looking up every tree. Every tweet of a bird, every rustle of a leaf, every honk of a horn is my enemy."

Her sister remained silent.

Lizzy attempted to rub the tension from her temples. "For too many years now I've been afraid of my own shadow. I can't do it anymore. I won't do it anymore. I'm going to learn what makes Spiderman tick, find out why he does what he does, why he—"

"What do you think every FBI profiler and criminal investigator in the country has been doing for the past decade?"

"Obviously not enough. They haven't caught the lunatic, have they?"

"Frank Lyle probably has friends on the outside with nothing better to do than make prank phone calls," Cathy said, ending with a sigh. "OK, OK. So you learn everything you can about Spiderman based on what little you remember, and then what?"

"And then I figure out his next step. I figure out what he's going to do before he does."

"And?"

"And then I set a trap for him and I wait." Lizzy looked at the door to her apartment, raised her arms, and aimed an invisible gun that way. "And when he walks through that door, I shoot him between the eyes."

"I don't like it."

"I didn't think you would."

"Why do you think he's doing this again...after all this time?"

"That's one of many unanswered questions I aim to find out," Lizzy said.

"If you insist on going through with this and getting involved in the Sophie Madison case, I can't let you hang out with Brittany. I can't risk having her life put in jeopardy."

"I understand."

Cathy huffed. "Your niece means so little to you that you would give up your time with her so easily?"

Lizzy laid an open palm over her heart. "She means so much to me that I would never risk hurting even one hair on her perfect head."

Cathy's head dipped.

Damn. Lizzy rested a hand on her sister's shoulder. "I don't mean to hurt you or stress you out, but after receiving that phone call and seeing Jared again, I had an epiphany. I can't live this way any longer. I can't run from my own shadow for another minute. It's killing me to live this way."

Cathy used her sleeve to wipe her eyes. "I can't do this anymore either. I'm done caring. You've always done exactly what you wanted without any care to any of us. You always took my things without asking, you lied to Mom and Dad. The choices you've made have ruined our lives. And now you're willing to give up your relationship with Brittany because you want to go after a maniacal, bloodthirsty killer." She raised her arms in the air before letting them drop to her sides. "I give up. I'm done." She grabbed her purse from the coffee table and then looked around for her sweater.

The doorbell rang.

Lizzy looked through the peephole. Jared stood on the other side. After unlocking the chain and deadbolts, she opened the door and gestured for him to come inside. He looked just as good in a blue button-down shirt and a pair of fitted jeans as he had in a suit and tie. The sleeves of his shirt were rolled to his elbows, revealing bronzed forearms sprinkled with just enough dark hair to tantalize. And here she thought she'd lost her appetite for the opposite sex. Who knew?

"Jared," Lizzy said, gesturing toward her sister. "I'm sure you remember Cathy."

Cathy had located her sweater. She headed for the door.

Jared said hello and offered his hand.

Ignoring his friendly gesture, Cathy stopped directly in front of him, her face a maze of angry lines. "Why did you have to call Lizzy and get her involved? Do you know how hard she's struggled to get where she is today?"

"I'm not going to let anything happen to her."

Cathy huffed. "You knew there was a killer on the loose fourteen years ago, but that didn't stop you from dropping her off in the middle of the street on a dark, starless night, now did it?"

"Knock it off," Lizzy said as she put a hand on Cathy's shoulder and ushered her away from Jared and out the door.

Once they were outside, Lizzy followed her sister down the steps to Cathy's silver BMW parked on the street. "What is wrong with you?" Lizzy asked. "I can't believe you're doing this to me."

Cathy's eyes blazed. "I'm doing this to *you?*"

"Yes. Why can't you understand that I don't want to hide from my own shadow for the rest of my life?"

Cathy slid behind the wheel of her car, turned on the ignition, and said, "Because I happen to believe that hiding from your own shadow is better than the alternative." Cathy gestured toward the apartment. "I hope you're not planning on getting romantically involved with that man again."

"Why would you care?"

"I've heard things about him, that's all. He's a heartbreaker… a love 'em and leave 'em kind of guy. Why do you think he's still single?"

Lizzy shrugged. "There's nothing going on."

"Well, good." Cathy shut the door with jarring finality and drove off.

As Lizzy watched her sister's BMW disappear around the bend, she noticed a green Jeep Grand Cherokee parked on the other side of the road. The Jeep wouldn't have caught her attention if the driver of the vehicle hadn't ducked the moment her sister drove away.

Lizzy walked toward her apartment, careful to keep her attention focused on the steps leading to her apartment because she didn't want whoever was watching from the Jeep to know she was on to them.

She entered the apartment and closed the door behind her. Jared said something, but she ignored him. Instead, she headed for the kitchen window and peeked through the blinds. Her heart raced when she saw the driver sit up. It was a woman. A baseball cap covered most of her face. A ponytail stuck out the back of her cap: thick, straight hair. Brunette.

Lizzy bolted for the Pembroke table near her front entry. She opened the drawer and grabbed her gun. Then she yanked open the front door, took the stairs two at a time, and hit the pavement running.

The screech of wheels drowned out Jared's curses behind her. Lizzy chased after the car by foot, gun drawn. The Jeep disappeared around the corner, tires squealing. If she went back for her car keys now it would be too late to chase after the woman. "Damn."

Jared was on her heels. "What the hell are you doing?"

"Lay off," she warned, pointing a finger at him as she headed back the way she'd come. Frustrated, she marched up the stairs to her apartment and saw Maggie trotting down the road in the opposite direction the Jeep had gone. "Maggie, come back here!"

"I'll get the cat," he said. "You get inside and lock the door behind you."

"Yes, sir."

Before setting out after Maggie, he shook his head at her as if she'd gone and lost her mind for good. Lizzy put her gun back in the drawer. She located the notebook and pen she kept by the phone and wrote down the part of the license plate she'd seen, along with a description of the driver: petite, dark hair, small nose. Forest-green Jeep with the numbers one and eight and the letter N in the first four digits of the license plate. She set down her pen. *Who was that woman and what did she want?*

A knock sounded, startling her. She'd already forgotten about Jared and Maggie. She hurried to the front entry and opened the door.

Maggie clawed at Jared's neck and chest. He groaned and tossed the cat in the general direction of her living room. He shut the door behind him and clicked the main lock.

"You're bleeding."

"You don't say."

She ushered Jared toward the kitchen, trying not to smile at the irritation lining his face. She found a clean cloth and ran a corner of it under cold tap water. Dabbing the cloth over the scratch across his jaw, she fought the urge to smooth a hand over his handsome face. It startled her to think he could have this effect on her after all these years.

"I hope that thing has had its shots."

"That thing is named Maggie." She smiled, and when she dabbed the cloth at his jaw again, he cracked a smile too. "It's good to see you smile," he said.

"It's either laugh or cry."

A moment passed before he said, "I guess your sister hasn't forgiven me yet."

"Cathy isn't the forgiving type. She's a lot like Dad."

"Yeah, well, you don't deserve to be treated that way."

"At some point in our lives we all have to learn to deal with the cards we've been dealt." She left his side and busied herself with feeding Maggie.

"About the Jeep," he said. "Did you get a look at the guy?"

She knelt down and scooped food onto Maggie's dish. "It was a woman."

"Anyone you know?"

She shook her head.

"You can't go chasing after every suspicious car you see parked outside your apartment."

She straightened. "I appreciate your concern, I really do. But please don't start telling me what to do."

"Still so stubborn after all these years?"

"I do my best." By the time she finished cleaning up in the kitchen, Jared was checking the windows in the front room.

"Cathy already checked the locks," she told him, but she knew she was wasting her breath.

"Jimmy wants to bring in a couple of his guys to set up a surveillance camera and a wiretap."

"Is that so?"

"Same goes for your office downtown."

"Great." Not.

"Jimmy also asked me to tell you to hold off on sending Spiderman any messages via the media."

"Why?"

"The agency doesn't want to put Sophie in any more danger than she's in already."

Lizzy followed him down the hallway, unable to bear thinking about what Sophie might be going through. "I think the agency is making a mistake. Sending Spiderman a message will distract him. He might not hurt the girl if we can divert his attention. He doesn't just torture his victims on a whim. Everything he does is carefully considered and calculated, designed for optimum pleasure on his part. He plans his next move in the same way an accomplished chess player would. If I send him a message it'll throw him off his game, cause him to concentrate on me instead of her—"

"Or he might get angry and take out his frustrations on Sophie."

She gnawed on her bottom lip, considering their options.

"I'll talk to Jimmy," he said before he disappeared down the hallway.

"When you're done checking windows, meet me in my bedroom," she said. "I want to show you something."

* * *

A few minutes later, Jared found Lizzy in her bedroom. A neatly made bed took up most of the room. The blinds were shut, curtains drawn. The walls were beige and the only hint of femininity in the room consisted of one well-used stuffed animal sitting front and center between the pillows on the bed. The stuffed animal was either a fox or a cat—hard to tell with its matted fur, missing tail, and one eye hanging from a thread.

Lizzy sat at a desk in the corner of the room farthest from the door. On the wall above the desk, a four-by-four whiteboard was covered with scribbles. The walls on both sides of the whiteboard, from ceiling to floor, were covered with lists and notes, all stapled or taped to the wall in an unorganized mess. Papers and notebooks were stacked high on the floor around her feet. "Looks like you've been busy," he said.

"After I returned home last night, I couldn't stop thinking about Sophie. You were right when you said that I need to remember everything I can in order to help her, but it's not easy. Scenes from my time spent with Spiderman pop into my head like film clips from a movie, flashing through my mind in bits and pieces when I least expect them. Some clips are blurred and choppy, others remarkably clear."

Jared didn't say anything; he just let her talk.

She gestured toward the papers taped to the wall. "I made lists of all of Spiderman's victims. Did you know that all except one of the girls was brown-haired and brown-eyed?"

He shook his head.

"I think that's more than coincidental."

"If there's even one girl with green or blue eyes," he told her, "it doesn't mean anything."

It was quiet for a moment. Her brow furrowed. "I still can't remember her name. A day hasn't gone by in the past fourteen years that I haven't seen her face, and yet I still can't remember her name."

"Whose name?"

"We were so close to getting away," Lizzy said, her eyes focused on the floor, her voice barely audible.

"Do you mean the girl you tried to save? The one you used to talk about when you first returned?"

She nodded.

After returning home, Lizzy had mentioned a small, malnourished girl without a tongue, but none of the bodies found fit the description. The original three girls Spiderman had been linked to had all been viciously tortured. They had spider bites on their legs and arms. All three victims had been left near a body of water: a community pool, a lake, and a reservoir.

While Lizzy was missing, another body had turned up in the same lake as the number two victim, tortured like the others… burn marks, spider bites, but no missing tongue. Since Lizzy's return, no other victims had been discovered, which was another reason some in the agency had a difficult time buying her story. Jimmy, among others, believed Lizzy was never caught by the madman at all, believing instead that Lizzy hid out for months until she tired of the game. Rumors quickly spread that she had made up the abduction story—all for attention.

Jared knew her well enough to know that wasn't the case. "What happened to the girl?" he asked, watching her closely.

She lifted her gaze to meet his. "All of those horrible things I talked about—"

"You mean the poison, the hot iron, the burns?"

"Yes, all of it." She stood. "It all happened to that poor little girl. Oh my God." She put a hand to her mouth. "And the other girls. These atrocities didn't happen to me, did they?" Her face paled. "You were right. All of those horrible, awful things happened to those other girls, but not to me."

He couldn't stand it another moment. The dark, haunted look on her face told him she hadn't had a moment's peace since her abduction. Jared pulled her close. He felt her wobble in his arms as if her legs might give out at any moment. Lizzy had transferred the shame and guilt that belonged with the killer onto herself.

She had also taken upon herself the disgust and horror of what had happened to his victims. More than likely, Lizzy had been engulfed by emotions until it became too much for her to bear. Unable to see the torture and beatings for what they were—inhuman acts performed by one human on another—Lizzy had been forced to deal with the horror in the only way she could in order to move on with her life.

Her forehead rested against his chest. Her body trembled. He rubbed her back. "Why did he keep you alive, Lizzy?"

There was a long stretch of silence before she said, "Because he thought I was a good girl. He wanted to keep me with him forever. He wanted me to watch and learn and see what happened to bad girls."

She was tense. Her voice raspy.

Jared moved away just enough so he could push flyaway hair from her face. "What did he want you to watch?"

"He wanted me to watch him do unspeakable things to the girls so I wouldn't make the same mistakes they did."

"How many girls?"

"Three. After the girl without a voice…three more girls. That I know of."

Jared had read every file, every note taken on the case, and Lizzy had never changed that part of her story, always stating that there were three more victims after she nearly escaped the first time. That would mean there were eight victims total, and four bodies were still missing, including the girl with no tongue. "How did he force you to watch?"

"He used manacles."

He drew in a breath. Lizzy had been one of the most compassionate, caring people he knew. Back in high school, she was the one who went out of her way to make new students feel welcome.

She was involved in a half dozen clubs, all having to do with raising awareness about animal cruelty, saying no to bullying, and helping to make the world a kinder, gentler place. The worst thing anybody could have done to her would have been to make her watch another person being harmed.

"The girls always looked the same at first," she said without prompting. "Scared, pale, shivering."

Lizzy appeared to be in a trance as she spoke, her eyes glazed and unblinking. "He would tie his victim up, usually to a bedpost or a chair, and use a blunt object like a steak knife to chop their hair at weird angles. Then he would ask them if they wanted to go home."

As she continued, her voice became clearer, easier to understand. "The moment Spiderman saw hope in their eyes," she said, "he would tell them they needed to pass a few tests if they wanted to go home." She looked up at him. "They never passed. Nobody could pass his tests."

He felt her shiver. "Days later—sometimes weeks later, once the hope was gone from their eyes—he would retrieve a glass jar filled with a clear liquid. It was always the same. He would dip a utensil into the jar. And then always, just when I thought his victim had nothing left, he'd drip acid into their eyes and the real screaming would begin." Her forehead fell gently against his chest.

He held her tight. Moments passed before her breathing calmed.

"And then what?"

"And then he'd bring me back to the room with the spiders. We were all in the same boat. We were all trapped with no way out."

"You and the spiders?"

He felt her nod.

"Most nights," she went on, "I just wanted to go to sleep and never wake up. But I couldn't sleep because those girls were always in my mind—the fear in their eyes, the horrors they'd endured. I could hear their screams…and sometimes I would hear a drilling sound."

"What kind of drilling?"

"High-pitched screeching…and never ending."

"An electric saw?" he asked. "Sawing or drilling?"

"I don't know."

Nobody other than the agents working the case knew that two of the three original victims had been blinded by acid. One victim had been found with needles protruding from her retinas. But the drilling noises didn't make sense, didn't tie into anything they had found on the bodies.

"Come on," he said, hating to see her look so broken. "I'm going to tell Jimmy you're not ready to get involved."

"I won't let you," she said, drawing in a steadying breath. "I need to do this…for me as much as for Sophie."

He led her to the kitchen, filled a glass with water, and held the rim of the glass to her lips. She took a few sips before he set the glass on the counter. Then he cradled her face between his hands. She had a pale, heart-shaped face, big eyes, and full lips. She was still the most beautiful woman he'd ever laid eyes on. He missed everything about her—missed their long talks about life, missed her easy laughter. "I never should have let you push me away."

"I hope you're not thinking of kissing me, because it's been so long since I've been kissed, I can't even remember how it's done. I don't think—"

He dipped his head and put his lips to hers before she could get another word out. Her lips were soft. He shouldn't be kissing her, certainly not now when she was vulnerable and weak. Maybe not ever. But he couldn't help himself. He'd spent a lot of time thinking about this kiss. It wasn't a matter of wanting to kiss her—he needed to kiss her, needed to hold her close and somehow let her know he would never let anyone hurt her again.

His cell rang. Lifting his head, he watched her eyes come slowly open.

"You're right," she said.

He grabbed hold of his cell when it rang again. "About what?"

"You never should have let me push you away."

He smiled and flipped open his cell. "Yes, I'm here with her now. She's fine with the wiretap."

He looked at her and she shrugged noncommittally.

"OK," he said, "see you in ten."

CHAPTER 8

Tuesday, February 16, 2010 11:00 a.m.

His heart drummed heavy against his ribs. He had dozed off. Sitting up straight, he glanced at the clock. He had a few more hours before he needed to get back to the office. "Cynthia," he said aloud, his dream still vivid in his mind. He longed to see her again, to be with her. He hadn't realized how much he missed Cynthia until this very moment.

For Cynthia he'd been able to stop killing. In fact, he thought he had kicked the habit for good. For nearly fourteen years, she had been enough. It hurt to think about the way she looked at him when he first told her the truth. But there was nothing he could do about that now. He had already hit the point of no return.

"Once a killer, always a killer."

There was no time for melancholy, he decided. He looked around the living room. He had a lot to do. The house hadn't been lived in for years. The walls needed a coat of fresh paint, maybe some new curtains. Cynthia had liked bright colors…reds and blues. He preferred more subdued colors like taupe. A mushroom yellow might work well to brighten things up some.

Movement inside a nine-gallon aquarium on the table in front of him caught his attention. Inside were two Australian funnel-web spiders he'd ordered online. Brownish-black in color and highly venomous, they were his favorite type of spider.

Cynthia had never been fond of spiders or snakes. His love for her had been strong, he realized. Still was. He'd overcome so much because of her.

He tapped the glass and smiled when the larger of the two spiders lifted its front legs and extended its fangs. "That's a good boy," he said. "Don't worry, you'll be eating soon."

Tuesday, February 16, 2010 11:55 a.m.

Lizzy couldn't remember the last time she'd had this many people in her apartment at once. Two men with the agency were working on her telephone, rewiring and connecting her phone to a black box resembling a miniature DVD player.

Jimmy Martin stood in the middle of her living room. He was on the phone again, telling law enforcement agencies to be on the lookout for a woman wearing a baseball cap and driving a green Jeep Grand Cherokee with the numbers she'd given him.

Lizzy didn't know what to think of Jimmy. He was stern in the face and rigid in movement. He didn't smile easily, if at all. In the kitchen, Jared opened another cupboard in search of a coffee cup and teabags. She didn't have the coffee he liked, so he'd opted for tea. Apparently, he was addicted to caffeine. And he was picky.

"Do you have any Indian black tea?" Jared asked.

She joined him in the kitchen, opened the drawer nearest the refrigerator, and pointed to a box. "Store brand green tea. It's the best I can do."

He took one of the packets from the box, although he didn't look happy about it. If she wasn't so tired she might have laughed at the displeasure scrawled across his face, unhappy with her tea collection. Picky or not, she already found herself enjoying his company. The kiss had sparked her imagination and had miraculously managed to take her mind off everything else for a few glorious moments.

"Did you ever leave Spiderman's house during those two months you were held in captivity?" Jimmy asked from the other room.

"No," Lizzy said with a shake of her head, wondering why the feds liked to ask the same questions over and over again. Leaving Jared to fend for himself, she headed back to the living room. Jimmy had moved from the chair to her couch where he hovered over her glass coffee table strewn with notes, pictures of Sophie, and a map of the Sacramento area surrounding the American River.

As she looked at the map, an image of the house from which she'd fled flickered through her mind. When Lizzy had escaped the second time, she'd gone through the bathroom window, the only window in the house without bars. In the beginning, Spiderman hadn't allowed her to use anything other than a bucket. Three weeks into her imprisonment, though, he led her to the bathroom and left her alone long enough for her to figure out she would need to lose a lot of weight in order to squeeze through the tiny window above the bathtub. She'd also known that she needed to stay alive long enough to make the attempt.

Lizzy looked at the map for another moment before she pointed at a specific street. "This is where I was picked up by Betsy Raeburn, the woman delivering dry cleaning that day."

Jimmy penciled a circle around an area nearly four blocks from the area she pointed at. "This is where Raeburn said she found you."

Frustrated, Lizzy looked at Jared. "Can somebody take me here—" she stabbed a finger at the map, "—to the spot where Betsy said she found me?"

Seemingly surprised by her request, Jared said, "According to the file, you've been there before. I don't think it's necessary."

"That was over a decade ago," she said. "Everything's different now. I've been seeing images of the house and the street in my mind. I need to go back there. Now."

"Are you sure you're ready?" Jared asked.

"For Christ's sake," Jimmy said. "I'll take her there myself."

Lizzy swallowed the lump in her throat. No, she wasn't sure. The truth was she felt as if she was teetering on the edge of a cliff. She could fall off at any moment. Been there, done that. But she'd already made up her mind and she wasn't going to turn back now. Glancing at Sophie's picture, she nodded at Jared. "I'm ready when you are."

"Before you run off," Jimmy said, "I have a few more questions."

She crossed her arms. "What do you want to know?"

"For starters—why now?"

Jared joined them in the living room and looked at Jimmy. "What do you mean?"

Jimmy's gaze never left Lizzy's. "I want to know why she thinks she can suddenly pinpoint the exact street where she was found, and yet for the past decade she couldn't zero in on a street within a mile radius of the spot given to us by Ms. Raeburn."

Refusing to cower, Lizzy stared back at Agent Martin with the same determination and grit she saw scrawled across his face.

"I believe she's been suffering from survivor's guilt," Jared cut in before she had a chance to respond. "Lizzy's guilt has caused her to repress painful memories, memories that could and can be triggered by almost anything…a particular smell, a song, a sound…anything at all. In Lizzy's case, I think it was the phone call she received from Spiderman or possibly the note that triggered some memories to return."

"I know you didn't believe me back then," Lizzy said to Martin, "and you probably don't believe me now, but I don't care what you think. The only thing I do care about is finding Sophie before it's too late."

Jimmy shoved his hands into his pants pockets. "I'm all ears."

"You two can speculate all you want," Lizzy went on, "but I'm telling you, Spiderman is back. And he already knows everything about Sophie, including what she's afraid of. If she's afraid of the dark, then she's in a basement or a windowless room."

"What about you?" Jimmy asked. "Did he keep you in the dark?"

"He didn't know me. I wasn't part of his plan. He used insects to scare me."

"Snakes and spiders never bothered you," Jared added.

"No, they didn't," she said. "Spiders and snakes intrigued me, but Spiderman didn't know that. His excitement when I showed fear was palpable. I knew that's what he wanted. If he acted as if he might place a spider on me, I cried out and begged him to stop. I let him think he'd found my Achilles' heel. He feeds on fear."

"You played him for a fool." Jimmy jangled the change in his pocket. "Sounds like this guy isn't as clever as he thinks."

She lifted her chin. "Clever enough to avoid the FBI for fourteen years."

Jimmy pretended to ignore her, but she could tell by the tic in his jaw he wasn't happy with her. Too bad. "Spiderman would also use things the girls enjoyed to calm them."

Jimmy lifted a brow. "For instance?"

"Hot chocolate, licorice, stuffed animals: you name it, he used it. He knew what they liked and he used it against them in the same way he used their worst fears to frighten them." She picked up Sophie's picture. "We need to find out everything we can about Sophie. Did she walk home or did she ride a bus? How did she treat her friends and family? Did she have any vices?"

"Why would that matter?" Jimmy asked.

"Spiderman thinks of himself as a hero," Jared answered. "In his mind, he's delivering justice by taking out girls he believes are disrespectful or 'bad.'"

"Disrespectful to whom?"

"To anyone," Lizzy said. "Adults...parents, friends. He used to talk to me about his victims being menaces to society. He didn't like girls sneaking out of the house after their parents were gone, girls who cut class or talked back, or who smoked cigarettes between classes."

"For the sake of argument," Jimmy said, "let's pretend we know everything about Sophie. How is that information going to help us find her?"

"She's looking for a link," Jared said. "Any link at all between Sophie and the other victims that might tie them all to one person, one man, one killer."

Jimmy huffed. "Aren't we all? What do you think we've been doing for the last fourteen years? Picking our noses?"

Lizzy shrugged as if that were a possibility.

"At this very moment," Jimmy said, "I've got someone talking to the principal at Sophie's school. Her piano teacher will be turning eighty next week, so we ruled her out. Sophie wasn't into sports and she gets straight As. Other than the fact that she's a teenager, there aren't any links to the other victims."

Lizzy held in a growl. Jimmy had already given up on finding any new clues. Before she could give him a piece of her mind, his cell phone rang and Jimmy excused himself before stepping outside to talk.

"Don't let him get to you," Jared said. "He's a hard head."

"He's an ass." She put her hands up in surrender. "I don't know why I'm wasting my time talking to him. He doesn't want to listen to anything I have to say. Can't you see he's already squeezed this case into a nice little box and given up?"

"Let's take a ride."

"What about your tea?"

"It can wait."

CHAPTER 9

Tuesday, February 16, 2010 12:04 p.m.

Karen Crowley was pleasantly surprised to see that her brother had chosen a beautiful, peaceful city in which to reside. Mountainous wilderness and the Sierra Nevada Range lay to the east, while rolling green hills could be seen to the west.

It was a miracle her mother had finally produced an address at all. Karen's mother lived in Arkansas and hadn't seen her only son since he had visited her fourteen years ago. According to Mom, that's when he had met his future wife, Cynthia. Mom mentioned that she received a Christmas card from Cynthia every year, which was how Karen was able to get her brother's current address. She hated to pop in on him and his wife unannounced like this, but his number wasn't listed in the phone book and Mom didn't have it either.

It was a shame, really, that her parents would marry, have two children, and then have absolutely nothing to do with them. Their father had died five years ago and nobody had bothered to let her know. That's when Karen broke off all contact with her mother. Enough was enough. Her mother never called her. She didn't care about anyone but herself.

Until a month ago, Karen didn't think she'd ever bother trying to contact her brother or her mother again. But recently, every time she looked into her own son's eyes, she saw her brother. That's when Karen knew it was time to find him and make amends, tell him how sorry she was. She'd even gone so far as to try to locate two of the three girls partly responsible for her brother's mental breakdown during high school.

But so far no luck.

Karen's cell phone rang. It was her husband. She picked up the phone and held it to her ear. "Is everything all right?"

"It's time for you to head home," he told her. "The kids miss you and I miss you."

"I can't come home. Not yet."

"You still haven't found him?"

"I just talked to Mom. She found his address. I should be there in a few minutes."

"I should have come with you."

Karen, her husband, and their two kids lived in Italy, above Cantiano and about two hours from Verona. She would have loved to have her husband come to the States with her, but the kids needed one of them at home. "I'll be fine."

"How do you know? From what you've told me, your brother can be a bit off his rocker."

"Mom said he was the happiest she'd ever seen him when he was with Cynthia. Mom said he no longer shows signs of his previous irrational behavior."

"I don't like it. What if he hasn't forgiven you?"

"I doubt he even remembers what happened." That was a lie, but she'd never had the guts to tell her husband the whole sordid story.

"You won't know that until you see him. Why don't you keep me on the line until you get there?"

"I can't. I'm not supposed to drive and talk on the cell phone without one of those ear devices. I shouldn't be talking to you now. I'll call you as soon as I find the house, OK?"

"Be careful."

"Don't worry. Everything will be fine." She clicked the phone shut. Wellington was the next street. A few more turns and she'd be at her brother's house.

There it was: 5416 Wise Road.

The house was a beautiful one story set on the top of a quiet hill. The house set her mind at ease. The lawn was well cared for, the fence freshly painted.

She pulled into the driveway, shut off the engine, and stepped out of the car. The walkway was swept clean. Other than a week's worth of newspapers piled up near the garbage bin, everything looked normal. For the first time in years, her heart lifted at the thought of seeing her brother. Usually she felt apprehension and fear at the idea of speaking to him, let alone seeing him, but not today. Despite the chill in the pine-scented air, she felt a warm glow inside.

With confidence in her spine and warmth in her heart, she knocked on the door. Then she rang the bell. After no one came to the door, she tried the door handle, surprised when the door came easily open. "Hello."

No answer.

"Is anybody home?"

The house looked well kept. No clutter or junk. She stepped inside. The furniture was high end, the rugs Persian. She never would have expected to find her brother living in such luxury. Although, why it would surprise her, she wasn't sure. According to Mom, he'd graduated from college with high honors. He was incredibly smart. So why had she expected so little from him? What was it about him that had always frightened her? Guilt? Guilt for what she and her friends had done to him? She could hardly face what had happened herself. How would she ever tell anyone else?

Thinking about that time in her life made it hard to breathe. And so did the horrible smell that seeped through the cracks and crevices as she walked toward the kitchen. *Wherever was that horrid stench coming from?*

CHAPTER 10

Tuesday, February 16, 2010 12:15 p.m.

Lizzy sat in the passenger seat of Jared's Denali and ignored the sloshing waves rolling inside her stomach.

Jared exited the freeway, heading toward the river. The closer they got to the area where Betsy Raeburn had found her, the more her chest tightened.

He made a left on Primrose Way. According to the map, they were almost there. Lizzy's body tensed, every muscle rigid. Her fingernails dug into the leather seat.

Jared pulled to the side of the road and turned her way. "Are you OK?"

No. She was drowning in a sea of nervous tension. She rolled down the window and sucked in some crisp, cold air. Once she could breathe easier, she leaned her head back against the headrest and tried to compose herself. "I'll be fine. I just need a minute."

It wasn't long before they were driving through the neighborhood. The homes looked nothing like the houses she saw every night in her sleep. These houses were smaller, older, single-family properties. Most were one-story detached homes built on less than a quarter of an acre. Shade trees were sparse and the majority of front lawns were in serious need of water. "Nothing looks familiar."

Driving at a snail's pace, Jared turned onto a quiet cul-de-sac. "This is where Betsy Raeburn said she picked you up."

Jared pulled the car around the cul-de-sac. He passed a mail truck and then made a left before continuing up the street. At a steady pace of fifteen miles per hour, they passed more of the same. An old rusty Pinto and a couple of beat-up trucks lined the street. Most of the driveways were cracked and stained with oil. Two kids who looked old enough to be in school played kickball in the street. Farther up the road, a couple appeared to be having a heated discussion as the woman followed a man to his car, gesturing wildly with her hands.

Nothing about the area looked memorable. "How are we going to find him? How are we going to help Sophie?"

Jared didn't answer.

"Sophie could be anywhere," she said. "Spiderman could have been any one of those men back there—the man working in his garage, the man arguing with his wife, the mailman. This is only one street, and I already feel as if I'm looking for a lost gem on a long stretch of sandy beach." She shook her head in frustration. "What the hell was I thinking? Cathy was right. I can't help you, Jared. I can hardly help myself." She gestured toward the row of houses. "Spiderman's house could be any one of these homes. They all look the same."

"You don't remember anything different about the house?"

She shook her head. "After escaping, I ran as fast as I could. I remember looking over my shoulder, hoping to see the house as I ran, but I was blinded by the rising sun. I hadn't seen daylight in months."

Jared made another turn and continued on.

She peered out the window, angry with herself for thinking she could make a difference. More of the same. Some houses were blue, some brown, some green. Had she truly thought she would miraculously recognize the house? They all had a front window and a— "Stop the car!"

Jared hit the brake a little too hard.

They both jerked forward.

She pushed the door open and stepped out of the vehicle.

Jared pulled to the side of the road and parked the car. He caught up to her. "What is it?"

"The tree in the backyard of that house—it's enormous. And the branches—see how they resemble gigantic arms reaching out to the sky. That tree is the first thing I saw when I stepped outside and almost escaped the first time." She marched determinedly toward the front of the house and rang the doorbell.

Jared stayed close on her heels. "What are you doing?"

"We need to talk to whoever lives here. We need to get inside."

"I'll call for backup. We can't just barge into every house that looks slightly familiar."

She pushed the ringer a second time. Seconds felt like minutes as she waited. *What if this was the house? What if he still lived here? Would she recognize him? Big ears. Strong jaw. Wide forehead.*

The door opened. A teenage girl stood inside. Long, stringy bangs covered most of her face. "Can I help you?"

Lizzy hadn't realized she was holding her breath. She exhaled and tried to peek over the girl's shoulder. "Are your parents home?"

The girl cocked her head and crossed her arms. "Whatever it is you're selling, we don't want any." Before she could shut the door, Lizzy shoved a booted foot inside to stop the door from closing.

Jared set a hand on Lizzy's elbow.

"This is the house," she told him. "I want to know if Sophie's here. I'm not leaving." Ignoring the girl's protests, and Jared's, Lizzy forced her way inside.

"Mom!" the girl shouted.

"I'm sorry," Jared said to the panicked girl. "She's been looking for her childhood home, and I'm afraid she's a little emotional."

The girl's mother rushed to her daughter's side. The older woman watched Lizzy march into her living room uninvited. "What the hell is going on?"

Ignoring the woman, Lizzy swept past her and made her way down the carpeted hallway.

The woman shouted at her to get out of their house. Nothing was going to stop Lizzy from checking the rest of the house. She needed to find Sophie before Spiderman could torture her with his mind games and—

A sharp, agonizing pain ripped through Lizzy's skull. She stopped and reached out, leaning against the wall for support. Images played through her mind's eye like a reel of 8mm film being played through an old projector. The images were so clear, she felt as if she could reach out and touch what she was seeing: a metal tray...and what looked like surgical tools...scissors...scalpels?

Spiderman was a doctor?

The pain in her head intensified. Her impulse was to shut her eyes, but she fought the urge and kept her eyes open. She needed to see what she didn't want to see. Sparks flared, lights bursting within her brain. And then his face flashed before her in living color. She put both hands to the wall to stop her knees from buckling. It was him—he wore a mask and rubber gloves. He was reaching for—

"What do you think you're doing?"

The woman grabbed her arm, breaking Lizzy from her trance. "Get out this instant! I'm calling the police!"

Lizzy broke free and ran to the bedrooms, one after another, checking the closets and under the beds. "Sophie, are you here? Sophie!" A few minutes later, frustrated and defeated, Lizzy returned to the front room.

Jared greeted her at the end of the hallway and tried to guide her toward the door, but she refused to budge. "I think he was a doctor," she said. "And this was his house." She pointed to the sliding door in the kitchen. "That's the door I went out the first time I tried to escape."

She could hear the woman on the telephone in the kitchen talking to the police. Lizzy's gaze fell to the spot in the living room where the couch had been—the place where she'd first seen Spiderman sleeping. Chills slithered up her spine as she remembered that day and how peaceful he'd looked. So normal.

There was a different couch there now—a fully padded couch with olive green, crown-shaped cushions and a sagging middle from overuse.

Jared put his arm around her and nudged her toward the front entrance. "We'll wait outside for the police to arrive."

The homeowner held the phone to her ear and a protective arm in front of her daughter as Jared ushered Lizzy out the door.

The door slammed shut behind them. The lock clicked into place before they heard the woman lecture her daughter about opening doors to strangers.

Tuesday, February 16, 2010 1:23 p.m.

After all these years, she'd finally decided to look for him. She'd finally come home.

He let the curtain fall back into place, then hurried down the hallway to the master bedroom. There it was, on his nightstand: his Nikon. He'd bought the camera in anticipation of what was to come. Over the years, he'd regretted not having any keepsakes. He'd stayed up late last night in order to read all about the tech specs and accessories. His Nikon had a built-in image sensor that would free images of dust particles using a special filter. It also had a 920,000-dot color LCD monitor and fast and accurate auto focus.

With camera in hand, he raced back to the large-paned window at the front of the house and cracked open the curtain, just enough to make room for the lens. He fiddled with the buttons, setting the camera to take continuous pictures—four to five pictures per second. He looked through the viewfinder. The camera was sleek and easy to handle. Magic. He zoomed in. He could literally see the sweat on her brow.

Tingles swam up his spine, shooting through his body like tiny sparklers on the Fourth of July. The picture was so clear it was as if he could reach out and touch her. His breathing quickened. His loins tightened. *Yes.*

Every picture was razor sharp. Lizzy Gardner still looked the same. Still so young. So vibrant. So alive. Her face was flushed. Her eyes bright. But not for long.

He never thought she would have the guts to come looking for him. He had called her because he wanted to hear her voice. And, of course, to let her know he was back. It saddened him to think he had actually cared for her…trusted her…believed in her.

She was a good girl. At least he'd thought she was. Now he knew otherwise. Back then, she had told him she would never leave him. She'd also said she never lied. *Click. Click. Click.*

After her escape, he thought she was going to lead the feds to his front door. Thinking the gig was up, he'd been forced to get rid of the other girls' bodies quickly and without any artistic thought to their disposal. A shame considering all the trouble he'd gone to, to dress the girls up proper for when they were found. Instead, he cleaned out the attic and the bedrooms and buried his beloved insects right along with the bodies in the backyard. A few days later, he'd asked a colleague to cover for him under the ruse that his mother was on her deathbed. Then he hopped on a plane and flew to Arkansas. Fate stepped in when he walked into his mother's house and met her neighbor, Cynthia Rose.

He and Cynthia fell in love almost instantly. At the time, he had considered closing his business and staying in Arkansas, but the voice in his head wouldn't allow it. Besides, nobody had contacted him or come to arrest him, which told him Lizzy hadn't gone to the authorities because she did, in fact, love him and didn't want to see him go to prison.

But everything had changed in an instant six months ago when copycat Frank Lyle kidnapped a girl named Jennifer Campbell and tossed her body in Folsom Lake as an afterthought. Authorities had caught the idiot within two days of finding the body.

Frank Lyle had ticked him off good when he tried to take credit for all of his hard work. Lyle told the feds he killed all four of the girls they found fourteen years ago. Not surprisingly, the media began to hound Lizzy Gardner. Journalists came out of the woodwork with tidbits of information. Evidently, the media had stayed away from Lizzy all of these years because her therapist said she was too "fragile" to talk with anyone. Apparently, Lizzy was getting better though, because the media no longer considered her off limits. In fact, he had seen news clips of Lizzy teaching young girls to defend themselves. She had hardly changed.

Lizzy might look the same, but things were different now. For starters, he knew the truth now. Lizzy was a liar. According to an interview her father did with Barbara Walters, the night Lizzy disappeared was the same night she had lied to her parents and snuck out with her boyfriend.

What had innocent little Lizzy been up to before he bashed her over the head and took her home?

Not only was Lizzy a liar, she was a whore. And yet he had bought into her bullshit.

He gritted his teeth. Thanks to Frank Lyle and Lizzy Gardner's endless string of lies, the voices in his head had returned in high-definition surround sound. The whore had lied to her parents and then left her girlfriends so she could go and fuck her boyfriend. And then she had made the biggest mistake of her life…she had lied to him.

For days, for weeks, for months. All lies.

The beat of his heart drummed against his ribs at the thought. His palms grew moist. Lizzy Gardner must now suffer the consequences of her actions. His chest rose and fell with each excited breath. Lizzy would know exactly what he was going to do to her once he caught her. She'd seen it all before. She knew what he was capable of.

But first he intended to have a little fun.

Click. Click. Click.

CHAPTER 11

Tuesday, February 16, 2010 9:25 p.m.

Jimmy Martin stepped out of his car and listened to the message from Dr. Lehman. He snapped his cell shut. He would have to wait until tomorrow to get the lab results. He already knew it was bad. Doctors had their assistants call the patient if they had good news to share. Otherwise, the doctor made the call personally. Not too long ago, Jimmy had watched his mother die a slow, cancerous death. He knew what to expect. He had a few more years before mandatory retirement. But it was beginning to look like he no longer had to worry about that.

Jimmy didn't like having regrets, but it seemed he had enough of them to go around. He'd been promoted to assistant special agent in charge of the Sacramento field office fifteen years ago, before anybody ever heard of Spiderman. For the first time in his long career with the bureau, he had felt an indescribable sense of accomplishment six months ago when they put Frank Lyle, a.k.a. the notorious Spiderman, behind bars.

Now everything was turning to shit.

Frank Lyle was turning out to be nothing more than a wannabe serial killer. The real Spiderman was back, and he meant business.

When it came to life, Jimmy thought, he had failed at every-thing. He and his wife were talking divorce. He still loved her, but she was tired of attending functions alone. She was ready for a real relationship with someone she could count on, someone who would be by her side when she turned off the lights at night. His daughters hardly talked to him anymore. Although his girls were often on his mind, he'd always put work before family. And now he was paying the price.

His phone vibrated. It was his wife, Marianne. "Is everything all right?"

"Where have you been? The girls just left."

Shit. Unfrickinbelievable. He'd forgotten about their dinner plans. "I'm sorry."

"What's wrong with you, Jimmy? How could you forget some-thing so important? You promised we would tell the girls together."

"Did you tell them?" he asked, hoping she hadn't, since he didn't want the divorce any more than he wanted cancer.

"I couldn't. Donna had important news she wanted to share with both of us. She waited hours for you to show up before she finally told me that she was going to marry Jeff."

"Oh, is that right?" He swallowed a bitter taste in his mouth. "That's nice. Have they set a date?"

"That's nice? You hate Jeff. What's wrong with you?"

"Nothing. I'm fine. I just want my girls to be happy. Including you, Marianne. I want you to be happy, you know."

"You don't sound like yourself. What's going on?"

"It's been a long day. I'm sorry I wasn't there tonight. I'll be home soon."

She snorted.

He clicked his phone shut. Jimmy scanned the area in front of Lizzy Gardner's apartment. Earlier today, when he arrived at the

Walker house with a search warrant, he'd seen something in Lizzy Gardner's eyes that he hadn't seen before. Fear.

Because of Spiderman, Jimmy had been tied to Lizzy Gardner by an unbreakable thread for the past decade plus. And yet he'd never known what to make of Lizzy Gardner. Now he was beginning to see she was more than likely a product of unspeakable madness and cruelty. She was a woman trying to make sense out of confusion and disorder, which had to be something like trying to do an autopsy on a rubber doll. It couldn't be done.

Jimmy was used to dealing with corpses, not survivors. For the first time since taking the oath, he found himself trying to put himself inside the victim's head instead of the killer's. He felt an overwhelming sense of empathy. He felt responsible, and most of all, he felt powerless.

Staring up at the stars, Jimmy took a moment to collect his thoughts before he looked about again, wondering if Spiderman was watching him now. Up the road, less than a block away, he spotted an unmarked sedan. John Perry was on watch tonight. He was a young rookie agent, eager to learn. He was also a newlywed. Jimmy liked the kid. A part of him wanted to warn the rookie, tell him to get out of the business before he journeyed too far into the darkness—get out while he could still look into his wife's eyes and believe there was more good in the world than evil.

Tuesday, February 16, 2010 9:32 p.m.

Jared got the call from his sister at 9:14 p.m. Her words still rang in his ears: "Come quick! Mom and Dad are at it again, only this time I think Mom's really leaving him. You have to hurry. Dad tossed Mom's car keys in the pond, and I swear I think he went back into the house for his gun."

Jared kept his eyes on the road as he recalled his first homicide. Tracey Baker, wife and mother of three, pointing a gun at her husband, daring him to try to leave her. Her kids, ages fifteen, twelve, and eight, all watching with wide eyes, praying their father would set his suitcase down, walk back into the house, and make everything better. Instead, Brandon T. Baker took the dare along with a bullet in the back of his head. It wasn't the blank look on Brandon's face as he fell to the ground or the horrified gasps of the onlookers that remained in Jared's mind. It was the kids' reactions that had stayed with him all this time. The way all three of those kids had pleaded with the officers not to take their mother from them. They had lost their only living grandparent a month before and they had no relatives to speak of. Regardless, Tracey Baker was hauled off. And the kids were taken in by Child Protective Services. Last time he checked, all three kids had been separated and put into foster homes.

After signing in at the front gate, Jared drove past a sprawling man-made lake that shimmered beneath the moonlight, making for an elegant setting that only the rich could afford.

An immediate right turn took him around a circular driveway framed by neatly trimmed hedges and well-manicured trees. He pulled into one of six designated parking spaces next to his sister's Jaguar.

He took the stairs two at a time. It was eerily quiet. He stepped inside, his footfalls quiet as he walked across a large expanse of marble tile. The house, with its wide entrance and spiraling staircase with custom-designed iron rails, looked like a high-priced resort instead of a home.

The front entry was bright and smelled like springtime with all of the fresh flowers adorning a marble-topped console carefully placed beneath a massive gilded mirror.

Mom was the first person he noticed as he entered the main living area. She was facing her left. Her hands were held up in the air like a cop trying to stop traffic. She stood tall. Her thick silvery hair was cut even with her jawline. The silver strands glimmered beneath the crystal chandelier. She wore a black cashmere jacket with a zip-up front and matching pants hemmed just above high-heeled shoes adorned with silver buckles. Strangely, he felt compelled to take in every detail. He saw his sister then. The movement of her eyes told him their father hadn't seen him yet.

"Jared," his mom said before he could head the other way and sneak up behind Dad.

Jared moved forward and stepped down onto plush white carpet. He looked at his father. "Dad, what are you doing?"

"Go home, son, and take your sister with you. This isn't any of your business."

Jared stepped closer, prompting his father to turn the gun on him instead. "That's great, Dad. You would shoot your own son? For what? What the hell are you doing?"

"Why don't you ask your mother?" Dad waved the gun between them. "Ask her why it's all come to this."

Jared raked a hand through his hair, relieved now that he'd had a chance to look into Dad's eyes. Dad was frustrated, but he would never shoot either one of them. So Jared went along for now. "Mom," Jared said. "What did you do to set him off?"

She lifted her chin defiantly. "I told him I was leaving him. Your father is a judge. Apparently nobody tells him they're leaving him."

His dad was handsome in a clean-cut, patrician sort of way with dark hair turning silver at the temples. His demeanor and looks usually radiated a bristling sense of confidence and leadership. But not tonight. Tonight his father looked ruddy-faced and haggard. Defeated.

"Tell your only son why you're leaving me."

"I'm in love with someone else," Mom said, her voice sad yet resigned.

"Tell him who!" He waved the gun again.

His mother's hands were shaking.

"Stop it, Dad," his sister shouted. "Just stop it. He's been drinking," she told Jared. "He's not thinking rationally."

"Your mother has been fucking the goddamn dentist!" That statement was followed by a round of bitter laughter. His father's head dipped, his chin hitting his chest. By the time Jared reached his side and took the gun out of his hands, his father's laughter had turned into a torrent of tears.

CHAPTER 12

Lizzy turned off the ignition but remained seated in her car. She listened to the whistling of the wind as it curled and coiled its way through the engine and seeped through unseen crevices. Outside, the gangly naked branches of the maple trees lining both sides of the street swayed back and forth as if dancing a Viennese waltz.

It was Wednesday. A lot had happened in the past few days. She had planned to sleep in this morning, but who was she kidding? She hadn't slept well, much less slept in, for years.

Yesterday, as she and Jared sat on the sidewalk in front of the Walkers' house, a.k.a. the house of horrors, and waited for the police to arrive, Jared called Jimmy Martin to fill him in on what was going down. It hadn't taken the feds long to get a warrant to search the house. While she and Jared waited, something told Lizzy they were being watched. When she'd mentioned as much to Jared, he gestured toward the house across the street where an elderly woman watched them from her kitchen window.

Lizzy had left it at that, but still her instincts were on high alert. He was close by, and he'd definitely been watching her. Instincts never lied. She'd learned that lesson the hard way.

Mrs. Walker and her daughter had not been pleased to learn that their house might have once been used as a place of brutal torture. Lizzy's main concern when they finally left the premises was that there had been no sign of Sophie. The Walkers had bought the house six years ago from a man, now deceased, who went by the name of Carl Dane. Jimmy Martin was looking into the matter and had promised to keep her updated.

Lizzy stepped out of her old beat-up Toyota. When she closed the door, the hinges creaked in protest. Since being inside the house of horrors, more and more images had been popping in and out of her head like Mexican jumping beans. Spiderman was a doctor. She was sure of it…and yet something didn't gel. *What wasn't she seeing?*

The street outside her office seemed oddly deserted for a weekday morning. More than likely the chilly weather had kept most people in their warm beds. The air was brisk and cold, and yet she couldn't solely blame the weather for the chill she felt in her bones. Reaching over her shoulder, she touched her holster to make sure her gun was where it should be. Old habits never died.

Maybe she should have waited for Jared after all. He'd called at eleven last night, said he'd been at his parents' house, and offered to stay at her apartment. He was worried about her. But she turned down his offer. She had a bad habit of pushing people away. She always regretted it in the end. But that didn't stop her from making the same mistake over and over. To make herself feel better, Lizzy had invited him to her place for dinner tonight, as long as he did the cooking. Jared agreed. He'd sounded distant, as if he were a million miles away.

Feeling like a gunslinger in the Old West—empty street, gun in the holster, evil in the air—Lizzy took steady steps toward her office. The rubber bottoms of her winter boots thumped against the pavement as she walked. The boots were five years old and counting, but still warm and comfortable with good traction. One of the perks of working for herself—she could wear what she wanted. Being a private investigator didn't require heels, nylons, or ironing. A pair of jeans, waterproof boots, a cotton V-neck T-shirt, and her favorite insulated fitted jacket were all she needed to get through the winter months.

Every time she exhaled, her breath came out as a puff of white fog. She glanced at her watch. The flower shop down the street wouldn't open for another hour; same for the salon across the street from her office. The only sounds were the whistling wind and the distant hum of traffic on the main boulevard a few blocks away. According to this morning's weather report, storm warnings were being issued. By Friday, wind gusts were expected to top eighty miles per hour.

As she drew closer to her office door, she slipped her key from her coat pocket. Shadowy movements reflected off the glass windowpane. She glanced over her shoulder. Nothing but dancing tree branches. Shit. Her imagination was getting the best of her.

Her hands shook. Not enough sleep. Her nerves were shot. No matter which way she turned the key, the metal grooves wouldn't match up. Damn lock. She dropped the keys. Murphy's Law, she decided as she pulled a glove off and then stooped over to pick up her keys.

A hand gripped her shoulder.

She reached between her legs and snatched the person's leg, bringing the intruder to the ground in an instant.

Hot coffee sloshed in a wide arc, hitting the side of her face and her jacket. Lizzy pivoted on her feet and reached over her shoulder for her gun.

"Don't shoot!" Jessica's eyes were wide with fear. A Styrofoam cup rolled to the middle of the street.

Releasing her hold on the gun still strapped in her holster, Lizzy released a stream of frosty air, making a hissing noise as she straightened.

She offered Jessica a hand up. "I thought you learned your lesson the other day." Lizzy looked past the girl. "Where's your car?"

"My brother dropped me off on his way to work. You weren't here so I decided to grab a cup of coffee. When I saw you, well, you know the rest."

"Did I hurt you much?"

"I'm fine."

Jessica didn't look fine as she rubbed her elbow and straightened her spine in an attempt to get the kinks out.

Lizzy reached for the keys on the ground. This time, because that's the way Murphy's Law worked, she managed to get the key into the lock on the first try. Opening the door wide, she waited for Jessica to enter first.

Jessica wrinkled her nose. "Sorry about your coat."

"No worries." Lizzy went back to the street to pick up the Styrofoam cup and saw the same damn green Jeep parked up the street in front of the café. *No way.*

Leaving the cup, she walked toward the Jeep, increasing her pace when she saw that the driver wasn't paying attention to her surroundings.

Same woman. Same baseball cap. Same ponytail.

Only three car lengths away...almost there.

The woman glanced out her window then, prompting Lizzy to break into a full-fledged run. She was close enough to see the woman curse under her breath. Lizzy lunged for the closest door handle and jerked the door open, but the driver had already started the engine and hit the gas hard.

The Jeep rammed into the car parked in front of it, causing the door to pull Lizzy forward. Lizzy bounced off the back bumper and hit the ground with a thud.

The Jeep backed up. Tires squealed. Lizzy rolled to her left, sending a jolt of fiery pain through her body. She choked on the acrid smell of burnt rubber.

Gray skies and dancing trees hovered overhead and then faded to black.

Wednesday, February 17, 2010 7:32 a.m.

Hayley Hansen stared at the popcorn ceiling and wondered how much of the toxic fibers one would have to inhale before it caused serious illness or, better yet, death. She lay on her bed fully clothed. Although why she bothered, she didn't know. Dressed or not, it wouldn't stop her mother's drug dealer from collecting payment. As she often did on days she knew Brian might visit, Hayley prayed to a God she no longer believed in. But whether the creator and overseer of the universe existed or not didn't matter. He was all she had left, the only one she could talk to.

Please, she began her heartfelt prayer, *let this be the day Brian overdoses on heroin. Please, oh please, your divineness, let Brian, spawn of the devil, wake up today, walk outside, and be the instantaneous recipient of a stray bullet, the fatal result of a drive-by shooting.*

She wasn't asking for a miracle. Drive-by shootings happened every week in her neck of the woods. It could happen. Her mother had been sober, doing so well for so long, until Brian came along and taught her mom how to "chase the dragon."

The sound of a car door opening and closing alerted her to the fact that once again her prayers had gone unanswered. No keys needed here. The front door creaked open followed by the familiar sounds of footsteps plodding across old floorboards.

He was coming.

She could run. Been there, done that. It only made things worse. Nothing good came out of prolonging the inevitable. If she ever found the courage to abandon her mother, leave her to fend for herself, she supposed she could escape. But could she live with herself? Her mother wasn't to blame. Her mother had done the best she knew how. Her grandparents, on the other hand, had been in a league all their own. Talk about ending up with the short stick. Her own life was a weekend in Disneyland compared to what her mother's childhood had been like.

More footsteps sounded in the hallway. Probably Mom just making sure it was Brian, the rapist drug dealer, and not some other dispossessed soul running amok in her pigsty of a house.

Hayley's bedroom door clicked shut. Yeah, it was Brian all right. Although her gaze remained on the ceiling, Hayley knew it was Brian standing in her room. She always smelled him before she saw him. A heady combination: cigarettes, stale beer, body odor mixed with remnants of puke and urine from whatever hellhole he came from.

Always the same.

She would never look at him if she had a choice. But she didn't. If she closed her eyes or tried to drift off to some distant nonexistent planet, he'd catch her off guard and try using his own personal shock treatment to wake her up.

Nope. She never shut her eyes.

Confused, she sniffed the air and had to summon every bit of power within to stop from gagging. There was a new smell. Oil? Rotted potatoes? A dead animal?

Oh, please God. No.

"Go ahead," Brian said to his friend. "You first."

CHAPTER 13

Wednesday, February 17, 2010 8:05 a.m.

"We need to get you to the hospital," Jessica said as she helped Lizzy off the pavement and back to the office.

"I'll be fine." Although the way Lizzy's head throbbed and her ribs ached made her wonder if it was true.

Jessica held the door to the office open. Then she followed Lizzy around her desk, making sure Lizzy was seated before she completely fell apart. "Oh my God," Jessica cried. "When I heard tires screeching I looked out the window and saw you rolling across the street. I thought for sure the car hit you. When you didn't move afterward, I thought you were dead."

Jessica was as white as a ghost.

"Jessica, you need to calm down."

"You need a doctor," Jessica said. "That knot on your forehead is the size of a tennis ball."

"Listen to me," Lizzy said. "I need you to go back to that coffee shop and see if there were any witnesses."

"There were three people huddled over you by the time I got to you," Jessica said. She pulled a business card from her back pocket. "This man gave me his card and said to tell you to call if you needed any help."

Hopeful, Lizzy took the card. She frowned. It was from an attorney. If he'd seen the license plate or the driver, he would have stuck around and followed them back to the office. "This is a good start," she said, "but I still need you to go back to the coffee shop before all potential witnesses are gone."

Jessica wrinkled her nose. "You didn't recognize the person in the car?"

Lizzy grimaced as a stab of fiery pain shot through her skull. "No."

"I really don't think I should leave you right now. You don't look good. You were unconscious."

"I'm fine." Lizzy pointed a finger toward the door. "Go check it out. Now. Please."

Jessica's gaze darted toward the door and then back to Lizzy.

"That's it." Lizzy began to lift herself from her seat. "I'll go myself."

Jessica was at the door before Lizzy could move another inch. "Man, you are one stubborn lady. I'm going. I'm going."

Jessica walked outside and picked up the empty Styrofoam cup still rolling around on the pavement before heading for the coffee shop.

Lizzy released a string of colorful words as she stood and then dragged herself to the bathroom to see the damage. The bump on her head wasn't nearly as big as Jessica made it out to be, but it was definitely the worst of her injuries. She cleaned her wounds and applied salve to a half dozen scrapes.

The phone rang just as Jessica returned. Lizzy hobbled out of the bathroom.

Jessica had answered the phone. She was holding the receiver to her chest, mouthing words Lizzy couldn't make out. Taking the phone, Lizzy held the receiver to her ear and sat gingerly back on her chair. "This is Lizzy Gardner. What can I do for you?"

She glanced at her watch. The first hour of her day already felt like an entire week. It was Victor, the man who refused to take no for an answer. "What can I do for you, Victor?" she asked again when he remained silent for too long.

Apparently, he wanted her to watch his wife, a woman named Valerie Hunt, from noon to one every day for the next two weeks. Valerie worked for a law firm in Carmichael, less than fifteen miles from Lizzy's office.

"OK, I'll do it," she said after he promised to pay her three thousand dollars in cash, assuring her the money would be delivered to her office by the end of the day. Ten hours of work for three thousand bucks. It was a no-brainer.

"Yes," she said into the phone as she delicately raised her arm to make sure it still worked. The pain hovered between tolerable and excruciating. She winced. "I understand. You'll call the office periodically for updates. Yes," she said again, rolling her eyes and making Jessica smile. "I have a duty to protect your confidentiality. I'm a professional. Besides, you haven't told me much and you're paying in cash. I've never seen your face and your telephone number comes up as restricted."

The last tidbit was a lie. Since the feds had wired her office yesterday, Lizzy was fairly confident they'd be able to trace the number on the black box sitting next to her phone. The red light was already flashing. But she didn't need to tell Victor that and lose out on the three thousand dollars. She had yet to show a profit. And she didn't want to borrow any more money from her sister—not that Cathy would loan her any more money now that they were no longer on speaking terms.

Lizzy would bet her favorite boots that Victor was using a false identity. But so what? After Victor finally said good-bye and hung up, she placed the receiver on its cradle and leaned back in her chair.

"That man is annoying, isn't he?" Jessica said. "I told him you were out, but he said he'd wait…as if he knew you were close by. Do you think this Victor guy is watching us?"

Lizzy turned toward the window so fast she put a kink in her neck and hurt her bruised ribs in the process. Her eyes darted from building to building, rooftop to rooftop, then window to window as she looked for movement or any sign whatsoever of somebody peeking through blinds or curtains.

Jessica moved to her side and stared out the window too. "Do you really think he's out there? You think he might be watching us, don't you?" Jessica chewed on her bottom lip. Her brows slanted inward. "Why was the woman in that Jeep trying to run you over?"

"I don't know who she is, but I don't think she was trying to kill me. If she was, she could have easily taken me out."

"She was wearing a baseball cap, wasn't she?"

"Yes," Lizzy said. "Did you see her?"

"I did. I saw her in the coffee shop right after my brother dropped me off. She wasn't wearing any makeup. My guess would be that she's in her forties."

"Did anyone else get a good look at her?"

"The only one who remembered anything about her was the lady behind the counter. She said that the woman in the baseball cap ordered a dulce de leche with toffee sprinkles. Nobody else saw her."

"Thanks, Jessica." Lizzy swiveled her chair back behind her desk and turned on her computer. "That same woman was parked outside my apartment yesterday. She's not that good at disguises. I would appreciate it if you could help me keep an eye out for her, OK?"

"If I see her car again, I'll try to get the license plate number."

"Perfect." Still waiting for her computer to warm up, Lizzy looked at Jessica. "Are you planning to be here all day?"

"All week if you need me."

"What about classes?"

"Nope. I don't have to be back to school until the middle of next week."

"Great." It wasn't spring break, but neither was it any of her business, so Lizzy decided to let it go.

Jessica grabbed a roll of paper towels from the top of the bookshelf lining the wall behind Lizzy's desk. She handed Lizzy a couple of paper squares and gestured toward the coffee stains on her coat.

Lizzy swiped at her jacket, but most of the coffee had already soaked in. She tossed the towels in the garbage and then reached for her backpack on the floor.

As Jessica shuffled through yesterday's mail, Lizzy unzipped the front of her backpack and pulled out a piece of paper. "I have a job for you," she told Jessica. She placed the paper on her desk and used the palm of her hand to flatten the creases. "We need to find out everything we can about these girls."

Jessica left what she was doing and came back to hover over Lizzy's shoulder. Jessica drew in a breath.

"What is it?" Lizzy asked.

Jessica seemed off-kilter, her face pale, but then she took in a deep breath and pointed to the last name on the list. "Is that the same Sophie Madison who went missing recently?"

Lizzy nodded.

"That explains the equipment," Jessica said, pointing to the black box by the telephone. "Are you helping the police?"

Lizzy gestured to the chair shoved close to the wall. "Pull up a chair and let's talk."

Jessica slid the chair over, took a seat, and waited.

"Fourteen years ago—"

"You were kidnapped," Jessica cut in.

Lizzy lifted a brow.

"I was only a child at the time," Jessica explained. "I liked to play with the next-door neighbors. Whenever I would leave the house, Mom would tell me to be careful and then remind me of the day you and those other girls were taken, never to be seen again. Except for you, of course."

"Does your mom know you're working for me?"

Jessica waved a dismissive hand through the air. "Mom has her own problems. She doesn't pay any attention to what I do any longer." She shrugged. "She's ready for me and my older brother to move out on our own and give her some space."

Lizzy nodded. "If you don't feel comfortable working on this case, I understand."

"Are you kidding me? This is exactly the sort of work that interests me. This is why I want to major in psychology. This is why I came to you looking for a job."

"OK, then," Lizzy said as she looked around for a potential work space. There wasn't one. "Let me clear this end of my desk off for you. Did you bring your laptop?"

"It's in the back."

"Good. We'll set up your laptop right here on my desk and use Internet search engines to find everything we can about these girls. Tomorrow, or later today if we have time, we can go to the library and scour old newspaper articles. We want to print any article ever written about Spiderman's victims."

"What are we looking for exactly?" Jessica asked as she helped remove stacks of papers and files from Lizzy's desk, placing them on the floor behind them. "Do we want details, like how they dressed or what hairstyles they wore? Or should we stick with interviews of friends and family, things like that?"

"Both. We want to learn everything and anything we can about each and every girl: weight, height, personality, you name it. Four of these girls are considered victims of Spiderman, but the other four girls are still considered missing children since their bodies were never found."

Jessica grew quiet as she looked over the list again. Once again her eyes seemed to water.

"Is something wrong?"

"No," Jessica answered a little too quickly. "I'm fine."

The girl was perplexing. One minute Jessica was talking her ear off and the next she was quiet and mysterious. Knowing she needed to focus on finding Sophie, Lizzy decided once again to let it go. "If one of the girls on the list took dance lessons," she told Jessica, "I want to know where and when. I want the names of every teacher, coach, friend, boyfriend, hair stylist, places they liked to hang out. I also want a list of each and every doctor these girls ever made contact with."

"Do you think the parents of the victims will talk to us?"

"It won't hurt to try. If not, we'll talk to their siblings or their aunts and uncles. We can't afford to take no for an answer. Someone will talk; somebody always does."

"So what we're really looking for is a connection between the girls—a commonality, whether it be the school they went to or an acquaintance they knew?"

"That's right. Any connection at all."

"Got it." Jessica stood and disappeared inside the file room to get her things.

Lizzy tore off another paper towel and used it to wipe dust from her desk where the files had been. She opened her top drawer and began searching for ibuprofen. The hairs on the back of her neck stirred. Somebody was definitely watching her.

Turning toward the window, she stared out past the street toward the empty storefronts. *He was there. She could feel him, sense him, and yet she couldn't see him.*

Her skin prickled.

Where are you, Spiderman? Come out, come out, wherever you are.

CHAPTER 14

Wednesday, February 17, 2010 11:30 a.m.

Jared pulled his Denali into a tight spot behind Lizzy's Toyota. Last night already felt like a world away. He'd never seen his father look so distraught. Dad had always been a conscientious man, a man with a strong sense of right and wrong. Holding a gun to his wife of forty years didn't compute. Jared's sister had taken their mother home while Jared stayed with their father. After sobering him up, Jared and his father had a long talk. It was the first time he ever saw his father cry, the first time he realized his father was human like everybody else.

He pointed his key at his Denali and pushed the lock button. His car whistled back at him.

Jared felt a chill in the air as he peered into the back window of Lizzy's Toyota. It was hard to believe Old Yeller was still drivable. Lizzy had driven the car back in high school. The cracked vinyl seats in the back were a familiar sight. He and Lizzy had spent a lot of time making out on those seats. *The good ol' days.*

"Lizzy, Lizzy," he said under his breath. He loved everything about that girl. The way she walked, the way she talked, the way she made him feel every time he looked into those expressive green eyes of hers. He'd loved her from the moment they first met. Kindheartedness pulsed through her veins—exactly why she spent most weekends teaching young girls to defend themselves. Although he'd been busy with college and then training at the academy over the years, a day hadn't gone by that he didn't think of Lizzy Gardner. He'd spent many sleepless nights filled with guilt for letting her walk home alone that night. If he had any regrets, that was it. He'd known better. But Lizzy had been stubborn. She still was. She'd also been full of life back then, brim full of promise before that lunatic snatched her off the street and tried to suck all that dazzling radiance right out of her. But Lizzy had lived to tell her story. She was a fighter. And if she allowed him back into her life, Jared wouldn't let her down again.

At the sound of uneven footfalls, he looked up to see Lizzy limping toward him. Her eyes were shadowed with exhaustion, but she smiled the moment she noticed him.

"Hey, beautiful," he said.

She answered with a stiff Mae West pose that showed off a well-worn jacket stained with coffee.

"Rough morning, huh?"

"You could say that."

"What the hell happened to your face?"

"The woman in the Jeep was back this morning. I snuck up on her. Just as I opened the back door, she took off and nearly ran me over in the process."

He hissed through his teeth. "Have you been to a doctor? That knot on your forehead doesn't look good."

"I'll be fine."

He exhaled.

"I'd love to chat, but I need to get going," she said as she moved past him.

"I was hoping to take you for a bite to eat."

"I can't. Something's come up…a surveillance."

"Insurance fraud?"

"An infidelity case." She unlocked her car and then looked over her shoulder at him. "If you want to hear the sordid details, you're more than welcome to ride along with me."

"Let's go."

Lizzy slid behind the wheel of her ancient Toyota and started the engine. The car coughed and sputtered. Jared climbed into the passenger side and glanced at the backseat. "Being in Old Yeller brings me back to another time."

Her cheeks flushed as she dug through her backpack. She handed him directions to where they were going and didn't waste any time before she set off down the road. "Have you heard any news from Jimmy about Carl Dane yet?"

"I talked to Jimmy earlier. Dane is the original owner of the house. He lived there with his family from 1980 to 1991. The house was a rental from 1991 until the end of 2002. The Walkers bought the house in January of 2003."

"Mr. Dane must have records of who rented the house during that time."

"His daughter tossed the files after he passed away a few years ago. The team is searching for a list of renters through the utility companies in the area."

"How about forensics? Has anything shown up in the bedrooms?"

"So far, the house is clean."

"There should be traces of blood, holes in the wall that have been patched up where the manacles were…something, right?"

"We need to hang tight. If this is the house, something will turn up. The backyard will be excavated first thing in the morning."

She kept her gaze on the road as they approached the entrance to the freeway. "What about a list of doctors from the victims' files? Any luck?"

Jared pulled a wallet-sized notebook from his shirt pocket. "I spent most of the morning going through the files. These are the names of physicians I found that were used by some of Spiderman's victims and family members. I didn't come across any duplicate names, but the list is all yours." He placed the notebook on the console between them.

"Thanks. I appreciate it."

"You're welcome," Jared said. "So who are we shadowing this afternoon?"

"Valerie Hunt."

"Her husband hired you?"

"He referred to Valerie as his wife, but I'm not sure I believe him. He said his name was Victor."

"Did you meet him face-to-face?"

She glanced Jared's way. "You think Victor could have something to do with Spiderman?"

"You can't tell me the thought didn't cross your mind."

"It did," she admitted, "but when Victor called me the second time I figured I'd be a fool to turn down the kind of money he was offering."

"What about his voice…did he sound anything like Spiderman?"

"Victor has a deep, husky voice. Spiderman uses a voice synthesizer. It's difficult to compare."

"What about Valerie Hunt, any idea who she is?"

"I did a quick search. She graduated from McGeorge in 1995. She's been a lawyer at Dutton and Graves for eight years. No children. I couldn't find anything that said she was married or had a child."

A quiet moment settled between them. "If Victor is Spiderman," Lizzy continued, "why would he hire me to follow Valerie?"

"He could be trying to lure you into a trap."

"Well, I won't follow Valerie or anyone else into an empty warehouse or a dark alley. And if this woman does have anything to do with him, then Spiderman is making our job a little easier."

An uneasy feeling washed over him. Jared hadn't liked dragging Lizzy into this mess to begin with. But if he hadn't, Jimmy would have. The note left by Sophie's abductor had sealed her fate. "How does Victor plan on paying you?"

"He's sending a courier to deliver the money today. I told Jessica to keep a close eye on the delivery person...name and description, vehicle make and model, license plate number, et cetera."

Lizzy pulled off at the next exit and stopped at the red light. "You don't think Jessica is in danger, do you?"

Jared was already punching numbers into his cell. "I'll send someone to watch your office until we know more about Victor."

* * *

Karen Crowley white-knuckled the steering wheel, her gaze jumping from the road ahead to the rearview mirror. Sirens sounded in the distance. Panic swirled within. She wanted nothing more than to swerve into the right lane and take the next exit off the freeway, but there was a car in her way and the last thing she wanted to do was hurt someone. She hadn't meant to hurt Lizzy Gardner when she'd taken off from the coffee shop. That was an accident.

She only meant to keep an eye on the woman, to make sure her brother wasn't hanging around and causing trouble.

Nothing was going as planned. Her weeklong trip had already turned into two weeks. Her husband and children needed her, but she couldn't return home now. Not yet.

She'd come to the States to find her brother and make amends. She hadn't seen him in over twenty years. Not since she left to study abroad in Florence, Italy. Within a month of living in Italy, she met Nicolas. They fell in love, and for the next two decades nothing else mattered. She and Nicolas bought a house in the country. Their firstborn was a daughter, Amber. Their second, a son. They named him Adam. Adam turned out to be a replica of her little brother, Sam.

She bit down on her lip as the police car zoomed past, lights flashing.

Six months ago, Adam turned thirteen, and every time she looked at him she saw her brother: same high forehead, same defined jaw, and same expressive blue eyes. But then, too often in her mind's eye, her son's face would distort, and she'd see the same horrified look she'd seen on her brother's face when she found him in the basement.

Her chest tightened.

She swerved to the side of the road, gravel spraying as she screeched to a stop. Her head dropped to the steering wheel. She gulped in breaths of air. "Oh my God," she sobbed. "What have I done?"

* * *

Nancy Moreno's high heels clicked on the floor as she rushed through the double doors leading into the news studio.

Caroline Mills, in charge of hair and makeup at KBTV, rushed toward her. "Where have you been? Mr. Cunningham has been trolling the halls, pulling out his hair looking for you."

"He's bald," Nancy reminded Caroline as she followed her into the room to the right and took a seat on a stool in front of the wall-to-wall mirror. Without missing a beat, Caroline brushed and teased Nancy's hair, her hands a whirlwind of movement.

Somebody shouted Nancy's name in the distance.

"She's in here," Caroline answered back.

Seconds later, Mr. Cunningham's beefy frame filled the doorway, his hands fisted at his sides.

There wasn't much he could say. *She was here, wasn't she?* Everybody knew Cunningham would never fire her. Nancy Moreno was the best thing the station had going for it. Since 1995 she'd anchored all three of News 10's highly rated and award-winning evening news programs. Now they had her doing the morning show to get the ratings up. She had received numerous professional honors over the years, including two Emmys.

The ring of her cell phone interrupted her thoughts. She pushed TALK and put the phone to her ear.

"Did you get the information I asked for?"

It was *him*. Nancy pressed the phone closer to her ear. "Not yet, but I'm working on it. These things take time." She glanced at Cunningham. "I can't talk now," she told the caller. "I'm due to be on the air in—"

"The green light came on two minutes ago," Cunningham barked. "The hair's good enough. She's gotta go. Now!"

"Get me what I asked for before the end of the week," the caller said, "or I'm giving my story to Gina Lockwell at Channel Three."

"Is that a threat? Because if it is—"

A low rumble of laughter cut her off. A *click* at the other end told her that their conversation was over.

Nancy shuddered. And yet the thought of Gina Lockwell getting the story overrode any concern she had that her caller might be a psychopathic killer.

"You're perspiring," Caroline said, ignoring Cunningham's wild gestures as he tried to get them moving.

Undaunted, Nancy slid off the stool and walked out the door. Caroline stayed at her side, powdering her face as they followed Cunningham down the hallway. Nancy's thoughts should have been on the morning news, but they weren't. The caller had yet to give her his name. The first time she talked to him was two days ago. He said he was the real deal—the killer known as Spiderman. He said Frank Lyle, the man arrested for the murder of Jennifer Campbell, was a copycat. She hadn't believed him at first, but neither had she hung up the phone.

What if he was telling the truth? Serial killers were notorious for wanting credit for their work. They were also known for making daring calls and sending packages to the media despite the risk of giving away their identities.

The caller promised to give her hard evidence proving he was the real deal after she provided him with the case studies on Lizzy Gardner. The killer wanted Nancy to steal files from Lizzy's psychiatrist. Somehow the caller knew that she too was being treated by Linda Gates, Lizzy Gardner's psychiatrist. The fact that he knew so much about her made her uncomfortable.

Stealing files was unethical. Nancy should have called the FBI after receiving the first phone call. But something had stopped her. She had interviewed her share of criminals over the years. When criminals lied they became nervous. Sure, some hardened criminals had been interviewed so often they'd honed their deception skills. But this man, she'd decided by the end of their first conversation, was telling the truth. And so she'd convinced herself she was actually helping the FBI by keeping her conversations with the killer private. For now, she would keep things simple: earn the killer's trust and learn whatever she could about the man. Chances were he was highly intelligent and would not be telling her where he lived anytime soon. But if she could piece together clues about him, pieces of his background, then maybe, just maybe, she would be able to give the authorities the information they needed to nab him. She could see the headlines now: "Nancy Moreno Leads FBI to Spiderman's Lair." She already knew where she wanted to put her third Emmy.

A smile came to her lips. Spiderman was no dummy. He had called her because she was the best in the business. By the time she entered the newsroom, the blood vessels in Cunningham's neck and face were enlarged, ready to erupt. The chaos in the studio reminded her of a tornado as she slid into her chair.

"THREE, TWO, ONE."

From across the newsroom, Cunningham pointed a finger at her. She zeroed in on the teleprompter and smiled. "Good morning, Sacramento. I'm Nancy Moreno with KBTV Morning News."

CHAPTER 15

Wednesday, February 17, 2010 12:35 p.m.

For the dozenth time, Jessica looked over the list of names. Spiderman's first three victims—Jordan, Laney, and Mandy—had a couple of things in common: their bodies were all left near a body of water and they all had spider bites on various parts of their bodies. One of the girls was a sophomore in high school when she disappeared. The other two were juniors. All three attended different high schools in Sacramento or Placer County. Four different high schools if she counted Rachel Foster, his fourth victim, and the only girl found during Lizzy's captivity.

Rachel Foster's body was found near Folsom Lake. At age fifteen, she was the youngest of his victims. A recent yet obscure article Jessica discovered mentioned that Rachel had been found with syringes stuck in her eyes.

Jessica winced and reminded herself to breathe. Just because these girls had been tortured didn't mean any of those horrible things had happened to Mary. She bit down on her bottom lip and took in a calming breath. Now wasn't a good time to lose it. Not if she wanted to help Lizzy find Spiderman. Her sister could still be alive. Although Mary was her older sister, she was tiny and everyone thought she was the youngest of three children even though she was the oldest. Mary was also smart. God, how Jessica missed their long talks.

Miracles happened every day, Jessica told herself. Whoever had taken Mary all those years ago could have given her a new identity and then moved to another state. Maybe her sister no longer knew who she was or where she came from.

Lizzy had escaped. The same thing could have happened to Mary. Her sister was still alive. She could feel it, sense it.

Jessica redirected her attention to her notes. Rachel's boyfriend at the time of her abduction was Ryan Arnold. A quick search on Ryan Arnold and a half dozen phone calls later, she'd found him. He was now a twenty-nine-year-old lawyer who liked to talk. With hardly any prompting, he spilled his guts, telling her that Rachel's kidnapping had changed his life. He'd stopped doing drugs and started reading and studying. Not only had Ryan Arnold read up on the Spiderman case, he'd gone out of his way to make some important contacts over the years in order to find out more. He'd seen the FBI files, including a letter Spiderman had sent to a local news station at the time. Arnold told Jessica that Spiderman considered himself to be one of the good guys, and he felt it was his job to eradicate the world of *bad girls*. Ryan Arnold believed Rachel was taken because she did drugs—lots of drugs. By the time Rachel was abducted, she had been in and out of rehab twice.

But it wasn't the drugs or the syringes that stood out. It was the eyes. Jessica's finger brushed down over the names and scribbled notes. She couldn't help but notice that every one of Spiderman's victims had had something done to their eyes.

Wednesday, February 17, 2010 3:02 p.m.

Cathy sat in the car and drummed her fingers against the steering wheel as she waited for her daughter. She looked from the statue of a bear, the school's mascot, to the group of teenagers huddled outside the gym.

Where was Brittany?

She dug around in her purse and retrieved her cell phone. No missed calls.

"We Can Work It Out" by the Beatles played on the radio. She shut it off. The song made her feel sad, brought her back to the days when her husband used to call her every chance he had just to say hi and tell her how much he loved her.

She placed the phone in the console between the front seats and inwardly scolded herself for even thinking of crying. She'd truly believed that everything would be OK after she met Richard…that life wasn't so bad after all. But then Brittany came along earlier than planned, Cathy gained fifty pounds, she lost her job at the bank, and two years ago Richard stopped calling home during his lunch hour.

Laughter caught her attention.

Her blood pressure rose as she watched a teenage boy reach out and grab one of the girls across from him. He pulled her close to his body so he could plant a sloppy kiss on her mouth. The girl wrinkled her nose, but her friends were amused, so the young girl let it go.

Cathy shook her head. Brittany would be attending high school next year. That worried her. Mostly because her own high school years had been such a nightmare. She was a senior when Lizzy was kidnapped. Lizzy had always been the cherished daughter; the beautiful, petite one; the smart one. And in the end, Lizzy had been the one who tore their family apart.

Cathy always felt like second fiddle to her sister. Before the kidnapping, she didn't think things could get worse. But they did.

When Lizzy was missing, Cathy realized she might as well be dead. Neither of her parents paid her any mind. Nobody asked her what she was thinking or how she was handling her sister's absence. Nobody asked her about the shit load of guilt she was holding onto like a lifeline. Nobody cared.

Thinking about such a horrible time in her life made her heart beat faster. She was about to climb out of the car and go in search of her daughter when she saw Brittany come around the corner. One of the boys said something to her as she passed by. Brittany ignored him.

"Hey," Brittany said as she climbed into the passenger seat and tossed her backpack to the backseat. Brittany smiled, her braces shiny and new. Then she pointed at her upper right eyetooth. "One of the wires broke today."

Cathy leaned closer for a better look. "Are you kidding me? For the amount of money we spent on those, they should last a lifetime."

"Sorry. I shouldn't have eaten that apple today. I think that's when it broke."

She couldn't exactly lecture her daughter for eating fruit. "Don't worry about it. I'll call and make an appointment with the orthodontist while you're swimming."

"Did you ever call the math tutor?"

"Why? What did you get on your math test today?"

Brittany scrunched her nose. "C minus. I swear my math teacher doesn't know how to teach. Did you bring my suit?"

Cathy pulled away from the curb. Her daughter's ability to quickly change subjects was not lost on her. "It's in the trunk. Who were those kids standing outside the gym?"

"I don't know," Brittany said. "I wasn't paying any attention to them."

Cathy could feel her daughter's eyes on her.

"Have you been crying again, Mom?"

"No."

"Your eyes are puffy and your nose is red."

"Oh, that. I was listening to a sad song on the radio before you showed up."

"Sounds like menopause. My science teacher talks about her hot flashes every day."

"I hope that's not my problem," Cathy said. "At thirty-three I'd like to think I'm a little too young for that."

"Are you going to stay at the aquatic center while I swim today?"

The question caught Cathy off guard. "Why? Do you want me to?"

"Yeah, that would be great. You haven't watched me swim in a while."

Brittany had never asked her to stay at practice. Usually her daughter tried to get rid of her. The concern in her daughter's voice worried her. "What's going on? Is someone on the team picking on you?"

"No."

"Then what is it?"

"It's nothing, Mom. Never mind. You don't have to stay."

Cathy kept her eyes on the road. She thought about the coach and wondered if he could possibly have anything to do with Brittany's unusual behavior. She'd met the coach twice now. He seemed like a nice man. All the mothers liked him. "I want to stay," she said with finality. "I want to see you break some records."

CHAPTER 16

Wednesday, February 17, 2010 3:05 p.m.

Jared pulled his SUV to the side of the road. He sat quietly for a moment before climbing out to take a look around. The sound of the car door shutting echoed across the field of tall grass. This was the spot where he'd dropped Lizzy off on the night she was kidnapped.

A cold wind nipped at his ears. He pulled the collar of his wool jacket higher around his ears and began walking, following the same path Lizzy had taken. Lizzy said it was unusually dark that night. No street lights and hardly any moonlight.

He turned off Emerald Street, and already he could see the willow tree at the end of the block. Lizzy's house—so close, and yet so far. He stopped to listen and watch. *Where had Spiderman been hiding that night?*

The wind whistled as if trying to tell him something. It was a quiet street with lots of shade trees and well-trimmed lawns. He turned until he was facing a wall of oleander. The leathery dark-green leaves quivered whenever a gust of air blew by. He moved closer to the tall shrub, reached out, and spread the branches apart. A likely hiding place for a killer. He would have been well hidden…even in the daylight. The ground beneath the oleander was covered with dead leaves and rotted tanbark. Specks of light filtered through from the other side of the bush, where he saw glimpses of a field. Once Spiderman had grabbed Lizzy, had he carried her across that field?

Stepping inside the wall of oleander, Jared left broken branches in his wake as he pushed through to the other side. The weeds and grass were thick, and he had to lift his feet high to take each step. The tips of the tallest weeds came to his chest. He imagined the killer walking the same path while carrying Lizzy. It pained him to think of it.

Up ahead, a flock of birds took flight. When he got to the middle of the field, he stopped to look around. A dog barked in the distance. There was a road on the other side of the field. He wondered where the road led. A city park lay to his left. It was no wonder there hadn't been witnesses that night. Few houses had a view of the field from where he stood, and even then, someone would have had to stand on a rooftop to see anything. There wouldn't have been many people, if any, at the park so close to midnight.

He exhaled. Dropping Lizzy off that night had been incredibly irresponsible. He'd known better. At the very least, he should have parked at the end of her road and watched her walk home. What was he thinking that night? He'd made love to her and then dropped her off on a dark street in the dead of night.

His phone vibrated. He looked at the number. Mom. He couldn't deal with her right now. Hell, he didn't know what to think of his own mother messing around with another man. She'd always been soft-spoken and demure. She babied their father. Greeted him every night when he came home from work with an adoring smile and a home-cooked meal. He and Mom had never been especially close. Nobody was good enough for her only son, including Lizzy.

Unlike his mother, Lizzy understood him. She was a great listener. She cared about everyone she met. He never understood why his parents hadn't warmed up to Lizzy, but the truth was, he no longer cared. His phone continued to vibrate. He ignored his mother's call and moved on. He had nothing to say to her.

A cold chill was plastered across his face as he walked. *Had Jimmy walked this same path all those years ago during the heat of the investigation? What had Jimmy missed? What weren't they seeing?* Walking through the tall weeds was like walking knee-deep in quicksand. He wanted to find out the name of the road on the other—

A scream jolted him. Every muscle tensed. He was alert now. Another piercing scream and then laughter—kids playing in the park. He took in a deep breath, exhaled.

Had Lizzy screamed out for help? If only he'd listened to his gut that night and followed her home. He shoved his hands deep into his jacket pockets.

He still remembered how Lizzy would stiffen when she was at his house and his father ordered his mother around. His mother never seemed to mind, but Lizzy had. And whether Lizzy knew it or not, that was why Jared hadn't pressed her when she insisted on walking home alone that night. He hadn't wanted to be like his father.

And now he was losing respect for his mother too. All these years she'd stayed with his father, but why? If Dad's controlling nature bothered her, then his mother should have stood up to him. Jared shook his head. He didn't need this right now. What was his dad thinking holding a gun to Mom's head, for God's sake?

Jared moved on, determined to focus on Lizzy. She said she'd forgiven him. But could he ever forgive himself?

Wednesday, February 17, 2010 6:38 p.m.

Hayley Hansen looked up at the sound of a car pulling up to the curb. She sat on the bottom stair, hugging her knees to her chest. Her shoes had too many holes, and since she'd left home without putting socks on this morning, her toes were icy cold.

Lizzy Gardner stepped out of her car and shut the door. "Hayley!" she called out the moment she spotted her.

Hayley couldn't believe Lizzy Gardner remembered her name. Nobody remembered her name. Suddenly Hayley felt guilty for coming. The last thing she wanted to be was a burden. But after Brian and his friend paid her a visit, she hadn't been able to talk herself into going home. Instead, she'd skipped school and wandered the streets. For hours she'd busied herself with people-watching at a park in midtown. Once it got too cold, she headed for the mall. On her way to the mall, though, she'd found Lizzy's flyer in her back pocket. Next thing she knew, she was sitting in front of Lizzy Gardner's house. And now she wondered why. If God couldn't save her, nobody could.

"Hayley, what are you doing out here in the cold? Come on, let's get you inside and get you warmed up."

Knowing she couldn't leave without some sort of explanation, Hayley stood and followed Lizzy up the remaining stairs. Then she saw the bruised knot on Lizzy's face. "What happened to your forehead?"

"All in a day's work," Lizzy said lightheartedly as she unlocked the door to her apartment.

Hayley didn't need to have the highest GPA in her class, although she was close, to realize the woman was putting on a brave front. Lizzy Gardner was the defender of the weak and small, after all.

The door opened and Hayley noticed Lizzy hesitate before she ushered Hayley inside. Lizzy entered and then proceeded to bolt the door as if she were protecting herself from every villain known to man. Hayley wondered if all of those locks could keep Brian and his friends out of her room. Something told her they wouldn't.

"Meow."

"This is Maggie," Lizzy said, bending over to pet her cat. "I think she's hungry. Why don't you follow me to the kitchen and we'll get some hot soup inside you. Where's your coat?"

"I really shouldn't have come," Hayley told her. "I saw your picture on television today. The news lady said the FBI was watching over you." Hayley's eyes widened. "Is it true? Is Spiderman after you?"

"I don't think so," Lizzy said. She opened an entryway closet, grabbed a coat, and wrapped it around Hayley's shoulders.

Too cold to argue, Hayley slid her arms into the heavily lined sleeves. Judging by the way Lizzy had stiffened when she mentioned Spiderman, something was definitely going down. "I think the FBI should use bait to catch the killer."

Lizzy settled her hands on Hayley's shoulders. "You shouldn't concern yourself with these things. I also don't like the idea of you walking around the streets at night. It's not safe."

In the light, Lizzy's face looked even worse. "So what really happened to your face?"

Lizzy plunked her hands on her hips. "I made the mistake of chasing after a car."

"I thought only dogs did that."

Their eyes met and they both chuckled. Hayley liked Lizzy. Nobody else ever appreciated her sense of humor.

"Yeah, well," Lizzy said, "I've never claimed to be the brightest crayon in the box."

Hayley watched Lizzy rush around the room, straightening decorative pillows, switching on the heat, and turning on the television. "Make yourself comfortable while I feed Maggie and get some soup on the stove. Hot soup will warm you right up and then we can talk."

Lizzy went to the kitchen, opened and closed drawers, fed the cat, and opened a can of soup. Watching the woman was like watching the Tasmanian devil in action. Hayley realized she should offer to help Lizzy. She wanted to, but for some reason her legs wouldn't move.

Hayley turned back to the door and looked at all of the bolts and locks. How was she going to get out of here? That thought brought her back to Brian. He could get past these locks. So why couldn't she? When had she lost her confidence? She used to think she could do anything she set her mind to. She was smarter than the average high school kid. She was in the top ten percent, and that was without trying.

Fortitude. That was a word she might have used to describe herself in the past. Grit, stamina, resilience. Yeah, sure, all of those things summed her up pretty well. She had all of that and more when it came to giving herself to a man clothed in iniquity. But somewhere, somehow, she'd lost her spine under the guise of "saving" Mom. *And what for? Was Mom any better off now than she was back then?* The answer sickened her.

"Soup is almost ready," Lizzy said.

Lizzy gestured toward the living room. "Make yourself comfortable. I'm going to change out of these clothes and then we'll eat, OK?"

Hayley nodded. She could tell Lizzy was worried about her... more worried than she was letting on. The poor woman looked like she'd had a bad day, but she was too nice to let it show. Once Lizzy disappeared, Hayley turned back to the door. She never should have come. Lizzy had problems of her own.

Wednesday, February 17, 2010 7:09 p.m.

"I don't want to hurt you, you know."

Sophie was sitting on the floor, the upper half of her body duct taped to the bedpost. Her eyes were shut tight. Thick ropes bound her ankles and wrists, only because he liked to use the ends of the ropes to guide her and pull her to the bathroom every once in a while to clean her off.

"Come on, Sophie, open your eyes. Look what I brought you."

Nothing. She was giving him nothing. Miss Popular dressed like a hooker and swore like a sailor, but today she trembled and sputtered like an eight-year-old.

"Listen," he said, plopping down on the floor so he was facing her, his legs crossed in front of him. "If you open your eyes and talk to me for a few minutes, I won't bring my pets here to play with you tonight, OK?"

Her lip twitched and tears streamed down her face, but that was all he got.

"If you don't open your eyes, Sophie, I'm going to have to cut your eyelids off so that we don't have to keep having the same conversation over and over."

Her eyes cracked open, and she cried out, surprising him. He jumped. "OK. That's more like it." He adjusted his mask so it didn't press down so hard on his nose. Then he smiled. "You caught me off guard there for a minute."

She blinked.

He pointed a finger at her. "Keep them open, Sophie."

Her legs shook so hard, her knees literally knocked together.

"Do you have any idea why you're here, Sophie?"

She sniffled and sputtered and shook her head.

"Do you think you're a good person?"

She managed a barely perceptible nod.

Unbelievable. Everybody in the world thought they were Mother Teresa. It didn't matter how many boys these teenage girls did in the locker rooms. It didn't matter if they stole, swore, or did drugs; they all thought they were good, decent, respectable human beings. Even his sister's friends used to think they were so cool. Even before they locked him in the basement, he'd hated the way certain girls would look at him with big, curious eyes as if they were looking at some rare bird in a cage.

"Have you ever lied to your parents?"

Sophie shook her head and that made him laugh. "Let's try another one. Have you ever kissed a boy?"

Another shake of the head.

But this time he didn't laugh. She was a liar too. He couldn't stand liars. He had already heated up the soldering iron, and it lay nearby on a metal stand. He didn't have to lift himself to his feet. He merely leaned to his right, grabbed hold of the preheated iron, and put the hot tip against her arm before she had a chance to protest.

She screamed and yanked her arm back as if he'd plucked out an eyeball. He waved the iron in front of her face, taunting her.

"Pl-please, stop."

His eyes widened in surprise. "She talks. Tell me about the last boy you teased and flirted with and then left standing alone like an idiot. Tell me about him, Sophie. I want details."

Her mouth clamped shut.

Smiling, he pressed the hot iron to her leg, below her knee. She kicked and screamed, but he kept leaning in, touching her flesh wherever he could despite her flailing around like a big ol' fish. The smell of burnt flesh filled his lungs, and he was already hard. After only a few minutes, she stopped flailing and took all his fun away.

"OK, Sophie. You win. I'm done. Sadly, you won't get to see the surprise I had for you. But because I sort of like you, Sophie, you get to ask me one question before we go for a little drive and I let you go."

For the first time in days, she stopped sputtering. Hope filled her eyes.

He set the iron to the side and crossed his arms. "We're not going anywhere until you think of a question."

"Why are you doing this to me?"

Disappointed, he stood and brushed himself off. His mask felt awkward across his face. His head throbbed. "Because you're vulgar and disrespectful, Sophie. I knew a group of girls just like you. They never should have done what they did." He raised his hands to the back of his head and looked toward the ceiling. Inhaling a lungful of stale air, he tried to erase the images spewing forth in his mind, but it was no use. He'd never forget what they did…never.

"I know who you are," she said.

That got his attention. His cowardly victim had a spine after all. He cocked his head. "Not too bright, are you, Sophie?"

Moving hastily to the dresser, he grabbed a roll of duct tape and returned to her side. Using his teeth to break off a section of tape, he wiped her mouth off with his hand and then plastered the tape over her lips. He grabbed the soldering iron again and held her head against the post.

It was time to leave Lizzy another note.

CHAPTER 17

Wednesday, February 17, 2010 7:33 p.m.

A glimpse in the mirror revealed a trail of bruises. Purples and blues blended together, starting at her ribs and ending midthigh.

Lizzy shuffled through her drawer for a clean shirt and thought about Hayley. She'd wanted to throw a blanket around the girl and sit her down on the couch. But Hayley looked confused and Lizzy didn't want to scare her off. Lizzy would take things slow, get some hot soup in the girl before she started asking questions. Hayley looked different tonight—exhausted and disoriented—nothing like the determined, tough-as-nails girl who showed up in defense class every month.

Maggie's long tail curled around Lizzy's leg. She leaned over and stroked Maggie's fur. "What's wrong, kitty? You don't like your new Seafood Delight?"

"Meow."

"Sorry. It's all we've got." On her way back to the kitchen, Lizzie retied her hair in a rubber band. Although Jared would be arriving soon, and he'd promised to cook, she figured he wouldn't mind sharing a meal with one more. Until then, hot soup would have to do. "I hope you like chicken noodle soup," she called out as she reached the kitchen. She gave the soup on the stove a quick stir before making her way to the front room.

The room was empty. "Hayley?"

Hands on hips, Lizzy looked around. The bolts on the door were unlocked. She opened the door and scanned the area. "Hayley?" She was gone. Damn. Lizzy ran to the kitchen, turned off the stove, and grabbed her coat and keys. A minute later, she was driving around the neighborhood looking for Hayley, but the girl had disappeared.

An hour later, Lizzy hovered over the stove, wondering if she should go ahead and eat the soup and call it a night. Hayley hadn't returned and Jared was a no-show. The antique clock hanging on the wall in the kitchen mocked her. *Tick tock. Tick tock.* Usually the sound of the pendulum soothed her, but tonight the rhythmic tick tock taunted her, telling her she was either running out of time or she was just a fool.

Jared was late. It shouldn't matter. This wasn't a date. They were getting together to discuss the case. But Lizzy never did like the idea of waiting around for a man—doing so made her feel vulnerable and needy.

She turned off the stove just as the doorbell rang. Lizzy sauntered to the door and peeked through the peephole. Jared stood back, waiting. His thick, wavy hair had that sexy windblown look and the stubble on his jaw made him look less like an FBI agent and more like a regular guy. He looked good in fitted jeans and an untucked, baby-blue button-down shirt beneath an open wool peacoat. In one hand he clutched a bag of groceries and in the other he held a bouquet of flowers: daylilies, her favorite.

Butterflies flittered inside her belly. *Silly girl.* This was merely dinner with an old friend. *Who was she kidding?* The mascara she'd brushed onto her naked lashes and the flowers in his grasp painted a different picture entirely. She watched him lean close to the peephole.

"Are you going to let me in, Lizzy?"

Inwardly smiling, she unbolted the locks and opened the door. He leaned forward and kissed her cheek before he handed her the flowers. "Sorry I'm late."

He smelled like soap and sandalwood, better than the daylilies. She wanted to wrap her arms around his neck and show him how glad she was to see him. Instead she held the flowers neatly to her chest like armor.

"After I left you this afternoon, I met with Jimmy and the rest of the task force." He held the groceries midair. "And then I went to the store."

She stood there for a moment, soaking all of him in. She wanted to forget why he was really here and just enjoy the moment.

"You're not going to let me inside, are you?"

"Oh, sorry." She opened the door wider and let him through. After locking the bolts, she caught up to him in the kitchen and watched him unload the grocery items from the brown paper bag.

"I hope you like salmon," he said.

"I love salmon."

He pulled out a box of presliced mushrooms and two crowns of broccoli. "How about mushrooms and broccoli?"

"I can't think of too many vegetables I would wrinkle my nose at."

"Not even peas?"

"I love peas."

He made a nasty face.

She laughed. It felt good to laugh.

The last thing he pulled from the grocery bag was an apron. He took off his coat, and she hung it in the entry closet. When she returned, he was sliding the apron over his head and tying the straps around his waist.

"Wow, this is serious business," she said. She maneuvered around the island so she could retrieve a frying pan from a cupboard. "Will this work?"

"Perfect." He looked around. "I'll need a cutting board and a knife and then I'll be set."

She found what he needed and put the items next to the pan.

He gestured toward the soup on the stove. "It looks like you were about to eat without me."

"I had an unexpected visitor. Hayley, a girl in my defense class, stopped by. Unfortunately she took off before I could feed her and warm her up."

"Is she OK?"

"I don't know. She didn't look OK. I drove around looking for her, but she was gone."

"Do you know where she lives? We could take a drive and check on her."

Lizzy gave Jared a thoughtful look. He'd always been compassionate and caring. That's what had attracted her to him all those years ago. "There's no listed number for the name Hansen. I usually pass out flyers in class and provide a sign-up sheet, but I don't require anything other than a name."

He took her hand and led her to the stool on the other side of the kitchen island. "Let's feed you first. You look like you could use some nourishment; then we can figure out what to do about Hayley."

"You don't want me to help cook?"

"I want you to relax." He kissed the knot on her head.

"Ouch."

"Sorry." He went back to his place at the stove and pulled a bottle of Cabernet from his bag. When she pointed to the cupboard where she kept the wineglasses, she noticed a black smudge on her finger. Mascara. "I'll be right back." She went to the bathroom, dismayed by what she saw in the mirror. Jared showed up looking like he'd stepped out of the pages of *GQ*, and here she was looking like the lady from the Black Lagoon. She used a wet cloth to clean under her eyes before making her way back to the kitchen. She took the wine he offered and said, "Thanks for telling me I looked like Rocky Raccoon."

"I thought you looked cute."

"Cute." She shook her head. "That's why I don't wear makeup. It's time consuming and it never stays where it's supposed to."

"But you took the time to put it on for me. I'm flattered."

"Don't be. This isn't a date."

His eyes sparkled beneath the fluorescent lights. "I swear I detected lipstick when you first let me in."

"You don't miss a thing, do you, Shayne?"

"I already told you…not when it comes to you, Lizzy." He stepped close enough for her to feel the heat from his body. That old familiar warmth sizzled between them. All these years apart, and yet put the two of them in a room together and it was as if they were back in high school. She'd felt the chemistry between them in the car today while they waited for Valerie Hunt to go to lunch. And she felt it now. Hell, she felt the same sizzling heat every time Jared Shayne stood within five feet of her. This wasn't a good time for them to get involved. They were both overworked and exhausted. They had too much on their minds. But that didn't stop Jared from leaning toward her. Nor did it stop her from tipping her chin upward until his mouth brushed against hers. His lips felt warm, intoxicating. He tasted like fine wine and all the best life had to offer.

He deepened the kiss.

She pressed her body closer to his.

He took her glass and set it on the counter. The weight of his body caused her to take a couple of steps backward until she was backed against the refrigerator.

His hand slid upward over her arm and across her shoulder. Shivers followed. He dragged his mouth from her lips to her ear. "I've missed you, Lizzy."

The tingling heat pulsing between her legs told her the feeling was mutual. Her hand slid beneath his apron and over his shirt. The soft cottony fabric beneath her fingertips was a stark contrast to all that hard muscle underneath.

His hands cupped her buttocks and brought her snug against him. A moan of desire slipped through her lips—the sort of noise that led to naked bodies and hot sex, reminding her of their first time…right before darkness swallowed her whole. She pulled away and sucked in some air.

"What is it, Lizzy?"

She peered into his eyes. It would be so easy to get lost in those eyes, in his scent, in his kisses. "Why now?" she asked. "After all this time, why now?"

"Because I'm an idiot."

She might have smiled at his honesty, but the ringing of the phone gave her a start. She followed Jared to where the black box revealed the incoming number. A cold chill swept over her. She didn't want to answer the phone, but she didn't have a choice. Thinking of Sophie, she lifted the receiver to her ear. "Hello."

"I wish you hadn't lied to me, Lizzy." His voice filtered through a synthesizer, robotic and cold. "Now I have to teach you a lesson."

"Is Sophie Madison with you?" she asked.

"I ask the questions first, Lizzy. If you tell me the truth, I might consider answering your question."

Jared was pressed close so he could listen in.

"Is your boyfriend there with you, Lizzy?"

"I don't have a boyfriend."

Laughter resembling a phlegmy cough sounded on the other end. "Let me reword the question for you, then. Is the boy you fucked before I found you fourteen years ago in the room with you now?"

She felt Jared stiffen.

"Is that clear enough, Lizzy? Have you met the woman he was engaged to? The woman he gave up because of you? Hair of gold and sweet, rosy lips. So beautiful, and yet he left her, Lizzy. And in the end, he'll leave you again too. He's a lot like his whorish mother. Love 'em and leave 'em, that's Jared Shayne's motto. Shame on him. Now answer me again. Is your lover there with you now?"

Jared's jaw tensed. She reached for Jared's hand and squeezed his fingers. She needed to keep Spiderman talking. "Yes," she said calmly. "He's here with me. Do you have the girl?"

"Not so fast, Lizzy. That was only one question."

Breathe, Lizzy, breathe.

"Do you still love me more than your daddy? I want the truth, nothing but the truth."

She waited as long as possible, hoping the red light would flash and they would have a connection. "No," she said. "No, I don't."

"Very good, Lizzy. Do you remember what I said I'd do if you ever betrayed me?"

Despite her anger, jolts of revulsion shot through her. "I do."

"That's a good girl. Now go ahead and ask me a question, Lizzy."

"Do you have Sophie Madison with you now?"

"Yes, but not for long. She's been a very, very bad girl."

"Tell me where you are. Let her go. Take me instead. I'll do whatever you—"

Click. The line went dead.

She looked at Jared, but neither of them said a word. They didn't need to. She hadn't kept him on the line long enough.

Wednesday, February 17, 2010 10:13 p.m.

Rain and wind thrashed at the hedges and shrubs in front of the house he was watching. Trees shed limbs and tossed branches and pieces of bark across the street.

The storm was brewing earlier than the weatherman had predicted. He wondered why he bothered watching the news at all since most weathermen never got it right. But who was he kidding? He watched the news to see Nancy Moreno in action. There was something about the anchorwoman that intrigued him... which was exactly why he'd handpicked her to help him.

Moreno was more than flawed; she was damaged goods. For starters, she'd been raped by both her father and her uncle at a young age. But instead of letting it destroy her, she'd used everything bad that happened to her to become stronger. She put herself through college and came out on top. From what he'd deduced, Nancy liked being on top. She also liked being in control. He wouldn't mind taking her to bed, but first he'd have to wine and dine her, and he hadn't decided yet if she was worth the trouble.

Despite her injured soul and broken psyche, Moreno always looked put together, never a hair out of place, not until this morning. Incredibly, he'd been able to do with a couple of phone calls what her father hadn't been able to do after years of fucking his own daughter. Only he had the power to unravel a cool exterior like Moreno's.

His fingers smoothed over his goatee. It wasn't real. In fact, he was eager to get home and pull the hair off his chin, and the mustache too. He no longer enjoyed hiding behind phony hair and uncomfortable masks, but neither did he want to sit in a cold, dank cell, so he did what he had to.

His gaze remained on the house across the street. Sophie was dead in the trunk. She'd been worthless, like playing with a dead fish.

Nothing was like it used to be.

He glanced at his brand new Perpetual Sea-Dweller. It was time to go. With all the wind and rain, he couldn't see much. Besides, he needed to get rid of the body. He reached over and snatched his Nikon from the passenger seat, deciding to give it one last shot before he left. Using the telescopic lens, he looked through the viewer until he could see inside Brittany Warner's bedroom. Her light was still on. Her bedroom light didn't usually go off until after eleven. A silhouette of a young girl walked by, giving him a rush. Seconds later, she returned. This time she paused directly in front of the window. *That's a good girl.*

Click. Click. Click.

Knowing that Lizzy Gardner's niece might be watching him made shivers shoot up his spine. *Yes.* He closed his eyes, savoring the moment. Maybe things weren't so bad after all.

Thursday, February 18, 2010 2:35 a.m.

"Stop!"

Jared sat upright. He peered into the dark at unfamiliar shapes and shadows. *Had he heard something?*

The only sound was the wind pressing against the building. It took him a few seconds to remember that he was sleeping on Lizzy's couch. After the phone call, Lizzy hadn't had much of an appetite—for food or sex. He didn't blame her. After the call, they spent a few hours scouring files and taking notes.

Lizzy didn't want him to drive home after finishing off a bottle of wine, but neither was she ready to invite him into her bed. He didn't mind. He just wanted to stay close and watch over her.

"Please don't!"

That definitely wasn't the wind. He jumped to his feet, rushed down the hallway, and opened the door to Lizzy's bedroom. She was having a nightmare. He went to her and smoothed the hair from her face.

"I'll never leave you," Lizzy said in her sleep. "I promise. Just leave her alone. I'll do anything you ask if you'll just leave her alone."

The desperation in her voice made his heart ache. "Lizzy, it's me, Jared. Wake up."

Lizzy reached for him, dug her fingers into his forearm. "She's had enough," she cried. "She doesn't mean to cry. She doesn't know any better…please, I'm begging you to stop."

Jared reached for the lamp and turned on the light. "Lizzy, wake up."

Her eyes opened and she let out a shuddering breath. "Jared? Thank God it's you." Eagerly, frantically, she pulled him closer and wrapped her arms around his neck. "You came. I knew you would come. I never gave up hope."

He'd never felt at such a loss. She was still asleep, but at least she knew he was there for her.

"It's me," he said as he slid onto the bed next to her. "I'm here."

She curled up close and rested her head in the crook of his arm. Within minutes her breathing calmed. He didn't bother shutting off the light. He lay still, his fingers gently sifting through her hair while he stared at the ceiling. She hadn't wanted him to drive home, but neither had she wanted him to stay the night. He'd known she was hiding something, but he never dreamed she was reliving the terror of her past every time she closed her eyes and went to sleep.

CHAPTER 18

Thursday, February 18, 2010 6:38 a.m.

Lizzy walked into her office, surprised to see Jessica already hard at work. "You're here early."

"I couldn't sleep," Jessica said without looking away from her laptop. "I can't stop thinking about these girls, especially Sophie."

Lizzy squeezed past Jessica's chair, took a seat, and turned on her computer. A cup of hot coffee awaited her. "Thanks for the coffee." She took a sip. "Looks like you've been getting a lot of work done."

Jessica plopped a pile of notes and papers in front of Lizzy. "Want to see what I've got so far?"

Lizzy took another sip of coffee and nodded.

"We've got four bodies all found near a body of water. Every victim had spider bites, burn marks, and their own distinctive mark left by the killer. For instance, the first victim found was Jordan Marriott—brown eyes, dancer, found floating in a community pool. Her family wouldn't talk to me, but I was able to locate two of Jordan's closest friends. They both agreed Jordan was a nice girl, but she had a big mouth."

Lizzy was about to comment, but Jessica raised a hand to stop her. "You said to find out every detail about these girls, so that's what I did. Maybe if we learn more about them, we'll learn more about Spiderman too."

Impressed, Lizzy waited for Jessica to continue.

"It seems Jordan had a tendency to tell people exactly what she thought of them—no holds barred. Her friends said her bluntness could get out of hand at times. She had been known on occasion to publically humiliate her mom. If you remember, Jordan was the girl found with soap shoved down her esophagus. She was also blinded by acid.

"Next victim was Laney Monroe," Jessica said without pausing. "The only blue-eyed victim. But guess what? She wore contacts."

"You're kidding me?" Lizzy was stunned.

"Guess what color her eyes were?"

"Brown."

"That's right. Brown. Laney was found on the edge of the American River, right before it flows into the Sacramento River. I talked to Laney's teacher and a couple of male friends who said that Laney was happy-go-lucky and fun to be around. Even her neighbors, fourteen years later, still remember her. They too had nothing but positive things to say about Laney. She was well liked and popular. But for some reason the killer did unspeakable things to her genitalia. And yet he didn't rape her."

So far, Lizzy was impressed with Jessica's findings. "So what do you think that means?"

"I'm not certain, but a few guy friends hinted that she was *so* well liked she might have 'gotten around' a little. I think Spiderman knew she could be a little 'too friendly' and didn't like it."

"OK, interesting take. Go on."

"Third victim was Mandy Rocha. Sixteen. Brown eyes. President of her class. Leader in student government. She was a student leader in twenty-five percent of the clubs at her school, which is unheard of. Mandy's body was found near Folsom Lake. All of the victims had burn marks, but unlike the others, Mandy's arms and legs were covered with cigarette burns. Guess what her vice was?"

"She was a smoker?"

"That's right. Cigarettes. Lots of them. Every person I talked to who knew Mandy well said she'd been smoking for as long as they could remember. She was up to a pack a day when she was abducted. She also snuck out of the house on weekends and met up with friends, mostly boys."

Lizzy watched Jessica with a newfound fascination. The girl was smart, and she seemed to have a knack for investigative work. Who knew?

Jessica skimmed over her notes. "The last victim, that we know of, was Rachel Foster. Rachel was also found near the American River, a few miles from where Laney Monroe was discovered. Rachel had syringes protruding from her eyes. Her family has since moved, but I located Ryan Arnold, an attorney. He was Rachel's boyfriend at the time she disappeared. He said Rachel was a drug user at the time of her abduction. She was fond of heroin. Ryan has done his own research on the case, and he faxed me an article written by retired FBI agent Gregory O'Guinn."

Lizzy nodded thoughtfully and waited for Jessica to finish.

Jessica held up a piece of paper. "I have a copy of the article right here. Mr. O'Guinn spent twenty years profiling serial killers. He calls Spiderman an outcast, someone who felt inadequate. To make himself feel better, Spiderman needed to be in control, and that's why he kidnapped young girls who would have less of a chance of defending themselves. But I wonder," Jessica said, pausing. "If you look at these four girls, you see a pattern. It seems that Spiderman thought he was doing the community a favor by getting rid of them: teenagers who were disrespectful to their parents, kids who smoked, did drugs, or had sex at a young age."

"That would mean most teenagers."

"Exactly, but that's why I couldn't sleep last night. If I put myself in the killer's head, I wouldn't know which girls were truly 'bad' unless I knew them on some level. Unless I saw them on a semiregular basis, which means—"

"He knew these girls," Lizzy cut in. "He saw them enough to decide that they were trouble. And who would see the girls on a regular basis?"

"Tutors, teachers, coaches, dentists—"

"And doctors," Lizzy finished.

Jessica's eyes widened. "But Spiderman also chose girls with brown eyes."

"Which makes it personal," Lizzy said.

"Yeah, teenagers with brown eyes must have reminded him of someone."

"Maybe he dated a girl with brown eyes and she broke up with him, or maybe it's the ol' mother-hate thing going on and the killer's mother had brown eyes."

Lizzy recalled what Jared had said. "Zeroing in on brown-eyed girls is not going to help us find Sophie."

"No, it's not," Jessica agreed, "but it did make me wonder if the killer could be an eye doctor."

Lizzy pointed a finger at Jessica. "You might have something there. It's worth a shot. We'll check out every eye doctor these victims visited, whether at school or out of school." Lizzy made a note of it on a pad of paper next to her computer. "And what do you make of his fascination with bodies of water? Why would every victim be left near or in the water?"

"I'm not sure. His obvious interest with water stumps me. And yet...I do think leaving the bodies near the water makes sense if he wants the victims to be found quickly, before nature takes its course and ruins his display."

"Good point. If he wanted to destroy the evidence, he would have buried their bodies somewhere in the woods or mountains."

"One more thing," Jessica said. "Every victim Spiderman chose was popular. I don't mean just 'well liked.' I mean popular with a capital P. Cheerleaders, overachievers, et cetera."

"So he goes for popular girls with brown eyes," Lizzy said. "And girls with a vice, whether it be sex, drugs, or cigarettes."

Jessica nodded. "I wonder if something happened to Spiderman to set him off. It's a known fact that some serial killers are set off by a specific type of victim. Ed Gein was provoked by middle-aged women who resembled his mother, while Ted Bundy went after women with very specific characteristics: young college students with long brown hair parted in the middle. There must be a triggering factor. Something happened to Spiderman to set him off. If this is the case, where has Spiderman been all this time and what happened to set him off again?"

"You've done a lot of research on serial killers?"

Jessica nodded. "I've thought about becoming a profiler someday. Although the more I learn, the easier it is to see why Sigmund Freud admitted defeat when it came to understanding why some people do the things they do."

"I think you'd make a great profiler." Lizzy reached into her coat pocket and pulled out the notebook Jared had given her yesterday. "I think it's time we focus on the girls who went missing during that same time period and see if we get more of the same: brown eyes, popular, et cetera. We need to start from the beginning, go about it as if these crimes happened yesterday. Let's start with every doctor these girls ever visited."

Thursday, February 18, 2010 10:33 a.m.

Twenty minutes after receiving a call from Jimmy, Jared pulled his car in front of Jimmy's sedan on Hazel Road and shut off the engine. Myriad police cars with roving lights and three unmarked cars made a neat line on the side of the road about a half mile from the freeway entrance.

Jared stepped out and followed the crime scene tape, starting at the curb and continuing down a muddied slope to the river's edge. At the bottom of the hill Jimmy was barking orders, trying to secure the scene as quickly as possible. He and Jimmy had been working together for three years now. Although Jimmy had the personality of a rock, he had an undeniable passion for his job that never failed to put a spark in his eye and a swagger in his step.

Jimmy already had a videographer on the scene. An intern, carrying a camera and a clipboard, followed Jimmy around like a puppy. The video camera was strapped to the kid's shoulder as he took copious notes, writing down everything from climate to the names and titles of people on the scene.

Jared recognized Joey Ritton, the same criminologist they'd used at the Madison house to record shoeprints. Ritton's assistant placed a ruler next to a muddied shoeprint and then photographed the print. Next, Ritton positioned a metal frame around the print before carefully pouring dental stone into the shoe impression.

Jared continued on, following the crime scene tape down a man-made trail that led to the American River Parkway. During the winter months, fishermen could be seen in the water, elbow-to-elbow in their cuffs and vests as they waited for salmon to catch their lines.

"The rain last night didn't help matters," Jimmy told Jared when he saw him approaching. "A little luck would be helpful about now."

"What about weapons?" Jared asked.

"None so far. The shoeprints might be our best shot at finding any evidence here, although the killer did leave us another note."

A few feet behind Jimmy, Jared saw two technicians using alternative light sources to look at the victim's body, searching for fibers and hairs before they would transport the body to a crime lab where another thorough search would be conducted.

A wave of biting wind nipped at Jared's ears as he followed Jimmy toward the body. "Where's the note?"

"You'll see."

Catching sight of the girl, Jared sucked in a breath as he drew closer. It was Sophie. He recognized her from the pictures. Her bangs covered her forehead, but the rest of her hair had been chopped at weird angles just as Lizzy had talked about. From where he stood he noticed burn marks and puncture wounds on both arms and legs. "Are those cigarette burns?"

"We believe the marks were made with some sort of iron," one of the technicians answered, "but we'll let the ME examine the body before anything is put in pen."

"Lots of bruises and cuts," the other technician said as she checked for loose fibers before readying the body bag.

"Strangulation?" Jimmy asked.

The male technician shook his head. "No contusions around the throat that we can see. Off the record, I don't think the victim has been dead for more than twenty-four hours. Eyes are clear and there's not much swelling of the body, but again, the ME will need to search the contents of the stomach to help determine the time of death."

"The body looks as if it was placed, not dumped," Jimmy told Jared.

"So that means you don't think the body washed ashore here. You think the killer walked down that trail," Jared said, gesturing toward the muddied slope he'd just come down, "and positioned her body exactly where he wanted us to find her?"

Jimmy rubbed the back of his neck. "That's what it looks like. Her lower torso was under water while her upper half was wedged within the rocks. Yeah, I think our man knew exactly what he was doing. Definitely Spiderman's MO to leave the body just so."

"How many of Spiderman's victims were strangled?"

"Not this one," the female technician said, "although I wouldn't rule anything out just yet. Based on what we've seen so far, my initial guess would be death from shock."

"How about clothing?" Jared asked. A victim's clothes were usually their best shot at finding evidence.

Both technicians shook their heads.

"Not a stitch of clothing on the girl," Jimmy answered before he was called away by the videographer. "Show him the note," Jimmy told the technician as he walked off.

Jared looked at Sophie.

The female technician pushed Sophie's bangs away from her forehead.

"Shit."

"Yeah," she said, "that's what I thought when I first saw it."

Burned across Sophie's forehead in bold letters:

LIZZY'S FAULT

The technician pulled her hand away and the bangs fell back in place. Her partner finished enclosing the body in the transport bag, then zipped the bag, starting at Sophie's feet. The bite marks on Sophie's ankles resembled the marks found on Spiderman's other victims.

Jared bent down for a closer look. Sophie's upper lip was swollen. She had two tiny cuts on her middle upper lip. "What about the mouth?"

Once the technician got the zipper as far as Sophie's neck, he stopped, reached into his kit, and pulled a tongue depressor from a plastic bag. He used the depressor to lift the upper lip slightly, just enough to reveal a nice even row of teeth. "No cracked teeth," the technician said. "No signs of bruising. Hard to say."

"OK," Jared said. "Thanks." He walked back up the trail, his insides churning. He'd worked on cases more gruesome than this, but never one dealing with a victim as young as Sophie.

CHAPTER 19

Thursday, February 18, 2010 12:10 p.m.

Yesterday Valerie Hunt had worn a tweed pencil skirt and matching jacket. Her jet-black hair had been twisted into a tight roll at the back of her head. Today Valerie wore a pair of tailored black knit pants and a checkerboard double-breasted jacket.

Lizzy rolled down the window, adjusted the lens of her camera, and took a couple of quick pictures. Valerie's long, wavy hair, free and flowing, cascaded down the middle of her back, blowing in the wind as she dashed across the street to her car.

Lizzy placed the camera on the passenger seat and started the engine. Then she waited. A minute later she was following Valerie's black Toyota Camry onto Sunrise.

For the next ten minutes Lizzy stayed a few car lengths behind the Camry. *Who was this woman? More importantly, who was Victor?* If Valerie was his wife, had he confronted her before resorting to hiring a detective? Had he tried to work things out first? Her thoughts quickly segued to Jared and why she'd felt compelled to push him away last night. The kiss they'd shared had made her feel alive, jolted her to awareness. Sadly, the kiss also brought back memories of that first blissful night turned to terror.

Her fingers tightened around the steering wheel.

Get a grip, Lizzy.

Even before Spiderman came back into her life, she had been living her life as if Spiderman were right there peeking in her window. She had allowed him to ruin her life by thinking about him every hour of every day.

She was done hiding.

She needed to move on and let her past stay in the past. She wondered about Jared; wondered if they had a chance together. If she could get through this as a better, stronger person, if she could get through the night without waking up in a cold sweat, then maybe, just maybe, they had a chance. Jared Shayne was an amazing man. The kindest man she'd ever known. Although she still wasn't sure this was the right time for the two of them to get reacquainted, who was she to question being given a second chance at something tender and real?

A new determination coursed through her veins. She would not allow Spiderman to continue to ruin her life. It was his turn to run cold, his turn to feel dread running through his veins, never knowing when he was being watched.

A silver Honda cut in front of her. Damn. She'd lost sight of the Camry. She merged into the left lane and stepped on the gas. Out of the corner of her eye, she saw the Camry make a right. Cutting in front of the Honda, Lizzy cut a sharp right onto Folsom Boulevard in time to catch sight of the Camry turning left onto East Point Drive. Lizzy caught up to Valerie and followed her into a hotel parking lot.

She watched Valerie pull her car in front of the hotel, step out of her vehicle, and hand the keys to a valet.

Lizzy drove past the front of the hotel and toward the public parking area. She didn't plan on entering the hotel lobby. Following her subject by foot would mean risking the possibility of running into Valerie. Private Eye 101: never allow your subject to become aware of your presence.

She tapped a finger on the steering wheel.

Screw it.

She took the first empty spot. A voice in her head said, "Curiosity killed the cat." She didn't care. After shutting off the engine, she climbed out and hurried to the back of her car. She opened the trunk and grabbed a knee-length jacket that she kept there for just this purpose. After wrapping a scarf around her head, she headed for the hotel's entrance. It was twelve twenty. If she was lucky, Valerie would be in the hotel bar or restaurant. If not, Lizzy would sit in the lobby until her hour was up and call it a day.

As promised, a courier had delivered the entire sum of three thousand dollars in cash yesterday afternoon. Unfortunately, the man Jared had sent to watch her office had arrived too late to be of any help. According to Jessica, the courier had not been wearing a uniform. He wore blue jeans and a long-sleeved sweatshirt. He'd arrived on a road bike that he'd left leaning against a building a block down the road from her office. After handing Jessica an envelope, the young man rushed off before Jessica could tip him or ask him about the person who hired him to deliver the package. Being a clever girl, Jessica had used her cell phone to take more than one picture of the courier as he ran off. Upon downloading the pictures to Lizzy's computer, they were able to enlarge the photos and see a Cosumnes River College Hawks sticker on the back of his helmet.

A gust of wind nearly blew the scarf from Lizzy's head as she walked across the parking lot. A silver BMW pulled up in front of the hotel, blocking her view of the lobby. *Get out of my way, buddy.*

A man dressed in a dark suit climbed out of the BMW and handed his keys to the valet. It took a few seconds for recognition to settle in. Stunned, Lizzy made an abrupt about-face. Pulling the scarf closer around her face, she focused on keeping a steady pace as she made her way back to her car.

Don't run. Walk. Don't call attention to yourself. Breathe.

Afraid he might recognize her car if he looked this way, Lizzy walked toward a gray Prius instead. Pretending to look for her keys, she dared to take a peek over her shoulder. He was gone. The valet climbed into the BMW and disappeared around the other side of the building. She ran back to her own car, tossed the coat and scarf into the backseat, and slid behind the wheel.

Her forehead fell against the steering wheel. *What the hell was Richard doing here?*

Sadly, she knew exactly what her brother-in-law was doing here. Yesterday she and Jared had followed Valerie to Seacrest and Associates, her brother-in-law's place of work. Although the coincidence had not been lost on her, Lizzy never for a moment questioned that Richard might be involved with Valerie Hunt. What the hell was going on?

When Lizzy told Jared that Valerie had entered her brother-in-law's place of business, Jared had asked point blank if there could be a connection between Valerie and Richard. Lizzy had scoffed at the notion. Richard Warner, her brother-in-law, was about as romantic as a two-by-four and about as friendly as a troll.

But now Lizzy's mind whirled with speculation and unease. She grabbed her cell, ignored the flashing icon telling her she had a voice message, and called her sister's house. Cathy answered on the second ring. "Hi. It's me, Lizzy."

Her sister's sigh on the other end was loud and clear. Clearly she wasn't ready to make amends.

"I'm sorry about everything," Lizzy blurted, talking fast, as she often did when she was nervous. "You've been so supportive and encouraging over the years and—"

"Are you still looking for that maniac?"

"To tell you the truth, I haven't had much time for the maniac," she fibbed. "I'm working on my first infidelity case and it's sucking up all of my time and energy." Her sister didn't need to know that "the maniac" had called her again last night. Her sister didn't need to know a lot of things. But Lizzy needed to talk to her, needed to hear her voice. Since her mother had moved away and Dad refused to have anything to do with her, Cathy was all the family she had left. And, of course, Brittany.

"I thought you didn't do infidelity jobs."

"I didn't. Not until a man named Victor offered me three thousand dollars to watch a woman for two weeks."

There was a pause before Cathy said, "Wow. I guess I would have taken the job too."

Some of the tension left Lizzy's shoulders and neck. "Yeah, well, I was sitting here in my car waiting for the woman to return and I started thinking about you and Brittany. I saw you three days ago and I miss you already."

"I miss you too, Lizzy, but until you're done with this obsession you have with Spiderman, a man who has very nearly succeeded in destroying all of our lives, I've got to do what's best for Brittany."

"I understand. How is she?"

"Hard to believe she'll be fifteen soon."

"Unimaginable." Lizzy squeezed her eyes shut. Cathy would be devastated to know what she had just witnessed. Lizzy couldn't do it. She couldn't tell her sister what she'd seen. *Innocent until proven guilty, right?* She refused to be the person to cause Cathy more heartache.

"What am I going to do when Brittany starts driving?" Cathy asked. "All the other moms I've talked to at the swim meets and school tell me I won't see Brittany much once she starts driving."

Lizzy sighed. After she'd escaped from Spiderman, she'd been shocked to learn that her sister was pregnant and was going to marry Richard. Her sister was eighteen at the time. "We have a while before that happens. But you're right; it's not easy watching our little Brittany grow up so fast, is it?"

"I hate it. I really hate it. Where did all the time go?"

"I don't know."

It was quiet for a moment, the silence filled with years of too many unspoken words. Although Cathy still had a relationship with their father, he refused to talk to Lizzy, and so Cathy and Lizzy never spoke of him.

"If you want to come to Brittany's swim meet at noon on Saturday, it's at the aquatic center in Roseville. I won't kick you out."

Lizzy's heart was breaking, knowing she should tell her what she'd seen, but also knowing it would only hurt her. "I wouldn't miss it for the world. Is Richard going to be there?"

"I doubt it. He's been super busy lately…working evenings and weekends. When he is home, he's too tired to do much more than fall asleep on the couch." Cathy let out a bitter laugh. "Maybe I should pay you to follow him around for a few weeks."

Lizzy's spine stiffened.

"I'm teasing, you know," Cathy went on. "Richard and I are doing fine. In fact, he took my car for me today to have it fixed. He left me with his Lexus. Unheard of, considering he's never let me drive his car before."

"What's wrong with your car?"

"Apparently everything. He called twenty minutes ago to read off a list of problems with the engine. The good news is everything should be fixed by the end of the day."

"Sounds like it might be time for Richard to buy you a new car."

"I don't think that will happen. We're pinching pennies as it is. But I'll let him know you think so," she said, her voice lined with amusement.

Lizzy rubbed the bridge of her nose. "I better go. Tell Brittany I said hello. I'll see you both on Saturday."

"I'll tell her. Take care of yourself, Lizzy."

"You too. I love you." Lizzy hung up the phone. She prayed she was wrong about Richard. Unwilling to leave without knowing the truth, she drove out of the hotel parking area and parked across the street where she would have a better view of the hotel entrance. She readied her camera, grabbed her binoculars, hunkered down in her seat, and waited.

CHAPTER 20

Thursday, February 18, 2010 2:03 p.m.

KBTV Sacramento anchorwoman Nancy Moreno sat on the chaise with its streamlined, no-frill design and waited patiently as her therapist, Dr. Linda Gates, fixed her a cup of hot green tea in the kitchen attached to Dr. Gates's third-story office.

Nancy had been coming to Dr. Gates twice a month for years, but today Nancy looked around the room as if it were her first visit. If she wanted Spiderman to give her an exclusive, she needed to steal Lizzy Gardner's file. And quick.

An executive-sized desk constructed of hardwood and painted black with a distressed finish sat before a large-paned window overlooking downtown Sacramento. Potted palm trees stood on either side of the desk, concealing part of the view of downtown. To the left of the desk was a bookcase crammed full of books on behavioral health, psychiatry, and physiology. To the right was a nine-drawer legal-sized decorative file cabinet where the client files were kept.

Nancy had considered asking Dr. Gates straight out for Lizzy Gardner's file, perhaps bribing her with a large sum of money. But Dr. Gates had married a banker, and judging by the jewelry she wore and the trips she took, she probably didn't need the money enough to risk ruining her reputation.

Dr. Gates exited the kitchen and came toward her with a cup of tea in hand. "Green tea without sugar, just the way you like it."

Nancy leaned forward and took the offered tea. Dr. Gates's dark hair was cut in a blunt A-cut set off by a beige collarless jacket and matching knee-length skirt. Nancy watched closely as Dr. Gates retrieved notepad and pen from atop her desk and then took a seat across from her. Dr. Gates crossed her legs. "How are you today?"

Nancy sipped her tea. "I've been better."

"What's on your mind?"

"I haven't been sleeping well," Nancy lied. "I've been having nightmares."

Dr. Gates remained expressionless. "About what?"

"The nightmares have been about you, Dr. Gates, and all the notes you take when I visit."

Dr. Gates stopped writing. "Go on."

"The nightmare begins with a shadow of a man lurking about in my home or at my office at work. He walks around with a file tucked under his arm. He opens the file and that's when I see all of your scribbling inside." She put a hand to her chest in exaggerated surprise. "I feel as if all of my dirty laundry has been aired before the world. I feel humiliated. I lose my job. And then I wake up." She exhaled. "It's always the same."

Dr. Gates did not laugh or even smirk. She took everything her clients said seriously, and Nancy's nightmare confession today was no different.

"Maybe it will assuage your fears," Dr. Gates said, "if I show you your file."

Nancy sipped her tea and waited for Dr. Gates to continue.

"The promotion you've been worrying about could be caus-ing your anxiety, making you fret about things you wouldn't nor-mally worry about. Perhaps if I show you that your file is safely locked away you'll feel better about things."

"It's worth a try," Nancy said, trying to keep her cool, pleased at how easily her ruse was working so far.

Dr. Gates set her notebook and pen aside, stood, and headed for the file cabinet. Nancy came to her feet too, bringing her tea with her. She watched Dr. Gates use a key hooked to a band around her wrist to unlock the file cabinet. As Dr. Gates thumbed through the files, Nancy spotted Lizzy Gardner's name on one of the thicker files. She waited patiently for Dr. Gates to locate her file, and when she did, Nancy feigned clumsiness and dropped her tea cup. The cup hit the hardwood floor and shattered. Tea sprayed across the floor and up against the file cabinet. "Oh! I'm so sorry. Clumsy me."

Dr. Gates handed Nancy her file and rushed toward the kitchen area to grab a towel. Nancy didn't hesitate. She reached into the file drawer, grabbed Lizzy's file, and rushed back to the couch where she quickly slid the file into the leather briefcase she'd brought for just that purpose.

"What happened to the file?"

Nancy jerked about, surprised by the doctor's quickness in returning to the room. She held up her own file. Her throat felt dry. "It's right here. Can I bring it home?"

"No, I'm sorry. I wouldn't feel comfortable. Why don't you go ahead and look through it, though, while I clean up this mess."

Nancy set the file on her seat cushion and hurried back toward Dr. Gates. She took the towel from the woman, wiped tea from the cabinet, and then clicked the drawer shut before the good doctor noticed anything missing.

When Nancy straightened, she saw a perplexed expression on Dr. Gates's face. The doctor's gaze fixated on the view outside her window. She looked concerned about something.

Nancy's heart pumped fast and hard against her ribs. "Is something wrong?"

Dr. Gates took a step backward until she was half hidden behind the potted palm. "There's a man outside…standing at the bus stop. I've seen that same man standing there before, more than once. That wouldn't be odd in and of itself except that he always walks away before the bus arrives." She shook her head. "Odd."

Nancy tossed the porcelain chips she'd collected into the garbage and moved closer to the window. "He's looking this way."

Dr. Gates frowned. "That's what I thought."

"Does he come often?"

"The first time I noticed him was last Monday. This is the third time I've seen him out there. I'm going to call the police. I'll feel better once he's questioned."

Nancy stood frozen in place while Dr. Gates made the call. *Could the man at the bus stop be Spiderman?* He didn't look like a killer. Standing there in a crisp black single-breasted coat, he looked like a businessman. His hair was dark. His full beard nicely trimmed. A pair of dark aviators covered his eyes. He was slight in build, and she guessed his height to be close to six feet.

Dr. Gates returned to her side. "The dispatcher said there was a patrol car close by. They should be here in a minute." She feigned a shudder. "There's something about him that gives me the creeps. Look at him, staring at us. Has he even once looked away?"

Nancy shook her head.

"If we can see him, he must see us watching him."

A bus pulled to the curb, blocking their view. The bus windows were tinted. Nancy couldn't tell if anyone was getting on or off. Dr. Gates's office was on the third floor. Nancy could see the police car approaching from two blocks away. No sirens. No flashing lights. The bus pulled away seconds before the police car approached and parked at the curb where the man had been.

Nobody was there.

Dr. Gates sighed. "He's gone."

Not once had the man looked away from their window. He could not have seen the approaching police car, and yet somehow he'd known to get on the bus. Chills raced up her spine. Nancy wondered if she was making a mistake. She would take Gardner's file for now, she decided, and give the situation more thought before she did anything rash. Yes. She needed to think this through before she did something she might later regret.

Thursday, February 18, 2010 2:56 p.m.

A little before three, Lizzy arrived back at her office. She locked her car door, surprised to see Jared waiting for her on the curb.

"Where have you been?" he asked.

"What are you, my father?"

"Hardly."

Frustrated by what she'd seen at the hotel and angry with herself for agreeing to take the job in the first place, Lizzy swept past him, her boots clacking against the asphalt as she marched toward her office. For over two hours she'd sat in her car across the street from the hotel waiting for Richard to exit the hotel.

Lizzy's hands fisted at her sides as she replayed the last twenty minutes over in her mind. Despite being locked up in a hotel room for hours on end, Richard and Valerie, having no idea they were being watched through a telescopic lens, had exited the hotel together. They kissed twice, passionately, and then proceeded to gaze into one another's eyes while they waited for the valet to retrieve their separate cars.

"Lizzy, please slow down," Jared said from behind.

She marched along, afraid of what she might say if she didn't. Richard's betrayal, his lies, it all swirled inside her like a swarm of irritating gnats. She'd taken dozens of incriminating photos. *And now what? How could she ever tell Cathy that her husband was a cheating, lying bastard?*

"Sophie's dead."

Lizzy stopped cold. Slowly she pivoted on her heels until she faced Jared. She put a hand to her chest. "What?"

"I've been trying to call you all morning. Her body was found on the river's edge off Highway Fifty."

"Oh my God. No."

"I'm sorry."

"I should have used the media to send him a message." She laid a palm on her forehead. "That would have distracted him, would have given us more time."

Jared took a firm hold of her shoulders. "It's not your fault, Lizzy. You can't blame yourself for every wrong he does."

She took a fistful of his coat sleeve. "We did nothing. We did nothing to stop him. This isn't right."

"There are dozens of people working the case. We're doing everything we can."

Jared didn't understand. She'd been spending her time following Richard and his mistress, a woman she knew nothing about, while Sophie was tied up and gagged, no doubt, praying somebody would find her...save her. Tears welled in her eyes while hatred boiled in her veins, bubbling and threatening to erupt in—oh my God. She peered up at Jared. Suddenly it all made sense. "Victor."

"What about him?"

"You were right," she said. "It's him. Victor is Spiderman."

"How do you know?"

"The note," she said. "In the note Spiderman left for me at Sophie's house he said he knows me. Maybe he knows me better than I first thought. Maybe he knew me so well he knew before I did that I was going to come looking for him. Remember when we were at the Walker house and I thought we were being watched?"

He nodded.

"I know Spiderman was watching me. He's probably watching us right now." She fought the urge to look over her shoulder. "He's been watching my sister too. He knew Cathy's husband was having an affair and he wanted me to know too."

"Slow down," Jared said. "Why don't you start from the beginning?"

She took a breath. "Remember how I thought it was odd that Valerie Hunt had gone to Seacrest and Associates yesterday?"

"The law firm where your brother-in-law works?"

She nodded. "It wasn't a coincidence. I followed Valerie Hunt across town to a hotel this afternoon. That's where I've been. Moments after Valerie Hunt entered the hotel, my brother-in-law showed up driving my sister's BMW. At that point it was his word against mine, so I parked across the street and waited until Richard exited the hotel."

"And?"

"And then I got the proof I needed but didn't want." She patted her backpack. "It's all here in my bag...dozens of incriminating pictures." She clutched his arm. "Don't you see? It's him.

Victor, the man who hired me to follow Valerie, is Spiderman. He knows my mother has moved away and that my father won't have anything to do with me. Somehow he knows Cathy and I are treading a slippery path when it comes to our relationship. Spiderman wanted me to know about Richard's affair so I could tell my sister and sever my last ties with my family." She shook her head. "I called Cathy, but I couldn't do it. I couldn't tell her the truth."

"We have to tell her."

"I can't."

"If Spiderman knows about your brother-in-law," Jared said, "then he's been watching their house…which means he's watching your niece too."

Lizzy's heart dropped to her stomach. Until that moment, she realized she hadn't truly known terror. Brittany was in danger. Cold electric currents shot through her body. "He's winning, isn't he?"

Jared put an arm around her shoulders. "Let's go to your office. I'll make a few phone calls and get somebody to watch your sister's house."

"When?"

"Now."

She noticed a muscle working in Jared's jaw. His eyes had a hollow, empty look to them. He'd been at the crime scene, no doubt. Her heart went out to him. And to Sophie and her family. She couldn't believe the girl was dead. Poor Sophie.

"The courier who delivered Victor's payment yesterday," she said to fill the silence, "appears to be a college student. He left before Jessica could question him. She managed to use her cell phone to take a picture though. When we enlarged the picture we were able to see a Cosumnes River College sticker on his helmet.

Although he's much too young to be Spiderman, he might be able to identify Victor. We need to find him."

Thursday, February 18, 2010 4:12 p.m.

He considered driving by his house in Auburn, the one he'd shared for fourteen years with his wife, Cynthia. He envisioned her returning from her trip back east to visit with friends. He imagined her wearing a pale pink sweater and beige slacks. Cynthia was a simple woman, easy to please. She had taken good care of him.

She didn't deserve to die.

The thought of Cynthia being gone forever caused his heart to beat rapidly against his chest. He turned on the radio and clicked on the CD player. Listening to Mozart, Piano Concerto 21 Andante, made him feel better.

Cynthia was alive and thriving, he told himself. More than likely, she and her friends were out painting the town red. He turned the music up, hoping to be swept up by the melody.

His smile disappeared.

Until he got his hands on the file, he wasn't going to be able to think straight. He thought about how easy it would be to snatch Lizzy up and finish her off once and for all, but then what? He needed to play the game. The only way to see this to the end as he envisioned was to be patient and focused.

Keep with the plan, Stan.

Keep Lizzy sweating; keep her in suspense. The last pieces of the puzzle would be found in the pages of Dr. Gates's file. That's where all of Lizzy Gardner's deep, dark secrets would be. That's when the real fun would begin.

The orchestral piece by Wolfgang Amadeus Mozart was lyrical and celebratory. The music filled him with a joy. Everything would be fine. He just needed to take care of unfinished business. Then he could go back to his house and pray Cynthia would forgive him and take him back.

Thursday, February 18, 2010 4:14 p.m.

Lizzy pulled into her sister's driveway and shut off the engine. She stepped outside and looked around until she caught sight of the government-issued vehicle parked across the street.

Jared shut the passenger door and met her on the sidewalk.

"Is that one of your men?" she asked with a nod toward the dark sedan parked across the street.

Jared nodded. "Ronald Holt."

She looked toward her sister's house. She didn't want to do this, didn't want to tell her sister that her husband was cheating on her. But she and Jared already agreed she had no other choice. Brittany and Cathy's safety came before all else. She had to warn her sister, let her know a madman might be watching them.

"I wish I didn't have to do this," she told Jared as they headed up the walkway.

"Do you want me to tell her?"

"No. That would only make things worse." She rang the bell and waited. Minutes ticked by before the front door opened. Cathy looked tired, as if they might have woke her from a nap. "What's going on?" Cathy asked.

Lizzy looked past her sister toward the staircase. "Is Brittany home?"

"She's at swim practice." Cathy's eyes narrowed as her gaze fell on Jared. "Why are you here?"

"Can we come in?" Lizzy asked.

Reluctantly Cathy let them enter. She shut the door and followed Lizzy to the living room. "What is it?" Cathy asked again. "What's going on? Tell me before I have a heart attack, for God's sake."

Lizzy reached for her sister's hand. "Brittany is fine. But after we talk, we should pick her up at practice and bring her home."

"She won't be finished for another hour." Cathy snatched her hand back. "Tell me what the hell is going on, Lizzy. Quit beating around the bush."

Jared remained close to the entryway, his hands tucked away in his coat pockets.

"I don't know where to start," Lizzy said.

"Anywhere, dammit. Start anywhere!"

"OK, you're right." Lizzy sighed, then just blurted it all out, "Richard is having an affair."

Cathy lifted a hand and slapped Lizzy across the face.

Jared stepped forward, but Lizzy raised a hand to stop him. "It's OK," she said, brushing her fingertips over the cheek where her sister's palm had struck. "It's true," she told Cathy. "I have proof, but that's not the only reason we're here."

Cathy's face was red with anger, her hands curled tightly at her sides. "That's why you called me earlier today, wasn't it? You thought you knew something about Richard but for some reason you didn't tell me."

"I didn't know *how* to tell you. You need to listen to what I have to say."

The anger, the hurt, the years of strained silence and guilt… it all hovered over their heads like thick black clouds waiting to burst open and wash away whatever ties were left holding them together. "I have reason to believe that the man I told you about, the man who hired me to watch his wife, is Spiderman."

Cathy's lips pressed together in a tight line.

"In the note Spiderman left for me in Sophie Madison's room, he said he knew me better than anybody. If that's true, Cathy, then he knows that you and I have been struggling to build a relationship. He's using this knowledge about Richard to try to put another wedge between us. That's why I believe he hired me to watch Valerie Hunt, the woman I was following today when I saw Richard and her together."

Cathy raised her chin. "Where were they?"

"At a hotel. The Hyatt."

"For how long?"

"I'll give you the details later, I promise. But first you need to let me finish. If Spiderman knows about Richard, then that means he's been watching him."

Cathy's eyes widened in horror as the truth dawned on her. "That madman knows where we live?"

"I believe so. It's possible that he's been watching all of you."

Cathy's face paled as she pressed her hand over her mouth. After a moment Cathy said, "What am I going to do?"

"There's a federal agent parked across the street," Jared cut in. "His name is Ronald Holt. He'll remain parked outside the house twenty-four-seven. He won't go anywhere unless he has a replacement."

"But I don't think that's enough," Lizzy added. "I think you should take Brittany to Dad's place and stay there until the feds catch him and put him behind bars."

Cathy's face paled. "You don't understand. Brittany has only recently begun to make friends. For the first time in her life she feels as if she's starting to fit in. I know what it's like to feel lost and out of place at school. I can't uproot her now and take away what little bit of confidence she's gained. I won't do it."

"But you can't take the added risk of keeping her in school or taking her to swim practice right now."

"She can't stop living." Cathy pointed a finger at Lizzy. "You said that yourself. You said you were miserable from all those years of hiding from your own shadow."

"But you were the one who was right when you said that hiding from my own shadow was better than the alternative." Lizzy didn't believe that for herself any longer, but Brittany had her whole life ahead of her, and Lizzy would say anything to make her sister understand that they needed to protect Brittany at all costs.

Cathy shook her head. "I can't do that to Brittany. She's too young. She wouldn't understand. I won't have her life turned upside down because of that maniac. I won't allow him to do this to me again."

"You must." Lizzy lifted a hand to comfort her sister.

Cathy backed away, her eyes feral. "Don't touch me. I want you to get out of here. Stay away from us, do you understand me?" She pointed to the door. "Get out. Both of you!"

"Don't do this," Lizzy said. "I never meant to hurt anyone. You know I would never deliberately try to mess things up for you and Brittany."

"Look what your lies did to Dad and Mom, and now to me. I won't let you destroy my family too. I won't. Don't make me say it again, Lizzy. Please go."

CHAPTER 21

Thursday, February 18, 2010 7:53 p.m.

Jared stood in Lizzy's kitchen. He snapped his cell phone shut and then rubbed the bridge of his nose. His sister had called to tell him that Mom had moved into a hotel. His sister was worried about Dad, who was drinking again. *Who could blame him?* The man needed time to sulk, Jared told her. His answer had angered his sister, and she'd ended the conversation as quickly as it had begun.

"Is everything OK?" Lizzy asked from the other room.

Jared headed that way. Lizzy sat in the middle of the living room floor surrounded by papers. Notepads and files had been placed in a neat row from one side of the room to the other. The television was on but the sound was muted. The cat weaved a figure eight around the wooden legs of her coffee table.

"My parents are having some difficulties," he told her.

"Oh, I'm sorry."

"They're adults. They'll work it out." Jared went to the stove and poured soup into a cup, then made his way into the living room. Jimmy would be coming by to give them an update.

Lizzy crawled around on the floor on all fours, using a black marker to make notes in the margins of her papers.

Jared had been with Lizzy for most of the day. He had yet to see her take a bite of food. Since taking a shower and changing into a pair of gray sweatpants and a white V-neck T-shirt, she'd been working. Her feet were bare. Her hair was pulled back into a ponytail.

"You haven't eaten anything," he said, handing her the cup of soup.

"Thanks. Do you mind putting it there on the coffee table?"

"Not until you taste it." Leaning over, he slipped a spoonful into her mouth.

Her eyes widened. "That's good. What sort of spice is that… are those capers?"

"It's a family secret."

She pouted.

"If you eat every last drop I'll write down the recipe for you."

"You're a pushover, Shayne."

He wanted to scoop her up in his arms, hold her close, and make all her troubles drift away. Instead he spoon-fed her another bite of soup and then set the cup on the coffee table.

"Thanks for going to my sister's with me today," she said as she returned to her notes.

"You're welcome." He stood there for a moment, watching her. Her eyes were framed by dark circles. The lump on her head was smaller today but darker in color. He knew her well enough to know she didn't like anyone to see her without her guard up. She didn't want anyone to see the pain caused by having all of her hopes and dreams stripped from her in an instant. For Lizzy, letting go of the past and moving forward was like waking up each day and trying to learn to walk all over again.

At eight o'clock sharp Jimmy Martin arrived, looking haggard. His suit was disheveled, shoulders stooped, face pinched.

Before Jared could usher him inside and shut the door, Lizzy's assistant arrived carrying a bucket of fried chicken from KFC.

"Come on in," Lizzy said from her spot on the floor.

Jimmy stepped inside and Jessica squeezed in from behind him. She said hello, then handed a bucket of chicken to Jared. "I'll be right back," she said. She opened the door and disappeared.

Jimmy looked confused.

Jared shrugged, letting Jimmy know it would be easier if they just went along with whatever Lizzy had planned. He took the chicken into the kitchen.

"I would have brought dessert," Jimmy said, "if I had known you two were throwing a party."

Jared and Lizzy ignored him.

Jimmy removed his wrinkled suit jacket and took a seat on one of two chairs Lizzy had arranged to face the couch for their impromptu meeting.

Jessica returned with her laptop and a stack of files. "If anyone is hungry," Jessica said, "help yourself to the chicken."

Lizzy smiled gratefully.

"OK," Jimmy said once they were all seated, "what's going on and who are you?"

Jessica reached out a hand toward Jimmy. "Jessica Pleiss, psychology student at Sac State and Elizabeth Gardner's sidekick."

Lizzy rolled her eyes. "She's my intern. She's interested in majoring in criminology and becoming a profiler."

"OK," Jimmy said as he looked at Jared, "remind me why I'm here?"

"You promised to update Lizzy on the Walker house."

Jimmy scratched his chin. "They started excavating this morning, but so far nothing has turned up. It'll be another day or two before we have a full report."

"What about Spiderman being a doctor?" Lizzy asked.

"What about it?" Jimmy loosened his tie. "You have no recollection of ever seeing his handwriting. No fingerprints were found on the note or at the Madison house. No signs of tire tracks or footprints outside. So far we have nothing to tie Sophie's abduction to Spiderman, but you want me to put an all-points bulletin out for any doctor who looks suspicious?"

"It would be a start," Lizzy said bitterly.

"Although we shouldn't generalize when discussing serial killers," Jessica cut in, "most serial killers are intelligent with an above-average IQ. Most are white males who have either been abandoned or who come from a highly dysfunctional family. It makes perfect sense that this guy could be a doctor."

Jimmy didn't say a word.

"It's better than doing nothing at all," Jessica added before anybody else could get a word in edgewise. "At the very least we should start with every doctor Sophie Madison had seen in the past, say, two years, and go from there."

The girl had gumption, Jared thought.

"What is this?" Jimmy asked Jared, his hands held wide. "Your special task force?"

Jared smiled. "Yeah, I guess you could say that. For the past ten years Lizzy has immersed herself in abduction cases all across the country. For three of those years she was a board member of the Missing and Exploited Children's Organization. From the sounds of it, Jessica here is on her way to becoming a profiler; so, yeah, I guess you could say that this is my task force. What have we got to lose?"

Jimmy shoveled his fingers through his hair. "Sure, OK. Fine."

Since Lizzy had done her best to distance herself from her own abduction case, she didn't know as much as she should about the FBI's investigative findings from fourteen years before, so it didn't surprise Jared when she asked, "Before Frank Lyle was arrested, were there any other suspects?"

"A few," Jimmy said flatly. "None were doctors. And I don't have the manpower to send my men off on wild tangents."

"Lizzy has experience," Jared said. "She's a private investigator and she wants to help. You've called in for outside help before. Hell, you used a psychic in the Smith case. Brush off that chip on your shoulder, Jimmy, and work with us."

The tension was thick until Jessica easily sliced through it with her I-have-nothing-to-lose attitude. "In 1998, four bodies were found," Jessica said, "and all four were believed to be the work of Spiderman."

Jimmy didn't look impressed.

"During that same time," Jessica went on, "at least three other girls within the same general area and age of the four victims went missing. Where are they? Has everyone forgotten about those girls?" Her eyes narrowed. "Without a body, are they so easily discarded?"

Jared looked at Lizzy, wondering what was going on. Jessica appeared to be emotionally connected to the plight of the missing girls.

"I want to know what happened to these girls, so I did a little research," Jessica went on.

Lizzy leaned forward, listening.

"Two of these girls were swimmers," Jessica said, "just like Laney Monroe, your number two victim. All the girls went to different high schools, but guess what? At some point or another, they all swam on swim teams outside their school. I haven't been able to connect a particular swim coach to all three girls, but this definitely puts a few more people on the list of suspects, don't you think? I also found one doctor connection when I added the missing-girls-but-no-body-yet-found to the list: Dr. Bruce Dixon, a family practitioner. And that's not all. Altogether, three of the missing girls and two of Spiderman's victims wore braces. That's a total of five girls with braces. I've started a list of orthodontists within a thirty-mile radius. I still have more work to do, but I'll keep you all posted."

Lizzy looked at Jimmy. "Now that you know what my assistant and I are working on, I'd like to know what the agency is doing about the possibility of Spiderman being a doctor."

"Let's make one thing clear," Jimmy said. "As far as the agency is concerned, we're still not one hundred percent certain we're dealing with Spiderman when it comes to Sophie Madison."

"He left me a personalized note," Lizzy reminded him.

"There's no concrete proof that either note was from Spiderman. It could be the work of a copycat."

"What do you mean by 'either note'?"

Jimmy looked at Jared. "You didn't tell her?"

Lizzy glanced at Jared. "What didn't you tell me?"

"We'll talk later."

"No, we won't." She straightened. "Please tell me what the second note said."

"'Lizzy's fault.'" Jared hoped that would be the end of it for now, but Lizzy pushed herself to her feet and looked him square in the eyes. "Where's the note?"

He had no words to describe what he'd seen scrawled across Sophie's forehead, so he remained silent.

Lizzy hardly moved. She just stood there for a moment before walking out of the room.

Jessica looked at Jared, wondering if she should do something.

"I'll talk to her. You two eat some chicken."

Friday, February 19, 2010 6:21 a.m.

He finished untying her hands. Then he took off her blindfold. "Go ahead, Lizzy. I trust you."

Lizzy looked up at him and tried to see through the holes in his mask. He seemed taller, bigger, broader in the shoulders. Last time she'd seen him he had a thick, wiry beard. At the moment, he appeared cleanly shaven. His jawline was square and even.

"I said go ahead, Lizzy."

Her heart thumped against her chest as she pushed herself from the hard ground and set off. Her knees wobbled from lack of use. That didn't stop her, though. She hobbled onward, careful not to knock into the case where he kept his precious spiders. She exited the room and quickly moved down the hallway toward the bathroom. A quick glance over her shoulder told her he wasn't following her, wasn't even watching her.

He'd only let her use the bathroom once before. She'd been starving herself for a month. If she was ever allowed to use the bathroom again, she knew she needed to be thin enough to squeeze through the window above the bathtub. She had no idea how many pounds she'd lost, but her legs and arms looked like bones. She felt unbelievably weak. Although she didn't have much in her stomach, she felt as if she might barf.

She turned the doorknob and entered the bathroom, then quietly locked the door. He wouldn't like that, but she had no choice. Her reflection in the mirror above the sink caught her by surprise. Her eyes looked hollow. Bones and skin. That's all she could see. Her hair was greasy, hanging in limp strands around her ears. She brushed her bony fingers over the cream-colored tiles around the sink, noticed the soothing blue color of the walls. It was all so clean, so different from the room he kept her in. Chrome towel rings, unadorned mirrors, a candle and a vase with flowers. The room didn't compute, didn't make sense. Clean and simple—nothing resembling the chaos going on in the rest of the house.

Before stepping up onto the edge of the tub to get to the window, she noticed a watch...his watch. Spiderman loved that watch. She knew this because he often lovingly stroked the watch around his wrist as if it was a beloved pet. She scooped it up and slid it over her arm, all the way past her elbow. Next she grabbed the liquid hand soap and stood on the edge of the tub to reach the twelve-by-twelve-inch window. She had been planning her escape for weeks. She squirted soap into the window frame to reduce noise; then, inch by inch, she pushed the window open.

Weak from lack of food and water, she tried to pull herself up, but her shoulders burned. Every muscle ached as she struggled to lift her body high enough so she could push through the opening. She was afraid to use her legs, afraid of kicking the wall and calling attention to herself.

"Lizzy!"

He called her name. She froze.

"Lizzy!" he called again.

This was it. This was her last chance, her only chance.

Time was running out. He had a temper. He was strong. He would probably kick the bathroom door open with one swift kick of his booted foot.

Use everything you've got, Lizzy. To hell with making any noise! She jumped this time, and then kicked and grunted and pulled herself upward until finally she was able to squeeze her shoulders through the opening.

The door rattled. He was coming.

Her heart beat so fast and so hard she thought it might explode. Without bothering to look to see where she might land, she dived headfirst out the window and landed on thick shrubs. Sharp branches dug into her skin. Fear threatened to clog her throat as she frantically untangled herself from the bush. It felt like forever before she managed to get her feet on solid ground.

He was shouting and banging on the door.

Don't panic, Lizzy. Whatever you do, don't stop.

Dressed in a T-shirt, her legs weak, her body sore, she ran as fast as she could. The sun was just beginning to rise. She saw a dark blue sky and white, billowy clouds. She saw freedom. She had no idea where she was or where she was going. She only knew she had to run fast if she ever wanted to see her family again.

Run, Lizzy, run.

Lizzy awoke with a start. She sat up in bed.

Another nightmare.

She looked about, her eyes darting from the closet to the curtains covering her window. Her gaze fell to the clock on her nightstand. Six thirty in the morning. Usually her nightmares included one of Spiderman's victims being tortured. This was the first time she had ever recalled her escape.

She fell back into the pillows and listened to her breathing until her breaths became shallow and even.

A scratching noise at her window reminded her that the red maple outside her window needed trimming. Twice she had called her landlord asking him to trim the trees around the building. Obviously to no avail.

Wearing sweats and a T-shirt, she slid off the bed and wondered what time she had finally drifted off to sleep last night. She hardly remembered saying good night to Jared before bolting the locks. She was still upset with him for not telling her about Sophie and the note, but she knew her anger was misplaced. Jared was only trying to protect her.

She headed for the kitchen and called for Maggie, surprised Maggie hadn't made an appearance by now.

"Here, kitty, kitty. Come on, Maggie. Time for breakfast." Maggie didn't like storms. With the wind rattling outside making the walls creak, it was no wonder Maggie was hiding out somewhere.

Lizzy looked around the living room. "Maggie. Come on, kitty. It's OK."

Maggie wasn't on the couch or under the coffee table, two of her favorite spots. Glancing at the papers laid out across her living room floor, she remembered all the work she had to do. She also sensed for the dozenth time that she was missing something crucial…something right there in front of her that had yet to click: *sports, dance, school, swimming, teenagers, brown eyes…what could it be? What wasn't she seeing? He killed Sophie. He would kill again.*

Once again Jessica had surprised her last night with all the work she'd done in such a short time. Apparently, she'd used the oldest trick in the book to get friends and family of the missing girls to answer her questions: she told them the truth, that she was working with a private investigator to try to uncover the truth about whether there were any links to their child's disappearance and Spiderman's victims. Family members and friends had been eager to answer her questions. The parents of the missing girls were tired of being ignored, tired of not knowing the truth. They wanted answers and they didn't care who got them.

She stacked papers into piles and placed them on the coffee table. The phone rang, and she answered it before it could ring a second time. "Hello."

"Lizzy," he said in his familiar robotic voice, "is that you?"

She remained silent as she watched the red light on the box. Jimmy had told her to keep the caller on the phone for at least sixty seconds. She'd thought she'd had him the last time. She counted to ten, swallowed, and said, "Of course it's me. I thought you knew me better than anyone."

His mouth was pressed close to the transmitter because she could hear him breathing. "You're getting too thin again, Lizzy. It's not appealing. When I first found you, you had some meat on your bones. What happened?"

Her teeth clenched together. Stay calm. More than anything, she wanted to tell him to go to hell and hang up, but she refrained.

"Cat got your tongue, Lizzy?"

"I'm here," she finally said. She looked at the red light, willing it to flash. "Why are you calling me? What do you want?"

"That's more like it. That's the willful, determined Lizzy I remember. I just wanted to hear your voice, Lizzy. Remember how we used to sing *twinkle, twinkle, little star?*"

She closed her eyes, tried to stop the bile from rising to her throat. She'd forgotten about the singing. She had purposely forgotten about a lot of things. The last thing she wanted to do was take a stroll down memory lane.

The red light began to flash. *Thank God.* "Yes, I remember," she said. "Do you want me to sing it to you now?"

He laughed. "No. I want to save that for later, you know, for when we're finally together again."

She sucked in a breath.

"I like what you've been writing in your journal, although I am surprised I wasn't mentioned more often."

Breathe, Lizzy. Just breathe. He couldn't have possibly read your journal. He's playing with you. But how would he know I keep a journal at all?

"Are you there, Lizzy?"

She waited. The red light was solid again. "I'm here." They had a definite connection. The little red light made her feel stronger—more determined than ever to put the first nail in his coffin. "What's your real name, Spiderman? Why don't you stop being a phony and a coward, stop hiding behind silly superhero names and ridiculous masks? Tell me your real name. Be a man, for God's sake. What's your name? Is it Hank? Jim? Fred? Are you afraid to tell me your real—"

"You're the liar," he said, cutting her off, his voice spiteful. "You lied to your parents. You're the coward and the thief, Lizzy. The raving whore. The slut. You had to give it all up just to try to get your boyfriend to stay put, but it never would have worked, Lizzy. You gave it all up for nothing. Your girlfriends were calling you a whore behind your back. At least I saved you from hearing about that. We'll be seeing each other soon. You do know that, don't you?"

Silence.

"I left you a present, Lizzy." He paused, his breathing growing heavier.

She was not going to hang up the phone. She'd let him talk all day if he wanted to.

"Go back to your bedroom, Lizzy, and look out your window if you want to see what I left for you. See you soon, Lizzy." *Click.*

Her hands grew moist. The receiver dropped from her hand. Slowly she walked toward her bedroom. A distant voice told her not to look, shouting at her to go back to the kitchen and call Jared. Call Cathy. Call the police.

Call anyone, but whatever you do, Lizzy, don't look out that window, the voice said. It was the same voice she had ignored fourteen years ago: *Don't listen to the screaming in the back room. Don't go back for that girl, Lizzy. Don't be a fool.*

She entered her room and then took slow, unsteady steps toward the window. The scratching noise had grown louder. She grabbed a fistful of mossy green curtain. *Don't do it, Lizzy!*

With a flick of her wrist, she pulled the curtain aside. There it was. Her gift from Spiderman. Her knees gave out, and she crumpled to the floor and sobbed.

CHAPTER 22

Friday, February 19, 2010 9:10 a.m.

Cathy checked her makeup in the rearview mirror before she stepped out of her car and followed Brittany into the orthodontist's office. She said hello to the women behind the front desk and signed her daughter in on the clipboard. The office was neat and orderly and the staff was friendly and efficient.

Her stomach did flip-flops as she looked around, hoping to spot Dr. McMullen. The office included three orthodontists; all were friendly, but Dr. McMullen was by far the most handsome. His good manners and charm were two reasons why she didn't mind coming in for an extra visit.

Brittany was already in the waiting area flipping through the pages of a *People* magazine when Cathy saw Dr. McMullen step out of his office. He glanced her way, giving her a subtle wink before the nurse handed him a file and ushered him toward a patient waiting in one of five chairs lined against the wall.

After Richard arrived home last night, Cathy had showered him with false thanks for taking care of her BMW. Then she'd served him a plate of grilled salmon and broccoli. After eating, he fell asleep on the couch, never once asking about her day. He had no idea what was going on at home. Apparently he was too busy with his mistress. In fact, he'd left the house so early this morning she never had a chance to tell him about Lizzy's visit or about the FBI agent parked across the street. She shrugged. *Fuck him.*

Cathy had lost two pounds this week. Funny what a little stress could do to one's appetite. This morning she pulled out her best pair of black slacks and favorite V-neck sweater that made her look ten pounds slimmer. The sweater revealed a little cleavage, her best asset. She'd also taken the time to curl her hair. Even the federal agent parked across the street had straightened in his seat when she exited the house earlier.

"Hey, Mom," Brittany said, "did you ever call the math tutor and make an appointment?"

"Didn't I tell you? You have an appointment with Mr. Gilman tonight. It was the only opening he had. He sounded like an older man, though; are you sure you have the right guy?"

Brittany nodded. "He used to be a math teacher at Carmen Junior High. Jenny says he's really nice. And she's getting As."

"That's fine, but I want to meet him. I'll go to the door with you when I take you. Or maybe he has a waiting area for parents."

"Mom, that's sort of lame. Can't you just drive home, and then come back after an hour?"

"It's twenty minutes away. I'll wait in the car and read my book." Cathy didn't miss the slight roll of her daughter's eyes. Although she didn't want to worry her daughter, she also couldn't take any chances leaving her alone.

"What about Lizzy?" Brittany asked. "Am I going to see her after school?"

"Afraid not. She's busy this week." Cathy wasn't in the mood to discuss Lizzy with her daughter. She needed time to think about things. "Maybe you can see her next Friday. We'll see."

"Brittany Warner," one of the nurses said. "Dr. McMullen is ready for you now."

Cathy's nerves got the best of her as she smoothed her hands over her slacks and straightened her spine. She followed her daughter into the room where Dr. McMullen was finishing up with one of his patients. The doctor's assistant gestured toward the chair at the end of the row. Cathy noticed the doctor watching her as she followed Brittany to the chair. She smiled at him and then looked shyly away.

It wasn't long before Dr. McMullen greeted Cathy with a friendly handshake. "So what do we have here? I didn't think I was going to see you two for another month."

Cathy blushed. "I-I didn't think we would see you for a while either. I'm afraid one of Brittany's wires broke."

A soft laugh rumbled from his throat, making her wonder if he was laughing because she was so obvious. *The hair, the nice outfit…had she made a fool of herself?*

Dr. McMullen took a seat on the stool next to her daughter's chair. Using his mirrored utensil, he looked into Brittany's mouth and checked all the wires. "Yep, a faulty wire all right."

Cathy blushed again. Ridiculous. She felt like a schoolgirl. "Should we have waited until the next appointment?"

"Of course not. You're on top of things by coming in so quickly. Good parents like you make my job easier." He reached over and took her hand in his. "You did the right thing."

Cathy looked at her hand clasped in his. She pulled away when she noticed Brittany watching with an odd expression on her face. Guilt flooded her, not because of Dr. McMullen, but because she had just decided that she was going to leave Richard. Maybe not today, but soon. Very soon.

Friday, February 19, 2010 9:15 a.m.

Her heels clicked against asphalt, causing an echo to hit the parking garage walls and bounce back at her. Nancy Moreno held her keys in one hand and her bottle of mace in the other. Her nerves were shot. After seeing her therapist, she had a creepy suspicion she was being watched.

Her eyes darted from one car to the next, checking for movement and unfamiliar shadows. The parking garage was well lit. Security made the rounds every thirty minutes and yet she felt exposed. She wanted to tell someone about the phone call and the deal she'd made with the devil, but who? She wasn't ready to go public. If she told Cunningham, he wouldn't think twice before airing the news about her conversation with the madman every hour on the hour.

She had stayed up late last night reading Lizzy Gardner's file—myriad notes made by Linda Gates, revealing two months of some of the worst horrors imaginable. Spiderman's atrocities appeared to be unlimited.

There was only one person Nancy should talk to, she realized, and that was Lizzy Gardner herself. A hollow thump of footsteps nearby caused her to glance over her shoulder.

Nobody was there.

She had been parking in the garage for years and had never felt unsafe. Until now. She quickened her pace. She never should have stolen Lizzy Gardner's file.

She had what the monster wanted.

If the contents of Gardner's file were anything to go by, nothing would stop Spiderman from coming after the file. The fluorescent lights above her head flickered.

Shit. Her heart jumped to her throat.

More footsteps. Closer, faster.

To hell with it. She broke into a full-blown run.

Friday, February 19, 2010 9:26 a.m.

Jared pounded his fists against Lizzy's door. *Where was she?* He'd called her office three times. The third time Jessica had picked up and said she was worried about Lizzy since they had planned to meet early this morning. Lizzy wasn't answering her home phone or the door to her apartment.

He climbed down the steps and tried to peek through her kitchen window. He needed a damn ladder. He went back to the door and knocked again. "Lizzy, let me in."

The wind was making a racket, stirring the trees and causing the branches to scrape against the building. His hair whipped back and forth across his forehead. "Lizzy," he shouted, "it's me. Let me in. Everybody is worried about you."

A branch snapped in half and tumbled across the street.

"Jared, is that you?"

Thank God. "Lizzy," he said again, trying to sound calm as he ran back to the door. "It's me, Jared. Look through the peephole, Lizzy."

He stood far enough from the door so she would be able to see him. "Can you see me?"

"Maggie's dead," she said.

He leaned his forehead against the door, saddened by the news but relieved to know Lizzy was alive. For the past twenty minutes, he'd had his doubts. "Where is Maggie?"

"Outside my bedroom window. I don't know what to do."

"Stay where you are. I'll take care of Maggie and then I'm going to come back to the door and knock. Until then, keep the door bolted shut. OK, Lizzy?"

He didn't wait for an answer. He took the stairs two at a time until he landed on the sidewalk. Looking toward the high branches, he took brisk steps toward the tall maple outside Lizzy's bedroom window. The tree was nearly sixty feet high and had thick, bare branches that intertwined. Hanging by a rope was a black-and-white fur ball. Maggie. Damn.

He needed to get Maggie down from there before Lizzy looked out the window again. He jogged across the street to his car and then drove the Denali up onto the curb beneath the tree. From his trunk, he retrieved a pair of gloves, intent on disturbing as little evidence as possible. Jimmy wouldn't be happy, but to hell with that. Jared climbed on top of the car and worked the knots in the rope. Within minutes he held Maggie in his arms. He emptied a box in his trunk and carefully placed Maggie inside. Then he made a phone call.

Twenty minutes later, Jimmy Martin and two others from the task force were making the rounds inside and outside Lizzy's apartment. Jared brought Lizzy a cup of hot tea. She sat on the couch with a blanket hanging limp around her shoulders. Her lists were spread out on the floor. She told anybody who tried to mess with her files to back off.

"It looks like you kept Spiderman on the line long enough to make a connection," Jimmy told her. "The call was made from a downtown Sacramento gas station off Broadway. We have some-one there now checking for prints."

"How about Lizzy's office?" Jared asked.

The tip of Jimmy's shoe crumpled the corner of one of Lizzy's papers. "More lists?"

"Yeah, and I'm checking them twice," she answered flatly.

"This last girl," he said, pointing at a picture stapled to one of her notes, "is definitely a runaway."

Lizzy scowled. "It's not your list. It's mine. With or without your cooperation, I'm going to find Spiderman."

Jimmy used his chin to gesture at Jared, letting him know he wanted to talk to him privately.

"Say whatever you want to say," Lizzy said.

"Across the street from the gas station," Jimmy said, "is a local news station. There were two calls made from the news studio to here." He looked at Lizzy. "Anyone you know of who might have called from the Channel Ten news station?"

"No idea," Lizzy said without looking his way.

"Stay away from the media until I give the OK."

She saluted. "Yes, sir."

"How did he get the cat if the doors were bolted?" Jimmy wanted to know.

"Maggie must have slipped out when I left last night," Jared said. "It's the only way he could have gotten to her."

Jimmy jotted something in his notebook. He looked at Lizzy. "You're not planning on going anywhere today, are you?"

"I'm going to the office as soon as you and your men clear out of here. At seven o'clock tonight I'll be at Granite Bay High School giving a talk to dozens of young girls, showing them how to stay safe in this crazy world we live in."

"Not a good idea."

"Too bad. The son of a bitch killed Sophie and now Maggie. I'm not going to let him stop me from living my life."

Jimmy exhaled.

"For the record," Lizzy added, "if that maniac comes anywhere near me, I'm going to blow a hole through his head and put an end to this madness."

Jimmy looked at Jared and lifted his hands in the air. "Talk to her." Then he disappeared outside where technicians were scouring the area searching for clues.

"Where's Maggie's body?" she asked Jared.

"She's in my car. I'll take care of her."

"I don't want her tossed in a garbage can or dumped somewhere."

"The technicians need to look her over. When they're finished, I thought I'd take her home and bury her in my backyard. Remember my retriever, Sadie?"

She nodded.

"She's buried there near a cherry tree."

She didn't say anything.

Jared took a seat next to Lizzy on the couch. Leaning close, he brushed his lips across her forehead. "Sadie never met a cat she didn't like."

Lizzy looked away.

"I'm sorry about Maggie. I should have been watching for her."

"It was my fault. She tried to sneak out all the time, but I wasn't paying attention last night. I was too busy worrying about Spiderman's next move. I don't know how much more of this I can take."

"We're going to find him, Lizzy."

She leaned into him, her cheek resting against his shoulder. "Don't make any promises you can't keep."

He had become an agent because he wanted to protect those he loved. But until this moment, he hadn't realized that *wanting* to protect someone you loved and *doing* it were two different things.

CHAPTER 23

Friday, February 19, 2010 1:30 p.m.

After working for hours on the Internet, searching and gathering information on the missing girls, Lizzy began to feel antsy. Jared had dropped her off at the office hours ago, and he wouldn't be returning until six. She needed to keep her mind off poor Maggie. She turned to Jessica. "Did you bring your car today or did your brother drop you off?"

"I brought my car."

Lizzy stood and waved her toward the door. "Come on then. I'll buy you a tank of gas."

Jessica grabbed her purse. "Where are we going?"

Lizzy held up her notebook. "We have at least a dozen doctors on our list of suspects. Let's get busy."

Jessica followed Lizzy out the door. "I thought you promised your boyfriend you would stay put until he returned."

"He's not my boyfriend."

"That's too bad."

Lizzy locked the door behind them. "Why is that?"

"He's hot, and, well, he also seems very protective of you, which I think is really sweet."

"I've been on my own for too long to have someone following me around telling me what to do."

"How old are you?"

"Never mind."

* * *

It was nearing four o'clock by the time Jessica and Lizzy left Dr. Griffin's office and headed toward Jessica's Volkswagen van, one of those retro vans so many kids in the seventies were conceived in.

Lizzy braced herself against the strong wind as she walked. The trees on the other side of the street swayed to and fro. Wind gusts were expected to reach anywhere from sixty to eighty miles per hour by eight o'clock tonight.

Lizzy climbed up into the passenger seat and shut the door. Jessica came around the front and hopped in behind the wheel. Neither of them said a word. They had visited five doctors, and so far all five had been crossed off the list. Two of the doctors were well into their sixties. For that reason alone they were no longer on their list of suspects. Another doctor was five foot three and much too young. The fourth doctor had been in Africa during the time of the first three murders. Patience was a virtue, though. This was simply a process of elimination.

Like the other offices, the one they had just visited had stark white walls, a strong antiseptic smell, and a biohazard box filled with used needles. Unlike the other doctors, Dr. Griffin fit the age bracket of the man they were looking for. He was also tall, broad-shouldered, and well dressed in a crisp blue suit. He wore steel-rimmed spectacles that balanced at the end of his straight nose, and he possessed a friendly smile that reached his eyes.

Jessica merged onto the main road. "Was there anything about Dr. Griffin that looked familiar to you?"

"No," Lizzy said. "He was the right age, height, and weight, but he had a bit of a cleft in his chin. Spiderman didn't have a cleft."

Jessica sighed. "The only thing dangerous about Dr. Griffin was his killer smile."

Surprised by Jessica's bluntness, Lizzy couldn't help but smile at the girl.

"We need to get this guy," Jessica said.

"There's something I need to talk to you about." Lizzy had had a premonition the other night where she'd seen Jessica lying in a pool of blood. If Spiderman was after her, it made sense that he might run into Jessica. "I don't want to hurt your feelings, Jessica, but I'm not sure it's a good idea for you to be working this closely with me. Don't get me wrong. I enjoy your company and I think you're a hard worker. You're worth every penny I'm paying you, but—"

"You've never paid me a dime."

Lizzy wrinkled her nose. "Are you sure about that?"

"Positive."

"My bad. Write down the hours you've worked so far and I'll take care of that ASAP."

"Are you firing me?"

"Of course not." Lizzy scratched her head. "It's just that I like you way too much to put you in any more danger than I already have. Whoever killed Sophie is just getting warmed up. Who knows who he'll go after next."

"You can't fire me, Lizzy. I've never told you anything about myself before because…well, because it's pretty obvious you don't want to know about my personal problems."

"I never said that."

Jessica snorted. "You don't have to lie to me. I'm not your boyfriend."

The girl was getting on her nerves. "He's not my boyfriend."

"Whatever. I'm a psych major, remember?"

Lizzy remained silent, figuring it wouldn't kill her to let Jessica vent.

"The reason I didn't go to New Jersey was because my mother recently fell off the wagon and she refuses to go to another AA meeting. Right before Mom started drinking again, my boyfriend joined the Marines. I haven't told anyone yet, but with everything falling apart around me, I received my first D in psychology. The dean informed me that I'm on probation."

"I'm sorry."

"That's not all. My brother can't handle watching Mom deteriorate, so he's planning to move in with a friend in New Jersey and leave me to deal with Mom alone. Sadly, this horribly dangerous nonpaying job that you've given me is the best thing I've got going for me right now. You can't fire me. I won't let you."

"Is that all?"

Jessica stopped at the light and glanced her way. "Yes. Unless you count a stubbed toe and a razor nick."

"You stubbed your toe? That's horrible."

Jessica looked at her as if she were crazy. Then she saw Lizzy crack a smile and she laughed.

Lizzy laughed too and pointed at the green light.

After a few moments of silence, Jessica looked into her rear-view mirror. "We don't know what kind of car Spiderman drives, do we?"

Laughing with Jessica felt good, but her question pretty much sucked all the fun right out of her. "Why do you ask?"

"Because I swear that's the same blue SUV I saw forty-five minutes ago on our way to Dr. Griffin's office."

Lizzy unbuckled her seat belt so she could twist around and get a better look behind her. She turned back and unzipped her backpack, shuffling around, looking for her binoculars. Damn. She'd left them in her car. The blue SUV was three cars back in their lane. "Move to the other lane."

Jessica did as she asked. Seconds later, the SUV moved over too. Lizzy couldn't make out any numbers or letters on the license plate. "Move back to the other lane."

Jessica merged back. After a moment, the SUV did the same. "I want you to pull over to the side of the road the next chance you get. If the SUV passes us, I want you to merge back onto the street and follow it."

Jessica's hands were steady on the wheel. Determination settled across her features, her mouth a straight line, her eyes focused ahead.

Lizzy kept an eye on the SUV as Jessica pulled off the road next to a public park.

The SUV sped by. "Let's go get him. It's a male driver. He's sporting a pair of aviators and a moustache."

Jessica pulled onto the road and gunned it. They were a car length behind when the SUV took off.

Lizzy grabbed a pen and scribbled 4L on the top of Jessica's notebook sitting between them.

"I think he spotted us," Jessica said as she swerved into the other lane and sped up. The van's frame rattled. All four tires felt as if they might come loose.

Lizzy tightened her seat belt and kept her eyes on the SUV as Jessica swerved in and out of traffic. At every turn, Lizzy was sure the van might tip over. The wind wasn't helping matters. The light ahead turned yellow. The SUV swept through the intersection. Jessica gunned it. Cars honked as they sped through a red light. "I'm not going to let him get away. He could have Mary."

Lizzy wasn't sure what Jessica was talking about, but she didn't have time to question her. She grabbed her cell phone and called Jared. He picked up on the first ring. "It's me, Lizzy. I don't have time to explain, but I need some help. I'm following a dark blue SUV, midsized GMC—"

Jessica yanked the wheel. Lizzy's phone flew from her hands. Jessica cut in front of more than one car in the right lane. The wheels on the left side of the van came off the road. Lizzy grabbed the console for support. She could hear Jared's voice, but she couldn't do anything about it. She braced herself for impact. The wheels hit the pavement with a clunk and Jessica slammed her foot back on the gas pedal. The girl was a maniac.

Lizzy leaned forward. She could almost make out the license plate on the GMC Terrain, but then the vehicle cut through a gas station, and Lizzy was sure they had lost him. Jessica maneuvered around a building, and once again they were behind the SUV.

The girl made the Daytona 500 look like child's play.

Lizzy snatched her phone from the floor as it slid back her way. "We're OK."

"What the hell is going on?"

"We were being followed by an unidentified man, but now we're following him. I think it's Spiderman. Get somebody on this guy before we lose him. We're on Sunset, passing by Pleasant Grove. He's driving a dark blue GMC Terrain."

Jared Shayne was even-keeled, patient, understanding, and calm under fire. He seemed downright inhuman at times. Just once she'd like to see him get a little riled up. "I called the police," he said. "They're connected in on our call. Were you able to see the driver?"

"He's wearing aviators. He has a moustache. It's hard to see much through the tinted windows."

Tires squealed as the SUV cut across a divider and headed into two lanes of traffic heading the other way. A red Honda swerved into the bike lane. The car behind it crashed into the Honda's bumper.

"Oh, shit!" The phone dropped from her hands again. She grabbed hold of the console as Jessica cut across the divider after him, taking out a row of small, newly planted trees.

The front right tire of the van hit something solid and they both jerked forward. The air was temporarily knocked from Lizzy's lungs as they came to a screeching halt on the grassy knoll. One of the van's back tires flew across two lanes of traffic and over a fence on the other side of the road.

Cars honked, angry drivers pumping their fists as they passed. Jessica honked at the last guy after he flipped her the bird. "Fuck you all!" she shouted out her window. "We're trying to catch a murderer, you dumbass morons."

Lizzy was speechless and at the same time glad to be alive. The girl had gumption, not to mention a colorful way with words.

Jessica squeezed the steering wheel. She looked ready to yank the steering wheel clear off and spit fire at the same time. "I can't believe we were that close! He was right there in our grasp!" Jessica jabbed a finger in the direction the GMC disappeared. "I can't believe we lost him. I let him get away." She shook her head in disgust.

"What's going on?" Lizzy asked, her blood pumping triple time. "Who's Mary?"

Jessica reached over Lizzy's lap, flipped open the glove box, and pulled out a picture. She handed Lizzy a five-by-seven picture of two girls posing for the camera in a backyard. "That's me and my older sister, Mary Crawford. She's the one sitting on the swing."

Mary Crawford, Lizzy thought. One of the missing girls on their list.

"Same mother, different fathers," Jessica said, explaining the different last names. "Fourteen years ago Mary went missing. I believe she's still alive. I want to find her. And I want to make sure the man who took her pays for what he's done to me and my family."

Lizzy looked at the photo. One girl sat on the swing. The older girl stood behind her, hands on the rope. They were both smiling. Both had big brown eyes and even bigger smiles. Lizzy's heart sank. There was no mistaking the older girl on the swing. *It was her*. The girl without a voice was Jessica's sister.

Friday, February 19, 2010 6:15 p.m.

Mr. Louis, a tall man with shocking white hair, stood at the front of an audience of seventy to eighty people all gathered inside the high school gym.

Lizzy stood off to the side, next to the projector, while Mr. Louis talked to the crowd of students and parents.

"My two youngest daughters are now sixteen and fifteen and, as many of you know, they attend Granite Bay High School," he began. "My oldest daughter, Dana, would have turned twenty next week had she not been taken from campus during her second week in college. That was two years ago."

Lizzy clicked the button to keep the pictures on the big screen behind Mr. Louis changing. The first picture was of Dana as a baby; next was Dana in her mother's arms in the hospital, followed by Dana on her first day of preschool, Dana attending elementary school on a pumpkin field trip, dressed as a princess, and so on.

A bit of light squeezed through the gym door as Jared entered and took a seat in the back row. Earlier today Jared had met Lizzy and Jessica at the scene of the accident. He'd talked to police and made sure Jessica wasn't ticketed for reckless driving, although she was lectured by more than one officer. Unfortunately, the police had yet to track down the SUV. After waiting for a tow truck, Jared drove them to Cosumnes River College where they passed around an eight-by-ten photo of the courier who had delivered cash to Lizzy's office. Since the campus was nearly empty, they posted the picture in the main office along with a note asking anyone with information to call.

"They found Dana's body," Mr. Louis was saying, "two days after she disappeared. Her body had been dumped on the side of the road as if her life didn't matter."

He paused to collect himself. "I came here tonight to tell you that her life *did* matter. Her life mattered to a lot of people. It took every bit of strength we could summon for me and my wife to keep going. At the time, we still had two daughters at home who needed us. Months after burying Dana, we enrolled our younger daughters in self-defense classes."

He paused for a moment to take a look around the room, making eye contact with the audience. "Many families over the years have contacted me because they're afraid for their children's lives, and yet they can't afford the financial burden of karate classes or sparring gear. No child deserves to be unprepared, and that's why I've made a self-defense video that you can download for free. Elizabeth Gardner has all the information here for those of you who are interested."

After the clapping died down, Mr. Louis took a seat and Lizzy turned up the lights. "Thank you, Mr. Louis."

"What about yelling 'fire'?" a young woman asked. "Would that be enough to scare off an abductor?"

"Do whatever you must to get away," Lizzy said. "Yell, scream, kick, fight. Do not let anyone get you into their vehicle."

"There are free programs out there," Lizzy added, "and people like Mr. Louis who want to help empower young women. And yet still most people don't realize that one in four teenagers risk sexual assault. In the US alone there are approximately one hundred thousand abductions a year. Right now, more than five hundred thousand registered sex offenders are walking our streets."

"No wonder they haven't found Spiderman," someone shouted.

Although Lizzy didn't want to talk about Spiderman, she couldn't let the opportunity to teach pass her by. "That's right. Finding these guys is like looking for a needle in a haystack. They don't have 'ABDUCTOR' tattooed across their foreheads."

She pointed to a young man who had his hand up.

"How do you know what they look like?" he asked. "I read in the paper that you don't remember what your kidnapper looks like even after spending two months with the guy."

Lizzy wasn't going to let the kid ruffle her feathers. She was about to explain that sometimes it's dark outside and that her abductor wore black clothing, including a mask, but another student stood up and beat her to the punch.

"What's your problem?" the girl asked. "She's here to help us, asshole."

It was Hayley Hansen. Thank God she was OK. Lizzy had been worried about Hayley ever since the girl had come to her apartment and then disappeared.

The boy laughed. "Why are you even here? You'd have to be the last girl on earth before somebody would bother abducting you."

Both Jared and Mr. Louis came to their feet at the same time. Before either man could reach the young man and escort him out of the gym, the double doors at the back of the room opened and a blitz of media and cold air entered.

Cameras clicked and lights flashed.

Jared left the kid with Mr. Louis and stopped the female reporter from charging up the center aisle where Lizzy stood. The woman reached over Jared's arm and held out her microphone. "Is it true that Spiderman left a personalized note for you in Sophie Madison's bedroom?"

Lizzy looked into the cameraman's bright light. She could hardly make out the woman's face or Jared's. "I'm teaching a class. Please take your cameras and exit the gym until I'm finished. I'll be glad to talk to you when I'm done here."

Another woman entered the gym. She marched past the reporter and came up to Lizzy. The woman's face was covered with blotchy red marks as if she'd been crying. She wore no makeup. Her nose was bright red, her eyes swollen and shadowed with dark circles. "Is it true?" the woman asked. "Did he take my Sophie because of you?"

Lizzy swallowed. It was Sophie's mother. "I don't know," she said. "I have no words to express how sorry I am about your daughter."

"That's all you have to say?" The woman's hands fisted at her sides. "My daughter is dead and you think 'I'm sorry' is going to help?" The woman's bottom lip trembled. "My Sophie did not deserve to die. You were with the killer for two months and yet you refuse to tell the authorities anything about him. Why didn't you tell the FBI what he looked like? Why don't you remember where he lives? What kind of person are you that you would let others die because of some sick, misplaced affection you have for the man?"

Lizzy's chest tightened. "You think I'm trying to protect a killer?"

"It's all over the news."

Lizzy looked toward the bright light where she knew Jared was standing. "What is she talking about?"

The reporter struggled to get past Jared, but he wouldn't budge. "Haven't you heard?" the reporter asked. "Spiderman sent a letter to the Channel Ten news station. He wants the world to know that he's back and it's all because of you."

"All you had to do was cooperate with the police," Sophie's mother said. "That's all you had to do to keep my daughter alive."

"You don't understand…I tried to help." Lizzy held out a hand to the woman, but Sophie's mother backed away as if Lizzy might strike.

"I'm trying to remember everything that happened," Lizzy told her. "More than anything in the world I wanted Sophie to come back safe." She wanted them all to come back safe, including

Mary. She still didn't have the heart to tell Jessica that her sister was dead.

Mr. Louis put a gentle arm around Mrs. Madison's shoulders and walked her toward the back of the room. Lizzy overheard him telling her it wasn't Lizzy's fault and that she was a victim too. But Mrs. Madison's words had already struck home, putting more doubts in Lizzy's mind. Maybe the woman was right. Maybe they were all right. Her mother had moved far away from her family and friends because of what happened…because of Lizzy's irresponsible actions. If Lizzy had obeyed her father, hadn't lied to her parents, they would still be together. Her father would be talking to her, and she and her sister would be close friends. If only she'd been a good girl, a good person.

The lights dimmed after Jared managed to get the reporter and the cameraman to wait outside.

Lizzy gazed out into the sea of people—all waiting to see what she had to say for herself. The room was jam-packed with people. *Where had they all come from?* She reached out a hand, reaching out to anyone who would listen. "I was only trying to help. I never meant to hurt anyone. I'm sorry. I am so sorry."

CHAPTER 24

Friday, February 19, 2010 6:26 p.m.

Cathy listened to the tutor explain how he was going to help Brittany with math. Mr. Gilman liked to teach his students to focus on skills such as handling whole numbers and fractions, he told her. Instead of drilling students on the same type of problems, he believed in conceptual understanding—whatever the hell that meant. He tutored dozens of kids who went to Brittany's school, and therefore he was familiar with the school's curriculum.

Cathy kept her eyes on Mr. Gilman's, but it wasn't easy because he had a crooked nose and big ears that begged for her full attention. The man talked fast, his words sounding like gibberish. But then again, she'd never been a math whiz, and she really had no idea of what he was talking about. As he rambled on about "computational fluency" her attention shifted to the interior of his house—quaint, but eerily quiet. Twice she'd detected a hint of mold, and yet the interior of the house appeared freshly painted. Other than the whooshing sound of the flag whipping about the pole in the front yard, there were no other sounds. No running dishwasher or television in the background. No distant humming of a washer or dryer. But there was something—an occasional hollow banging sound in the backyard or basement, most likely caused by the wind—hard to tell.

Mr. Gilman finally turned his attention on Brittany. Her daughter flipped through her math book to show him what chapter her class was on. Despite the smell, the living room was neat and orderly.

Brittany lifted a brow when Cathy looked her way—Cathy's signal to "go to the car and wait outside."

"It was nice meeting you," Cathy told Mr. Gilman. "I better let you two get to work."

The man seemed nice enough. But there was something odd about Mr. Gilman that made her feel uneasy. "I'll be waiting in my car," she said, pointing outside.

His eyes widened. "It's much too cold. Find a magazine over there and make yourself comfortable in the family room if you're not heading home."

"I'll be fine," she assured him. "I have a book in the car and I can always turn on the heat." Now that he'd offered to let her stay, she felt better about waiting outside.

A spider skittered across the floor in front of her. She jumped and then laughed at the high-pitched squeal that had escaped her.

Brittany shook her head, clearly embarrassed. "It's just a bug, Mom."

The spider scampered away, disappearing in some hidden crevice. "Looks like it's time to call the pest control people," Mr. Gilman said.

Cathy managed a tight smile and headed out the door. A flurry of cold air hit her face. She walked down the walkway toward her car, aware of every sound, every movement. She breathed in a lungful of newly mowed grass, which brought her some sense of normalcy. The moon was bright and full, lighting her way to the car.

Was Lizzy's madman out there now watching her?

Tempted to shout out at him, she held her tongue. For the first time in all these years, she realized she might be experiencing a tiny bit of what Lizzy had been going through.

Shivers coursed over her.

Is this what it felt like to be afraid of one's own shadow?

Cathy looked at the house across the street. The television flickered in the living room. With her hand on the car handle, she looked back over her shoulder, relieved to see the kitchen light in Mr. Gilman's house reflecting in such a way that she could make out her daughter's silhouette. She opened the door and slid in behind the wheel of her car. Then she locked the door and waited.

Friday, February 19, 2010 7:48 p.m.

Hayley Hansen watched Lizzy being ushered away by the same man who had protected her from the media inside the gym. The two of them took off in his car before Hayley had a chance to talk to Lizzy. She'd wanted to tell Lizzy she was sorry she left so suddenly the other night and that she appreciated Lizzy taking the time to help kids like her. There weren't too many good people left in the world. She knew that firsthand.

Hayley didn't like what the ignorant boy had said to Lizzy. Even the reporter had known better, but at least it was her job to ask dim-witted questions. Not one person in that gym tonight had any idea of what Lizzy Gardner had been through. Hayley didn't know all the details either, but she knew a troubled soul when she met one.

She sat on the curb, elbows propped on her knees, and watched the media people pack up their cameras and lights, filling their trucks and vans with expensive equipment without any care as to the trouble they had just caused. Tonight, some students might have learned something if they'd been given half a chance to listen to what Lizzy had to say. Hayley had heard it all before, but nobody ever touched her heart in the way Lizzy did when she spoke. Lizzy talked to the kids as equals, as someone who had been there. Lizzy had spent time with the devil himself and lived to talk about it.

Hayley didn't have to be abducted to know what it was like to play with the devil's fire. She lit up a Marlboro and took a long drag, filling her lungs with formaldehyde, ammonia, and hydrogen sulfide.

As the news truck revved its engine and the last of the cars pulled out of the parking lot, the petite reporter sitting in the passenger side of the truck rolled down her window and stuck her head out.

Hayley blew smoke from her lungs and watched the woman's shiny brown hair fly every which way around her heart-shaped face.

It was so windy tonight the smoke disappeared the second it seeped through Hayley's lips. There would be no blowing smoke rings in this weather.

"Do you need a ride somewhere?" the reporter asked.

It was Friday night. Where would she go? Back home to be sodomized by one of her mother's drunk friends? "No, thanks. I'm good." Hayley took another drag off her cigarette.

"Are you sure? Is someone coming to pick you up?"

"Yeah. They should be here any second." It wasn't like one more lie was going to stop her from going to hell.

"OK, if you're sure."

Hayley watched the reporter roll the window back up. It must be one of those older model trucks because the reporter had to actually put some muscle into working the handle to get the window rolled up tight. Hayley wondered if that was the most work the woman had done all week. She felt a twinge of guilt for judging the reporter. Hayley knew firsthand that a person really couldn't judge a book by its cover. She had learned that lesson right after she was sent to live with her grandfather when she was eight years old. Her grandfather had looked like such a nice old man. *Who would have guessed?*

Even as the truck pulled away, the reporter stared at her worriedly. Hayley waved, hoping to ease the woman's mind. Nice jewelry, perfect hair, straight white teeth…she wished the woman no ill will just because she might have been dealt a better hand in life than most.

Hayley took one last drag before dropping the cigarette on the asphalt. She used the heel of her boot to snuff it out. It would be easy to start a fire in this wind. But she was no pyro. She never understood people who liked to damage others' property just for the hell of it.

She looked around. The lot was empty. Darkness quickly descended as dark, billowy clouds gathered overhead. The temperature had dropped dramatically since she'd arrived an hour ago.

She thought about heading off, but then she felt his eyes on her. Yeah, he was here all right. He'd come. She knew he would. He was watching Lizzy. According to the media, he had left her a personal note, letting Lizzy Gardner know that he was back in business.

Sophie Madison had attended more than one of Lizzy's self-defense classes, which told her that Spiderman was targeting anyone who had anything to do with Lizzy Gardner. The media had also mentioned that Lizzy would be speaking at the school tonight, which meant he was here…somewhere…watching.

Yeah, the crazy asshole wanted Lizzy, but tonight she hoped he would settle for someone a little younger and a little tougher. She knew enough about him to know he wouldn't want anything to do with her. But here she was sitting in the dark, all alone; how could he resist?

Bait.

Cops used bait all the time to catch drug dealers and prostitutes. It worked on fish and it worked on humans who couldn't say no to a little temptation.

She'd read all about Spiderman. She probably knew more about him than he knew about Lizzy. He stalked his victims, learned all about their fears—their likes and dislikes.

He didn't know a thing about Hayley Hansen, though. He had no idea that the scariest thing he could do to her was take her home. She inwardly smiled as she dug deep into her coat pocket to make sure her three-inch knife with the gut hook was there. Clipped to her boot was a double-edged boot knife, a basic survival tool. And last but not least, a sleek tactical folding knife was tucked away in her nylon gym shorts beneath her jeans in case of emergency.

She had anticipated his arrival. What puzzled her, though, was if she knew he'd be watching Lizzy, why hadn't the FBI figured that out? Where were the guys in black when you needed them?

She'd come up with the plan a few days ago. That was the real reason she went to see Lizzy—to talk about baiting Spiderman out of hiding. But the exhaustion on Lizzy's face had prompted her to change her mind…at least until she saw Lizzy's face plastered on every news station tonight. That's when Hayley decided to catch the killer on her own. Apparently Hayley and Lizzy had something else in common. They both took in misplaced guilt as if it were nourishment. Why else would Spiderman have sent Channel 10 a letter putting all the blame for his actions on Lizzy? Because he *knew* she would feel guilty, and he relished the thought of making Lizzy miserable. Spiderman didn't like the idea of Lizzy getting stronger every day.

In case this didn't go as planned, Hayley pulled out the letter she'd written to Lizzy and shoved it into the crevice between the moist grass and the cement curb. She didn't want Spiderman to see what she was doing, nor did she want the wind to blow the paper away. If he came after her, she planned to kill him. But just in case something went wrong, she wanted to leave evidence. Lots of kids waited for their parents on this very curb day after day. Sooner or later, somebody was bound to find the letter.

The claps of thunder and swoosh of the wind didn't drown out his approaching footfalls.

She wanted to light up another cigarette. Instead, she reached down and unclipped the knife from her boot. Killing him and taking out her frustrations on a hateful killer sounded a lot better than going home and being raped by one of her mother's drug-dealing boyfriends.

He was right behind her. She could smell his aftershave—a killer who took showers on a regular basis. *Who knew?*

The moment she felt his hand slide around her neck, she lifted her body upward and plunged the knife hard and fast over her shoulder. The blade sunk deep. A grunt along with a sickening suctioning noise sounded as she pulled the knife out of him. Despite the blood spurting in all directions, mostly onto the side of her neck and face, he hadn't keeled over.

What the hell?

He reached for her again.

She lunged with her knife again, but he sidestepped and grabbed hold of her face. He held a damp cloth over her nose and mouth. Twisting and turning, she managed to get a look at him, but he wouldn't give an inch. He was strong. And he was suffocating her.

Again and again she swiped at him with her knife, but her arms hardly moved. He grinned, the same sort of lewd smile plastered on Brian's face every time he unzipped his pants.

The only difference was that Spiderman didn't look spaced out on drugs and alcohol. He knew exactly what he was doing. His eyes were wide and alert. With his full head of hair and a strong, square jaw, he looked like he could be a teacher or a lawyer. He looked like a law-abiding citizen, for God's sake.

Her body was losing ground, her legs and arms limp. He refused to let go of her face, his hands tight against her mouth and nose. *Was this it? Was she dying?* Her muscles were relaxed. She couldn't move. With the last bit of strength she had left, she opened her mouth wide and bit down with all the force of a pit bull. She tasted his blood, relished the sound of his high-pitched squeal as he turned away.

Before he saw what she was up to, she spit out gobs of his blood onto the sidewalk where the letter was, hoping somebody would see it before it rained. Infuriated, he took a fistful of her hair and dragged her body across the lawn. He walked fast enough that her hip bounced off the curb and onto the pavement. She couldn't feel a thing. Her body was numb, but her mind was alert. She screamed at the top of her lungs just as Lizzy Gardner had said to do, but no sound came out.

CHAPTER 25

Friday, February 19, 2010 8:24 p.m.

Standing in front of the bathroom mirror in an oversized T-shirt and a pair of sweats, Lizzy towel dried her hair as she stared at her reflection. Her left eye twitched. She pointed a finger at her reflection. "Come on, you can do it. Cry, dammit! Do you hear me? You've got to feel something. Cry and get it all out. Everybody is blaming you for everything bad in the world and you still can't cry?"

She grabbed her toothbrush from the top drawer, squirted toothpaste onto the brush, and scrubbed her teeth and gums a little too hard. After a good rinsing, she dragged a comb through her hair.

Done primping, she found Jared in the kitchen making tea. He wore slacks and a white button-down shirt. His sleeves were rolled to just above his elbows. His tie was draped over a canvas bag by the front door. Because of last night's incident with Maggie, he'd informed her he was moving in for a while.

She looked at the spot where Maggie's dishes used to be and noticed Jared had put everything away. Their eyes met. "The shower is all yours," she said.

"Thanks."

Thumbing through the phone messages, she tried to pretend everything was OK, tried to concentrate on little things like breathing. Another good example of why she couldn't live with anyone. She tried to put on a brave front, tried not to jump every time a car honked outside or a tree branch creaked in the wind.

She was a wreck. She was damaged goods. She couldn't cry. She couldn't feel. But shit yeah, she could jump at the snap of a finger.

"You have two phone calls from Nancy Moreno, the news anchor from Channel Ten," Jared said as he poured hot water over the tea bag in an ugly brown mug.

"She probably wants an interview," Lizzy said. No way was she calling Moreno back. Feeling on edge, she watched Jared fix his tea. She wondered if he remembered making love to her all those years ago. She was in one of her moods. Exhausted, jittery. She already knew she wouldn't be able to sleep after everything that had happened.

Jared looked so damn prim and proper, a perfect gentleman. For some reason it pissed her off. She wanted to mess his hair and rip off his shirt, see what was hidden beneath that cool exterior of his. See what his reaction would be. She wanted to nibble on his ear, taste him, feel him hard against her. She wanted to be on top.

She went to the refrigerator and grabbed a beer from way in the back. "Do you want a beer?"

"You've been holding out on me." Leaving his tea behind, he opened both beers and handed an open bottle back to her.

She took a swig, hardly tasting a thing as the cold liquid slid down her throat. She went to the front room, plunked down on the couch, and took another swallow. Nothing. She couldn't cry and she couldn't taste the fucking beer.

Jared joined her.

"Tell me about the woman you were engaged to," she said.

"Peggy?"

"Was that her name?"

"You want to know about Peggy?"

Yes and no. "Yes."

He sat on the other side of the couch, too far to reach out and touch him unless she stretched out a leg and put her foot on his lap. *What would he do if she rubbed her toes against his crotch?*

He sat back and held the beer between his thighs. "Peggy was a sweet girl. We met in college. She was studying law. I was studying psychology."

"Have you seen her lately?"

He took in a mouthful of beer and swallowed. "No."

"Do you miss her?"

"I think about her sometimes."

Shit. He couldn't even spit out a little white lie? "What do you think about when you think of her?"

Jared looked at her, his gorgeous eyes making her want to jump into all that blueness and swim around for a while.

"When I think of her, I only wish her the best."

Lizzy took another drink, hoping to catch a buzz.

"Nothing that has happened is your fault," he said, obviously sensing her distress. "You know that, don't you?"

"Logically, yes. Emotionally, no." She sighed. "So what does Peggy look like?"

"Why so curious about Peggy?"

She shrugged. "Humor me."

"She's happily married and has two children."

"Ahhh, so she has big hips and circles under her eyes?"

He smiled wryly.

She took another long swig of beer. *To hell with it.* She set the bottle on the coffee table and then scooted closer and put his beer on the table too. Then she straddled him so that they were face-to-face, chest-to-chest. Her legs were folded, her knees tucked into the couch on both sides of his hips. "I feel numb," she told him as she leaned close and brushed her mouth against his ear. "I can't remember the last time I felt something other than cold and numb. Help me feel again."

She felt a slight twitch of his stubbled jaw.

She kissed his neck. He smelled like soap and beer and sandalwood. "Do your parents still hate me?"

"They never hated you. Nobody hates you."

"Sometimes I hate myself." She kissed his jaw. "I have nightmares." She kissed his ear. "I see horrible things. Every morning I wake up and wonder if I'll ever be free of him."

"I want you to be free of him," he said. "You've suffered long enough."

He was talking, but he wasn't touching, wasn't doing. She kissed his jaw and dragged her mouth to his mouth. His lips were warm. "Do you remember our first time together?"

Finally he moved. His hands cupped her face. His gaze locked on hers. The way he was looking at her made her heart skip a beat. Finally. She felt something.

"I'll never forget our time together," he said.

She grabbed hold of the hem of her T-shirt, pulled it up and over her head, and tossed it aside. She wanted to pull his mouth to her breast, feel his tongue roll over her skin, but he seemed content with just looking at her.

She ran her fingers through his hair and said, "I can't remember the last time I cried. Touch me, Jared. Kiss me like you used to when we had nothing to worry about but our next exam." She wanted his hands and his mouth to take her to another place in time, a time when birds sang and the sun warmed her from the inside out.

She unbuttoned his shirt, one button at a time, working her way downward. His chest was smooth and hard, his arms strong and well defined.

"Lizzy," he said, "maybe this isn't the right time."

"There might never be a right time. I need you. Don't make me beg."

He smoothed damp hair from her face and pulled her mouth to his. The kiss was long and deep and hot. She pressed against him and realized he'd been holding back because he was already hard. Jolts of desire shot through her, urging her onward. Feeling as if time was running out, she slipped off his shirt and then worked on unfastening his belt. She unzipped his pants, and that's when he grabbed her hands and held her back. He moved her to his side and stood. Then he scooped her into his arms and carried her to the bedroom. "We've got all night," he said. "I've waited a long time for this and I don't want to miss a thing."

He moved easily through the hall and into her bedroom where he set her gently on the bed and slid her sweats off in one clean sweep. He climbed out of his pants and boxers and she drank in the sight of him as he stood before her in all his glory. He stared at her for a few minutes longer than her patience saw fit, but the intense look in his eyes filled her with a longing she hadn't felt in a very long time. A knot settled in her chest and a pulsing need throbbed between her thighs.

He crawled over her, leaving a trail of soft kisses on her neck and across her collarbone. She arched upward until he took her breast into his mouth. She raked her fingers through his hair, pulling his mouth closer and relishing the feel of his raspy jaw against her skin.

Blurred images flickered within her mind. She started to panic, afraid she might see something she didn't want to see, but Jared dragged his mouth back to her ear and told her she was beautiful, drawing her back to the moment.

"I've missed you," he said, as if sensing he needed to keep her here with him now. He kissed her again, his body covering her with warmth, careful not to crush her beneath his weight. "You have no idea how much."

"I've missed you too," she said as she breathed in the smell of lingering aftershave before finding his mouth again. She felt his arousal hard against her thigh. Swept up in a haze of desire, she arched her hips, urging him to slide into her, afraid that time was running out.

He didn't question her actions or her impatience. Instead he filled her completely, taking what she offered and matching her movement for movement.

They climaxed together, shuddering in each other's arms, everything perfect until he relaxed against her and said, "I love you, Lizzy."

Friday, February 19, 2010 8:53 p.m.

Karen Crowley paced the hotel room and dialed the number one more time. On the fifth ring, her mom answered. Thank God. "Mom, I can't find him anywhere. Are you sure he's working in Sacramento?"

"Karen, it's late. Why is it so important for you to find your brother now after all this time?"

Karen sighed. She had forgotten about the time difference, but she didn't care. She'd hardly slept since arriving in the US. She needed to find her brother and get it all out before the guilt ate her alive. "Mom, do you remember when you and Dad traveled to Europe and left me in charge of Sam?"

"Are you still upset about that? For God's sake, how many times are you going to make me pay for living my life, Karen? I've already told you I'm sorry. You were almost seventeen. We thought you could handle the responsibility. You could hardly wait for us to pack our suitcases and walk out that door."

Karen shut her eyes. It was true. She and her friends had made big plans. A party at the Jones's house, everyone! Booze, drugs, fireworks. "You're right," Karen said. "I wanted you to leave. But that's not why I'm here or why I'm calling you. This isn't about you and me. It's about Sam. It's about something that happened when you and Dad were gone that summer."

"Whatever it is, Karen, you've got to let it go. It's not healthy to hang on to the past like this. Sam is happily married. He's successful. He's living in a beautiful home with his beautiful wife. Did I ever tell you how he never would have met Cynthia if it weren't for me? She was my neighbor and—"

"Mom! Stop! Please. You've told me the story a thousand times. I know—if it weren't for you, Sam would never have met Cynthia. Sam is so perfect. Sam is so smart! Sam this and Sam that." Nothing had changed. Exactly why she'd done the things she did back then. But it wasn't Sam's fault that their mother doted on him and put him on some ridiculously high pedestal.

"I don't know what you want from me, Karen."

"I want you to help me find him. I went to his house. Nobody's there. I've been calling his number every hour on the hour. No answer. Today I knocked on his neighbors' doors. Not one person has any idea what Sam or Cynthia do for a living. Nothing is making sense, Mom. Where are they?"

"Perhaps they went on vacation."

Karen couldn't believe her ears. Her mother was either in denial or she just didn't care. Plain and simple. All this time she thought her mother doted on Sam instead of her, but maybe it wasn't true at all. Her mother cared about no one but herself. Her parents were two of the most selfish, uncaring people she'd ever met. She closed her eyes. Inhaled and then exhaled slowly. "I need you to remember where he works, Mom. That's all you need to do for me and then I'll leave you alone."

"I told you he was a doctor."

"Do you have any idea how many Dr. Joneses there are in the Sacramento area alone? Hundreds, maybe thousands."

"You know...I do remember Cynthia sending me a postcard when Sam moved into a new office building a few years back."

Karen's heart beat faster. "When? Where?"

"No, that's right...he didn't move, he partnered with another doctor."

Karen let her mother mull it over for a moment. If she tried to yank it out of her, it would only frustrate her mom and they would argue again.

"I can't remember the name of his partner...hmmm. I might still have the postcard, but it'll take me a while to find it. I have so many boxes in the garage, though...I don't know."

"Just call me if you find anything. You have my number."

"All right, dear. You get some rest. You sound tired."

"Good night, Mom." Karen shut her cell and plopped down on the edge of the hotel bed. The headlines on this morning's newspaper taunted her: "KILLER ON THE LOOSE. LIZZY GARDNER CAUGHT IN HIS WEB ONCE AGAIN."

Sam, she thought. *Where are you?*

The last time her brother had contacted her was fourteen years ago when he'd called to ask Karen the names of the three girls who had stayed at their house when their parents were away that summer. She had lied and told him she didn't remember. A month later, she heard from an old friend that one of the girls had died in a freak car accident after her car went off a bridge. A bridge she traveled over every day of her life. Months after that, another of the same three friends who Sam had asked about lost her house in a fire. The last of the girls involved had a little sister…Jordan Marriot, the first of Spiderman's victims.

Karen had lived in Italy at the time, where she still lived. She never would have heard about Spiderman if her brother hadn't sent her an envelope stuffed with newspaper clippings of the car accident, the fire, and the killings. On the bottom of the envelope he'd written: "Good you moved far away from this place where evil lurks around every corner and death awaits those who deserve it most."

She hadn't told her husband about the clippings. Instead, she'd stuffed the envelope away in a shoebox in her closet and tried to forget about it. Her brother had always been an odd duck. But lately, the clippings and the odd note called to her, begging her to do something.

Watching her kids grow, loving them so deeply, made Karen realize she couldn't ignore what she was feeling anymore. She needed to talk to her brother. Not only to tell him she was sorry and ask for his forgiveness, but to find out why he'd sent the newspaper clippings to begin with. She needed to know the truth, once and for all.

CHAPTER 26

Saturday, February 20, 2010 8:30 a.m.

They were almost to the Federal Building on Marconi when Jared took his eyes off the road long enough to glance at Lizzy. She'd been quiet all morning. "Was it the omelet?" he teased.

"The omelet was fine."

"Something I said?"

"No."

"Ever since I told you I loved you, you've been quiet."

She turned on him then, her expression grim. Bingo.

"How could you love me when you don't even know me any longer? I'm not whole. I'm all screwed up in the head. Not because of lack of trying either...because I am trying to forget what happened and move on. I've been trying to get better for a long time. I'll never give up. But I'm not whole and I'm not relationship material."

He made a left and pulled into the parking lot. He shut off the engine and took her hand in his. "I love you, Lizzy. I always have. I'm sorry if that bothers you so damned much."

Her eyes narrowed. "Then why did you leave me?"

Her words cut deeply. "Because I knew if I stayed, if I kept coming around, you would spend so much time worrying about me that you wouldn't stand half a chance at getting better. You never put yourself first, Lizzy. You never did, you never will. But you should. That's why you've struggled with the demons inside you for so long. You always put everybody else first. You've taken full responsibility for your mother and father's divorce, your sister's problems, and your father's inability to cope. Now you're trying to figure out how to balance the rest of the world on your shoulders."

"Ridiculous."

"What was one of the first things you did when you began to slowly crawl out of the cave you had found yourself in?"

He didn't give her a chance to answer. "You committed yourself to helping others. You joined the Missing and Exploited Children's Organization and began volunteering your time helping young girls learn to defend themselves. You got involved, Lizzy, and whether you want to see the writing on the wall or not, you've made a difference. You haven't hurt anyone. You've only helped. That's only one small reason why I love you. That's why I've always loved you. And that's why I'll never stop loving you. I'm sorry if it bothers you, but I'm not going to lie to myself and I'm not going to fight it anymore. And you're right. I never should have left you alone. Not for one day, not for one minute."

She was looking out the window again. She had taken her hand back and now her arms were crossed. She wasn't ready for confessions of love. She obviously didn't think she deserved to be loved by anyone, not even herself. But he didn't give a shit. She could ignore him all she wanted. He wasn't buying it. And he wasn't going anywhere, no matter how hard she pushed this time.

Saturday, February 20, 2010 8:52 a.m.

The door to Jimmy Martin's office was wide open when Lizzy and Jared entered.

"Good timing," Jimmy said as he gestured to the chairs in front of his desk. "I just finished talking to Betsy Raeburn's brother."

Jared pulled out a chair for Lizzy and took a seat in the chair next to her. "Does he know where Betsy is?"

"She's practically around the corner," Jimmy said. "After getting her third DUI in less than a year, Betsy Raeburn is being held in the Sacramento County Main Jail."

"Has anyone talked to her?"

"I thought the two of you could stop over there after you leave here." Jimmy shuffled through papers on his desk. "Sean Davis isn't a fan of his sister. He was more than happy to tell me she's been drinking and driving for as long as he can remember—including the day she found Lizzy."

Lizzy's gaze fell on Jimmy's watch. It was a Rolex. A Sea-Dweller.

"Sean Davis told me Betsy admitted she had no idea of her exact location when she picked up Lizzy," Jimmy finished.

"Lizzy?" Jared reached over and touched her arm. "That means you were right about the house not being where they've been looking all this time."

Lizzy wasn't paying any attention. She was focused on Jimmy's watch…it was unusual and she was sure she'd seen it before. But where? The answer hit her hard and fast. "Can I have a closer look at your watch?"

Jimmy slid it off his wrist and handed it to her.

"That's what he was talking about," she said, "when he accused me of being a thief and taking things that didn't belong to me."

"Who?" Jimmy asked.

"The killer," Jared said. "Spiderman."

"When he called me," she reminded Jimmy, turning the watch over in her hands, "he said I never should have gotten away and I never should have taken something that didn't belong to me. He called me a thief, but until this moment I didn't know what he was talking about."

Neither man said a word.

"He was talking about his watch," she said. "Before I escaped I saw his coveted watch on the bathroom counter. I scooped it up, stepped onto the bathtub, and squeezed my way through the window."

"Where's the watch now?" Jimmy wanted to know.

"It was a Rolex very much like this one," she said again as she thought about what she'd done with the watch after she escaped. "I never saw Spiderman without his watch. He would constantly touch it as if it was his pet." She closed her eyes. "I had a dream the other night. I was escaping. I fell out of the window and I had to climb out of the bushes that had broken my fall. I was bleeding, but I didn't care. I wanted…needed to get away. I ran as fast I could. I remember feeling the watch bobble against my arm." She rubbed her temple as she tried to remember. "I was afraid I was going to lose the watch because I'd lost so much weight." Inwardly, she wondered why she had worried about losing the watch at all, and then she remembered the feeling of elation when she'd scooped it up, knowing she'd taken something that mattered to him, something she knew he loved.

"Take your time," Jared told her.

She recalled running down the street and seeing a dry cleaning truck parked in front of a house. She saw Betsy Raeburn leave clothes wrapped in plastic hanging on the front door. Lizzy cried out to her and grabbed a fistful of the woman's coat as Betsy made her way back to her truck. Betsy was friendly and tried to calm Lizzy. After Lizzy was seated in the truck, Betsy took the watch.

Lizzy's heart raced. She opened her eyes. "Betsy told me she would hold the watch for me. She placed it in her pocket and promised to keep it safe."

"Looks like we have another reason to pay Betsy Raeburn a visit," Jimmy said.

Jared's phone rang. He flipped it open and held it to his ear. Thirty seconds later, he clicked it shut. "Somebody recognized the picture we left at Cosumnes River College. They've contacted the student and he's willing to talk."

Jared stood. "Come on. The kid who delivered the money is going to meet us at Starbucks downtown, next to the school. After that we'll visit the jail and have a talk with Betsy Raeburn."

Jimmy also came to his feet. "Odds are the watch is long gone. I'm heading over to the Walker house to see where they're at with the excavation."

After Lizzy disappeared through the door, Jimmy pulled Jared back and said, "The ME found spider bites on Sophie Madison's thigh and on her right arm. We were also able to use the wire found around the cat's neck and match it to the markings on Sophie's wrists."

"Lizzy mentioned Spiderman's affection for tarantulas," Jared said. "Tarantulas don't often bite, not even after being provoked. If we can determine the breed of spider, we could do a search on where these particular spiders are sold."

"A field biologist is examining the bites," Jimmy said. "I also called in a tool examiner to determine what sort of wire was used on both the cat and the girl."

Jared nodded. "If the student we're meeting with got a good look at the man who hired him to deliver money to Lizzy's office, I'll need to call in a forensic sketch artist."

"Yeah." Jimmy's mouth tightened. "If Betsy was drunk when she was making deliveries, it looks like I might owe your girlfriend an apology."

"I'm not his girlfriend," Lizzy said from outside the door. "But I'll accept your apology."

Jimmy shook his head as he made his way back to his desk.

Jared exited the office and put his arm around Lizzy's shoulders. He escorted her through the maze of cubicles and out the main entrance. Outside, the wind had died down although dark clouds still huddled in the south. The storm had pulled down a few trees last night. According to the morning news, more than one neighborhood was left without power this morning.

They walked through the parking lot in silence. Jared aimed his key at his car and hit the unlock button. His car whistled back. Once Lizzy was situated, he came around the front, slid in behind the wheel, and looked at her.

"What?"

"You're not my girlfriend?"

She rolled her eyes. "Until Monday night I hadn't seen you in years. Last night was great, but one roll in the hay does not a girlfriend make."

"You sure know how to cut a guy to the quick."

"It takes years of practice." She sighed. "Besides, you only called me because of the note."

"I called you because we needed your help. But I always intended to call." He started the engine. "So how long or what do I have to do before I can call you my girl?"

"Just drive," she said.

ABDUCTED

Saturday, February 20, 2010 9:08 a.m.

"So who are you?" Hayley asked the man when he peeked inside the bedroom door. "Just some pervert who gets his kicks scaring young girls with spiders?" Her arms were held high above her head, her wrists duct taped to the bedpost behind her. The asshole had also wrapped wire around her wrists for good measure.

Her shoulders were sore.

He shut the door. "That's so sad," she shouted after him.

For some reason, the sick bastard had taken off her shoes, socks, and pants, but she still had on her snug nylon undershorts and her death angel reaper T-shirt. For just this occasion she'd worn her favorite T-shirt with a detailed picture of the grim reaper using a human bone as a flute.

Hayley had felt nauseous this morning when she'd first awoken. To her surprise, the small folding knife she'd slipped inside her nylon shorts was still in place. *What had he given her to make her sleep for so long?*

Blurred images of fighting him, kicking and screaming, swirled around in her mind. She must have scared him off. With her arms raised high above her head, she wasn't sure how she was going to get to the knife tucked neatly under her ass. She strained her forearms, trying hard to push her arms apart and loosen the tape and the wire, but the wire kept cutting into her skin. Blood trickled down her arm and over her elbow.

The weirdo looked like a moron in his little Batman mask. He used some trippy voice device too that made him sound like a ridiculous robot. The bedroom was no bigger than the room she slept in back home.

The room smelled like mothballs. She had smelled worse.

She leaned closer to the bed and took a whiff. OK, maybe not. She listened. There he was again, pacing the hallway just outside the door. Every once in a while he would stick his head in as if to make sure she was still there. Earlier this morning, he'd come all the way inside and she'd spit on him, right in the eye. She had laughed too. He hadn't been happy about that. It was almost comical the way he seemed to be almost afraid of her. Clearly he hadn't planned to abduct her. She obviously made him very nervous. Rightly so.

She'd made it so damn easy for him to take her, though, how could he resist?

The door creaked open and the weirdo leaned inside and placed another ugly spider on the floor a few feet from her bare feet. The last spider he'd let loose had disappeared under the bed. Through the tiny holes in his mask where his eyes were, she could see excitement beaming from wide, wild eyes.

What a dumb asshole. A spider the size of a golf ball. *Is that all he had?*

Her legs, starting at her ankles and ending below her knees, were bound with duct tape and wire just like her arms, but she could bend her knees and stretch out her legs without much pain or effort if she wanted to.

She watched the spider. The insect was big enough that she could hear its little feet pitter-patter across the wood floor as it came toward her. She watched the spider closely. *Just a little closer. Come on, spider, you can do it.*

A little excited gasp came out of the man's throat the moment the spider's hairy leg brushed against her big toe.

Hayley pretended to shudder. Yeah, he was excited all right.

Gritting her teeth, she lifted both feet in the air and dropped them to the floor, hard, slamming her bare heel downward, making contact with the spider's round, semisoft body. The insect literally exploded, covering the floor with a sticky, yucky mess. The sick bastard's pet spider was dead.

"Ooops," she said. She lifted her foot so he could see the mess on her heel. "Could you get me a wet rag and clean up this mess?"

He clicked on the little voice button and said in his fucked-up robotic voice, "You're going to regret that."

"Yeah, yeah. That's what they all say. So what's your deal, old man? Are you a copycat or are you the real deal?"

Ignoring her, he left the room, returning a few minutes later with a broom and a dustpan. He cleaned up the mess, and when he returned the second time he had a wet cloth in his hand. He knelt down in his neatly pressed beige slacks and began wiping her feet.

She pulled back. "That tickles."

The mask made it difficult to figure out if he was mad or amused or anything at all. It didn't really tickle, but she wanted to get him closer so she could slam her foot into his face, but apparently he wasn't as stupid as he looked.

He kept his distance as he finished wiping her heels clean, squeezing her toes tight when she tried to pull away. He was stronger than he looked, too. She'd thought she had hurt him last night when she'd stabbed him. Apparently not.

"So what's the deal?" she asked. "Did your daddy and mommy play with your private parts when you were little? Or maybe your twin uncles liked to play doctor?"

"Shut up," he said through his synthesizer.

"Why can't you take off the mask? If you're planning on killing me anyhow and making my skin into a pillowcase or something, then you might as well come clean right now. Come on, show me what a real bad guy looks like."

Ignoring her, he stood. When he got to the door, he looked back at her, unmoving. Although she'd never admit it, the mask was kinda creepy. "Do you have that mother-hate thing going on…you know, where you have to torture women to vent because of all the sick, heinous things your mother did to—"

The door slammed shut before she could finish.

She laid her head back against the bedpost and let out a long, shuddering breath. And then she began to work her arms again, wincing as the wire cut deeper into her flesh.

CHAPTER 27

Saturday, February 20, 2010 9:32 a.m.

Jared and Lizzy sat at a table in the coffee shop, waiting for the college student to arrive. Jared took a sip of the coffee he'd ordered and grimaced. "Good thing you didn't order anything. Not good."

"Have you always been so picky?"

He ignored her.

Lizzy glanced at her cell phone. "Our guy is two minutes late. Speaking of which, does our guy have a name?"

Jared shook his head. "The caller said that the student was scared and didn't want to reveal his name yet."

Lizzy grew quiet, worried about Brittany, hoping her niece was safe.

Jared leaned across the table, his eyes on hers. "We're getting closer, Lizzy. We're going to get him."

She prayed he was right. "Look," she said, gesturing with her chin toward the door, "there he is now." She could tell by the curly hair alone that the young man entering the coffee shop was the same courier in the picture Jessica had taken on her phone.

Lizzy waved him over to their table. He was tall and lanky, and at closer view he looked like a seventeen-year-old kid. Jared stood and pulled out a chair for him. "I'm Jared Shayne and this is Lizzy Gardner."

The young man glanced at Lizzy, his grim expression making it clear this wasn't a friendly visit.

He took a seat. His eyes darted about the coffee shop and then he looked over his shoulder at the view of the parking lot. "I don't have much time."

"We ordered you a latte." Jared slid the steaming coffee closer to him.

"Thanks." He took a sip.

Lizzy noticed his hand shake as he held the cup to his lips.

"What is it you people need to know?" he asked.

Jared spoke first. "Who hired you to deliver a package to Ms. Gardner's office the other day?"

"I don't know his name. It was a man who I would guess to be in his midforties."

"How did he find you?"

"He was hanging around the campus the other morning when I pulled up on my bike. He asked if I knew anyone who would be interested in making a quick three hundred dollars to run an errand. He said the job had to be done right then or no deal."

"Why are you so nervous?"

"There was something disturbing about the dude. He told me he would find me and take care of business if I talked to anyone."

Lizzy looked at Jared and then back at the young man. Excitement rolled through her at the notion that they might actually be talking to someone who saw and spoke to Spiderman. They needed his help. She leaned forward. "What did he look like? Was the man thin? Heavyset? Any scars or tattoos?"

The boy exhaled. "He was a white man. He had a beard, a thick beard with lots of gray. The beard looked strange, almost fake, but I couldn't see any glue. The man was of average weight."

"How tall?"

"Not sure." He looked Jared over. "About your size and height, I would guess."

"What about his eyes?" Lizzy asked, desperation lining her voice. "Big eyes? Narrow slits?"

"That's all I remember," he said, his face pinched, feeling the pressure.

"Three hundred dollars in cash," Jared said, "if you'll agree to meet with an artist."

"Why?"

"We need you to give the artist a description of the man who hired you. The more details the better. The artist will make a sketch from your description so we can get his picture out to the public."

"Who is this guy anyhow?"

"He's a cold-blooded killer," Lizzy said, hoping to make him understand how important it was for him to cooperate.

"He's already killed one little girl that we know of," Jared said. "We need to find him before he harms anyone else."

"What about me?" The kid's eyes widened. He put a hand to his chest. "He's going to come after me."

Jared handed him his card. "You're a big guy. He'd be foolish to try to mess with you."

The boy looked scared to death as he pushed his chair away from the table and stood. "I need to think about this. If I agree to meet with the artist, you'll need to pay me at least a thousand bucks."

"Call me once you decide," Jared said.

Lizzy stood too. She couldn't believe Jared was going to let him walk away. He was all they had and they didn't even know his name. "Do you have any sisters?" she asked.

He turned, hesitated, and then nodded.

"You might want to think about them when you're making your decision. What would you want someone else to do if this maniac ever got his hands on someone you cared about?"

"I'll think about it," the young man said before he turned and marched out the door.

Saturday, February 20, 2010 1:42 p.m.

Lizzy clapped when Brittany Warner's name was announced on the loudspeaker. She watched with pride as a gold medal was placed around Brittany's neck. Eight days had passed since she'd seen her niece, but it felt like months.

Lizzy waved at her, but Brittany didn't see her amid the sea of kids wrapped in towels. Lizzy turned to Jared seated next to her on the bleachers. "I'm going to say hello to Brittany before we head off. Do you want to come with me?"

"I'll wait here. I'm already getting the evil eye from your sister."

Brittany's face lit up the moment she spotted Lizzy heading her way. Brittany dropped her towel and duffel bag and rushed to meet her halfway. They hugged for a long moment before Lizzy took a step back so she could take a good look at her niece. "You were amazing!"

Brittany grinned. "Thanks."

"Wow!" Lizzy said. "When did you get braces?"

"Less than a week ago. Dr. McMullen said I only have to wear them for one year."

Lizzy tucked a loose strand of dark hair behind Brittany's ear. Although she'd seen Brittany at least once a week for most of her life, it was hard to believe how fast she'd grown.

Brittany looked around. "Are you here alone?"

"I'm here with a friend." She pointed to the stands and smiled when Jared waved back at them.

"He's cute. Who is he?"

"We're working on a project together at the moment, but we dated back in high school."

"Cool. Can I meet him?"

Cathy called Brittany's name before Lizzy could answer.

Lizzy waved at her sister, but Cathy avoided making eye contact and instead gestured for Brittany to come speak to her in private.

"I'll be right there, Mom." Brittany turned back to Lizzy. "I guess you two aren't getting along again?"

"She's mad at me," Lizzy said, "but she'll get over it. We'll be fine. We always are. How's school?"

Brittany shrugged. "It's OK, although I feel pretty tired today after spending an hour and a half with my math tutor last night."

"My poor baby," Lizzy teased. "Math was never my favorite subject either. Is your tutor helping?"

"Too early to tell. I was only supposed to be tutored for an hour, but Mr. Gilman got so wrapped up in equations he forgot all about the time. He's a nerd."

"Bummer," Lizzy said, and she meant it. "Is that your new swim coach?"

Brittany followed Lizzy's gaze to the group of girls wearing the same red suit. They were all huddled around a man who Lizzy guessed was in his early forties. He sported a pair of beige slacks, a white polo shirt, and a baseball cap with a dolphin emblem.

"Didn't I tell you about him?" Brittany asked.

Lizzy's skin prickled. "No, why, what's going on?"

"Don't tell Mom because she'll freak out, but he's a little creepy, that's all."

"How so?"

"He stares at me and some of the other girls sometimes." She feigned a shiver. "Gives me goose bumps."

Lizzy frowned. "Has he ever touched you inappropriately?"

"No. I promised Mom I would tell her if any coach or teacher ever made a move."

Lizzy watched the coach closely. She tried to picture him with a beard. "What's his name?"

"Henry Sullivan."

"Is he from around here?"

"Not sure."

One of the girls called Brittany's name this time. Apparently, they wanted to take a team picture.

"You better go," Lizzy said. She gave her niece a hug. "I love you. Keep me updated on your math progress…and on that coach of yours."

"I will. Thanks for coming," Brittany said as she started off toward her team. "And next time I want to meet your boyfriend."

He's not my boyfriend, Lizzy was about to say when Brittany turned toward her again and said, "Oh, Lizzy, one more thing."

Lizzy waited.

"How did you like your new ringtone?"

"Cute. Very cute." She watched Brittany walk off singing "Louie, Louie." She thought about trying to talk to Cathy, but her sister's stiff body language told her now was not the time.

Lizzy inhaled long and deep as she turned her attention back to the coach. *Henry Sullivan.* Nothing about the man looked familiar, but that wasn't going to stop her from putting him at the top of her list of suspects.

Saturday, February 20, 2010 3:10 p.m.

"I don't trust Coach Sullivan," Lizzy told Jared for the second time since they left the aquatic center. Jared was driving and Lizzy was fretting. "We need to get a warrant and search his house," she said. "Your father is a judge. You could get a warrant quick, couldn't you?"

"Lizzy, slow down. Let's do this the right way. We don't want to scare him off before we've had a chance to check him out thoroughly. You said yourself he didn't look familiar."

"It's been fourteen years. Spiderman could look completely different by now. What if he had plastic surgery?" The idea of such a thing unsettled her greatly. He could have made a lot of changes in the past fourteen years. "How many of Spiderman's victims did Jessica say were swimmers? Three? Four?"

"I'll call Jimmy and get someone to follow Sullivan. In the meantime let's visit the county jail and have a chat with Betsy about the watch she promised to hold for you."

"If she was drunk at the time, it won't matter what she saw."

Jared sighed.

"What if something happens to Brittany?" Lizzy asked, unable to let go of the fact that Spiderman could be absolutely anyone. "I wouldn't be able to forgive myself if something happened to her because I did nothing to protect her from Sullivan."

"Would you feel better if we checked him out ourselves? Follow him around, see where he lives?"

"I would."

He pulled to the side of the road and made a U-turn. "We'll follow him home. See what he's up to."

"Thanks. I'd feel much better if we could keep an eye on him, although I don't think Cathy was too happy about us staying after the swim meet to talk to him."

"Your sister should be glad you're concerned about Brittany and that you're watching over her."

"Yeah, well, maybe in a perfect world."

"Your sister has never been a happy person."

"Seriously? That's news to me."

Jared kept his eyes on the road. "Cathy has been jealous of you since high school."

"Cathy? Jealous?" She huffed. "What are you talking about? My sister doesn't have a jealous bone in her body."

"Are we talking about the same Cathy Gardner that was in my graduating class?"

"Give me one example of a time when she was jealous of me."

"Let's start with your first car."

Lizzy snorted. "Cathy was jealous of Old Yeller?"

"No, your first car. Cathy was driving a Honda, a gift from your parents, but she borrowed your little red sports car—"

"Little Red was older than dirt," she reminded him. "That car had over a hundred thousand miles on it."

"Doesn't matter," Jared said. "I still remember the look on Cathy's face when everybody made a big deal about how cute Lizzy looked in her shiny red convertible."

Lizzy's brain felt like mush. She had no idea where Jared was going with this crazy car story. "What happened?"

"When Cathy brought Little Red back, the car was ruined— no longer drivable."

"That wasn't her fault," Lizzy said defensively. "Her friend backed into it with his truck."

"Annie Smith said she saw the whole thing. Cathy watched her friend back into Little Red and did nothing to stop him."

"Annie Smith told a lot of stories that weren't true."

"You've always been blind when it comes to your sister," Jared said.

"That's not true."

"What about that white lacey dress you saved up for, only to find it in your closet with ink stains?"

Lizzy racked her brain trying to remember. "Lacey dress? Ink stains?"

"I thought women remembered these kinds of things."

"You're wrong about Cathy. She was never jealous of me. It's not her style. And although most women might remember a favorite dress, I'm not like most women, remember?"

It was Jared's turn to be perplexed.

"You used to tell me that's what you liked most about me—that I was different from all those other girls."

"Ah, so you do remember some things," he teased.

"I remember many things. For instance, the way my stomach knotted and my heart broke in two when you kissed Amanda Rocha at Winter Ball."

"You had broken up with me," he said in his defense.

She held up seven fingers. "One week. We had broken up for a total of seven days, and in that amount of time not only did you ask Amanda to the ball, you kissed her right there on the dance floor in front of everyone."

His smile worked its way to his eyes. "I only kissed her to make you jealous."

"Well, it didn't work."

He laughed.

She liked the sound of his laughter. "We made a lot of plans back then, didn't we?"

"We did," he said quietly.

The ring of Lizzy's phone interrupted her thoughts of better days. She clicked TALK and regretted doing so when she realized the caller was Nancy Moreno, the news anchor from Channel 10.

"I'm not interested," Lizzy said before the woman could say more than two words. It made her stomach turn to know that the media, as always, put the BIG story above all else.

"Please don't hang up."

Lizzy was about to do just that when Nancy followed with, "I'm calling about Spiderman."

"No doubt."

"He's been following me."

"How do you know?"

"I have something he wants."

Lizzy could hardly believe the lengths Moreno would go to get a story. "What could you possibly have that he would want?"

"I have your file."

"My file?"

"Your file from Linda Gates's office," Nancy said.

"How could you possibly—" Then it dawned on her. "You stole my file from my therapist?" She had heard way back when that Nancy Moreno was one of Linda Gates's clients. She also knew Linda would never willingly give the file to anyone without talking to her first.

"When I took your file from Linda's office, I thought I could help the FBI by talking to the killer and finding out as much as I could about him."

The woman wasn't making any sense at all. "What have you found out?"

"Only that he'll stop at nothing to get what he wants."

Nancy Moreno sounded scared. "Where are you now?" Lizzy asked.

"I'm at home. He's out there now. I know he is."

"Did you call the authorities?"

"I needed to talk to you first."

So that's why Nancy had been calling, Lizzy realized.

"I was supposed to meet with him this morning to give him your file," Nancy said, "but I changed my mind. I was getting ready to leave for work when I heard a noise outside my front door. I keep hearing noises, but I can't see anything. There it is again. Please come. I live at thirty-five sixteen Skyview in Rolling Hills."

Lizzy glanced at her watch. It would take ten to fifteen minutes to get there. "Nancy, I want you to hang up and call nine one one. Do you hear me?"

"I can't. I'll be the laughingstock of America. They'll play my nine one one message over and over after they find out that I stole your file."

Lizzy covered the receiver and told Jared what Nancy Moreno had told her. They needed to get to 3516 Skyview in Rolling Hills, a primarily upscale suburb outside Sacramento.

"You have to hurry," Nancy said over and over.

"We're on our way."

Jared retrieved a teardrop-shaped beacon from beneath his seat, opened his window, and placed the flashing light on the top of his car.

"What should I do?" Nancy asked.

"Call the police right now and then find a safe place to hide until we can get there."

It sounded as if Nancy was rushing around the house. Lizzy could hear the soft patter of footsteps and then what sounded like a rattling of dishes. Next came a clicking sound followed by… silence.

"Nancy, are you there? Can you hear me? Shit."

CHAPTER 28

Saturday, February 20, 2010 3:22 p.m.

Only two of the doctors on Lizzy and Jessica's suspect list worked on Saturdays. Jessica crossed the first doctor off the list the moment she saw him. He had a long neck, a thin face, and he was Indian. The second doctor, Dr. Harold Long, an eye doctor, was a possibility. He was about the right height and age. His ears might be considered big by some, but he didn't have a strong jaw or a high forehead—two other characteristics Lizzy had said to watch for.

Jessica walked to her car. "Don't worry, Mary," she said under her breath. "If I have to visit every doctor in Northern California, I'll do it. I'm going to find him. And then I'm going to find you. We'll be a family again."

After Jessica's beat-up Volkswagen bus was towed away, she had borrowed her mother's Honda Civic. Sitting in the car, she listened to voice messages on her cell and went over the list of suspects one more time. There was a message from Lizzy telling Jessica to add two more names to their list. A math tutor named Mr. Gilman and Henry Sullivan, a swim coach.

A frosty chill slid down Jessica's spine the moment she repeated his name aloud. Why hadn't she thought of him before? She quickly dialed Lizzy's number.

Ring-ring. Ring-ring.

Answer the phone, Lizzy.

Jessica started the engine. She needed to get back to the office. She waited for Lizzy's answering machine to click on. "Lizzy, it's Jessica. I think we might finally have the connection we've been looking for. Call me back ASAP."

Saturday, February 20, 2010 3:23 p.m.

Lizzy knocked on the front door to Nancy Moreno's house for the third time. "Nancy," she called out, "it's Lizzy Gardner and Jared Shayne from the FBI. Open the door. Everything's going to be all right." *Liar, liar, pants on fire.*

When no one came to the door, Lizzy went to the front window and peeked inside. The main room had an elegant yet eclectic look to it. Cozy and warm with no sign of struggle...and yet... she strained her eyes, trying to see past the furniture and into the dining area. The table was set, complete with tablecloth and silverware. Part of the tablecloth was pulled too far to one side. A wineglass had been knocked over. "Jared," she said. "We need to go around back."

The side gate was open. She followed Jared through the gate. There was a peanut-shaped pool surrounded by a water fountain and well-manicured grass. The tranquil sound of water cascading from a mermaid's tail contrasted greatly with the wild thud of her heart. The French doors leading into the house were wide open.

Gun drawn, Jared gestured for her to stay put.

Lizzy had no intention of standing outside alone…waiting. Careful not to disturb anything, she tracked Jared's every step as she followed him inside. Not only had a wineglass toppled over, a porcelain bowl had fallen to the floor and shattered into pieces.

The kitchen was to the left. The sink was empty, the stainless steel sparkling. The granite counters were wiped clean, everything in its place.

Jared headed down the hallway while Lizzy went for the stairs. Holding her Glock between sweaty palms, she took the stairs two at a time. She jerked open the first door she came to. The shades were drawn. She flipped on the lights. Nothing appeared out of order. Slow and steady, she moved through the room, stepped toward the closet, and then slid the mirrored closet door open. Plastic bins neatly stacked. A couple of winter coats neatly hung. No bad guys. No dead bodies.

Her pulse raced. She realized she was holding her breath. She exhaled as she exited the room. Slowly she worked her way down the hallway. "Nancy? Are you here? It's me, Lizzy Gardner. You can come out now."

There was no answer. She hated the quiet nearly as much as she hated the dark. It had only taken eleven minutes to get here. Was Nancy able to hide in time? Was she huddled in a dark closet waiting to be rescued? He couldn't have gotten to her so quickly. And yet the open patio doors, the broken bowl…they told a different story.

The carpet was thick and so pearly white that anything would show, including the trail of blood drops leading to the master bedroom. Shit.

"Lizzy! Down here!" Jared shouted.

Holding her gun straight ahead, she wanted to call out to Jared and ask him what he'd found. If he'd found Nancy, then what the hell had she found?

He called Lizzy's name again, louder this time.

She couldn't respond. Each step she took was muffled in plush carpet. She was in the master bedroom now. The trail of blood led across the wide expanse of floor and into the master bath. The killer could be standing a few feet away. Maybe he was injured, still hoping to get away. She'd never fired her gun other than on a firing range. But she wouldn't hesitate to pull the trigger if she had to.

Stay calm. Be ready.

Had he seen her? Did he know she was coming? Did he know she was standing right outside the bathroom door?

Now, Lizzy, now! Just do it!

She took one last step, gun drawn, two fingers on the trigger, and found herself staring into Nancy Moreno's eyes. "Shit!"

Saturday, February 20, 2010 4:21 p.m.

Jessica walked into her mother's house and found her brother in the kitchen. She took a seat at the picnic table that served as a kitchen table while her brother, Scott, scrounged around inside the refrigerator. After a few moments, he gave up. "I'm going to go get something to eat. Want to come along?"

"Where's Mom?"

"Where she always is—passed out on the couch in the other room."

Jessica hadn't expected to find her brother at home. He and Mom were fighting a lot lately, and so he'd spent the last few nights at a friend's house. Next week he was packing up and leaving for Jersey. Jessica had come to get the gun their mother kept in an empty box of Tide in the cupboard above the washing machine.

She hadn't planned on telling anyone, but as she peered into her brother's eyes, it just sort of popped out of her mouth. "I think I know who took Mary."

Grim lines bracketed his mouth as he plowed his fingers through his hair. "Wow." He turned toward the kitchen sink and stared out the window overlooking a dead lawn. A quiet moment settled between them, and she wondered what he was thinking. She didn't have to wonder for long.

"When are you going to get over your obsession with finding Mary?"

"Probably when I find her."

"After all this time you're still in denial. I had no idea."

"It's happened before," Jessica said.

"What?"

"Missing people have been found. Alive and thriving, in fact."

"Name one."

"Elizabeth Smart. Shawn Hornbeck—"

Her brother walked to the picnic table and took a seat across from her. He looked tall and broad shouldered. Somewhere along the way, he had grown up. He looked older and wiser, making her wonder if he looked anything like the father they hadn't seen since Mary disappeared. Mom had torn every picture of him from photo books and framed pictures around the house. Not one memory of her father remained. Her brother reached an arm out and put his hand over hers. "It's time to let it go, Jess."

"I can't."

"I loved her too, but Mary never would have run away."

"What if whoever took her brainwashed her? You know, convinced her that we didn't love her. After a few years, she might have started to believe what she was hearing. Maybe he changed her name. I've been doing a lot of reading lately, and it happens."

He pulled his hand away. "I think—oh, never mind, it doesn't matter what I think. You sound like Mom." He stood.

She blinked. "What do you mean by that?"

He leaned forward and dropped his hands palms down on the table. "If you're not careful, Jess, you're going to end up just like her. After Mary disappeared, she lost it. She gave up on herself and on us." He gestured with his chin toward the other room. "Go look at her. For years now she's been in limbo, unable to move on. Now she's drowning herself in booze. If you don't let it go, that's going to be you." He straightened, and before Jessica could tell him the rest of the story, about working with Lizzy Gardner and finding the connection, the key to their older sister's whereabouts, he was gone. The door slammed shut behind him.

Jessica had already gone back to Lizzy's office and made a couple of phone calls. Sure enough, the man had a record a mile long. He'd served time for indecent exposure and for selling videotapes of teenage porn.

The moment Jessica had stepped into the house and seen her brother, she'd hoped he might come along for the ride. She sighed. Lizzy had yet to return her call, which worried her. Had Lizzy already gone to his house? Since Lizzy was the one who had asked her to add his name to the list, it made sense that she might have gone there already.

There was no way Jessica was going to call the police. They would need a search warrant. Realizing she'd already wasted too much time, Jessica went to the laundry room. The gun was right where she saw it last. She scooped the gun up, pushed detergent and fabric softener out of her way, and grabbed the Tupperware bowl filled with ammunition.

The sound of her mother's voice caught her off guard. "Mary," she called.

Mom was stretched out on the couch just as her brother had said she was. Her eyes were half-open as she reached out a pale hand. An empty gin bottle lay on the floor. "Mary, is that you?"

Jessica took her mom's hand, surprised by how cold she felt. "Yes, it's me. It's Mary."

The corners of Mom's mouth tilted upward. "You came home."

Jessica squeezed her frail hand and tried to picture her mom the way she used to be...vibrant and full of life—Donna Reed in the flesh. "I have to go, Mom, but I'll be back soon. Everything's going to be OK."

CHAPTER 29

Saturday, February 20, 2010 4:33 p.m.

Jared, Jimmy, and Lizzy stood in the backyard near the pool outside Nancy Moreno's house. They watched as two separate body bags were hauled off to the crime lab where the contents of each would be carefully examined for blood, hair, fibers, and prints belonging to anyone other than Moreno.

Jared had found Moreno's body in the laundry room clothes hamper downstairs. Lizzy had found Moreno's head upstairs in the bathroom sink. If Nancy Moreno had worried more about her life than her reputation, Lizzy thought, she might still be alive.

For the last five minutes, Lizzy had been holding her phone to her ear. She finally gave up and clicked her cell shut. "Jessica's still not answering."

"We'll stop by your office after we're done here," Jared offered.

Jimmy stood next to Jared. As always, Jimmy wore a dark suit, well-polished shoes, and a cynical scowl. Seconds ago, a crime scene technician had handed Jimmy a plastic bag. Inside the bag was the paper stuffed in Moreno's mouth, a bloodied note from one of Lizzy's therapy sessions with Linda Gates.

"How could Nancy Moreno have gotten into Linda Gates's office?" Jimmy asked.

"Nancy has been one of Linda's clients for many years," Lizzy answered.

"Has anyone talked to Dr. Gates?"

"I called her at home," Lizzy said. "She was shocked to hear what had happened. She called me back ten minutes ago to let me know she'd gone to her office and my file was, in fact, missing."

"How would Moreno steal the file in the first place?"

"Dr. Gates believes Nancy took the file during her last visit only a few days ago. Dr. Gates also mentioned seeing a strange man hanging around the bus stop. Apparently, the man was watching them from the street corner while Nancy was at her office. Linda called the police the moment she spotted him, but the man disappeared before they arrived."

"We need to get someone over there and get a full report."

"It's done," Jared said. "Hank is on his way."

"What about the kid you met at the coffee shop this morning?"

"He's afraid."

"Of what?"

"The man who hired him to deliver the money to Lizzy's office threatened to come after him if he talked," Jared said. "I had someone follow the kid after he left the coffee shop, though."

Lizzy raised an eyebrow. She'd had no idea.

"He lives in an apartment building close to Cosumnes River College. His name is Russell Parker."

"He said he'd have to think about meeting with a forensic artist," Lizzy told Jimmy.

"Does he realize we're dealing with a serial killer?"

Lizzy nodded. "We told him."

"He's scared," Jared repeated. "He's not thinking straight. I think he'll come around, though."

Jimmy stopped a detective as he passed by. "What did you get from the neighbors?"

"So far, nothing. Nobody saw anything suspicious. No strange cars parked near the house. The woman across the street is a stay-at-home mom. She said her kitchen window looks directly at Moreno's house. She didn't see anything out of the ordinary when she was washing dishes around the same time Moreno would have been on the phone." He excused himself and walked off.

Jimmy scratched the back of his neck. "This guy never leaves a trace. How the hell does he do that? Look around us. There are no fields or parks for the killer to hide in. So how does he get in and out without anyone noticing?" Jimmy rubbed the area between his eyes. "And why the hell would the killer go after a news anchor?"

"She had something he wanted," Jared said. "Once he got Lizzy's file from her, he was finished with her."

"And now what?"

They all knew verbatim the message scrawled in blood on the mirror in the bathroom, but Lizzy repeated it anyhow. "'Darkness awaits,'" she said.

"What do you think it means?"

"He has my file," Lizzy said. "He's obsessed with knowing everything about his victim before he strikes."

"And how does 'darkness awaits' fit in?"

"I'm afraid of the dark," she said without elaborating.

Jimmy understood then. They all did. Spiderman was almost ready.

Jimmy's cell rang. He stepped away to answer it.

Lizzy hadn't bothered to tell Jimmy that not only was she afraid of the dark, she was paralyzed by it. Spiderman would also learn when he read her file that she hadn't cried since she escaped, that the mere sight of a spider now made it difficult for her to breathe, and that she couldn't sleep through the night without reliving the horror of what he'd done to those girls. Lizzy wrapped her arms around her waist.

"Come on," Jared said, "let's get out of here."

Saturday, February 20, 2010 5:05 p.m.

Lizzy was asked to leave her cell phone, gun, and backpack at the front counter of the California Department of Corrections facility. Next she was searched for pepper spray, tear gas, alcohol, and explosives. Finally she and Jared were led to the appointment-only noncontact room and reminded more than once that it was a crime to assist an inmate. They were also asked if they had any cameras or recording devices on their persons, to which they both answered no.

They passed through a metal detector and then entered the CDCR noncontact visiting room, where they would have twenty minutes to talk to Betsy Raeburn.

The room was quiet. There were four areas set up for inmates to meet with a maximum of two visitors at a time.

The security officer pointed to the first two chairs within a booth partitioned off by glass. There were visible speakers so they would be able to carry on a conversation.

By the time Jared took a seat next to Lizzy, Betsy Raeburn was being led to the booth on the other side of the glass.

The woman was tall and well muscled. Her brown hair was clipped back. She had wide-set hazel eyes, a full, round face, and a mouth that appeared to be set in a permanent frown.

Betsy took a seat. The security guard took a few steps back and set the timer on his wristwatch.

"Ms. Raeburn," Jared said. "I'm Jared Shayne and this is Lizzy Gardner."

The woman leaned forward until her face was an inch from the glass. "You're not Lizzy."

"I am Lizzy. I remember you." Lizzy's throat clogged with unexpected emotion. "I can't thank you enough for what you did."

"I didn't do anything," Betsy said.

"You were a friendly face when I needed one most. You helped me into your truck. You helped me get away."

"Well, I'm glad you're OK."

Awkward silence followed before Jared said, "We're here for a couple of reasons, Betsy. We need to know if you saw anyone or anything unusual on the day you helped Lizzy."

"No," she said, shaking her head. "The feds asked me the same question a hundred times, and the answer is still the same."

"What about the watch Lizzy had with her the morning you picked her up?"

Betsy's face reddened. "I don't know anything about any old watch," she said. "You didn't have a watch, did you, Lizzy honey?"

Clearly Betsy had gone on the defensive. Lizzy put a hand on the glass. "It's OK, Betsy. You're not in trouble. In fact, nothing you say or do will ever change the gratitude I feel for what you did for me that day. But we need to ask you about the watch because the sicko crazy bastard is back in business."

Betsy's eyes widened. "No shit."

"No shit," Lizzy echoed. "We need to know what you did with the watch. We don't care if you sold it or hocked it or tossed it in the garbage, but we need to know where it might be because the watch could have a serial number…something to give us a clue as to the killer's identity."

Betsy gnawed on her bottom lip. It was hard to tell if she was deciding whether or not she wanted to say what she did with the watch or if she just didn't remember the watch at all. Betsy leaned close to the glass again as if she were about to tell them a secret.

Lizzy leaned close too.

"Did you happen to bring me some cigarettes?"

Lizzy turned to Jared.

"I saw a vending machine in the lobby," Jared said as he stood. "What kind do you smoke?"

"I'll take two packs of Marlboros."

"Inmates are only allowed one pack through the glass," the guard told him.

"Come on, man," Betsy said over her shoulder, "cut the lady a break."

The guard ignored her.

Jared was back in under five minutes. He placed a pack of Marlboros in the metal tray, and Betsy pulled on a device that delivered the cigarettes to the other side. She took her time packing the cigarettes against the palm of her hand before removing the plastic wrap. She placed a cigarette in her mouth and looked over her shoulder at the security guard.

The guard pulled out his lighter and lit it for her.

Betsy sucked in a lungful of nicotine and exhaled. "Thanks."

Jared nodded.

Lizzy glanced at the clock. "We need your help, Betsy."

Betsy took another drag. "The last thing I need is to give these assholes another reason to keep me locked up."

"You did nothing wrong," Lizzy said emphatically. "I gave you the watch, remember?"

Betsy's eyes brightened. "You're right. I remember. You gave it to me, didn't you? I have nothing to worry about?"

"That's right," Lizzy said. "You have nothing to worry about. You did nothing wrong, Betsy."

Betsy took a long pull from her cigarette. "I'd like to help you," she said, "I really would, but the thing is, I tried to sell that watch but I couldn't get more than two hundred dollars for it because of the engraving. Really pissed me off because my brother said it was a Rolex and that it was worth thousands."

Jared hardly flinched. He was a pro, Lizzy thought. He had patience and then some. Lizzy, on the other hand, wanted to reach down the woman's throat and pull the words out for her. But now that Betsy had her smokes, she wasn't in any hurry. She had nowhere to go.

"You wouldn't happen to remember what the engraving said, would you?" Lizzy asked.

Betsy took in another lungful of nicotine. Smoke fogged the window between them. "If I tell you, will you send me another pack of these?" She held up the Marlboros.

Lizzy nodded. "If you tell me, I'll send you a whole carton as soon as the post office opens."

Betsy's smile revealed a row of crooked yellow teeth. "Like I said before, I was pissed off about the engraving. I mean why would someone go and ruin a perfectly good watch like that? The engraving had the initials SJ and then a small heart symbol followed by the initials SW."

Shivers coursed up her spine. Lizzy had no idea if this tidbit of info would lead anywhere, but the notion that they might have something, anything at all, even a few initials, made her dizzy with excitement. "Are you sure it was SJ and SW?"

"Yeah," Betsy said with a snicker, "that was it. I remember because I told my brother that the letters stood for Stupid Jackass loves Stupid Whore." Her laughter bounced off the walls. "If that son of a bitch hadn't ruined the damn watch, I could have made some real money. Speaking of which," she added midpuff, "do either of you have any cash?"

Lizzy looked at the guard.

"Up to fifty dollars in one-dollar increments," he said.

Jared pulled sixteen ones from his wallet and Lizzy found another nine, wrinkled and folded. They placed the dollar bills in the tray.

Betsy pulled the device and guffawed as if she'd just won the lottery. The guard stepped forward and said it was time for Betsy to get back to her cell.

Jared stood and Lizzy did the same. "Thanks for everything," Lizzy said.

"Yeah, anytime. Just don't forget that carton of cigarettes."

"I won't forget." Lizzy watched Betsy push herself to her feet and then follow the guard back to her cell. After Betsy disappeared, Lizzy followed Jared away from the private booth, through the facility, and to the front lobby where they collected their belongings.

Jared's phone rang the moment they exited the main door. His brow furrowed as he listened. He nodded and hung up.

"What's going on?"

"We've got to get to the high school where you spoke last night."

"Why?" Lizzy asked.

"They think he might have struck again."

Her heart dropped to her stomach.

"They found a letter and blood at the school."

"This can't be happening." She grabbed hold of Jared's coat sleeve and peered into his eyes as awareness settled in. "The letter…was the letter to me?"

"Yes, but this one was signed by Hayley Hansen."

CHAPTER 30

Saturday, February 20, 2010 6:00 p.m.

"It's Lizzy Gardner's fault that you're here. You know that, don't you?"

Hayley's stomach gurgled. She hadn't eaten in at least twenty-four hours. The blinds were shut tight. Spiderman had dragged in a spindly wooden chair. He'd been sitting in the corner watching her for at least an hour now.

"What are you going to do?" she asked. "Just sit there and stare at me all day and night?"

He didn't answer. His mask was in place, but there was something different about him. For starters, he didn't look well. He wore his usual starched collared shirt and beige-colored pants, but his clothes were wrinkled and he was slouching. His game was definitely off. When he looked to his right, she saw bits of gauze sticking out from under his collar. She'd almost forgotten that she'd stabbed him last night. Had he gone to the hospital? The knife had gone deep. And the house had been quiet for a few hours before he entered the room.

The mask he wore covered the middle section of his face: eyes, nose, upper half of cheeks. His forehead, jaw, and chin looked pale, a sign that he'd lost some blood.

He was a creepy man. Not once had Brian ever come into her room and just sat there and stared at her. Brian just got right down to business.

But not Spiderman.

It was disturbing the way his eyes looked through that mask of his. "What are you looking at, asshole?"

"You."

"The only reason I'm here," she said, gathering confidence at the thought that he might be in pain, "is because I *let* you take me."

His head tilted to the right. "How so?"

He wasn't using his voice-changing device, which could bode badly for her. Maybe he'd listened to her earlier and realized she was right. If he was going to kill her in the end, what did he have to hide? And yet he still bothered to wear a mask.

"I didn't have to be Einstein," she told him, "to figure out that you had a bone to pick with Lizzy Gardner." She also didn't need much in the way of brains to figure out the only way she might have a chance at getting away would be to befriend him and get him to untie her arms from the bedpost. Although she was well aware that her idea could just be wishful thinking on her part.

"After watching the news, I figured you were watching her," she said when he didn't respond. "And if you *were* watching Lizzy that meant you would probably show up at the high school. So I found a comfortable spot after everyone else left last night. And I waited."

"Why would you do that?"

"Because I was bored."

He laughed, a weedy, pathetic laugh, but a laugh all the same. "You could have spent your time getting another tattoo," he said bitterly. "Looks like you enjoy using your body as a canvas. You could die from that."

She laughed. "Now that's funny. You're a killer, right?"

"A seeker of justice," he corrected.

He had a deep, soothing voice, she thought. He was articulate. Nothing like the losers her mom hung out with who couldn't pronounce the simplest of words. "A seeker of justice. Hmmm. How so?"

"I do my best to help rid the world of useless teenagers who serve no purpose—teenagers who seduce and tease young men, speak rudely to their elders, fill their lungs with smoke, and carve their limbs with foolish designs with no respect for themselves or their bodies." He looked at her tattoo. "Did you know that during MRI scans the metallic salts in a tattoo can cause the skin to burn as if the flesh is being cooked?"

She lifted her legs, bending them at the knees so they both had a better view of the tattoo on her ankle above the tape. She also had an angel tattooed on her collarbone and a barbed wire tattoo around her baby finger. She shrugged. "I like my tattoos."

He sneered.

She gestured with her chin toward her ankle. "That was my very first tattoo. It's hard to tell from far away, but the writing on my ankle says 'Brian.' Brian talked me into getting my first tattoo…years ago, when I still trusted him. Brian is my mom's drug dealer. He started out as Mom's boyfriend, and then he got her hooked on meth. Years later, when Mom couldn't pay him the money she owed him, she let him have his way with me. I was fourteen at the time. After that, I guess I became fair game. He and all his drug dealer friends have since had their way with me…sometimes at night, but mostly in the morning," she added as if she were talking about the weather. "If you're really a seeker of justice why don't you go after guys like that instead of girls like me who never stood a chance?"

He seemed to ponder that for a moment before he said, "I'm sure you weren't perfect."

She didn't bother telling him that she was a straight A student or that she worked most weekends and nights at a smoothie shop and gave every penny she made to her mom to help pay the rent. In her spare time, she read books. Lots of them. She liked the classics as much as she enjoyed a good romance or mystery. There was nothing like a well-told story to make her forget her troubles. "You're right," she finally answered, "I definitely wasn't perfect."

Beneath the mask she saw his eyes brighten.

"What did you do?" he asked.

"Sometimes when those men made me suck on their dicks," she said, "I gagged. They didn't like that at all."

"What did they do about it?"

Although she spoke the truth, the maniac seemed to have missed her sarcasm. Whatever. If she wanted him to be her friend she needed to keep talking…entertain him until she figured out how she was going to get out of this predicament. "Most of the druggies didn't care if I gagged," she said. "One drug dealer, a fat, hairy dude, would pinch me real hard every time I choked. The pinching was worse than the retching, so I got a lot better at opening my throat. Sort of like a sword swallower does."

He nodded his head as if he understood. *Sick bastard.*

"A couple of guys would wait until they were done getting off before they knocked me around."

"Hmmm."

"See my nose?" she asked, turning her head slightly so he could get a better look at her profile.

276

"What about it?"

"It's crooked. It's been broken three times by various assholes." Her stomach grumbled, louder this time.

"Sounds like you're hungry."

She shrugged as best she could under the circumstances.

"Tomorrow we're going to make a phone call," he said as he stood, his body stiff. "If you do as I say, you might get something to eat as a reward."

Hayley watched him walk toward the door. Judging by the grimace, he was definitely feeling some pain. Good. He should be dead, she thought as she released a long sigh.

He usually shut the door after he left, but this time he left the door open. She hoped he would go to bed. Before he'd entered earlier, she'd felt the bindings around her wrist finally loosening. Her flesh beneath the tape was raw, but the pain had subsided to a dull throb.

She was hungry, but more than anything she needed to go to the bathroom. She had already peed once, but her shorts were dry now. If she soiled herself she worried he might try to clean up the mess and find her knife. The pocketknife in her undershorts was uncomfortable but it was also her last hope.

A million thoughts raced through her mind, including thoughts she used to have about killing herself. Back home, there was a fan above her bed. The scarred wooden blades would go around and around and she often imagined her dead body dangling from the fan: eyes bulging, face pale, tongue hanging limp from her mouth. The suicidal thoughts had increased in intensity over the past few months, another reason she hadn't worried about the maniac catching her.

Although her intent had been to kill the monster, she had considered the possibility that she might die in the process. She wasn't stupid. Shit happened. And now, twenty-four hours after she set out to get the bastard, she was half naked, hungry, and tied to a bedpost with a pocketknife tucked under her ass.

Despite all of that, she realized more than anything…she wanted to live.

Saturday, February 20, 2010 6:17 p.m.

Lights flashed in Lizzy's face despite Jared's best efforts to shield her from the blitz of reporters surrounding the school. Media vans lined up on one side of the street while patrol cars with rolling lights outlined the entirety of the school premises.

"Lizzy," a reporter shouted from the crowd. "Is it true that Spiderman has been calling you?"

Lizzy kept her eyes focused straight ahead. Jared lifted the crime scene tape and ushered her through.

"Did he kill Nancy Moreno to get to you?" someone asked. "And what about Sophie? Is it true he left another note for you?"

"Did you know the girl who was abducted last night?"

"You're doing well," Jared whispered into Lizzy's ear. "Ignore them. We're almost there."

Lizzy tried not to pay any attention, but that didn't stop the hurt from wrapping its achy fingers around her heart and squeezing tight.

Jimmy Martin, she noticed, was bent over a crime scene technician who was using a scalpel to scrape dry blood samples into sterile containers. Portable floodlights were set up so investigators and technicians could work fast and hopefully beat the rain forecasted to hit the area in the next few hours. Closer to the gym,

Lizzy noticed the same reporter from the other night, the woman who had barged into the gym and put a stop to her class, talking to an agent. The reporter was dressed in jeans and a T-shirt. "Is she being interviewed?" Lizzy asked.

Jimmy stepped away from the technician. "Apparently, the reporter saw Hayley Hansen sitting alone last night, and she asked her if she needed a ride. It was getting dark. The girl told her somebody was on their way to pick her up." He looked over his shoulder at the reporter and added, "She's taking it pretty hard."

"Where was the letter found?" Jared asked.

"Right here," Jimmy said, "the same spot where the reporter saw the girl waiting for a ride."

Lizzy looked around. "Where is the letter?"

"They're making sure the blood is dry before they bag it. We won't be able to take a good look at the letter for another hour at least."

"Any theories?" Jared asked.

"I have one," Lizzy said. "Hayley decided to use herself as bait. She mentioned doing just that when she showed up at my place the other night. All she had to do was watch the news to know that Spiderman has been keeping tabs on me. So she comes to the school where she knew I would be, and after the talk ends, she sits down and waits for Spiderman to show up, knowing the odds are in her favor if she makes it easy enough for him."

"That's ridiculous," Jimmy said. "What kind of kid would get themselves abducted on purpose?"

"She's lonely and lost," Lizzy said, wishing she'd had a chance to sit down and talk to Hayley the other night. Maybe then she could have talked some sense into the girl.

"Has anybody contacted her parents?" Jared asked.

"Eric Holden is with Hayley's mother now. She had no idea her daughter was missing. In fact, she said it wasn't unusual for Hayley to disappear for days at a time."

Lizzy couldn't believe what she was hearing. What kind of mother let her child disappear for days at a time?

"If this is the same guy who decapitated Moreno," Jimmy said, "I want to know how the hell he's getting from point A to point B without anybody noticing him."

The technician finished gathering blood samples and started packing up. Jimmy wagged a finger at him. "I want the results ASAP. And I want every sample from this location compared to all blood samples collected from the Moreno residence."

The technician nodded, picked up his metal case and duffel bag, and walked off.

"At this rate," Jimmy said, "I'm going to run out of technicians. Who the hell is this guy? What happened to sticking with an MO?"

"He no longer has an MO," Jared said.

Jimmy frowned. "What are you talking about?"

"This is personal now," Jared said. "The media's right about that. Spiderman's playing us all, watching us run from one crime scene to the next. He's angry, and his rage is taking him down an unfamiliar course. Serial killers like to fantasize and plan. Spiderman is used to feeling as if he has all the time in the world. But things have changed."

Jimmy's frown deepened. "Who is he angry with?"

"Me," Lizzy said.

Jared didn't argue. "The way I see it, Spiderman was getting ready to come back for an encore when Frank Lyle confessed to the world that he was Spiderman—the killer who had taken the lives of four young girls. That set our man off. Serial killers like to get credit where credit is due. And then Lizzy's father agreed to do a couple of interviews on national television…"

"Why would Spiderman care?" Jimmy asked, unconvinced.

"I don't think he cared so much as he was interested to hear what Lizzy's father had to say. Lizzy was, after all, the reason I believe he must have stopped killing, at least at first. He had to be afraid she would identify him or at least point to his where-abouts."

"And then my father said too much," Lizzy added, "and Spiderman must have gone berserk."

Jared nodded. "More than likely he worked himself into a frenzy knowing he'd been betrayed and lied to."

Jimmy was having trouble staying on track. "Betrayed by who?"

"By me," Lizzy said. "I had convinced him that I cared about him and even loved him as any young girl would love and respect her own father. It didn't take long for me to realize he knew his victims well. But he didn't know me. He thought he was doing the world a favor by eliminating teenage girls he considered to be bad. I knew I had to convince him I was one of the good girls if I was going to have a chance at staying alive."

"That was his MO," Jared said. "Find a girl who fit his depic-tion of a 'bad' girl. Then wait, watch, and learn. But now he's angry at Lizzy's betrayal and he's getting sloppy."

"Hayley Hansen was on to something," Jimmy murmured.

Lizzy looked at Jimmy. For the first time since she'd met him she felt as if they might be on the same side. "Are you thinking what I'm thinking?"

"I won't let you do it," Jared said.

"You don't have a choice."

"Spiderman is growing restless," Jimmy said. "He's losing his patience, which could ultimately work to our advantage."

"We need to work fast," Lizzy agreed.

"He'll know exactly what you're doing," Jared said. "He's getting sloppy, but he's not stupid. Bait might have worked for Hayley, although I'm sure her plan didn't include being dragged off by the man. I want to know whose blood this is. Spiderman won't be fooled twice."

Jimmy took hold of Jared's shoulder. "We'll be all over Lizzy. She'll have more wires hooked to her than the cable company."

Jared shook his head.

Lizzy took Jared's hand in hers and squeezed. "I have to do this."

Saturday, February 20, 2010 7:02 p.m.

A loud POP sounded and the car lurched forward. Jessica held the steering wheel in a death grip and somehow managed to steer the Honda to the side of the road. She stepped out and saw the problem. The back left tire was flat. She looked up at the sky as dusk settled overhead, and without any warning, she started crying. She couldn't stop the tears from coming as she plunked her hands on her waist, her gaze never leaving the one lone star in the sky. She couldn't remember the last time she'd cried, and yet she knew the floodgates had not opened because of a stupid flat tire. She could handle a flat tire.

After Mary disappeared, her family fell apart. Her father packed up and left, unable to handle the guilt he felt every time he looked into their eyes. It wasn't long before Mom started drinking and her brother began experimenting with drugs. Jessica did everything she could to preserve what was left of her family. She started working at the mall to help pay the bills. When she wasn't working and doing chores around the house, she studied. Even back then she'd known she wanted to study human behavior, find out why some people killed while others gave their lives saving complete strangers. She wanted to know what made people angry enough to do the unthinkable. Mostly she wanted to find out what kind of people abducted children, because she was certain Mary had been kidnapped. Mary never would have run away. And yet the cops working the case were certain she had done just that. They said kids often ran off when family members were constantly fighting.

Mary never would have left, Jessica thought as she wiped tears from her face. She and Mary weren't only sisters; they were best friends. They had vowed to protect and look out for one another. When they were small and their parents fought, they made tents out of blankets in the room they shared and played make-believe.

Mary might have grown tired of the yelling. She might have even gone to sleep at night dreaming of happier times when their parents used to get along. But Mary never would have left without talking to her first.

Saturday, February 20, 2010 7:22 p.m.

Back at the apartment, Jared and Lizzy checked the phone. No incoming messages on her main line. Once again Lizzy dialed Jessica's number. "Jessica still isn't answering her phone," Lizzy told Jared. "She left me a message at three thirty this afternoon. She sounded excited about the two names I had given her to add to the list of suspects. She asked me to call her back ASAP. That was four hours ago."

Lizzy grabbed her laptop sitting on the coffee table and booted it up.

Jared went to the kitchen. "Do you have her home phone number?"

"I called her there too. No answer." Lizzy heard the kitchen cupboards opening and closing. The water faucet was turned on and off before he asked, "How long have you known Jessica?"

"A few months."

"Didn't you say you were short on funds and couldn't afford an assistant?"

"She's pushy and wouldn't take no for an answer. Jessica's persistence didn't make sense until yesterday when I discovered that her sister is one of the girls who went missing fourteen years ago."

Jared poked his head around the wall dividing the kitchen from the main room. "What?"

Lizzy's fingers rattled across the keypad before she looked over at him. She sighed. "I just found out yesterday. I haven't had time to give it much thought. We've been sort of busy." She jotted down an address in her notebook and then stood. "Jessica thinks her sister is still alive."

"If she's a runaway, then it's a possibility."

Lizzy shook her head. "Jessica showed me a picture. It was her, Mary, the girl I almost saved."

"Did you tell Jessica?"

"I couldn't." Lizzy put on her coat, went to the door, and then looked over her shoulder at him. "Are you coming?"

"Where to?"

"I have to find Jessica. I need to make sure she's OK. I was hoping you could drive by Gilman's house while I take a look at Coach Sullivan's."

"Where does Gilman live?"

"Not too far from here."

"I don't like it. Let's do this together."

"I think it's sweet that you want to protect me, Jared, but I'm a big girl. We're running out of time. I'll call you when I get there. You do the same."

He sighed, then glanced at his watch. "I'll take Sullivan. I have his address. You take Gilman. What car is Jessica driving?"

"Her mother's Honda Civic. Silver."

"If you see her car, call me. I'll do the same."

She nodded.

"Don't do anything crazy."

They stepped outside, and Jared waited for her to finish locking the doors before he surprised her with a kiss, a brief but warm brush of his lips against hers. She hadn't had time to think about what had happened last night between them and what it meant, if anything. "What was that for?"

"Tell me you won't knock on any doors or barge inside if you see something you don't like."

She nodded.

He waited.

"What is wrong with you?" She lifted a brow when he didn't answer. "OK," she said. "I promise. I'll be a good girl and call you if I see anything suspicious."

Saturday, February 20, 2010 7:36 p.m.

Jessica pulled up to the curb outside Gilman's house and shut off the engine. She glanced at her cell phone on the seat. If the battery hadn't died, she could have called a towing service. Instead she'd been forced to change the tire herself. No wonder Lizzy hadn't returned her call—a dead battery tended to make it difficult for people to get through.

Jessica shut the car door, shoved her hands into her pockets, and walked toward the creeper's house. The wind whistled through the trees. Dark clouds curled around the moon while her fingers curled around her mother's Kel-tec P3AT snug within her front pocket. She had accidentally discovered the gun eighteen months ago. She hadn't given the gun another thought...until today.

The walkway leading to the front door was cracked. The hedges needed trimming. Branches scratched against the house and leaves danced at her feet. The wind caused a flag to flap against the flagpole. Once she reached the door, she realized she probably should have gone to Lizzy's apartment instead of coming here alone. She'd never been the patient sort, though. When she got an idea in her head, it was impossible for her to sit around and wait. She was an act-now-regret-it-later sort of person.

She looked over her shoulder, scanned the street. All was quiet. A light was on in the house across the street. Having no idea what she would say or do if someone answered, she raised a hand and rapped her knuckles against the door. After a few seconds, she knocked again. Then she shoved her hand into her pocket and wrapped her fingers around the gun. She'd never fired a gun before. *How hard could it be?*

CHAPTER 31

Saturday, February 20, 2010 7:55 p.m.

Lizzy looked inside the front window of the Honda. She recognized the bag on the passenger seat as Jessica's. She also noticed the cell phone with all the glittery bling. Jessica's phone. Damn. She jogged across the lawn and peeked through the kitchen window. Except for a sliver of light coming through a door at the end of the hallway, the house was dark. But she heard music.

There was no sign of Jessica. She reached into her pocket and realized that in her haste she'd left her cell phone in the car. She was about to turn back when a crash sounded from inside the house. Shouts sounded, followed by a couple of loud thumps.

"Jessica!" she shouted as she ran back to the window. Inside, she saw the door down the hallway open and a naked man appear. He looked like he was heading toward the front door, but then he disappeared inside another room. Then she spotted Jessica.

"Jessica!" she cried. What the hell was she doing in there? Nobody could hear Lizzy over the loud music. Shit! She yanked her gun from her holster and ran back to the door. She knocked hard and then rang the doorbell, but nobody was paying her any mind. She ran to the side gate, flipped open the latch, and ran past a row of garbage cans toward the backyard. A sliding glass door leading into the house had been left wide open.

Saturday, February 20, 2010 8:01 p.m.

The snakes had arrived yesterday. Six in all. Two eastern diamondback rattlesnakes, three Mohave rattlers, and his all-time favorite, one puff adder with a very bad disposition. He put his face close to the glass aquarium and instinctively sprang back when the snake struck at him with amazing force.

He held a hand to his chest and even found himself needing to take a seat. Anger and resentment bubbled inside him. He had a tremendous urge to toss all of the snakes into the bedroom where the bitch was tied up and watch her die a slow death. But then a voice told him he needed to keep his wits and stick to the plan. His anger subsided. He hadn't meant to kill Sophie so early in the game, but the girl had literally bored him to death.

He needed to keep Hayley alive for now. The thought of Lizzy being forced to watch him torture the girl excited him beyond words. He closed his eyes and let the blissful images renew him with the strength he needed to stay the course.

Lizzy needed to be taught a lesson once and for all. An intensely sharp pain gnawed at his shoulder and side, keeping him from enjoying the moment. He had cleaned his wounds last night after tying the girl to the bedpost. He had stitched himself up using sewing thread, alcohol, and a sharp needle. But he'd run out of antibiotics, and he didn't want to show up at the office looking pale and sick. The nurses were nosy as hell and they never missed a thing, or so they thought. Not even his partner knew that he was working side by side with a seeker of justice, a real-life hero. Most people were pathetically unobservant. All these years and nothing had changed. Sad but true.

Standing in front of a mirror, he unbuttoned his shirt and took a look at his wound. The cut was long and deep. Too deep. He might even be forced to visit the hospital. He could tell the emergency doctor that he'd been mugged. The area around the wound was red and swollen, foul-smelling with purulent drainage.

Annoyed by what the bitch had done to him, he stood and went to where the diamondback snakes were kept. He slid on a handling glove, reached into the aquarium, and grabbed the largest snake. One bite wouldn't kill her, but it sure as hell might make him feel better.

Saturday, February 20, 2010 8:03 p.m.

Jessica didn't bother running after the naked man. Instead, she entered the bedroom and looked at the king-size bed. The room was hazy with smoke and reeked of marijuana. The music was deafening and the scene before her was surreal. It took her a moment to take it all in, especially the person tied to the bed, wrists and ankles all tied to separate bedposts. Despite amazingly long lashes and the flowing red hair layered around high cheekbones, the woman tied to the bed was actually a man. The feathering of dark hair disappearing beneath a leopard Speedo was a telltale sign. His mouth was gagged and his eyes were round with fear.

She had no idea what exactly she'd interrupted, but whatever it was, it wasn't right. The loud music made it difficult to concentrate. The man was trying to say something, but his words were muffled by the gag. There had been three men when she'd opened the door. Where was the third guy?

She raised her gun. Her hand shook as she moved toward the closet where heavy metal music blared from a six-foot speaker on the floor. There was a video camera perched on a tripod inside the closet. The camera was still filming. A red light flashed.

What the hell was going on in here?

At closer view she could see that the man tied to the bed had bruises, and he was bleeding. She bent down to shut the music off and that's when she saw the third man—shirtless and low to the ground as he snaked his way across the floor toward the half-open window. "Stop!" she shouted.

He turned and fired.

Psss.

The gunshot sounded like a leaky gasket. She would have shot first and asked questions later if she'd thought he was carrying a gun.

The gun dropped from Jessica's hand as she sank back against the wall. A mind-numbing sting swept through her left side, then quickly became a searing hot burn. "Where's Mary?" she asked the man on the bed.

He shook his head, his eyes wider than before—like big round moons with a black speck in the middle. His hair was so red it made his face appear as white as a ghost. She wanted to help him, wanted to pull the gag from his mouth, but her legs wouldn't cooperate. His image became distorted and blurred around the edges. The shooter escaped through the window. Nothing she could do about that now. She drew her fingers away from her side. Blood stained her fingertips. Images of Mary kept popping into her mind's eye.

Was she dying?

The room spun out of control. Jessica's legs gave out first, and the rest of her body quickly followed suit.

Saturday, February 20, 2010 10:30 p.m.

Brittany was in the middle of downloading a song from iTunes when she saw a message pop up from i2Hotti.

Finally.

She was beginning to think he'd forgotten about her. Feeling reckless and bold she started typing.

> Brit35: what took you so long?
> i2Hotti: what do u mean?
> Brit35: i haven't talked to you for a million years
> i2Hotti: 3 days
> Brit35: too long
> i2Hotti: sorry been busy
> Brit35: doing what?
> i2Hotti: things
> Brit35: what's wrong? u seem different
> i2Hotti: i need to see u

Brittany's heart went pitter-patter, and she smiled with relief.

> Brit35: i was worried u didn't like me any longer
> i2Hotti: u joking? i think i have fallen madly in love w/u
> Brit35: stop teasing
> i2Hotti: serious
> Brit35: i need to see u too
> i2Hotti: i thought u might never ask

Brit35: how? mom is watching me 24/7 cuz of stupid killer and house is being watched

i2Hotti: tell her u have broken wire and need to go to ortho

Brit35: good idea…and then what?

i2Hotti: get out of school early on monday I will pick u up

Brit35: car?

i2Hotti: black BMW

Wow, Brittany thought, he must have rich parents or a really good job. She felt like the luckiest girl in the world.

i2Hotti: r u there?

Brit35: yes. i am excited to finally meet face to face

i2Hotti: not as excited as me

Brit35: mom coming gotta go

i2Hotti: see u soon

Brit35: not soon enough

i2Hotti: ♥ u

Sunday, February 21, 2010 12:55 a.m.

Lizzy paced the hospital waiting room, back and forth, hoping the doctor would appear and let her know if Jessica was going to be all right. The main door opened. A rush of cold air came inside followed by Jared.

"You're OK," he said, relieved.

"I meant to call earlier," she said, "but everything got crazy fast. I have no idea where my phone is and—"

"You're OK." He put his arms around her and held her close. "That's all that matters." Jared pulled away and said, "Coach Sullivan is clean as far as I can tell. He moved here after a bad divorce. He didn't mind letting me have a look around. What happened at Gilman's?"

"Gilman, it turns out, is not only Brittany's math tutor, but he's in the porn business. Apparently his films are unique in that he invites strange men to his home. Once he has his new guest neatly tied to the bed, his buddy comes out of the closet and they play dress up with their victim. They doll up their man to look like a transvestite and then proceed to perform all sorts of acts on his body. They call their videos Shameless Shemales. The poor man they were working on when Jessica appeared was scared to death. He's here at the hospital on the fifth floor. He's in shock."

"Where's Jessica?"

"Gilman's partner shot her before escaping through the window."

The doctor came through the door. "You can see her now," he said, "but only for a few minutes. We want her to get some rest."

"How bad is it?" Jared asked.

"It was a low velocity gunshot wound to her left side. She was lucky in that no major arteries were hit. The bullet was removed and she's been given a sedative."

Lizzy's shoulders relaxed. "How long will she need to stay in the hospital?"

"A few days at least. We'll know more tomorrow after we see how she does tonight."

They entered Jessica's room. A nurse was adjusting the IV. Lizzy went to the side of the bed and took Jessica's limp hand in hers. The poor girl was pale and she had a tube in her nose.

"I'm sorry," Jessica said weakly. "My phone died."

"Don't worry about any of that," Lizzy told her. "You need to focus on getting better."

"I don't suppose Gilman is our man?"

Lizzy shook her head. "No. But he's certainly not innocent either." More than anything, she wanted to lecture Jessica, tell her she never should have gone into that house alone. And the gun, where had she gotten hold of a gun? What the hell was Jessica thinking? She could have been killed.

The door opened and a young man walked in. His eyes were bloodshot.

"My brother, Scott," Jessica said as the young man approached her bedside.

Scott frowned. "What the hell were you doing at that guy's house? I told you he was a weirdo, didn't I?"

Jessica licked her lips. "He was on our list of suspects. I wanted to find Mary."

Scott's face turned a deep shade of red. "Mary's dead. If she were alive she would have come back to us. How many times do we have to go over this? Look at you." He raised his hands and dragged them across his face in utter frustration. "I can't believe you would do this to me. Mary disappears. Dad abandons us. Mom drinks herself into oblivion. And now you're running into strangers' homes wielding a gun, trying to get yourself killed."

Lizzy was about to cut in when Jessica raised a hand to stop her from saying anything.

"We'll give you two some privacy," Lizzy told Jessica. "I'll be back in the morning to check on you, OK?"

Jessica nodded.

Scott's shoulders slumped as he shook his head. Lizzy wanted to tell Jessica and Scott about their sister, give them some closure, but Jessica looked too fragile to handle another blow tonight. It would have to wait.

Sunday, February 21, 2010 3:03 a.m.

Something wet and heavy slithered over her legs.

Hayley's head snapped up. She'd fallen asleep. Apparently the bastard had waited for her to fall asleep so he could let loose another one of his pets.

Her heart pounded. The room was dark. Pitch black. She'd been struggling to get her wrists loose for two days with no luck, but this time when she yanked her arm downward her right hand came free.

She reached for the thick-bodied snake crawling over her thighs. A hiss sounded right before the snake struck, sinking its fangs into her leg. She grimaced, sucking in a painful breath as she got a firm stronghold around the snake's body and then heaved it across the room. The snake's heavy body slid across the floor and hit the wall with a thud.

Frantic, she reached her free arm upward and began working on releasing her other hand. The wire seemed never ending as she scrambled to find the end of it so she could unwind it from her other wrist. When the wire was off, she got to her knees and used her mouth to rip the duct tape off. Her arm came free, but the pain was excruciating. Adrenaline combined with determination kept her moving. Using her right hand, she felt around in her own stench in search of the knife she'd been sitting on for over forty-eight hours. Panic threatened to consume her until her fingertips connected with the knife's handle. She sat down on the floor, unfolded the blade, and quickly pulled her knees to her chest so she could cut the wire and the duct tape around her ankles.

Ripping the last remnants of tape away, she then set the knife on the bed and used her good arm to push herself to her feet. Her legs wobbled, threatening to buckle as she grabbed the knife and headed for the door. She nearly slipped to the floor as she went, her arm stretched out in front of her. She couldn't see a thing.

But she was free.

She had taken so much for granted before now. She could move her arms and she could walk. She would never return home to be abused by her mother's druggie friends. She would leave her mother's home and she would never look back. Never again would she allow anyone to touch her.

It took her another three steps before her fingertips touched a wall. She felt around, sidestepping until she felt the doorknob. Her fingers curled around the cold metal. Her heart thumped against her ribs. She turned the knob. Nothing. Locked. Bastard.

The window. She needed to find the window.

Using the wall as guidance, she moved slowly, inches at a time, careful not to make any noise as she went. If the window was locked, she would find something to break the glass.

She'd broken windows before. She would take the sheet from the bed and curl it around her good hand, then shove her fist right through the glass. Then she would run for her life.

She could do this.

She could escape. Just like Lizzy Gardner.

For the first time in her life, she felt as if she had purpose. She had to escape. She wanted to go to college. She wanted to live.

Her knee knocked into a chair. Damn. She held still for a moment, praying he hadn't heard the noise. She maneuvered around the chair in the dark and inched onward. Her bare foot touched the snake's body and she kicked it out of the way. Gross.

She used her right hand to guide her. *Stay calm. Don't make any noise. Don't wake the monster up.* If he knew she'd gotten loose, he'd make her pay. She still didn't understand his anger toward her and the other girls, but he'd made it clear he expected her to follow his rules. Escaping was not obeying. If he found out she'd tried to leave him, it would only give him an excuse to torture her further. The room wasn't that big. Where the hell was the window? She knew there was a lamp on the table near the window. She would have to be careful when—

Click.

The light came on.

She jerked her head around.

The monster was sitting on the edge of the bed. No mask. No beard. How the hell had he returned to the room without her noticing? She'd dozed off for such a short time, waiting for him to do the same.

"Did you really think I was that stupid?" he asked.

She grabbed her knife, snapped the blade open, and pointed it at him.

"I must admit, I never guessed you were still armed. You're a clever girl."

"I don't want to use this on you, but I will if I have to," she said. "You look pale. You really should have gone to the hospital for that knife wound."

"Look what you've done to the room." He looked around, unbothered by the glint of her sharp blade, more upset by the mess on the floor.

She looked at his chest. If she was going to live to see another day, she needed to strike him hard and deep. She needed to plunge the knife into his heart, because even the devil possessed a beating, pulsing heart.

"It stinks in here," he said. "Tsk. Tsk."

"Let me go," she told him, "and I'll leave you alone. I won't tell anyone what you've done. I'll walk away. It's not too late for you to put this whole ugly mess behind you. They'll never catch you if you stop before you've gone too far."

The smile on his face was creepy.

He was never going to let her go.

He lifted his hands. His fingers were short and stubby. He wore a wedding ring on his left ring finger. She hadn't noticed the ring before.

"I believe in justice and the American way," he told her. "Fairness and respect above all else. If you don't have respect for your peers and your elders then you're worthless to society." He wore slacks and a running jacket. When he reached into his jacket pocket, she lunged for him, but he was too far away and she came up short. The blade struck the mattress instead of his heart.

Before she could take another swipe at him, he put a metal device into her side.

Zap.

She jerked forward. It was as if she'd been hit by lightning. Her body stiffened and cramped. She couldn't move. She gasped for breath. Every muscle contracted. The pain was unbearable. She crumpled to the floor.

He stood over her.

She wanted to tell him to fuck off, but it was useless. She couldn't say a word, couldn't move an inch.

Dull, lifeless eyes looked down at her. He unclasped the knife from her hand, and without any warning, he leaned over and used its sharp edge to slice off the pinky finger from her right hand. She couldn't see what he was doing but she could feel it.

When he was done, he held up the bloodied digit. "I don't like tattoos. They can kill you, you know."

She could feel her muscles begin to relax. Blood oozed from her hand as she watched him set her severed finger on the bedside table. Then he reached into his pocket again and this time he pulled out a syringe. He walked back to where she lay and plunged the needle into her arm.

CHAPTER 32

Sunday, February 21, 2010 9:02 a.m.

Nine o'clock the next morning Lizzy and Jared were once again at the FBI headquarters in Sacramento. Ten minutes ago, they were ushered into a conference room where three men were already seated.

Lizzy sat across the table from Jared. She recognized Ronald Holt, who sat next to Jared. The other two agents were unfamiliar to her.

Jimmy stood in the hallway talking to a woman before finally joining them in the conference room. He shut the door and then took a seat at the head of the table. Before saying a word, he slid two eight-by-ten sketches across the table toward Lizzy.

Lizzy held the picture up. It was a penciled drawing of a man wearing a mask. The other picture was of the same man sporting a beard. The man's eyes had been drawn to reflect a light color. In her sleep, Spiderman's eyes were always dark. The eyes in the picture bored into hers. Whoever had drawn the pictures had an incredible artistic knack for this sort of work. The eyes were downright chilling.

"This looks like him," Lizzy said as she stared at the eerily accurate sketch: the high forehead, strong jaw, larger than average ears. Chills crept up her arms.

"The artist spent the past two days working with the student from Cosumnes River College and your therapist, Linda Gates," Jimmy told her. "They both agreed that this is a good likeness of the man they saw."

"Except for the eyes," Lizzy said. "Didn't they both say he wore sunglasses? If so, they couldn't have seen his eyes."

"That's why the eyes weren't drawn too wide or too narrow."

Jared reached across the table for one of the pictures and took a long look. "Have these sketches been distributed?"

Jimmy looked at his watch. "As of six o'clock this morning, both pictures were shown on news stations across America."

Jared looked pleased.

Lizzy wasn't sure what to think, although she was glad the public was being informed even if the picture wasn't one hundred percent accurate.

Everyone in the room looked tired and overworked. Jimmy looked around the room and said, "OK, people, I want to hear some chatter. What have you got? Give me something to chew on. Surprise me. Anything." He gestured at the big man at the far end of the table. "Matt, what about the phone taps? What have you got so far?"

Matt cleared his throat. "Unsub has been using disposable phones and apparently tossing them after one use."

"Doesn't he have to sign a contract to buy a phone?" Lizzy asked.

Matt shook his head. "He pays cash."

"Prepaid cell phones offer anonymity," Jared explained. "No names. No contract. He uses the phone and then tosses it."

"What about you, Holt?" Jimmy rambled on. "Who's watching the Warner house?"

"Cameron's on duty today. I haven't seen anything unusual since I've been parked there. It's a quiet street."

Lizzy was relieved to hear it. For the past few nights she'd been waking up in a sweat, worried about Brittany and Cathy.

"We've got two notes now." Jimmy looked around the room. "Fingerprints? Anything?"

Matt shook his head. "Unsub wears gloves, and he's just real meticulous with everything he touches. No fingerprints at the Moreno location or on either of the notes."

The door to the conference room opened. A young woman poked her head in the room to tell Jimmy he had an important call on line seven. Jimmy picked up the receiver and hit the button. By the time he hung up, his eyes looked haunted, as if he'd received some sort of death sentence.

He took a moment to refocus before he spoke again. Jimmy entwined his fingers and looked at the picture of the man with the mask. "I want to get the bastard. I want him today. Hayley has been gone for two nights. We're running out of time."

"What about Frank Lyle?" Jared asked the team of investigators. "Has he changed his story?"

Matt spoke up again. "Frank Lyle is sticking to his original story. He adamantly refuses to back down. Says he killed all of the girls fourteen years ago, including the ones who went missing. But he doesn't have any proof. Won't say where the bodies are buried. Most who have interviewed him believe he's lying. He likes the attention."

"What about the house of horrors?" Jimmy asked, his voice lined with frustration. "The excavation, the Rolex, the spiders, the bite marks?"

"Excavation was clean," a man named Tom said. "Nothing but dirt and rocks." Tom removed his glasses and used a cloth from his coat pocket to clean the lenses as he spoke. "I was able to locate the pawn shop where Betsy Raeburn sold the Rolex. Problem is the owner of the shop has no record of where the watch went after it was bought. Unlike the purchasing receipts, the sales records go back seven years, not fourteen."

"What about going public with the Rolex and describing the inscription, SJ loves SW," Lizzy said. "Maybe somebody will recognize the initials."

"That's not a bad idea," Jimmy said.

Ronald scribbled something in his notebook.

"If this is Spiderman we're dealing with," Matt said, "why is he killing random reporters and girls straight off the curb? What happened to his meticulous plotting and carefully laid out plans I've heard so much about?"

"Spiderman is not the same man he used to be. He's desperate," Jared said. "Spiderman has switched his MO from serial killer to killing spree. It doesn't happen often, but my bet is Spiderman found a way to live his life for the past fourteen years without killing. Whatever he was doing worked for a while...at least until Frank Lyle came into the picture. Serial killers like to take credit for their own work. Getting away with murder, time after time, year after year, makes them feel superior. But then Frank Lyle kills a young girl in the same manner as Spiderman, and after Lyle is captured he tells the world that he's our man, the guy responsible for at least six murders. This enrages Spiderman. So much so, he can't help but come out of hiding. His anger toward Lyle throws him off balance. He's older now, but not necessarily wiser. He desperately wants the world to know that he's back. He watches the news, reads the papers, learns that Lizzy was not who he thought. All that pent-up anger inside him turns away from Lyle who is locked up behind bars and is instead directed at the girl who got away."

Lizzy rubbed her arms.

"All right," Jimmy said, "let's get down to business. The reason Lizzy is sitting in today is because she has offered herself up as bait."

All eyes fell on Jared, who was shaking his head. "I don't like it and I don't think Spiderman's going to fall for it, especially after being set up by Hayley. But Lizzy has a mind of her own and she's stubborn as hell."

With a nod of her head, Lizzy confirmed what Jared had said.

"OK," Jimmy said, "I guess the only questions left are when, where, and how?"

Sunday, February 21, 2010 5:07 p.m.

"Hey there," Lizzy said when Jessica opened her eyes.

"Hey."

"How are you feeling?"

"Great."

Lizzy smiled because the question was more ridiculous than Jessica's answer. The girl had tubes running in and out of her body, and she looked like shit.

"I had no idea the man had a gun," Jessica told her in a hoarse voice.

"What made you think Gilman was our man?"

"He used to be my brother's math teacher. He was also a tutor. My brother, Scott, stayed late one day because Gilman offered to help him study for an exam." Jessica swallowed. Her lips were dry and cracked. "I still remember the night my brother returned home after being tutored. He wasn't the same. I teased him, which wasn't unusual because we always teased one another. But this time my brother got angry and I started crying. Before I knew it, my brother was crying too, and suddenly he was telling Mom and Dad that his math teacher had touched him. It was a horrible time for our family. Dad went to the school the next day and raised hell."

"Was Gilman arrested?"

"I don't remember what happened after that because days later Mary went missing and Gilman and my brother were all but forgotten."

Lizzy reached over the railing and took hold of Jessica's hand. "I'm so sorry."

"When I listened to your message," Jessica said, "and you told me to add Gilman and Sullivan to our list of suspects, I thought for sure Gilman was Spiderman. At the very least, I figured he was the person who took Mary. It all made sense, you know, since two days after Dad complained to the authorities, Mary went missing. I couldn't believe I hadn't made the connection years ago. I still can't believe I was wrong."

Lizzy found a tube of Vaseline and held it out so Jessica could smear some of the gel onto her dry lips.

"You know something about Mary, don't you?" Jessica asked after rubbing the ointment on her lips.

Although Lizzy was surprised by the statement, she found herself nodding.

"I thought so. You had a strange look on your face after I showed you the picture. You saw her, didn't you?"

Lizzy swallowed hard. "I'm so sorry."

"You have to tell me. I need to know. Was she tortured like the others?"

Lizzy didn't know what to say, couldn't bear to tell Jessica what she'd seen, but she knew she had to try. "Two nights after I was abducted, I awoke in an unfamiliar room in an average-looking house. I was tied up, but I managed to get myself untangled from the ropes. My leg was messed up. I was at the back door, about to escape, when I heard someone cry out from inside the house. The moment I heard the cries, I knew I couldn't leave without helping. I found your sister right away. I don't remember untying her, but I remember holding her in my arms." Lizzy's voice cracked as she squeezed her fingers tight around the railing, recalling how frail and weak Mary had been. "We were so close to escaping." She exhaled. "Mary and I almost got away."

Jessica's hand slid over Lizzy's. "It's OK. It's not your fault, Lizzy. You went back for my sister and paid a terrible price. You tried, and that's all anybody could have done."

"I wanted to save her." Lizzy's eyes burned from the memory. "More than anything in the world, I wanted to bring Mary home to her family. That's all I wanted."

Sunday, February 21, 2010 11:23 p.m.

The day dragged on in the same way Christmas Eve drags on when you're a child waiting for Santa to come down the chimney. Lizzy wanted tomorrow to come. She wanted tomorrow to come because she had a hunch their plan just might work. Once she saw Spiderman face-to-face, she could tell him what she'd always wanted to tell him—to go to hell where he belonged.

Lizzy sat motionless in front of the television thinking about tomorrow while Jared sat next to her doing paperwork. The interview between her and Detective Holt had already hit the local news stations, many of which played the interview every hour on the hour. The public was being warned to keep an eye on their children and lock their doors. Most news stations had been led to believe that the taped interview had been leaked by an FBI insider. The media executives had no idea they'd been set up. Even if they had known, Lizzy thought, they wouldn't have cared. A story was a story.

After this morning's meeting, Lizzy was taken into a room where Detective Holt interrogated her. Lizzy was purposely asked questions that would enable her to answer in such a way that would aggravate Spiderman. After losing Sophie, Jimmy had decided that Lizzy's idea to provoke Spiderman was worth the gamble. They would try to distract him and give Hayley a chance at staying alive for another day.

Lizzy watched, praying she had done the right thing.

"What do you know about Spiderman?" Holt was a big, burly man, his booming voice intimidating.

Lizzy had remained calm throughout the interview. "He's a coward," she'd replied as rehearsed. "A sniveling, gutless coward." Lizzy wanted to poke Spiderman's pride where it would hurt the most.

"Where do you think Spiderman is now?" Detective Holt asked.

"He's hiding," she said. "Cowards hide."

"Do you think he'll come after you?"

"No."

"Why not?"

"He's afraid of me."

"How so?"

"Because I'm the one who got away. I'm smarter than he is, and he knows it."

"Did he ever tell you anything about himself or talk about why he does the horrific things he does?"

"He has a problem with his father."

"How so?"

"He wanted his father's love, and he obviously never got it. Spiderman wore a Rolex, a Perpetual Sea-Dweller, just like the one his father used to wear. Spiderman loved his Rolex. He liked to touch it lovingly as if it were a pet. That's why I took his watch from him before I escaped."

"What did you do with the watch?"

She shrugged nonchalantly. "I gave it away."

"Why?"

"It meant nothing to me. I didn't want anything to do with his watch. I took it because I didn't want him to have it. I wanted to take something from him that mattered to him."

"Do you know Spiderman's name?"

"No. But 'SJ loves SW' was engraved on the watch, so his name could be Shawn, Sebastian, Simon, Scott…who knows?"

Lizzy pointed the remote control at the television and pushed the OFF button. She'd seen enough.

Jared stopped writing and put his papers to the side. "You should get some sleep," he said. "Tomorrow is going to be a long day."

She leaned against him. Her head rested on his shoulder. The apartment was quiet. Too quiet. She missed Maggie. After a moment she said, "If I hadn't been taken that night, do you think we would have stayed together?"

"There's no doubt in my mind."

"Really?"

"Really."

"Would we have married?"

"Definitely."

"What about children?"

"Two girls and a boy. You would still be complaining about the extra weight you gained from the last pregnancy."

She smiled inwardly, hoping to be swept away in their fantasy game. "What are their names?"

"Our firstborn would have been named Katherine Elizabeth, Kate for short."

"I like that." She reached for his hand and curled her fingers between his. She liked the way her fingers felt lodged between his. "What about the other kids?"

"Our second child would have been named Savannah Ruth, and our boy would have been named Adonis because I don't think that name has been used enough."

She chuckled. "Kate, Savannah, and Adonis. What would we have done with all those kids?"

"We would have gone hiking at Yosemite, rode bikes around Lake Natoma, and every once in a while Adonis and I would have gone fishing while you and the girls read books on the grassy bank overlooking the lake."

She raised a brow. "What? Girls can't fish?"

"Girls are too loud. Fish don't like loud noises."

She elbowed him playfully in the side. It felt good to tease and laugh and smile. "What would you have done with the girls," she asked, "when Adonis and I went on our mother and son field trips?"

"Good question." He rubbed a hand over her back. "I would have taken the girls to lunch and then…hmmm…we would have gone dress shopping, no doubt. Not in that order though because females don't like to try on clothes with a full stomach. Nothing ever fits right after a meal."

"You're a shopping expert?"

"I guess you could say I have a gift."

She brushed her thumb over his knuckles and smiled thoughtfully before her thoughts shifted in a new direction. "I didn't think I was ever going to see you again. And then when I finally did I felt so much guilt for what had happened to the other girls, I didn't think I deserved to be happy. That's been the hardest part."

He didn't say anything, just rubbed her back.

"I told Jessica about Mary today."

"How did she take it?"

"Better than I expected. I should have told her sooner, although she won't have closure until we find Mary's body, but it's a start."

He nodded.

"It's the not knowing that eats away at the victims' families."

"Lizzy—"

She put a finger to his lips. She knew he was worried about tomorrow. He didn't want her to be used as bait to catch a killer. "Don't say it, Jared. I have to do this. I know I've put you and everyone else in my life through hell, but for the first time in a long time I'm not afraid. I'm doing exactly what I need to do."

Monday, February 22, 2010 2:45 a.m.

Lizzy tried to sleep, but she couldn't stop thinking about Hayley. The minutes crept by as if in slow motion. Nothing new there.

Jared slept next to her, his breathing deep and even. Surreal. That was the word she'd been looking for earlier when she and Jared were talking as if they had no worries. Surreal. It was hard to believe Jared was back in her life, sleeping in her bed, protecting her as if his life depended on doing so. She reached for him, letting her fingers rest against his arm. She realized then, for the first time since she was a small child, that she felt safe.

Lizzy stared at the ceiling. She needed to sleep, but she also knew that if she allowed herself to close her eyes she would be taken back to another time. A time when minutes felt like hours and death became synonymous to life. She had never believed in evil until the night she was snatched up like a mouse caught within sharp talons. It was a sad thing to lose all innocence within the blink of an eye. Nobody in the world died unscathed. Nobody.

Lizzy thought about calling her sister to find out how Brittany was doing, but Cathy still wasn't talking to her.

Lizzy shut her eyes. It didn't surprise her that the moment she did, the telephone rang.

Jared was at her side before she reached the bedroom door. He followed her to the kitchen. Lizzy picked up the phone. She nodded at Jared. It was him. She had known he would call. She just hadn't known when.

"I saw the interview."

"They cut out all the good stuff," she said.

His laughter echoed as it came through the weird device he was so fond of using.

She had been looking forward to the call because she knew it would mean he was doing the expected and falling into their trap. But she was too exhausted to muster up much enthusiasm.

"I thought your interview was explosive."

"Why is that?"

"I can't put my finger on it exactly. Seeing you on television, Lizzy, up close and personal like that, made me yearn for what we used to share."

"We never shared anything. We never will."

"You're wrong. Even now, we share the same longing for a perfect world."

"My perfect world includes you being dead," she told him.

"See? We do think alike."

"I'm tired," she said, trying to use reverse psychology to keep him on the line. "I have to go."

"You're not going to ask about Hayley?"

Was that desperation she heard in his voice? Lizzy gritted her teeth. Hayley was all she wanted to talk about, and he knew that. She was tired of the crazy man and playing by his rules. "You're going down, asshole. We're so close now we can smell your dirty secrets. We know exactly what you've been up to for the past fourteen years and we're coming after you."

Jared looked taken aback by her change in tactics. If and when Spiderman called, Lizzy was supposed to stay calm. She'd screwed up. If there was one thing Spiderman hated, it was a loose tongue and dirty words.

"All the therapy in the world isn't going to save you now, Lizzy," Spiderman said calmly, as if unruffled by her sudden outburst.

"It can't hurt," she said bitterly.

"I beg to differ."

"Why is that?"

"No reason," he said. "I look forward to seeing you tomorrow."

"You and me both."

"Before I go," he added, "I want to tell your boyfriend how much I've enjoyed chatting with his mother. She has a beautiful smile."

Jared took the phone from Lizzy's grasp, but it was too late. The line was dead.

CHAPTER 33

Across the street from the building where Lizzy and her therapist, Linda Gates, were meeting, Jared peered through a pair of binoculars. He had a clear view.

For the past hour, the two women had talked, taken notes, and sipped tea. Jared set his sights on Lizzy's mouth. The corners of her mouth turned upward. Until now her expression had been serious, bordering on severe.

So far, no sign of Spiderman.

Every other Monday Lizzy visited Linda Gates for an hour of therapy. Spiderman had Lizzy's file. He knew exactly where Lizzy spent her Monday afternoons. And if he was the same man Linda Gates had seen standing at the bus stop last week and the week before that, then Spiderman knew his way around the area.

Lizzy was stubborn. Nothing new there. Once she had Jimmy on her side, Jared hadn't been able to convince her to skip this therapy session. Why not wait to see if someone recognized the sketch and identified their man? Lizzy had refused to wait another minute, let alone another day. She was sure they could lure Spiderman away from Hayley. And that's all that mattered to

313

her. Hayley, she said, needed time without her captor hovering over her.

Music sounded from the hotel room next to him. Sinatra, his mother's favorite singer. Ever since Spiderman had mentioned chatting with her last night, Jared had been hard pressed to get her out of his mind. He'd tried calling his mom this morning, but she hadn't answered. Then he called his sister who, in turn, called their mother at the hotel where she was staying. Apparently, Mrs. Jacqueline Shayne had checked out of the hotel the same night she had checked in. Neither he nor his sister knew what to make of that bit of information.

Jared's life was literally unraveling. Rules, order, organization: three staples he'd grown up with. When there was a problem, his father had taught him there was always a solution. And then Lizzy had disappeared, throwing all of his father's teachings to hell. Jared felt as if he'd been trying to pick up the pieces and stack them in an orderly manner ever since. Strange, he thought, how one man, one crazy lunatic, could wreak havoc on so many lives. Not just on the victims' lives but also the lives of their friends and families. And now, fourteen years later, the madman was back, like a ghost, invisible, elusive, doing it all again…wreaking havoc, causing pain. And nobody could stop him.

Since the sketch of Spiderman had circulated, the agency had received hundreds of tips. They just needed the manpower to sort through the calls. Frustration coursed through his veins as he looked from the empty street to the parking lot, to the bus stop, to the coffee shop on the corner. Not a lot going on. There was an agent on the rooftop across the street, an agent parked in the same lot where Lizzy's car was parked, and another two agents working undercover inside the building. All bases were covered. So why did he have a feeling there was something they were overlooking?

If Spiderman was anywhere in the vicinity, they would have seen him by now. Spiderman was playing with them. It was as simple as that. They had fallen into his trap; everyone was right where he wanted them.

A delivery truck pulled in front of the building where moments before Jared had seen Lizzy through the plate glass window on the third floor.

Jared straightened, setting his sight on the driver as the man stepped out of the truck and came around to the back.

"Matt," Jared said into the transmitter. "Get outside and check out the driver of the truck that just pulled up outside the building."

"Will do," Matt answered.

Jimmy was stationed inside the building where Lizzy and Linda chatted. He was on the top floor and had a bird's-eye view of the back of the building. Jimmy's voice rang loud in Jared's earpiece. "What's going on?"

"We've got an express delivery truck out front. Matt's checking it out."

Monday, February 22, 2010 1:06 p.m.

Karen kept her eyes on the road as she cracked the window and let in some fresh air. Five more minutes and she would arrive at the car rental area next to the airport. Twelve hours after that she would be wrapping her arms around her husband and her kids.

It was time to go home.

She'd come to the United States to find her brother, but it seemed he'd disappeared off the face of the earth. And nobody seemed to care.

Poor Sam.

She sucked in a lungful of air to calm her nerves. After her mother failed to call her back with the name of her brother's partner, she'd decided to pack up her bags and head for home. Her husband was worried and her kids needed her.

But something wasn't right, and the irritating niggling at the back of her mind refused to go away. She could feel it in her bones. Something was very wrong.

The music failed to keep her mind off her brother, so she clicked through the radio channels until she heard a soothing voice. It was Tammy Spencer, a how-to author who had written books on everything from raising children to growing herbs. Today Ms. Spencer was talking to her listeners about getting down on all fours to clean the kitchen floor. Back home, whenever Karen was stressed out, she would clean. There was something comforting about the smell of cleaning products. Maybe she thought she could scrub her problems away...if only it were that easy.

"Mops and brooms don't get into the nooks and crannies like good old-fashioned scrubbing," Ms. Spencer told her listeners.

Karen nodded in agreement. Next, the woman gave instructions on cleaning out the pantry and ridding the house of all those nasty smells that easily accumulate from things like rotting potatoes. "You don't want people to visit and think you've got someone buried in the basement, do you?"

No, Karen thought as she parked her rental car, nobody wanted their house to smell like that. But that's exactly how her brother's kitchen smelled.

Since nobody came to help her, Karen retrieved her belongings from the trunk of the car and made her way inside the building. As she waited in line behind a gentleman reading the newspaper, she caught sight of the newspaper headline.

"IS SPIDERMAN BACK?

A YOUNG GIRL AND A NEWS ANCHOR DEAD. ANOTHER GIRL
MISSING. HAVE YOU SEEN THIS MAN?"

Below the headlines were two sketches of the man thought to be Spiderman. Karen looked from one picture to the next. "Oh my God," she said, drawing a hand to her mouth. "No."

Monday, February 22, 2010 1:21 p.m.

The driver was cleared and sent inside to deliver the package.

"Just received a call from the office," Jared said, updating Jimmy. "They received a call from a woman named Karen a few moments ago. The woman thinks her brother might be the guy we're looking for. She's not ready to give up his name until somebody assures her he won't be hurt."

"What is it with these crazy people? A serial killer is loose, but they don't want the killer to be hurt?"

"Who knows," Jared said. It was quiet for a moment as Jared watched the building. Every nerve ending quivered with foreboding. "We've been set up, Jimmy."

"Why do you say that?"

"Lizzy isn't the only bait we're using today. We're all bait. He's doing his best to distract us."

"Why is that?"

"It's all a game to him." Jared saw movement inside the office where Lizzy had been seated for nearly an hour now. "Something's happening. I'll get back to you." He lifted his binoculars for a better look inside Linda Gates's office. "Matt," he said into his receiver, "who was the package addressed to?"

"A Linda Something-or-other."

"Linda Gates?" Jared asked.

"Yeah, Linda Gates."

Every word of your interview was explosive, Lizzy...all the therapy in the world won't save you.

"Matt! Get inside that building and make sure nobody opens the damn package!"

"The package was from a well-known store. The driver had ID. He was legit."

"If you're willing to bet your life on that, get your ass up there and open the damn package yourself."

"I'm on it."

"What's going on?" Jimmy shouted into his earpiece.

Jared growled his answer as he looked through the viewfinder, "The driver of the truck happens to be delivering a package to Linda Gates. I don't believe in coincidences."

Jared looked through his binoculars. Both women looked toward the door at the same time. Linda stood and pointed to another part of her office. Lizzy seemed to hesitate before she glanced toward the window and then disappeared from Jared's view.

Jared's heart was racing. Don't open the door. Shit. Where the hell was Matt?

Linda opened the door, signed for the package, and carried it back to her desk.

Jared moved the binoculars over the room, one side to the other. His adrenaline rocketed. *Where are you, Lizzy?* The driver was gone. Lizzy was gone. The door to Linda's office had been left wide open.

Jared turned the viewfinder on Linda and zoomed in close. Preoccupied with the package, she examined the box thoroughly. Her expression was calm, unruffled.

"Matt," Jared said into the receiver.

No answer.

Jared left the equipment where it was, hurdled over a cement ledge, and flew down the stairs. In less than a minute, he was across the street and running through the entrance to the building. The elevator was in use.

He ran to the stairwell and took the stairs two at a time. At the third floor, he shoved through the door to the hallway and to the sounds of screaming.

Jared raced through the hallway, angry at himself for letting it come to this. People stepped out of their offices to see what the commotion was about. Jared rushed into Linda Gates's office and saw Lizzy. Alive. She was alive.

His gaze fell to the open box and the puddle of blood at Linda Gates's feet. At closer view, he saw clearly the contents that had fallen from the package—one bloodied finger belonging to Hayley Hansen, no doubt.

Monday, February 22, 2010 2:48 p.m.

Cathy glanced at her watch. She'd been waiting in the hotel lobby for nearly three hours. Sex with her husband had never taken more than five minutes, ten minutes tops. But Richard had been cooped up in the hotel room with that woman for hours now. She reached inside her purse for her cell phone, but realized she'd left it in the car.

It was nearly time to pick up Brittany from school. She looked from her watch to the elevator. She didn't want to miss Richard when he stepped out of the elevator with his mistress. She wanted to confront her husband at the hotel, where he would be unable to deny having an affair with the woman.

She glanced at her watch again. *What should she do?*

Brittany had another appointment scheduled with Dr. McMullen after school. Another wire had broken.

It didn't take Cathy long to figure out what she needed to do—she needed to call Lizzy. She hated to call her sister after she'd sworn never to talk to her again, especially after the way she'd treated Lizzy at the house and then at the swim meet, but she knew Lizzy would help her out. Lizzy could be naïve at times, but her intentions were always honorable, which was exactly why Cathy worried about Lizzy and treated her like a child instead of a sister at times. Cathy had known all along she couldn't stay mad at Lizzy for long. Lizzy was family. No matter how angry she was with her sister, no matter how hard she tried to blame Lizzy for everything that had gone wrong in her life, she knew it wasn't true. Lizzy had a good heart. She didn't deserve her or their father's scorn. And yet that's all Lizzy had gotten over the years.

Every time Cathy found herself in a lurch, she thought of Lizzy. Every time she needed a shoulder to lean on, it was Lizzy who cheered her up. Not her father. Not her husband. Always Lizzy. And yet Cathy had never once told Lizzy how much she meant to her or that she worried about her because she couldn't imagine a life without her sister in it.

She went to the front desk and asked if she could use their phone to make a local call. The woman nodded and told her to dial nine first.

Swallowing hard, Cathy dialed Lizzy's number and hoped Lizzy would pick up.

Monday, February 22, 2010 2:49 p.m.

Jared followed Lizzy up the stairs to her apartment. He went inside first, checking the place thoroughly before telling her it was clear. After leaving Jimmy and his men to take care of the bloodied digit, Lizzy and Jared had taken Linda to the emergency room where the doctor determined that Linda had experienced a severe panic attack.

No sooner had Jared made Lizzy comfortable on the couch when his phone rang. Minutes later he hung up the phone and told Lizzy he needed to leave for an hour or two. "Do you want me to make you some tea before I go?"

"I'm fine. What was that about?"

"We've got a couple of leads. A Dan and Renee Winters in Citrus Heights called in today. They recognized the man in the sketch. They believe he's the same boy who stalked their daughter back in high school. Her name was Shannon Winters. Shannon died after choking on a jawbreaker on her way home from school. Apparently the boy's initials match those on the watch. The Winters have always believed the boy was responsible for their daughter's death."

"How could anyone be responsible for someone else choking on candy?"

"They believe he watched her die and didn't do anything to help her."

"What's his name?"

"Samuel Jones. Most people knew him back then as Sam."

"SJ loves SW."

Jared nodded. He stood there watching her for a moment longer. "You've done good, Lizzy. Because of you, we're going to catch the bastard."

She didn't respond.

Jared leaned over her and kissed her forehead. "I'll be right back."

CHAPTER 34

Monday, February 22, 2010 2:53 p.m.

After Jared left, Lizzy locked the door behind him. She was about to do her own research on the name Samuel Jones when her cell phone rang. "Hello?"

"It's me, Cathy."

Lizzy knew her sister wouldn't call unless it was an emergency. "Is anything wrong?"

"Everything's fine. I need to ask a favor, Lizzy. I need you to get Brittany from school and take her to an orthodontist appointment. Are you busy?"

"I can get her."

"Sorry about the late notice, but you'll need to be at the school by three thirty."

Lizzy didn't bother mentioning the bloodied finger. It would only upset her sister. The truth was Lizzy was glad Cathy was entrusting her to pick up Brittany. Lizzy wanted to see Brittany and make sure she was OK. Lizzy glanced over her shoulder at the clock. It was nearly three. It wouldn't take her long to get to the school.

"The orthodontist's office is off Eureka Road in Roseville. I don't have the exact street address on me."

The frustration in Cathy's voice was palpable. Her sister was frazzled. She was probably confronting Richard. "That's OK," Lizzy told her, "I took Brittany for her consultation. I know how to get to McMullen's office. Don't worry about a thing."

Monday, February 22, 2010 3:07 p.m.

Cathy watched Richard exit the elevator with a gorgeous woman hooked to his arm. His mistress had deep, rich hair the color of chocolate. Her almond-shaped eyes were also brown, her cheeks high, her mouth plump. She didn't look a day over twenty-five.

Cathy stepped in front of the adorable couple and poked a finger at Richard's chest. "You made me hate my own sister. You blamed Lizzy for all of our troubles, and all the while you were screwing another woman."

Richard calmly helped the woman with her coat and told her he'd call her later. The bastard didn't even try to hide his affair or pretend it wasn't happening.

The woman appeared unaffected, refusing to look her way. What a bitch.

"You're a home wrecker," Cathy shouted at the woman before she could escape the hotel unscathed. "You're a whore and I'm going to make sure everybody in your life knows it."

The woman walked across the lobby. Her heels clacked loudly against the marble tiles before she disappeared through the revolving door.

"You won't tell a soul," Richard said. "If you slander Valerie in any way, I'll make sure you don't have a penny to your name after I leave you."

Cathy snorted. "I can't believe I let you ruin my life."

"You ruined your own life. You've never once taken responsibility for your own actions. Even now. Look at yourself. You've gained fifty pounds since I met you. Have you ever once gone to the gym or taken a walk? No. You blamed your own daughter for your weight gain. I never cared about the extra pounds. I thought you were beautiful; more of you to love, I used to tell you. But when someone tells you over and over that she's fat, guess what? You start to believe it, and then you even begin to see it."

"That makes perfect sense coming from someone who doesn't see a thing. Do you have any clue what's been going on at home lately?"

"Why don't you tell me?"

"I bet you didn't know you were being trailed by a serial killer who hired my sister to follow you and your girlfriend around."

Richard stood silent.

"Apparently the killer wanted Lizzy to see what you were up to so that when she told me about your affair I would blame Lizzy instead of you. His plan worked perfectly."

"What are you talking about?"

"If you weren't spending all of your time screwing Valerie Hunt you might have heard that Frank Lyle isn't the man who kidnapped Lizzy fourteen years ago. He's a copycat, a wannabe. The real killer has been getting his kicks out of following you. And because of *you*, the FBI is afraid the killer might now have his sights on our daughter."

Richard stepped close. Only inches separated them. His face was a maze of angry lines as he grasped her shoulders and gave her a shake. "This better be some crazy tale you dreamt up, because if it's the truth, Cathy, and you didn't tell me, you will be dead to me from this moment on."

She flinched. She was angry, but she wasn't sure if she was ready to give up on their marriage. Standing here in the lobby, she'd had visions of Richard falling to his knees and begging for her forgiveness. But this...this hadn't been part of her plan.

"Tell me you're making this all up, Cathy. Tell me our daughter isn't in any danger!"

She wanted to lie, but she couldn't do it. She might not have been the perfect wife, but she'd never lied to him before.

"Where is she?" he asked, his face pale. "Where's Brittany?"

"Lizzy is picking her up from school."

He pulled his cell phone from the clip on his waistband. "I have two missed calls from Brittany."

"Why would she call you?"

"She only calls me," he replied, "when she can't get hold of you."

Overwhelming fear set in as Cathy shuffled through the contents of her purse before recalling that her phone was in her car. She looked at Richard. "Why didn't you answer your phone?"

He didn't move, not even a twitch of a muscle.

They both knew exactly what he'd been doing when his daughter called. At that moment his face changed before her eyes. Nothing about Richard resembled the handsome young man she'd married fifteen years ago. She didn't want him to beg for her forgiveness. She didn't want him at all.

Monday, February 22, 2010 3:25 p.m.

Lizzy waited in the long line of cars moving at a snail's pace into the school parking lot. Seeing all of the kids running around brought her back to the days when she and Jared would meet at the quad for lunch. They had lots of friends back then, and they had a lot of fun too.

She and Jared had a strong connection from the start. Her father, of course, hadn't liked the idea of Lizzy dating an older boy, and he'd been glad to see Jared go off to college, always reminding Lizzy that there were lots of fish in the sea. But from the moment they met, Lizzy never wanted anyone else. Jared was special. He was caring and compassionate. He deserved more than she could ever give him. He deserved to be happy.

She tapped her fingers against the steering wheel as she scanned the parking area. She pulled her car into a parking space and then called Brittany's cell. After three rings, Brittany's voice-mail came on.

"This is Brittany Warner. Please leave a message and I'll get back to you."

"This is your aunt Lizzy. I don't know if your mom told you, but I'm picking you up today. I'm at the school now." Lizzy looked at her watch. Three thirty-one. The kids got out of class six minutes ago. She couldn't have missed her. "I'll wait for you by the bear statue at the front of the school."

Five minutes later she called Brittany's number again. "Where are you, kiddo? And why aren't you answering your phone?" She looked at the time. "I have to get you to your orthodontist appointment in ten minutes. Call me back."

She clicked the phone shut and tried not to panic. *She's OK. She's with her friends. Teenagers are notorious for being late.*

She attempted to relax her shoulders as she looked about the parking lot. She wasn't ready to think about what was inside the box delivered to Dr. Gates's office. *Hayley*, she whispered before sucking in a breath. She couldn't go there right now. She couldn't handle that. Linda Gates was OK. That was something to think about. Linda had been in her life for fourteen years. Linda was the person who had helped her to see the light at the end of the tunnel. Linda was OK. *But what about Hayley?*

At the sound of laughter, Lizzy had had enough. She got out of the car and walked at a brisk pace toward the gym.

"Can I help you?" a woman asked.

"I'm looking for my niece, Brittany Warner."

"She's not on the team, but you might want to check the front office to see if she's waiting for you there."

"Good idea." Lizzy thanked her before leaving. After checking the front office and finding it empty, Lizzy ran from building to building and room to room. Brittany was nowhere to be found. Every muscle grew taut as full-fledged panic set in. She questioned anyone and everyone still wandering the halls. Inside her car again, she called Cathy's cell and left a message. Next she left a third message on Brittany's phone and then she called Jared. He picked up on the first ring.

"Thank God," she said.

"What's going on?"

"Cathy called after you left the apartment. She needed me to pick up Brittany at school. I've been here for at least twenty minutes and she's not here. I can't find her anywhere. What am I going to do?"

"Stay calm, Lizzy. Take a deep breath. Were you supposed to take her home after school?"

"No. Cathy asked me to take Brittany to her orthodontist appointment. It's scheduled for three forty-five. Five minutes ago."

"Do you think Brittany could have gotten a ride to the orthodontist?"

"I don't know; I just don't know."

"Lizzy," he said, his voice firm. "Whatever you do, don't panic. It'll only make things worse."

Her hands were shaking. She couldn't breathe.

"Do you want me to call the dentist's office?"

Lizzy inhaled and then exhaled. "The office is five minutes away. I'm going there now," she said as she rushed toward the parking area. "Do me a favor and keep your phone close."

"Will do. Call me when you find her."

Lizzy ran across the parking lot. *Breathe, Lizzy, breathe.* She jumped into her car, started the engine, and drove off. Who would Brittany accept a ride from? There was no conceivable way Brittany would have climbed into a car with a stranger. She'd taught her niece better than that. Brittany knew what to do if a stranger approached her. Maybe a friend had offered her a ride. Maybe she'd forgotten about her appointment.

Lizzy shot through a yellow light before she forced herself to slow to a steady forty miles per hour. Her hands shook as she made a right turn and then another. Moments later she pulled into the handicapped spot in front of the orthodontist office and jumped out of the car. She pushed through the door.

The woman at the front desk smiled. "How can I help you?"

"I'm Brittany Warner's aunt. Is she here by any chance?"

"We haven't seen her. Diane was just asking about Brittany."

"Is the doctor in?"

"Dr. McMullen works three days a week in this office and two days a week in the Auburn office. Diane Givens fills in when he's not here. She's in the back."

Lizzy walked into the main room where Dr. Givens was treating a patient. Lizzy wanted to see for herself whether Brittany was there or not. The receptionist followed her around with a worried expression on her face, then walked Lizzy to the exit and followed her outside. The woman pointed to the other side of the parking lot. "See that coffee shop over there?"

Lizzy nodded.

"A lot of kids from the school like to hang out there. You might want to check—"

Lizzy didn't give her a chance to finish. She jogged across the parking lot. The cold air turned her nose to ice. She pushed through the door to the coffee shop, overwhelmed with relief when she spotted a brown-haired girl sitting at a booth with two teenaged boys. "Brittany," she said, tapping the girl on the shoulder. "You almost gave me a heart—"

Brittany turned about, a frown on her face. Only it wasn't Brittany at all. Lizzy maneuvered around the table for a better look. "I'm sorry. I thought you were my niece. Do any of you know Brittany Warner?"

They all shook their heads. Clearly they thought she'd lost her mind. With her bruised forehead and exhausted state, she knew she looked a wreck, but she didn't care. She had to find Brittany. She checked every table in the coffee shop, talked to the manager, and then checked the restroom before heading back to the doctor's office. Her body was shutting down. Her head throbbed, every thought jumbled. Her knees wobbled. *Don't stop now, Lizzy. Stay calm.*

Images of a man in a mask flashed before her, his eyes cold, his voice robotic. Everything that had happened this past week had been leading to this very moment. She saw that now. Déjà vu.

"Brittany wasn't at the coffee shop," Lizzy told the woman who had helped her only moments before.

"Your sister just called. She wants you to wait for her. She's on her way here now."

Lizzy nodded. "I'll be outside if you hear anything." A squeal and a whine sounded in the other room. Lizzy stopped and listened. "What's that noise?"

The woman appeared wary of her, but she answered just the same. "It's a high-speed drill the doctors use for orthodontic implant pilots."

Lizzy listened for a moment longer.

"They're used when the doctor needs a good anchor to attach a wire or a spring."

The drilling lasted only a few seconds, but the noise set Lizzy's teeth on edge. Her head was throbbing. Lizzy managed a "thanks" and then went outside to wait for Cathy. She plopped down on the curb and stared at her cell phone, willing it to ring.

Monday, February 22, 2010 4:11 p.m.

By the time Lizzy hung up the phone after updating Jared, Cathy pulled up to the curb. Lizzy climbed into the passenger seat.

"What happened to your forehead?"

"It's a long story," Lizzy said. "Let's get to the house and find Brittany."

Cathy pulled out of the parking lot and merged onto the main road. "She's not answering her phone," Cathy said. "Brittany always answers her phone."

"Jared is going to meet us at your house."

"It's him, isn't it? Spiderman. He has her, doesn't he?"

Lizzy couldn't think. Her mind was a big fat blank. He couldn't have Brittany. That statement did not compute.

"This is my fault," Cathy said as she stepped on the gas.

"No. This is not your fault," Lizzy said, her voice raised. "This is nobody's fault, dammit."

Cathy's fingers white-knuckled the steering wheel. "I never should have let her out of my sight. I should have moved in with Dad. I should have listened to you. You were right about Richard too. After I received a call telling me where I could find Richard and his mistress, I drove to the Hyatt and I waited for them. Sure enough, Richard came out of the elevator with that woman on his arm."

Lizzy's pulse quickened. "Who called you?"

The light turned red, but Cathy didn't notice right away. She slammed on the brakes. Tires squealed and Cathy's head jerked forward.

Lizzy's hands stopped her body from slamming into the front console. Once the car came to a stop, Cathy looked at Lizzy. "Are you OK?"

"I'm fine. Do you want me to drive?"

"No. We're almost there." The light turned green. Cathy pushed down hard on the accelerator.

Lizzy tightened her seat belt.

"Who do you think called me?" Cathy asked.

"The same man who hired me to follow Valerie Hunt. He wanted to get you out of the house and out of your usual routine."

Cathy sped up.

"Slow down. We won't be able to help Brittany if we're in the hospital."

Cathy slowed, but not nearly as much as Lizzy would have liked. Trees and houses swept by in a blur.

"What if he has her, Lizzy? What will we do?"

"She'll be home," Lizzy told her. "She has to be at home."

Cathy made a sharp right at the stop sign. She sped down the residential street, finally slowing when she spotted a child throwing a ball to a dog. She pulled the car into the driveway and came to a screeching halt. Cathy shot out of the car and made her way to the house before Lizzy could unbuckle her seat belt.

Lizzy climbed out and took a look around. The air was crisp, colder than usual. Smoke spiraled from more than one chimney in the neighborhood. The government-issued sedan was parked across the street. She wanted to talk to the agent, ask him if he'd seen anybody at the house. Ronald Holt sat in the front seat reading a newspaper.

At closer view, she noticed something odd about the way his head was angled to one side. And then she saw blood and her only thought was that it was over. He had won. Spiderman had gotten what he wanted. He knew her all right. He knew the only way to destroy her was to destroy those closest to her.

Ronald Holt's skin was ash gray. His neck had been sliced clean through. Blood had oozed from his wound and onto his newspaper. She opened the passenger door, leaned toward him, and put her thumb and fingers around his wrist, checking for a pulse. Nothing. He was dead. She shut the door and moved quickly toward the house, keeping a steady pace as she pulled her phone from her pocket and crossed the street. Her hands shook. Her body too. Before she could call Jared, her phone rang.

"Lizzy—"

"Brittany! Thank God! We've been looking all over for you." She put a hand to her chest. "Where are you?"

"I'm scared, Lizzy."

The front door was wide open. Lizzy could see her sister rushing through the house.

Brittany's voice was small and frightened. Lizzy sank to her knees right there on the sidewalk. "He has you?"

"Please help me, Lizzy."

"Is he there with you now?"

"Yes."

She had to think fast. "Where are you?"

"I'm—"

Brittany's voice was cut off. Someone was still on the line. He could hear every word. "Brittany," she said.

"Yes," a small voice answered.

Lizzy talked fast. "Talk to him, Brittany. You must talk to him. Distract him. Talk about everything, anything. Don't stop talking until I can find—"

Click. Silence. No!

Cathy was hovering over her. Her sister's eyes were wide, her face pale. She reached for Lizzy's phone. "Is that Brittany? Can I talk to her?"

The phone dropped from Lizzy's hand and onto the lawn. "He has her. Oh God, Cathy, he has our Brittany."

CHAPTER 35

Monday, February 22, 2010 6:14 p.m.

The crime scene had been taped off and a half dozen law enforcement agencies scoured the grounds surrounding Cathy and Richard Warner's house. Ronald Holt's vehicle was being checked for fingerprints. His body had been bagged and taken to the lab for analysis.

Jimmy Martin was inside the house asking Cathy questions about Brittany, about her friends and her hobbies. Brittany's room was being examined for clues. It didn't take them long to discover that Brittany had been spending a lot of time on the Internet.

"I have no idea who i2Hotti might be," Cathy said. Her eyes and nose were red and blotchy from crying. She was sitting on the couch rocking back and forth when Richard shot through the door, demanding to know what was going on.

He marched up to Lizzy and wagged a finger in her face. "What the hell did you do with my daughter?"

"Ease up," Jared warned.

"Who are you?"

Jared flashed his badge.

"Spiderman has Brittany," Cathy said from across the room.

Richard lifted a fist as if he was about to take a shot at Lizzy. Jared took hold of Richard's wrist and twisted his arm around his back. "Are you going to calm down or am I going to have to cuff you?"

"I'm sorry," he said.

After a moment Jared released him. Defeated, Richard made his way to the couch and took a seat next to Cathy. "Will somebody please tell me what's going on?"

Tuesday, February 23, 2010 1:15 a.m.

Brittany opened her eyes. Everything in the room looked unfamiliar and blurry. She blinked, hoping the dizziness and nausea would pass.

"Are you awake?"

Brittany's heart raced as she tried to zero in on the voice and where it was coming from.

"I'm down here."

Disoriented, it took Brittany a moment to recall bits and pieces of her day. This morning, she had asked her mom for a note to let the school know she would be leaving ten minutes early for her orthodontist appointment. Then she had changed the time on the note and left school an hour earlier so she would have time to meet with i2Hotti. Her plan was to leave her mom a message, telling her that her braces were fine after all, and they could cancel the appointment. Nobody would be the wiser.

But nothing had gone as planned.

Instead of her dream boy, Brittany had been surprised to see Dr. McMullen pull up to the curb. He rolled down the window and told her to hop in. When Brittany hesitated, he said her mom had called his office to say she would be late, so Dr. McMullen had offered to pick Brittany up himself. None of it had made much sense at the time. If Mom had called him, why was he so early? And how could she tell her orthodontist she was waiting for a boy? Her only choice was to go with him.

Still, she'd been reluctant to get into his car. He was a stranger, wasn't he? But if she didn't go with him, Mom would be angry and probably ground her for life. Then her computer would be taken away and she'd never meet i2Hotti.

Noticing her reluctance to get into his car, Dr. McMullen told her to call her mom, which she did, but there was no answer. She called Dad next, but again no answer. So Brittany climbed inside his SUV and put on a seat belt.

Besides, he wasn't really a stranger. And her mom liked him. A lot.

She hadn't worried after that…not until Dr. McMullen passed the road they needed to take to get to his office. That's when she knew something weird was going on. The last thing she remembered was coming to a stop and seeing the white cloth in his hand right before he shoved it over her nose and mouth and held tight.

"Can you hear me?"

Brittany lifted her chin. She had dozed off again. "Yes," she said. "I can't see very well. Everything's blurry." Brittany tried to move her arms, but her wrists were held in metal cuffs stuck to the wall. She tried to pull free, but it was no use. She saw movement on the floor in front of her. "Is that you on the floor?"

"Keep your voice down. The man who took you is a nut case. I think I heard the front door open a moment ago, but I'm not sure. If he knows you're awake, he might come in here to check."

"Are you bleeding?" Brittany asked the girl.

"Do bears shit in the woods?"

"Oh."

"Yes, I'm bleeding. If he comes back," she whispered, "shut your eyes and let your head slump forward so he'll think you're still passed out."

"Why? What will he do?"

"Who knows? He's a sick bastard, that's for sure. You're not afraid of spiders, are you?"

"A little."

"That sucks. I hate to be the bearer of bad news, but if you act afraid he'll just keep doing whatever it is that scares you. He feeds on fear."

Brittany tried to wriggle her arms free again, but it was no use. The metal bands were fastened to the wall by thick chains on each side of her. As her vision improved, she noticed one of the fasteners loosen from the wall. She tugged harder. Crumbs of sheetrock fell to the ground.

"What are you doing?" the girl asked.

"Trying to get out of here." Brittany looked at the girl and gasped. The girl was naked. Her arms and legs were tied with ropes fastened to metal hooks in the floor. Her legs were spread wide, her hands tied above her head in a Y. There was blood everywhere.

Brittany squeezed her eyes shut and tried not to barf. Reddish blotches covered the girl's stomach, legs, and arms. Tears trickled down Brittany's face.

What had he done to the girl? Did Dr. McMullen do that? Or someone else? Her gaze focused on the girl's hand. "Did he cut off your finger?"

"Yeah. He didn't like my tattoo." Hayley gestured toward the wall where the sheetrock had crumbled. "Is that screw loose?"

Brittany wiggled her arm again. The sheetrock crumbled some more.

"Do you think you can break loose from the wall?"

"I don't know," Brittany said. "Maybe. I'm afraid I'll make too much noise if I pull too hard." She didn't want to see the man who had done these horrible things. *Why was she so stupid? Why had she gotten into his car?*

"Just keep doing what you're doing for as long as you can," the girl said. "What about your other arm?"

Brittany tried to move her other arm. It was no use. Nothing happened.

"One arm might be enough. If you can break free, you can use the chain to strangle him."

"I don't think I'm strong enough to do that."

"It's amazing what you can do when you set your mind to it. He's a crazy bastard and he's going to kill us if you don't. Just remember that. Besides, he's injured. You can do this. I know you can."

Tuesday, February 23, 2010 1:31 a.m.

Jared picked up his phone on the first ring.

The woman on the other end said hello. She said her name was Karen, the tipster who had called the FBI to say she thought her brother might be the killer.

"Is this Jared Shayne?"

"This is him."

"I need you to meet me at fifty-four sixteen Wise Road in Auburn. Take Interstate Eighty to Ophir, then make a left on Wise Road."

Jared swallowed his frustration. "There are two girls missing. We need a name, Karen."

"Please come quickly."

She ended the call, and Jared had no choice but to check it out. Unable to sleep, he'd been driving around. The car was one of the places where he did a lot of thinking. He pulled over and shuffled through the glove compartment for his portable navigator. Pictures fell from an envelope and onto the passenger seat, pictures his sister had given him months ago. He glanced at a few of the photos taken at a family reunion years ago, then grabbed the navigator, logged in the address Karen had given him, and headed for Auburn. The night was cold; the streets were empty. He grabbed the photo on top and gave it a closer look before returning his gaze to the road. In the picture, his parents stood tall behind Jared and his sister. Everyone looked happy, everyone except his mother.

His phone rang again. This time it was Jessica, Lizzy's assistant. Two o'clock in the morning and suddenly everyone wanted to talk. "What's going on?"

"Do you know where Lizzy is? I've been trying to get a hold of her."

"She's staying at her sister's house. It's a little early for phone calls, or late depending on how you look at it. Where are you?"

"I'm still in the hospital. The doctors won't sign a release yet. I wanted to talk to Lizzy, but she's not answering her phone. That's odd, don't you think?"

"Jessica."

"Yes?"

"Go to sleep. I'll be seeing Lizzy in a few hours. I'll make sure she calls you."

Jessica didn't respond, but he could hear her breathing. "Jessica, please stay put. I don't need any more missing people, all right?"

"OK," she finally said. "But please call me the moment you hear something."

Fifteen minutes later, Jared pulled his car into the driveway at the address Karen had given him. The neighborhood was upscale: every house color coordinated, complete with flagstone walkways and tranquil water features. He stepped out into the chill air. The brightness of the moon provided enough light to see unread newspapers piled around the garbage canisters. The lawn was green and well manicured. The front door was open. A woman stood there, holding a cloth over her nose.

"I'm Karen," she said as she lowered the cloth and offered her hand. "Thanks for coming."

He shook her hand and followed her inside. The cloth over her face suddenly made sense. The stench was overpowering.

"Is this your house?"

She shook her head. "As far as I know this is where my brother used to live."

"You're not sure?"

"I haven't seen him since I left for college over twenty years ago."

"That's a long time."

"Yes."

"Where is your brother now?"

"I don't know. I live in Italy with my husband and kids. I came to the States to find him."

"Why?"

Her gaze fell to the floor. "I wanted to apologize to him for something that happened a very long time ago…when Sam was only ten."

"Is that your brother's name? Sam?"

She nodded. "Samuel Jones. His wife is Cynthia."

He heard sirens in the distance.

"After I called you, I called the police."

"Mind if I look around?"

"Go ahead," she said with a subtle flick of her wrist. "I was here days ago. I looked around but didn't find anything. I figured the stench was from a dead rodent. At least until I saw the sketch of the killer on the front page of the *Sacramento Bee*."

"And then what changed?"

"I recognized the man in the picture. That's when I knew the killer was my brother and that the smell in his house wasn't because of a dead rodent at all."

"What's causing the smell, Karen?"

"Cynthia. I'm guessing he killed his wife, but I don't know where he put the body."

She followed him from room to room as he searched under beds and in closets. The smell was strongest at the end of the hall. He looked up at the outline of an access door leading to the attic, and that's when he knew exactly where Cynthia's body had been hidden.

Tuesday, February 23, 2010 2:14 a.m.

"Lizzy! Let me in!"

This was it. It was now or never.

Lizzy's heart thumped hard against her chest. Her time was running out. If she was going to escape, it was now or never.

She jumped from the edge of the tub to the window ledge. It was no simple jump. She was small, thin, and weak, but she had made it. Her arms burning, her legs pumping, her feet pushing and then slipping and sliding against the tile wall as she tried to squeeze her body through the ridiculously small window.

The door rattled. No. Not yet. He was coming.

Her heart pounded against her chest. She was never going to make it. The thumps against the door grew louder, stronger. She was almost there, halfway out the window, but what was that ringing?

Lizzy jolted awake. It took her a moment to find her cell phone under the covers. She flipped open her phone. She'd fallen asleep in Brittany's bed. Remnants of her dream clung to her foggy brain as she held the phone to her ear.

"We found his house, Lizzy. The house belonging to Samuel Jones."

"Thank God."

"Apparently he was married. He killed his wife, stabbed once in the heart, left her to rot in the attic. I'm at the house now."

"What about Hayley and Brittany? Are they there?"

"I'm sorry, Lizzy. Nobody else is here, and we haven't been able to trace Samuel Jones to a place of work or any other address. I'm working on it," Jared said. "I have to go. I'll call you when I'm done here."

Lizzy hung up the phone. She had to do something. She'd fallen asleep fully dressed. She grabbed her coat from the chair in front of Brittany's desk. Her phone vibrated, which meant she had a text: "Meet me at the corner of Granite and Third Street in ten minutes. No car. No one else is to know you've left the house. Come alone or your niece is dead."

Spiderman was texting her.

How far away was Third Street from her sister's house? Lizzy went to the window. Two unmarked cars were parked out front.

She grabbed pencil and paper and scribbled a quick note. Time was running out. She took quiet steps down the stairs. Somebody was in the kitchen. She made it out the back door in under two minutes. Eight minutes left.

CHAPTER 36

Tuesday, February 23, 2010 2:27 a.m.

Lizzy stood on the corner of Third Street, her hands propped on her knees as she caught her breath. Through the fog she saw approaching headlights. She couldn't see the color or make of the car, but she knew it was him. He stopped the vehicle in front of her. She didn't hesitate to open the door and climb inside. There was nothing she wouldn't do to save her niece, and he knew that.

"It's been a long time, Lizzy."

"Not long enough." She looked to the backseat. Nobody was there. "Where's Brittany?"

"Patience, my dear. First we'll take a little drive…make sure we're not being followed."

"Nobody saw me leave."

"I'll be the judge of that." He kept the SUV at a steady thirty-five miles per hour.

She pulled out a gun, released the safety, and rested her finger on the trigger. Then she raised the barrel to his head.

He smiled. "Give me the gun, Lizzy, or you'll never see Brittany again."

"You're going to take me to her and then I'm going to—"

He jerked the steering wheel hard to the right, causing Lizzy to slam into his side. Then he hit the brakes and grabbed the gun from her in one fluid motion.

What the hell had just happened? He looked at her as a father might look at a child who refused to obey and said, "Put your seat belt on, Lizzy."

"If you've hurt her, I'll kill you."

He smiled. Tonight, other than one brief moment fourteen years ago, was the first time Lizzy had seen him without any disguise. No beard, no wigs, no mask. "Sam Jones," she said, angry at herself for being so damn stupid. She'd lost her chance at gaining control. She should have shot him the moment he opened the door, but then what? She wouldn't have been any closer to finding Brittany. They knew his name, but they had no idea where he was keeping the girls.

He laughed at her as if the name Sam Jones meant nothing to him, as if the name disgusted him.

"Shannon Winter's parents were right. You killed their daughter, didn't you?"

"I did no such thing. The stupid girl choked on her favorite candy. That's no fault of mine."

"But you watched her die. How could you stand by and watch a loved one die?"

"I didn't love her."

"Of course you did."

His body stiffened.

"You were madly in love with her, but for some reason you stood there and watched her die when you could have saved her life. What happened?"

"When Shannon died," he said, "when her face turned reddish blue, the only face I saw was Trish's." He sighed. "No, that's not entirely true. I also saw Julia's face and Lisa's and Karen's."

"Girlfriends?"

"My sister and her friends," he said without any emotion.

"Why did you hate them so much?"

"Let's just say they deserved to die. They needed to die."

"You killed them all?"

"Not all of them. And not my sister. She was too far away, so I had to send her news clippings and such to let her know her friends were all dying, dropping like flies around me."

"Nobody deserves to die."

"Trust me, Lizzy. Each and every one of those girls deserved what they got." It was quiet for a moment before he shook his head as if he were trying to get rid of images running through his mind. "You just don't do those things to a ten-year-old boy."

"What did they do to you, Sam?"

"I'm done talking about it."

"What was it about their eyes that made you do the things you did?"

"Let's just say I didn't appreciate the way they looked at me. I deserve respect. In fact, I demand it."

Within minutes, he exited the freeway.

She recognized the neighborhood. They weren't too far from the Walker house, the house she'd thought was the house of horrors. "It helps to talk about things."

He smiled as he hit the remote at his side, as if he knew she was trying to keep him off guard by striking up a conversation. They hadn't driven far, but they were already pulling into a garage. She reached for the door handle, jiggling it before she realized he'd locked it from the inside. The garage door closed behind them. He turned off the engine, and as she thought about what her next step would be, he plunged a needle into her arm.

Tuesday, February 23, 2010 4:16 a.m.

Immediately after Cathy Warner called Jared to tell him Lizzy was missing, he left the crime scene in Auburn. Samuel Jones was their man, and yet it appeared the man did not exist. His driver's license information had been logged into every possible database, but his name came up clean. Karen Crowley insisted her brother was in the medical field, and yet state records showed no license information for Samuel Jones, which meant he had a second identity.

Karen Crowley had no idea where her brother might be. Guilt and shame had brought her back to the States to make amends. Decades ago, she had been entrusted by her parents to take care of her younger brother, Sam. Something horrible had happened while their parents were gone, but Karen wasn't willing to say anything more than that. She wanted a lawyer before she would agree to say another word.

Cynthia, Sam Jones's wife, the only other person who might have been able to shed some light on what Sam had been up to over the past fourteen years, had been murdered and left to rot in the attic. The neighbors had known her as Cindi, but no one had ever said more than two words to Samuel Jones. Apparently, Cindi and Sam had kept to themselves.

As Jared pulled out of the driveway and clicked on his earpiece, his phone rang.

"It's me again…Jessica."

Jared focused on the road, eager to get to Lizzy's apartment where he hoped to find her. Unable to sleep, she must have gone to her office or to her apartment to do some investigating of her own.

"Sorry to bother you again," Jessica said, "but the more I thought about it the more I realized I should at least tell you why I was trying to find Lizzy in the first place."

"OK, shoot."

"Before I called you earlier, I received a call from Sophie Madison's mom. I was going to wait until morning to tell Lizzy, but I won't be able to sleep until I tell someone what Mrs. Madison said."

"Mrs. Madison called you that early in the morning?"

"She doesn't sleep much these days."

Understandable, he thought.

"I told her to call anytime she needed to talk. She likes me to keep her posted on what's going on with the case, so that's what I try to do."

"Tell me what's on your mind, Jessica."

"Remember when you mentioned the other day that Sophie Madison wasn't wearing braces when they found her body?"

"I remember."

"Well, as I was talking to Sophie's mother I happened to comment on how many of the missing girls had braces. She went on to tell me that Sophie had just gotten her braces put on two weeks before she was abducted. I didn't tell Mrs. Madison what you said about Sophie not having braces because I didn't want to upset her, but I thought you should know."

His jaw tightened. "Did you ask her who Sophie's doctor was?"

"I didn't have to. She just told me."

"Who is it, Jessica?"

"I thought I told you already. Sophie's orthodontist was Dr. McMullen, the same orthodontist Brittany Warner uses."

Tuesday, February 23, 2010 4:21 a.m.

The door creaked as it opened, prompting Hayley to shake her head at Brittany, letting her know now was a good time to pretend she was asleep.

Brittany clamped her eyes shut and bent her head low until her chin rested on her chest.

Spiderman peeked inside, his gaze settling on Brittany. After he stepped into the room, Hayley realized she was holding her breath. She prayed Brittany wouldn't twitch or give herself away. The iron manacle around Brittany's left wrist was still chained to the wall, but the hook was coming loose. They just needed a little more time.

He turned his gaze to Hayley. "You're still alive," he said.

"No shit, Sherlock."

"You think you're funny, don't you?"

"You know what they say. The more you laugh, the longer you live."

His gaze went to the knife on the table next to the bed. He'd left it there to irritate her, knowing she wouldn't be able to think about anything other than getting to the knife and slitting his throat.

"When our new little friend wakes up," he told her, "I'm going to teach her what happens to fools. After watching me carve you up like a Thanksgiving turkey she'll be the best-behaved girl in town."

"Don't forget the cranberry sauce."

"You're a wild one, aren't you?"

"And you're an asshole."

The corners of his mouth turned downward right before he marched across the room, his fingers curling into fists at his sides. Although he had a limp to his gait, and he was paler than before, he still had a lot of life to him. Shit. She'd gone overboard. He picked up the knife he'd taken from her the other day and clicked the button. The blade shot up, its sharp metal edge making her wish she'd kept her mouth shut for once. He usually laughed at her smartass comments, but tonight he seemed different—on edge, angry, and restless.

Usually his every move was cautious and purposeful, but not tonight. Instead of taking his anger out on her as she thought he would, he went to stand by Brittany.

"What are you doing?" she asked, hoping to calm him.

He put the sharp blade against Brittany's cheek, the tip of the blade sinking into her skin.

Hayley prayed Brittany would stay silent, but Brittany cried out. How could she not? Blood oozed from the wound.

"Thought you could fool me, didn't you?" He pointed at Hayley as he spoke. "Don't listen to a word that girl tells you. Not if you want to live."

Hayley watched Brittany's lip quiver. She wanted to tell Brittany to stay calm and take a deep breath, maybe count to ten, but she held her tongue. She'd already told the girl to show no fear. He fed on fear.

He grabbed a fistful of Brittany's hair and cut it off. She was trying so hard to be brave that Hayley had to bite down on her tongue to keep from begging him to stop. If she begged, things would only go from bad to worse.

He put the knife to Brittany's throat. "What do you think, Hayley? Do you want to watch her die today or would you rather lose another finger?"

"I think you should go fuck yourself."

He moved the blade slowly across Brittany's throat and down to her chest. He wasn't cutting her. He just wanted to scare them both. Tears rolled down Brittany's face.

"Look at her porcelain skin, Hayley." He continued to move the blade of the knife over her nose and across Brittany's chin, excitement showing in his eyes whenever she gasped or whimpered. "She's had a good life," he said. "She doesn't know what it's like to go to bed hungry. I bet she's never been fucked by her mother's boyfriend. Doesn't that bother you, Hayley?"

Hayley kept silent, gritting her teeth.

The tip of the knife trailed over Brittany's cheek. "Your mother wanted me. God, she wanted me bad, didn't she? You saw the look in her eyes when she brought you to my office."

Brittany spit, spraying saliva into his face and eyes.

He turned away to wipe his face with his sleeve.

Hayley laughed, not because she thought it was amusing but because she wanted to draw him away from the girl.

His face crimped into a maze of fury. "Shut up!"

Hayley didn't stop. She laughed louder and harder until finally he left Brittany and came to Hayley's side. He picked up her left hand and put the knife to her middle finger. "I think this finger should be the next to go, don't you?"

Brittany screamed.

Tuesday, February 23, 2010 4:26 a.m.

The minutes dragged by as he raced across town. Jared issued an APB on Dr. Samuel McMullen. Unfortunately the only address connected to Dr. McMullen was the house in Auburn where

Cindi had been left to die. The man was an orthodontist. Lizzy had talked about hearing drilling noises, and although many of his victims had worn braces, none of the victims were wearing braces when their bodies were found. Had the killer used drills to remove evidence pointing to Dr. McMullen?

Jared parked outside Lizzy's place, climbed out of his car, and ran up the stairs. The apartment was empty and dark. Every muscle tensed at the thought of Lizzy being with Spiderman. Jared walked through her living area and into the kitchen, looking for clues, a note, anything. He walked into her bedroom and picked up the scraggly, one-eyed stuffed animal lying on the middle of her bed. He couldn't bear the thought of losing Lizzy. Not again. Not ever.

His phone rang. It was his mother. She must have seen the news. Or maybe she was finally returning one of his half dozen calls from earlier. That was his mother in a nutshell. He couldn't remember a time when she'd been there when he'd needed her. Not once. But that didn't matter any longer. Nothing mattered except finding Lizzy.

It was nearly five in the morning by the time he arrived at Cathy and Richard Warner's house, which was buzzing with activity now that Lizzy had disappeared right under their noses. Richard sat on a couch, his hands wrapped around a mug of coffee. Cathy had greeted Jared at the door and then dragged him to her daughter's room where Lizzy had slept last night. She showed Jared a note Lizzy had left on the bed, half hidden beneath the pillow.

He said he would release Brittany if I went with him. I refuse to let him have Brittany.

Spiderman had called Lizzy and made her a deal, Jared realized. Lizzy for Brittany. Of course Lizzy would have agreed to the exchange. The way her mind worked, she had no other choice. But neither Lizzy nor Brittany had returned home, which meant Lizzy had been betrayed. Had she expected Spiderman to keep his word?

Unable to stand there with nothing to do but gaze at the pleading look in Cathy's eyes, Jared told her he would do all he could to find them. Then he left the house.

He was on the freeway, driving fast, before he realized where he was going. He thought about using his LED dash light once his speedometer hit eighty, but then decided against calling any unwanted attention to himself. In less than six minutes, he exited the freeway and drove over the Sacramento River. He had to follow his instincts. It was all he had left. Spiderman's sister had no idea where they might be able to find her brother. What had she and her friends done to a little boy all those years ago?

He stopped the car in front of the Walkers' house where the excavation had taken place last week. It was still early and it was cold. Not even the crickets were out tonight.

He left his car and stopped in front of the Walker house to take a look around. He stood at the same curb where he and Lizzy had waited for backup. Lizzy had told him on more than one occasion that she was sure Spiderman had been watching her that day. Jared peered across the street where the elderly woman had watched them from her kitchen window.

The neighborhood was like any other neighborhood: row after row of single-family homes, most of them built in the seventies or eighties. Many with families and young children. Houses in varying degrees of preservation.

His gaze wandered from house to house. Lizzy had said that after she escaped, she looked to her right in order to try to see the house from which she'd escaped, but she'd been blinded by the rising sun.

Jared stepped into the middle of the street, turning about so that his right side faced the east. If she had looked to her right to see the house she'd just escaped from, and the rising sun had blinded her, then that would mean the Walker house was on the wrong side of the street.

It was dark out. Jared began walking down the middle of the street. A dog barked in the distance. The moonlight threw shadows across his path. There were more than a dozen houses on the other side of the street, six or seven of which had a decent view of the Walker house. If Lizzy was right about being watched that day, then he was close. Tonight, though, close might not be good enough. Spiderman might have seen the news that they had found his dead wife. An APB had been issued in the names of Samuel Jones and Dr. Sam McMullen. He was running out of time. They all were. His phone vibrated, and he opened it without looking at the caller ID.

"Jared, I need to talk to you."

He kept walking. "Mom, not now."

"Jared, don't hang up."

He readied his gun.

He couldn't hear past her sobbing. He gritted his teeth, ready to toss the phone in the bushes. "What do you want to tell me? The world doesn't revolve around you and your problems." Guilt might very well creep up to bite him in the ass later, Jared knew, but right now he didn't give a damn. He'd had enough of his parents' antics. Grow up. Get a life. He was about to hang up when his mother said, "I think I know where you can find Dr. McMullen."

"Why? How?" She made no sense.

"He's the man I told your father about, the man I've been see-ing. Recently he stopped returning my calls. So I waited for him to leave his office the other day and I followed him."

CHAPTER 37

Tuesday, February 23, 2010 4:32 a.m.

Lizzy opened her eyes.

Darkness. Pitch black. She couldn't see a thing. He'd done his homework. If there were any windows, they had been covered well. She could feel her throat closing, making it hard to breathe. *Don't panic, Lizzy*. If she wanted to help Brittany and Hayley, then she needed to stay calm.

Death.

The room smelled like death. Her arms were tied behind her back just like old times. That son of a bitch. She fought with the ropes, pissed off, but then it dawned on her. He thought he knew her so well and yet he still didn't know she could dislocate her shoulder the way other people could crack their knuckles. If he'd known, he would not have tied her the way he did. If she could dislocate her shoulder, she could catch him off guard.

She listened for a moment. Her head hurt. Intense pain rippled through her skull. Whatever Spiderman had pumped through her veins had put her out in a matter of seconds. Although her eyes were adjusting to the darkness, her vision was hazy at best. She looked around the room. White walls and beige carpet, stacks of cardboard boxes.

Had nothing changed?

Spiders and centipedes climbed on top of one another, trying to escape from their glass cage. One blink of her eyes and the bugs disappeared.

Knives and needles, drilling sounds, and endless torture threatened to break her focus. What had he given her?

Swallowing, she shut her eyes and concentrated on getting untangled from the ropes. Dislocating her shoulder would take focus. Could she still manage it? The door opened before she could answer the question.

He stood there…watching her.

So many things she wanted to shout at him: he was going to hell; he was evil; he'd never get away with this. Instead, she said nothing. He entered the room. Without a word, he grabbed her and pulled her to her feet. Since her feet were tied at the ankles, she hobbled alongside him as he dragged her through the house. He stopped at the room at the end of the hallway, the room where she'd found Mary so long ago.

He opened the door.

Lizzy bit her tongue to stop from crying out. Brittany was fastened to manacles chained to the wall while Hayley was tied to hooks on the ground. Poor Hayley—bloodied and naked, the pinky finger on one hand sliced clean off. "Hayley," she said, wondering if she was still alive.

He forced her to sit in a wooden chair set up just for her. A true gentleman. She knew the drill. Brittany's face was bruised, her lip and the right side of her face cut and bleeding.

The man was going to die. "Let them go," Lizzy said, her voice flat, "and I'll do whatever you want."

Spiderman stood between Hayley and Brittany. He shook his head, smiling. No mask. No robotic voice. "Lizzy, Lizzy. How many times have I heard that before?"

"Just let them go."

"Did you really think for one moment I would let you go? Everyone must pay for your lies, Lizzy. You're a liar." He pulled a switchblade from his pocket and waved the knife in front of Brittany's face.

Lizzy screamed at the top of her lungs, moving the chair up and down, making as much noise as possible, prompting him to come at her instead. He used the back of his hand to knock her in the side of the face.

Brittany sobbed, her tears mixing with the blood oozing from the gash on her cheek.

"Why are you doing this?" Lizzy asked. "Why couldn't you just leave us alone?"

He let out a hearty laugh. "You don't know?"

Hayley's arm moved. She was alive.

Lizzy needed to keep him busy, keep him talking. Keep him away from Brittany and Hayley.

He moved the knife over Lizzy's forehead, stopping every inch or so to pierce her skin with the tip of the blade. "You promised me you would stay with me forever," he said. "I believed you, Lizzy. I loved you as I would have loved my own daughter."

"Leave them alone and I'll go with you now. We can start over. I never should have left you. I've missed you—"

His laughter bounced off the walls, cutting her off before she could finish her sentence. His eyes appeared dark and vacant as he tapped the blade of the knife against the tip of her nose as if he were deciding what to cut off first. Blood oozed down her forehead and into the corner of her right eye.

"I have a surprise for you," he said excitedly before he disappeared from the room.

"Brittany," Lizzy said, talking fast. "You have to be brave." She had so much more she wanted to say, but there wasn't time.

"Hayley."

Hayley opened her eyes. "I'm all ears."

Lizzy was filled with relief at hearing Hayley speak. "I need you both to make noise while I dislocate my arm so I can loosen these ropes. He won't know what I'm up to when he comes back. He'll think we're trying to attract attention from the neighbors. Now!"

They didn't need to be told twice. Brittany screamed at the top of her lungs while Hayley shouted obscenities, drowning out any noise Lizzy made as she used the floor to knock her shoulder out of its socket, crying out in pain as she did so. She hadn't dislocated her arm in years. The pain wasn't anything like she remembered. It was much worse.

Spiderman rushed into the room just as Lizzy managed to wriggle back onto the wooden chair. He was clearly annoyed by the racket they were making, and he quickly shut the door behind him. "Quiet," he said, "or I'll cut all your tongues out. You know I will, Lizzy."

In a gloved hand, he brought forth one of his beloved spiders. "Now that we have an audience, I'd like to show Brittany one of my prized possessions."

"Leave her alone."

"This isn't just any spider, Lizzy. This is a prized Australian funnel-web spider, the most poisonous spider in the world." He dangled the spider above Hayley's face as he made his way to Brittany.

For years Lizzy had thought the worst was behind her. But she'd been wrong. She'd never felt so helpless in her life. She should have called Jared on her way to meet Spiderman. He would have done the right thing. He wouldn't have called in the troops and risked Brittany's life. He was a good man. But there hadn't been enough time to think things through.

Spiderman held the spider inches from Brittany's face. It was a glossy, hairless, black thing. Lizzy bit her lip and shook her head, letting Brittany know she needed to stay calm, say nothing. And yet the crazed look she'd seen in his eyes told her Spiderman was on a mission and nothing was going to stop him.

"You didn't deserve what you got from your sister and her friends," Lizzy said in desperation. "Trish and Julia and what was her name? Oh yes, Lisa. They deserve to rot in hell for what they did to you. I know what they did, Sam. I know about your parents and how your father never paid any attention to you. You didn't deserve to be treated that way."

It was working. He turned to face Lizzy.

"Put the spider away," Lizzy said. "Let them go. Everyone knows why you've done the things you've done. They understand. They'll forgive you as I've forgiven you."

His lip curled into a sneer.

"Now, Brittany!" Hayley shouted. "Do it now!"

Brittany's arm swung away from the wall. The thick chain broke away from the metal ring and whipped Spiderman in the face. The spider dropped from his hand. He covered his face with both hands and screamed in agony.

Lizzy struggled to get free from the ropes. She needed more time. Lizzy saw Brittany struggling to release her other arm from the manacle but realized it was no use.

Spiderman fell to his knees. He removed his hands from his bloodied face and pointed an accusing finger at Lizzy. "She almost had me there, didn't she? Guess who's going to die first?"

Lizzy used her free arm to untangle one knot and then another. Endless knots. Spiderman was coming out of his stupor, and his face, she noticed, wasn't the only part of his body that had been injured. Even in the car he'd looked pale. He'd obviously lost a lot of blood, which meant Hayley must have put up a good fight.

He got to his feet, then stumbled to the bedside table and shuffled around inside the drawer until he realized the knife he was looking for was lying on the end of the bed.

Another knot came free.

The man was unstoppable.

Just like Lizzy.

She pulled free.

Using every ounce of dead weight, every bit of strength she could summon, she lunged for him. They crashed to the floor, Lizzy on top, their combined bulk barely missing Hayley, who didn't move. Spiderman lifted himself from the floor, and suddenly, as if he was the Hulk, he picked Lizzy up and tossed her to the side.

Brittany kicked and screamed as Spiderman approached her. Clearly she was done staying calm. She'd had all she could handle.

Lizzy hadn't had time to push her shoulder back into place. Her arm hung limp at her side. The pain was excruciating. If she had more time, she would bend her elbow to a ninety-degree angle and then use her other arm to coax her shoulder into place. But this wasn't Disneyland. She made a fist instead, used her good hand to hold onto her bad arm, and slammed her dislocated shoulder into the floor. White-hot pain shot through every nerve ending.

Lizzy turned toward Brittany just as Spiderman lunged forward with his knife. Lizzy screamed, unable to stop him.

A shot rang out at close range.

Jared stood beneath the doorframe, gun aimed, ready to fire a second shot.

Spiderman fell forward. Brittany used both legs, bent at the knees, to kick him off her, sending him staggering backward onto the floor.

"Brittany!" Lizzy cried out.

After checking Spiderman for weapons, Jared dragged him unconscious across the room and cuffed his wrists behind his back to the bedpost.

Lizzy untied the ropes from her ankles while Jared made his way to Brittany. Free from the ropes, Lizzy stripped the bedcover from the bed and covered Hayley's body. She knelt down beside her, thankful to see that she was breathing. "Hayley," she said. "Don't you dare think about leaving us."

"I'm not going anywhere," Hayley said, her voice weak.

Relieved, Lizzy worked on getting Hayley untied.

"Tell your boyfriend the keys to the manacles are in the dresser drawer."

After he had freed Brittany, Jared helped Lizzy cut Hayley's bindings.

Lizzy and Brittany held onto one another while Jared swooped Hayley, blanket and all, into his arms.

Lizzy brushed the hair from Brittany's face so she could take a good look at her. Despite the nasty cut on her cheek, her niece was going to make it out of here alive.

Brittany stopped Jared at the door. She looked at Hayley, trying not to cry as she said, "You saved my life. Thank you."

"You saved your own life," Hayley said.

The sound of sirens grew close. Jared gestured with his chin for Lizzy to take the gun from his holster. "Keep an eye on him while I take care of Hayley. She's lost a lot of blood."

"Go with Jared," Lizzy told Brittany. She didn't want Brittany in the same room with the man. He was still alive.

Brittany looked from Samuel Jones to Lizzy, hesitating.

"Now," Lizzy said. "Call your mother. She needs to hear your voice."

Brittany nodded and then disappeared through the same door Jared had just exited.

Lizzy kept the gun pointed at Samuel Jones. He didn't deserve to be called Spiderman. He was no superhero. He was a killer, a man without a conscience.

Samuel Jones lifted his head.

Before she knew what he was up to, he pushed himself to his feet, easily pulling the wooden bedpost from its holding.

"Stay where you are," she said, the gun aimed at his chest, her hands shaking.

Although his hands were cuffed behind his back, he was now free to move about. He'd been badly injured even before Jared shot him, and yet he still managed to get to his feet.

"You've always been too soft," he said when she failed to fire the gun.

"Stay where you are or I'll shoot."

"Why did you lie?" he asked.

"Because I wanted to live." She took a step backward toward the door. "Why did you kill those girls?"

"I told you. They were menaces to society."

"They were kids. It's not easy being a teenager. You haven't done anyone any favors. You're no hero, Sam."

He took another step toward her, and that's when she saw his beloved spider climbing over the stiff outer collar of his blood-ied button-down shirt. The arachnid must have crawled on him when he was on the floor cuffed to the bedpost.

"I'm warning you. One more step and I will shoot."

"I know your worst fears. I know everything about you. I had so many plans for you. You have no idea."

"You're a sick, disgusting man. And you don't know me at all."

"I know you better than anyone, Lizzy. And I know you won't shoot me," he said. "They may put me behind bars, but this isn't the end. I can promise you that."

He stepped closer. The spider disappeared inside his shirt. "Give me the gun, Lizzy."

"I might not have to shoot you after all," she told him. "Not if your Australian friend gets you first."

He caught her meaning and looked around, unsure if she was telling the truth or not. Agitated, he pivoted and then stopped cold. Their eyes met, and that's when Lizzy knew he'd been bitten. He winced. And then his eyes grew round with shock and fear, perhaps even with pain.

He'd been right about one thing, Lizzy thought. She wasn't sure if she would have shot him. She'd wanted to. She'd felt the trigger beneath her finger, cold and deadly, but she hadn't been able to do it. She wondered if he'd been right about her all along.

Lizzy watched him struggle to find the spider, no easy task with his hands behind his back. She hoped she was looking at Samuel Jones for the last time. He didn't look like a serial killer. He didn't look like a killer at all. He looked normal, like someone you might pass on the street without notice. A man turned evil by chance. A man who lived and worked in their community and who had single-handedly taken the lives of too many girls…girls who deserved a chance to mature and grow…girls who would have learned from their mistakes and made a difference in the world just by being in it.

Every part of Samuel Jones began to twitch, including his tongue. Not a pretty picture. Saliva covered his bottom lip, and a thick sheen of sweat formed over his brow. "Help me," he said as he fell to his knees.

But Lizzy had already left the room.

CHAPTER 38

Sacramento, California
Sunday, March 21, 2010 2:00 p.m.

"Mary was my sister and my best friend," Jessica told the crowd, comprised of family and friends, but mostly strangers, people who had lived in the community for decades. People who wanted to see Mary put to rest so that they too could move on, knowing their children were safer now that Samuel Jones was dead.

"She was the kind of friend everybody should have. Mary and I used to play on the swings at the park and make grandiose plans for the future. We were going to travel, learn new languages, and explore the world together. There wasn't anything we couldn't do. We had our whole lives ahead of us." She paused to wipe a tear. "Unfortunately, Mary was taken from me and my family too soon. But let's not be sad. Not today. Mary wouldn't want us to be sad. She was the happiest person I've ever known. Look around you," Jessica said, holding her arms wide. "It's a beautiful March day and we are here to celebrate Mary's life. I am going to remember her smile, her laughter, and her dreams. I am going to return to school, learn a new language, and get my degree. Afterward, I will travel and explore the world. And everywhere I go Mary will be right there with me because I will carry her in my heart and I will never forget her. Never."

Lizzy stood at the front of the crowd. Jessica's gaze locked on hers, and Lizzy smiled at her new friend, thankful that Jimmy and his team had located Mary's body along with three other girls buried in Samuel Jones's backyard.

Last week, Jared had spoken with the associate dean for undergraduate studies at CSU, and after explaining Jessica's situation, the dean had agreed to give her another chance. She would be returning to school in the fall.

Today's memorial was being held outside at the Sierra Hills Memorial Park on Greenback Lane in Sacramento. The air was warm for this time of year, the sky a deep blue brushed with a few strokes of ivory. Mature oaks and sixty-foot sycamores dotted the seventy acres of rolling hills.

For this memorial, Lizzy thought, the Sacramento community had come together. People were showing their compassion by giving generously to the Mary Crawford Fund, allowing Jessica and her family to give Mary a proper burial.

Samuel Jones's name would not be mentioned today. Two days after Samuel Jones died, his older sister, Karen Crowley, finally told her story. A young Samuel Jones had been tortured by his sister's friends, two of which had since died under peculiar circumstances. After Karen's parents had left for vacation, leaving Karen in charge of her younger brother, she and her friends had drank, smoked weed, and snorted crack cocaine. After Sam threatened to call their parents, Karen's friends took Sam to the basement where they taped him to a chair, covered his eyes and mouth with duct tape, and poked him with cigarettes. But Karen hadn't realized what her friends had done until three days later when she picked up the telephone and called her brother's friend, thinking he was hiding out there. When Karen finally located Sam, he was a mess. Found on the floor, still fastened to the chair, he'd been bitten by a black widow. Karen knew this because when she found him the dead spider was clutched tight in his fist. Although Karen Crowley was clearly remorseful, she insisted no harm was intended. She was released and had already returned to her family in Europe.

Lizzy spotted Hayley in the distance. Hayley lifted her bandaged hand in acknowledgement, and Lizzy walked that way. It had been four weeks since Jared had come to their rescue. Hayley had burn marks on her arms, legs, neck, and face. Like Brittany, her hair had been cut short at weird angles, so Lizzy had paid a stylist to cut Hayley's hair in a short, sideswept haircut with a long, sweeping bang. Although Hayley wasn't the type of kid who liked to be gushed over, Lizzy didn't care. She slipped an arm around Hayley's side and gave her a long squeeze.

Cathy had offered to take Hayley into her home, grateful for all Hayley had done to keep Brittany safe. After much coercing, Hayley had agreed. "How did you get here?" Lizzy asked.

"Your sister let me take her car."

"Wow, she must really like you."

Hayley smiled, but she sounded sad when she said, "I guess I sort of got carried away, didn't I? Getting caught by that lunatic and then letting him get the best of me. I really thought I could take him out."

"You never should have put yourself in danger, Hayley, but you did good. You did real good."

"So did your niece. She's a tough kid—you know—for a cheerleader."

Lizzy nodded and couldn't help but think of how proud Cathy had sounded when she told Lizzy how well Brittany was doing in school and how Brittany had made the cheerleading squad. The side of Brittany's face had required nineteen stitches in all, but her wounds were healing nicely and the doctors said the scars would be hardly noticeable by year's end.

Cathy had also taken Brittany to talk with Linda Gates so Brittany could discuss what happened and also talk about her feelings about her parents' recent separation. With everyone's support, Lizzy felt confident Brittany would be able to move forward and go on to live a normal, healthy life.

Hayley gestured toward Jared, who had parked his car. He was running late after stopping by the hospital to visit Jimmy. Jimmy was having tests done after discovering he had cancer.

Jared looked exceptionally handsome in his dark suit and tie.

"Are you going to marry that guy?" Hayley asked.

"No, I don't think so." Lizzy tilted her head for a better look at him. "Besides, he hasn't asked me."

They shared knowing smiles before Lizzy quickly changed the subject. "I was wondering if you would be interested in traveling to schools across the country. Together the two of us could teach children everywhere how to defend themselves against the evils of the world."

"Sounds like a job for a superhero," Hayley said.

"Exactly."

Hayley rubbed her heavily bandaged hand. "I don't know. I'm not as courageous as I sometimes pretend to be."

Lizzy sighed. "Neither am I."

"I was really scared."

"I'm still scared."

"I'll think about it," Hayley said at last, and then she held up her bandaged hand. "But how will I ever play the piano again?"

Lizzy's face fell. "You play the piano?"

A twinkle lit up Hayley's eyes. "No. I'm just shittin' you."

Lizzy shook her head at the girl's off-the-wall humor.

"For the first time in my life," Hayley said, her voice serious, "I realized I wanted to live. How screwed up is that? Tortured by a madman and I suddenly want to live?" She huffed. "It doesn't make any sense."

"No," Lizzy agreed. "But if nothing else, it's kind of nice if all the bad can somehow make the good that much better."

"Yeah, I guess," she said as Jared approached. The three of them made small talk for a moment before Hayley said good-bye and headed for the parking lot.

"She's a trooper," Lizzy told Jared as they watched Hayley walk off.

"Yes, she is. Sorry I'm late," he added. "Looks like I missed Jessica's eulogy."

"She'll understand. She did a great job. How's Jimmy doing?"

"He starts chemo first thing in the morning. Prognosis is uncertain."

"That's a shame. I like Jimmy. And even if I didn't, I wouldn't wish cancer on anyone."

"I told him we'd drop by the hospital tonight."

Lizzy nodded as they weaved through the crowd to find Jessica. She knew Jared was having a hard time. Jimmy was his friend and mentor, and he was very sick. And then there were Jared's parents and their failing relationship. Although he hadn't said much about his parents' separation, she knew it was something that weighed heavily on his mind. Although Jared was an adult, Lizzy knew firsthand the effects of a split household and how it could make a person reevaluate and look at life a little differently.

They stopped a few feet from where Jessica and her brother were placing flowers at Mary's gravesite, giving them a chance to mourn privately.

"It's hard to believe it's finally over," Lizzy said to Jared.

Jared took her hand in his. "It's just the beginning, Lizzy. Just the beginning."

ACKNOWLEDGMENTS

I would like to thank every writer I ever met, online or off-line, who inspired and encouraged me along the way. Years ago I critiqued with Susan Crosby, Susan Grant, and Brenda Novak, not necessarily in that order and not all in one group, but I learned something from each of these writers, and I am thankful to have worked with them. I have also learned so much from various organizations and writers' groups including RWA, the Wet Noodle Posse, the Sacramento Valley Rose, and the Pixies Chicks. Thank you all.

ABOUT THE AUTHOR

T. R. Ragan grew up in a family of five girls in Lafayette, California. As an avid traveler, her wanderings have carried her to Ireland, the Netherlands, China, Thailand, and Nepal, where she narrowly survived being chased by a killer elephant. Before devoting herself to writing fiction, she worked as a legal secretary for a large corporation. She is the author of *Dead Weight*, the second Lizzy Gardner book. Also, writing under the name Theresa Ragan, she is the author of *Return of the Rose*, *A Knight in Central Park*, *Taming Mad Max*, *Finding Kate Huntley*, and *Having My Baby*. She and her family live in Sacramento.